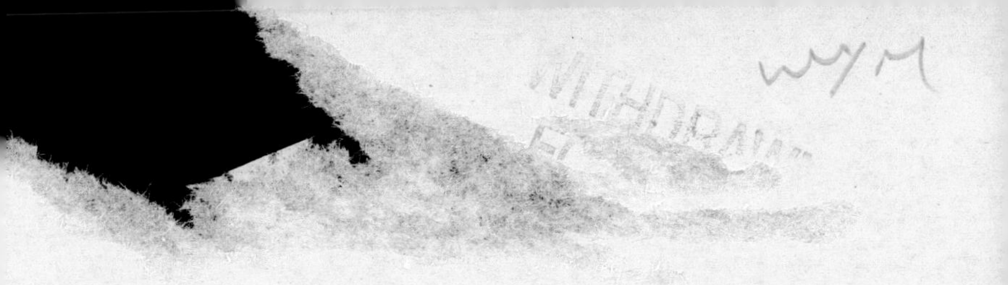

The Concubine's Child

Born in Brisbane, Australia, Carol Jones taught English and Drama at secondary schools before working as an editor of children's magazines. She is the author of several young adult novels as well as children's non-fiction.

The Concubine's Child

CARRO JONES

First published in the UK in 2018 by Head of Zeus Ltd
This paperback edition published in the UK in 2019 by Head of Zeus Ltd

9 7 5 3 1 2 4 6 8

A catalogue record for this book is available from the British Library.

ISBN (PB): 9781786699831
ISBN (E): 9781786699800

Printed and bound by CPI Group (UK) Ltd, Croydon, CR0 4YY

Head of Zeus Ltd
First Floor East
5–8 Hardwick Street
London EC1R 4RG

WWW.HEADOFZEUS.COM

For Max and Lorna

Prologue

IN THE SLATTED light, she glimpsed a flash of white slipping past the open door of the bedchamber. She closed her eyes and in the golden shadows behind her eyelids, saw her again. The girl in white. Long hair flowing loose as she floated across the garden and disappeared between the mango trees into the jungle.

Neuih gwai. Ghost maiden.

Haunting them still.

She considered calling Ho Jie, but the old woman would only ridicule her fears. And it was too early to ask for the shutters to be opened, for there would be no cooling breeze, only searing midday sun. Outside, the neighbourhood dogs snoozed in shady sanctuaries and the macaques had taken to the trees to rest and groom one another. She was alone. The doctor had departed hours ago, leaving the pungent scent of herbs lingering in the room. She had tried to wave him away, but Ho Jie overruled her feeble protest. Once upon a time, the amah wouldn't have dared question her will, but these days servant had become mistress. The amah's black trousers and white blouse were merely a cunning disguise, as deceptive as her mild old-lady face and her habit of nodding when she meant no.

So the doctor pounded his dried fungi and desiccated roots into a foul paste, before setting them to boil while he tormented her with needles that wound in a trail along her spine, like the quills of a porcupine. She could have told him it was pointless.

Almost as futile as prayer, no matter how many joss sticks you lit.

Now she lay prostrate in her bed, immobilised by the humid air, the medicinal aroma of herbs and her own impotence. Half a century ago she had first lain in this bed, a nervous sixteen-year-old bride, trusting to phoenix and peonies to bring her luck. She had had such expectations, if not of happiness, then at least of the ancestors' approval. Yet all the dragons and phoenixes in the world hadn't managed to bestow upon her their promised benevolence.

She glanced again at the open door, wishing that it could all end here. Her son would return soon, tapping at the door to ask after her health. But they both knew she would never recover. She scanned the room, her eyes roaming over gilded cabinets, table and stools inlaid with mother-of-pearl, washstand and dresser littered with pills and potions, before settling on the small desk tucked beneath the window where her writing tools lay. Perhaps it was time for the truth.

Sliding across the silk coverlet, she dropped her feet to the floor and stood holding the bedpost for support. Thick rugs dotted the parquetry like islands. She ventured a few steps, lurching across a field of white chrysanthemums to the table, then a further reel to the desk. She lowered herself onto a stiff-backed chair, dribbled water onto ink-stone, and began grinding ink-stick. Then, weighting a sheet of rice paper, she selected a brush. Yet just as she was about to commit to paper the truth, as she knew it, sharp pain lanced her lower back, spearing into her abdomen and blurring her vision. She had to hurry now or they might never be free.

She had to hope that if her son knew the truth he might

stand a chance of surviving a dead girl's spite. He might find a way to save them, even if he came to despise his mother. Even if he cursed her, all the while burning hell money for her soul.

His hatred would be her penance.

1

Kuala Lumpur 1930

YU LAN WAS finding it difficult to concentrate on the teacher's words, for across the courtyard of the clan house a woman was remonstrating with her ancestors. She wasn't a poor woman, a seller of vegetables or a loud-voiced aunty from one of the stores along Petaling Street. Yu Lan saw at a glance that she was wealthy. She wore a long silk *cheongsam* printed with diagonal stripes, patent leather shoes and stiffly waved hair in the latest fashion. Her outfit would have cost more than the entire Lim family wardrobe. Yet she seemed heedless of this fact as she knelt on the dusty stone floor, with ash drifting about her shoulders from the enormous brass brazier that smoked with incense day and night.

The teacher's dull monotone couldn't compete with the woman's theatrical worship, her sweeping arm movements, exaggerated bows and high-pitched caterwauling of complaint. She might have been an actor in a Cantonese opera troupe. It was apparent, however, that her prayers weren't being answered, for she was shaking her fist at the heavens. If Yu Lan were the woman's dead relative, she wouldn't be inclined to intercede in her affairs either. Not for a few paltry joss sticks and some stale rice buns. She would be more inclined to shut her heavenly ears and hope the woman never joined her in the celestial realm.

Looking beyond the reproachful woman, she tried to focus her thoughts. Her eyes wandered to the banner hanging from the roof above her head, emblazoned with three gold characters. She recognised the word *tong*, which meant hall, but she was yet to learn the other words. And above the banner, above the swinging red-paper lanterns and the gold-leaf frieze, were the bamboo-styled tiles crowned with carvings of gods, animals and plants, and the capricious dragons that prowled the rooftop.

'Ah Lan!' shouted Lou-si, startling her out of her reverie. 'Have you more important things to do with your time than listen to your teacher?'

'Not important, Lou-si. I was thinking about what you said,' she answered, drawn back to earth by the sound of her teacher's angry voice.

'And what was that?'

'You said... you said...'

Around her the other children giggled. At sixteen, she was the oldest student in the afternoon class held by the Chan Clan Association, where the students shared the building and its central courtyard with the ancestral tablets, altar and gods. Yet she knew no more than eight-year-old Ping, the son of the newspaper seller. Her own younger brother had started school when he was six, with her second brother following soon after. But their father had decided long ago that school was a waste of money for a daughter, since girls were temporary. Girls would one day belong to their husbands' families. Yu Lan was more useful helping her mother or sorting herbs in her father's apothecary shop on High Street than wasting her time at school.

Ma was glad of the help too, for she had been born in China and her tiny lotus feet often gave her pain, particularly if she had to walk far. So it was only recently that Ma had prevailed upon Ba to let her attend class, saying it would help them find her a better husband if she could read and write. She would also be more useful in the shop, able to read labels and doctors' prescriptions.

Yu Lan already had a boy in mind as a husband, a fact she dare not tell her father. If she could read, perhaps that boy's father would see her worth. He might be inclined to accept a modest dowry. If she could read, she might have more choices. She might have some say in her destiny. She was grateful to her mother for the opportunity to attend class at the clan association, but so far reading and writing had proved illusory. Memorising characters was like learning to count stars. Just as she had one in her sights it escaped into the infinite sky above.

'Perhaps this will jog your memory,' said Lou-si, striding over to the low stool where she sat with her slate upon her knee, and striking her hand with the bamboo cane he kept expressly for that purpose, his infallible teacher's aid.

'Thank you, Lou-si,' she said, bowing her head. It wouldn't do to be ungrateful because she might receive another whack. At least she had learned that lesson well.

Once she had believed she was clever. She had no trouble learning the names of hundreds of dried plant and animal parts that her father sold in his shop. She memorised which ingredients were stored in each of the small wooden drawers. She even knew the uses for most of them. But since coming to the clan house she realised that she was a know-nothing girl, more stupid than an eight-year-old. Characters that Ping had no trouble learning twisted and turned like snakes, slipping away before her eyes. Just like her choices.

'Stand up! Now, what does this say?' asked Lou-si, pointing his stick at two words he had written on the blackboard.

Setting her slate on the floor she stood, arms rigid at her sides. She wished she could shrink her long gangling body so that she took up less space. The other girls at the clan house were slightly made with fine-boned wrists and tiny waists that you could span with two hands, whereas she was as big-boned as any of the European women who took tea at the Selangor Club. Somewhere amongst her father's southern Chinese ancestors a tall northerner must have intruded. Like her father, Yu Lan stood out even on the crowded streets of Chinatown. When her parents had named her for the jade orchid, that elegant flowering tree with dark, glossy leaves and sculptural white flowers, they could never have imagined she would grow into a tall, clumsy girl who stood tongue-tied before children half her age.

Now, as well as being singled out for ridicule and stinging pain, she felt her palms begin to sweat and her throat constrict. She recognised one of the characters on the blackboard, two downward curving strokes crossing each other with a horizontal stroke above, but the other escaped her.

'Um... female... woman...'

'But what kind of woman? A young woman? An old woman... a *stupid* woman?'

Her classmates sniggered again, not bothering to hide their laughter from the teacher. Even the rich woman chastising her ancestors turned to stare at the sound of giggling children, frowning at the girl whose plight had so rudely interrupted her conversation. They were all about to witness her shame. Her ignorance. Squinting her eyes into slits, Yu Lan tried to make sense of the shapes on the blackboard. She could see the shape for 'mouth' but there were so many squiggles that the meaning of the word was beyond her.

'Ah Ping, tell her the word.'

'The word is "ghost",' the boy said, throwing a superior glance in her direction.

'And what was our lesson about?'

'We've been reading a story by the famous scholar Yuen Mei, about the Widow Ma. She hanged herself from a roof beam then returned as a ghost to haunt the stepson who wronged her. It was very scary.' He shivered ostentatiously with the thrill of it. Everyone enjoyed a good ghost story.

'And what did we learn from the tale?' asked Lou-si.

'We learned that it's not a good idea to let a woman hang herself from a roof beam in your house,' answered Ping, and the other children laughed.

Yu Lan thought that perhaps it wasn't a good idea to wrong your stepmother either. But she kept that to herself. Who was she to say, when she had deciphered only one word of the story?

'So you must practise at home, if you want to learn.'

'I will practise.'

'Do you wish to remain a know-nothing girl? Or do you wish to have some choices in your life?' the teacher asked, his frown softening for a moment. He was harsh, but he wanted her to learn.

'I don't wish to remain a know-nothing girl,' she said, looking down at the red welt that was already forming across the back of her hand. She didn't think to question her punishment. She expected to be beaten for stupidity, or laziness, or a myriad other sins. She expected to respect and obey her elders or suffer the consequences. That was the way of her world. Shoving the offending hand into the pocket of her trousers, she closed her fingers around a small round object nestling there and slipped it over her thumb. She relished the smooth cold feel of stone, the comforting fit on her hand. Clenching that hand into a fist, she begged the gods for the courage to endure the taunts of her fellow students and the disapproval of her teacher. She must try harder. Ma had given her this chance. She must not squander it through her own stupidity.

In the brazier across the courtyard a thicket of incense ignited. The unexpected flames briefly drew the attention of teacher and students and bathed the features of the gods in a golden glow. She watched as the joss sticks flared for several moments before flickering out, sending a pungent smoke wafting darkly towards the ceiling to float there in an acrid cloud. She felt her eyes burn. But the pall of smoke didn't seem to bother the angry woman kneeling before the altar. She had stopped complaining and was staring. First at the half-burnt joss sticks, before swivelling around to regard Yu Lan. Then she steepled her hands in thought, almost as if she was considering a purchase or making a judgement.

Across the courtyard, Yu Lan met her eyes and in them she spotted something familiar. Something almost hungry. The woman's eyes scanned her from the ends of her untidy hair to the worn-down heels of her clogs as she wet her painted red lips with her tongue. As if Yu Lan was a steaming pork bun or a slice of shiny, crisp-skinned duck.

2

AS HER FELLOW students exited the clan house in a noisy swarm, Yu Lan lingered behind. She didn't want to be caught in that swift current of jostling, teasing children or listen to their taunts of 'cabbage head' and 'tall man'. She didn't need to feel any more stupid, big or clumsy than she already did. She had already forgotten about the angry woman with the hungry eyes. From now on, she resolved, every lesson would have her full attention. Even if she learned one new word, it was one more than she'd known before. One word closer to being able to read. One word closer to earning her teacher's respect. So when she finally stepped over the high doorsill – careful not to let her wooden clogs slide from her feet – she didn't notice the angry woman complete her worship and follow. She passed through the red doors and ventured once more into the outside world where the ancestral hall dazzled in the late-afternoon sun. Its green-tiled façade gleamed like jade, while two ferocious white lions guarded the entrance. Sited at the foot of a hill, with the river not far away, the clan hall was perfectly positioned to provide refuge for newly arrived clan members from China. But Yu Lan found little refuge here.

She headed off down Petaling Street, not setting too fast a pace, for a girl never knew when someone might catch up to her. Especially if that someone expected class to finish at about this time, and knew which route that girl took home: someone whose face lit up her day with his wide smile. In the pocket of her *samfu* she relaxed the tense fist of her hand. The jade ring circling her thumb had warmed to the heat of her body. Once, a long time ago, it had belonged to a Chinese warrior. The slot carved on its outer surface held the string of an archer's bow in place. Then it had graced the ink-stained hand of a scholar. Now it belonged to her, a simple apothecary's daughter, far away in Malaya, given to her by her friend Ming, passed down in his family for generations. It was a silent promise for the future. She wanted to show it to the world, but Ming said that the time was not yet ripe. He said that he must wait for the most auspicious moment to ask his father. Yu Lan supposed he was right. Plucked too early, young love might never ripen. Even a simple apothecary's daughter knew this to be true. She must wait and trust in Ming and the gods to bring them together.

Turning down Sultan Street and then right into High Street, she was grateful for the shelter of the five-foot way keeping the worst of the sun from her back, as she stepped around cobblers and other hawkers who plied their trade there. One old aunty made a spare living selling needles and thread, combs and tongue-scrapers, ear-diggers and wood shavings – the ladies' hair styling necessity which her mother soaked in water to make a sticky gel. There were always a few clog sellers, nailing rubber straps onto wooden clogs, and numerous food hawkers such as the woman who sold sweet potato balls outside the tobacco shop. A small group also gathered around the letter stand on the corner, listening to the letter writer read out news received from people's relatives and friends in China.

She passed the soaring gate-tower of the Hindu temple, peopled with intricate carvings of the many Hindu gods; elephant-faced Ganesh and Shiva the destroyer, almost as fierce as Guan Di, the Chinese god of war who was worshipped at the temple across the road. She would have liked to purchase an afternoon snack from the *rojak* seller who squatted outside the temple. It smelled so good that she could almost taste the spicy mix of fried seafood and salad in sweet peanut sauce, but she had no money to spare for snacks. Then someone interrupted her thoughts by falling into step beside her.

She knew who it was even before she turned to see him grinning at her. She could tell by the light touch of his upper arm against her shoulder, by the shivery feeling in her lower belly. He was the only person whose steps matched hers stride for stride, whose presence set her heart to popping like a firecracker.

'Oh, it's you, Ah Ming,' she said loudly for the benefit of any big ears that might report back to her father, as if the tall boy with too-big feet who strode alongside was any other boy she might bump into on her way home. As if he wasn't the boy who was more important than anyone in the world, the one person who made her feel clever and almost pretty.

'It's me. Are you on the way home from the clan house?' he said, taking her free hand in his and hiding them both in the loose tunic of his *samfu*.

'I am. Are you running errands for your father?' she said, looking up at him shyly. Then too softly for other ears to hear, no matter how big, she added, 'I'm wearing your ring inside my pocket. I wish I could wear it for everyone to see.'

'I do too, but we must wait until my father is satisfied with his business. Once he is certain of our prosperity he'll be happy to welcome you into our family.'

She nodded, although inside she felt less sure. Ming was confident that one day he would convince his father that the apothecary's daughter was exactly the right daughter-in-law for the owner of one of the busiest *kopi* shops in Petaling Street. Yu Lan wasn't so sure. Anyone could see that the Wang family was on the way up. Each year Madam Wang's arms glinted with more gold, and Ming's father was the owner of a brand-new Vauxhall. Whereas Yu Lan knew that her mother had sold her one remaining bracelet just last week to pay her brothers' school fees, and that her father spent more time playing mahjong than selling herbal remedies. She worried that waiting might only make matters worse.

She felt the heat of his hand caressing hers against the coarseness of his tunic. The heat seemed to travel up her arm, into her breasts and course through the organs of her body into her secret place. Not the sweltering heat of Malaya, but a subtle fizzing that melted her insides to liquid.

They had known each other since they had toddled beside their mothers shopping for vegetables at the Central Market. They had played tagger in the worn grass triangle where High and Petaling Streets meet. They both shared homes above their fathers' shops with other families, sleeping in rooms made gloomy by timber shutters that kept out the dust and noise of the street below. The rhythms of their days had followed each other. But in those days, if she had thought of him at all she would have seen just another rowdy boy from the neighbourhood, throwing stones at stray dogs or messing about on the riverbank with floating sticks. And then one day, she glanced at Ming and instead of seeing a skinny boy with too-big feet and ears that stuck out like an elephant's, she saw a handsome young man with strong arms who stared at her as if she was the only girl in the world.

'Are you going to the market for your mother tomorrow morning?' he asked, his eyebrows lifting hopefully.

'I think so. Unless my father needs me and then she will have to go herself.'

'Ba wants me to do the marketing tomorrow because he has a business meeting with an important new associate. So…'

'So… it might be so hot tomorrow that I have to stop and rest in the shade of the *banyan* trees before I carry my heavy shopping home,' she said.

'It might be so hot tomorrow that I have to sit and drink two glasses of *cendol* before I walk home.' Or perhaps they might find a moment to sneak down to the riverbank, out of sight of prying eyes, where once he had pressed her against the trunk of a monkeypod tree and leaned the whole length of his body against hers.

'It might,' she said with a giggle.

'Since it's always hot.'

'And boys are always thirsty.'

Two doors from Lim's Authentic Herbal Remedy Shop, he released her hand. A woman stood in front of them, her lips set in a disapproving line. Her hair was pulled back so tightly that her face could barely move. She looked like a particularly scary demon.

'Good afternoon, Madam Chu. My mother was talking about you only this morning. She wondered how you're getting on with your rheumatism.'

'Did she now? Does she also wonder why her daughter wastes so much time talking to boys?'

Yu Lan thought quickly. Their neighbour loved any excuse to gossip and soon it would be all over Chinatown that the Lim girl was making eyes at Wang's eldest son. 'Please tell your mother that I will set aside those herbs she requested,' she said to Ming, stepping a little away from him and hoping this would be enough to silence the woman's tongue.

'Thank you, Ah Lan. Good day, Madam Chu.' He nodded to them both and turned away.

She watched his tall straight back as he strode down High Street away from her, still feeling the warmth where his hand had cradled hers. She wished that they didn't have to hide their feelings from the world, or more particularly from their fathers. She wished that she could hold his hand openly. But they were sixteen and their lives didn't belong to them. She was still watching as he flicked his head back for a last quick smile before disappearing onto Pudoh Street. She didn't notice the well-dressed woman leaning back in a Chevrolet that had slowed to a crawl behind her, forcing rickshaw pullers and bullock drays to veer around it. Nor did she notice that the woman's hungry expression had altered to one of speculation. Yu Lan had room in her thoughts for one person only.

She waited until her heart slowed to a normal pace then sucked in a great lungful of air and turned towards the shop. Already the scent of home reached her nose, a mixture of barks, berries, roots, fungi and the unassailable stink of dried, dead sea-creatures.

*

MADAM CHAN WATCHED thoughtfully as the tall girl entered the apothecary shop. Her sharp eyes had noticed how closely the girl walked next to the young man. She also noticed the girl's strong physique and healthy glow. Despite her loose cotton *samfu* it was clear that her hips were made for bearing children. Thirty minutes previously, Madam Chan had been grovelling in the courtyard of her husband's clan hall, begging his ancestors to answer her prayer. It was the same prayer she had offered every day for the past seventeen years. To send her a child. Or, to be more precise, to send her a boy child. Thirty minutes ago she was despairing, sure that the celestial realm would forever be deaf to her pleas. And then like a bolt from above, the ancestors answered. Her joss sticks blazed into life, the answer written in the flames. They had sent her this girl to be the mother of her sons. Her piety hadn't been for nothing. Her sons would be all the more precious for being so hard-earned, so long-desired.

'Ah Kong, do you know the owner of that apothecary shop?' she asked her driver.

The Chans' driver seemed to know everyone in Chinatown. The sort of man who would associate with anybody, he had plenty of time on his hands to frequent *kopi* shops while he waited for his employers. Now he put his head on one side as he considered his employer's question before nodding slowly.

'Perhaps I know, Madam. Perhaps I might have seen him at Lee's *kopi* shop.'

'Is he a prosperous man, would you say?'

'He spends too much time playing mahjong to be prosperous. Other people are taking his prosperity from him,' he said with a knowing chuckle.

She wasn't surprised to hear this. Gambling was an almost full-time occupation for many residents of Chinatown. Apothecary Lim wasn't unique in that respect. She herself enjoyed a game of mahjong or dominoes with her lady friends now and then, but she always ensured that she won. There was no fun in losing.

'So he might be a man open to offers, do you think?'

'Any man is open to the right offer.'

Madam Chan nodded at her driver's wisdom.

'You can take me home now.' She released a satisfied sigh. The ancestors were showing her the way. For seventeen years she had offered her husband's venerable antecedents the freshest fruits plucked from her garden, orchids picked by her own hand, just-steamed delicacies from her kitchen. For years she had endured regular chastisements from her husband's family in Guangdong and the snide innuendo of her friends at her barren state. All that time she had kept a light burning on the ancestral altar of their home and in her heart.

Finally she had received an answer.

Her driver guided the Chevrolet through the busy streets of Chinatown and out onto Lornie Road, following the Klang River through its valley. Low hills undulated in all directions, as if a giant hand had scrunched the landscape into a fist and then relented. The Klang and its tributary the Gombak were timid at this time of the year but during the monsoon season regularly overflowed their banks. The floods of 1926 had been so bad that Kong had to wade through the streets of Chinatown to replenish her husband's supply of Chivas Regal. It wasn't until the Klang was straightened two years ago that the floods were mitigated to some extent.

Here the river flowed a dull, slow brown, bordered by banks covered in long grass with trees on either side. They passed the occasional bungalow and the thatched roofs and timber-stilted houses of Malay *kampungs*. But as they continued their journey towards her own spacious bungalow on the outskirts of the city, houses became fewer, jungle fringed the road, tin mines dotted the landscape and Madam Chan began to plot. There was a lot to do and no time to be lost.

3

YU LAN STOOD at the counter pounding dried herbs as she watched her father usher a stranger through the shop. She didn't know the woman's name but recognised her as a matchmaker and brides' aide. She had often seen her trailing a bridal chair as it wove through the city to an expectant groom, or popping in and out of houses in the days before and during a wedding. She was always dressed in an embroidered jacket of thick black silk over a mid-calf skirt of dark blue. Close up, Yu Lan saw that her face was powdered to the colour of chalk, her eyebrows plucked bare and traced to a fine black arch.

The woman glanced at her through narrowed eyes as she passed through the shop. Yu Lan's breath caught in her throat at the thought that Ba might be consulting a matchmaker. Surely not yet? Although she was old enough to be married, she had hoped she wouldn't have to go away, not before Ming had enough time to convince his father that she would make the perfect daughter-in-law. It couldn't be so. But of course, she reminded herself, her father was an apothecary. People often discussed their more intimate ailments with him privately. And he had shown no signs of wanting to marry her off. She was more useful to him in the shop, especially now that he was devoting more time to his mahjong. The matchmaker was probably consulting him about her haemorrhoids.

Her father welcomed the woman effusively, showing her through to the crowded parlour that doubled as a storeroom at the rear of the shop, and immediately shouting to his wife for tea. This woman must be important for he was rarely so welcoming. Yu Lan tried loitering in the doorway to listen in on their conversation, confident that it would be of more interest than her mortar and pestle. But her father ordered her back to grinding and mixing, so she was surprised several minutes later when he called out for her to join them in the parlour.

'Daughter, please pay your respects to our esteemed guest, Madam Foo.'

'Good morning, Madam Foo,' she replied with a small bow.

The woman looked her up and down, saying, 'Come closer so that I can see you properly.'

Yu Lan walked forward, trying not to worry about why the matchmaker was showing interest in her. Adults rarely took any interest in children and young people who weren't related. Perhaps her father was thinking of finding employment for her with this woman. She wasn't sure what she thought about that. She liked working in her father's shop. She liked helping sick people, even if it was only by grinding ingredients for her father's remedies. And she had learned so much already from watching him. One day, she allowed herself to hope that he might even let her make up remedies. Once she learned to read she would be able to decipher the instructions, which their customers brought from their doctors. Perhaps if the gods were kind, she might be permitted to continue working in her father's shop after she and Ming wed, rather than helping out in the Wangs' *kopi* shop like most daughters-in-law.

'Show me your hands,' Madam Foo ordered, indicating that Yu Lan should pull back the sleeves that covered her wrists. 'Such big hands,' she said, frowning in distaste. 'And her feet are so large and clumsy,' she added, looking down at Yu Lan's feet in their woven straw slippers.

'She is a tall girl, it's true,' her father said in an apologetic tone, 'but she is strong and she is accustomed to hard work. You won't find fault with her health. Show Madam Foo your teeth.'

Yu Lan drew the lips back from her teeth in a grimace. She didn't understand what this interview was about but knew not to disobey her father openly. It was usually best to disobey in secret and hope he didn't find out.

'Well, she's not very pretty but her figure isn't bad and as you say, she appears healthy. Tell me, girl, can you add numbers? What is thirty-three and seventy-nine?'

Yu Lan quickly calculated the answer, saying, 'One hundred and twelve, Madam.' Could it be that this woman was hiring staff for a restaurant or an office? Or was she testing Yu Lan's intelligence?

'And do you read, girl?'

'I am learning, Madam, but I cannot read yet.'

'Well, no matter, reading isn't an essential requisite for this role,' the woman said, her lips twitching. 'Perhaps you will do. You may return to your twigs while your father and I discuss matters.' She waved Yu Lan away and returned her attention to Lim.

Thirty minutes later, her father was again bowing and ingratiating himself with pleasantries as he escorted the woman to the street, past the glass cabinet scattered with baskets and scales for sorting and weighing ingredients, around the sacks of dried sea cucumber and scallops, between stacked crates of cuttlefish and shark fin, and all the way to the door where he made a final bow of farewell.

'A pleasure to meet you, Madam Foo. A great pleasure.'

'And you, Mister Lim,' the woman nodded. 'I'll set things in motion then. My client will be pleased to hear we have concluded our arrangement satisfactorily.'

'It's an auspicious day,' he responded, rubbing his hands together. 'Most auspicious.'

Madam Foo reached into the black leather handbag looped over her arm and offered him what looked to be two small squares of cardboard.

'For you to keep,' she said, lifting her chin in Yu Lan's direction as her lips twitched again in that almost smile.

Yu Lan looked down. Ba would be angry if he caught her staring.

'Thank you, Madam Foo. My wife will be grateful.'

'The residence is large and gracious. Your daughter is a lucky girl indeed.'

'My daughter is a know-nothing girl who doesn't deserve her good fortune,' he said with a wide smile. 'Ah... and when do you think your client will want to conclude our arrangement?'

'Soon, Mister Lim. Very soon.'

The words hung in the air as the woman exited the shop and climbed into a waiting rickshaw, the driver who had been resting in the shade of the five-foot way scrambling to accommodate her.

'Ba? What did the lady want?' Yu Lan ventured, as her father returned, an unaccustomed bounce in his step. She kept her eyes fixed on the dried mulberries in the basket before her. She doubted now that Madam Foo had come to buy an aid to constipation or a preparation to improve blood flow.

'Heh, heh, never you mind, girl. You'll find out soon enough,' he rasped, less sternly than usual, gazing at her almost fondly. Then with a brisk, 'Mind the shop until I return,' he skipped to the back of the premises, returning a few minutes later wearing his hat and heading no doubt for the mahjong parlour above the *kopi* shop where he liked to spend time.

Later that day, in the kitchen at the rear of the building, Yu Lan tackled her mother. The kitchen steamed in the early evening sun, heady with the scent of chopped green onion, ginger and garlic, as her mother cut fresh chicken into bite-sized pieces for the evening meal. The cleaver sliced through bone with a loud thwack. Ma's dainty limbs were deceptive. She wielded the chopper with an efficient flick of the wrist, flipped mounds of ingredients in a burning hot wok with a light toss. But today she seemed to apply her skill with added force.

'Ma, what did the lady want?'

'What lady?'

'The wedding lady who called on Ba.'

Her mother ceased chopping, holding the blood-smeared cleaver in mid-air before turning to face her daughter with a frown that drew her pencilled brows together. She considered her daughter for a moment, her gaze travelling from the loose pigtails, down past the gentle curve of her breasts and the long trouser-encased legs to the feet in their straw slippers. She seemed to be taking an inventory. Either that or she was embedding the image of her daughter in her memory. Neither possibility appeared promising to Yu Lan.

'What did your father say?'

'Ba said I'd find out soon enough.'

Pressing her lips into a tight line, Madam Lim set the cleaver on the chopping board and wiped her hands on a wet rag hanging on a hook for that purpose.

'Come with me,' she said, swivelling on her golden lotuses and tottering through to the parlour where she withdrew something from a drawer in their one good mahogany cabinet, inlaid with mother-of-pearl and kept for best. Yu Lan followed as she returned through the house to the air well. The air well was the coolest place in the house and the only spot with a touch of green in the form of a potted frangipani, a cumquat bush and a shiny green lime tree. Madam Lim sat on one of the ceramic stools and indicated for her daughter to take another. Then, with a sigh, she handed over an item she had taken from the drawer. Yu Lan looked down at the object she held in her hand, her chest tense with foreboding.

It was a photograph of a house. Perhaps a mansion. Having never been inside a mansion, she couldn't say for sure. But it was certainly large. The house was two storeys – constructed in ornate Straits style – and surrounded by a garden threatened with jungle at its edges. It was symmetrical; the central section jutted forward with a wide, shady portico beneath and wings flaring to either side. It seemed to Yu Lan that everything about the house was constructed in threes: three front rooms, each with triple-arched shuttered windows, three wide arches to the portico, three gables to a roof of curving Chinese tiles.

'It's very grand, Ma,' she said, knowing as she said it that she didn't like the house and hoped she would never need to. She couldn't understand what it had to do with her… unless Ba was arranging to send her away as a servant. She was too old now to be sent away as a *mui jai*. Those girls were sold off by impoverished parents when they were as young as ten, old enough to work but young enough not to cause trouble. They were contracted to work for their bond-masters until the age of eighteen when their masters were obliged to arrange a marriage for them. Sometimes they actually did.

'The house belongs to the *towkay* Chan Boon Siew,' her mother said.

She looked at her mother questioningly.

'The *towkay* is a very important man, the owner of a tin mine, perhaps two tin mines,' her mother continued, handing her a second photograph, with the image facing down, as if to give her daughter a brief respite. A moment in time to remain herself: Lim Yu Lan, a tall girl of sixteen years, eldest child of Apothecary Lim, elder sister to Lim Wang Yu and Lim Wang Seng, precious daughter to her mother Tan Hoi Wah, know-nothing student of Ng Lou-si, promised bride to Lee Ming Ho...

A moment in time before her world changed for ever.

'Your father has settled that you are to become Chan Towkay's secondary wife.' Her mother's voice was devoid of expression but she couldn't hide the sadness in her eyes. Every mother worried when her daughter left home to be married. And only a callous, unfilial daughter wouldn't weep until her eyes grew red and swollen on her wedding day.

'His first wife is barren and he seeks a mother for his sons.' Sons that Chan Towkay didn't yet have, sons that someone would have to get for him, Yu Lan thought, but she remained silent. Her voice was tangled somewhere inside, trapped by her father's plans and Chan Towkay's desires. No one was interested in her desires.

'You will be a valuable member of his household.' She noticed that her mother used the word *gwai,* meaning expensive, rather than *jihk,* meaning of worth. Presumably her father would be well remunerated for giving away his daughter. And once she was sold as a concubine she would no longer be part of the Lim family; she would belong to the Chan family. If she became a first wife, a *chi*, she would be expected to make visits to her birth family on all the major holidays, and her children would call her parents Gung Gung and Po Po. As a first wife she would receive a handsome dowry and her parents would be clothed in respect.

But as a concubine, a *chieh*, her husband would decide when and if she might visit her birth family. As a concubine she would receive no dowry of gold and jewellery, own no property. She wouldn't return to her parents' home on the third day after the wedding with gifts of roast pig and other delicacies. There would be no red posters outside the apothecary shop announcing to all that her father was receiving a gifted son-in-law into their family. There would be no street urchins singing foolish nursery rhymes outside her house and no riding in a red sedan chair to the home of her groom wearing an embroidered red jacket and pleated skirt, her arms tinkling with gold, and firecrackers announcing her departure.

As *chieh,* Yu Lan might never see her birth family again. No wonder her mother was sad.

'And if you bear him a son...'

She stopped listening as her mother extolled the virtues of motherhood. Ma spoke of bearing sons as if it was a small thing. As if it wouldn't entail the intimacy of the bedroom with a man she had never met. Yu Lan was innocent but she was far from ignorant. Growing up in a small house shared with other people, she knew that in order to get sons a man had to put his penis inside a woman, inside the soft parts she sometimes touched in secret beneath her sheet. To bear this *towkay* a son she would have to let him put his thing inside her. He would probably want to touch her breasts and look at her naked and other things she didn't have a name for.

And he wouldn't be a boy named Ming.

She flipped over the picture clutched in her hands.

A man looked out at her, dressed in a western-style suit with his hair carefully oiled and slicked back from his face. It was a thin face with high cheekbones and might have been handsome once. But now it was old, with lines dragging down the mouth and a shrewd look to the eyes.

'You will be mother to the next *towkay*.'

But this man with the shrewd eyes would want to put his penis inside her private parts, whenever he grew hard with his needs, whenever the whim took him. Her body was the only thing that was hers and her father would sell it to a stranger.

'He already has a wife. I will be his concubine,' she whispered, finally finding a few worthless words. She spoke in a flat voice. She didn't speak out in anger, for what would be the point? Her father had spoken. Chan Towkay had spoken.

'Better to be a rich man's concubine than a poor man's wife.'

It was true that a poor man's wife would be subject to the whims of her mother-in-law, serving not only her husband's parents, but perhaps a tribe of younger siblings, cooking and cleaning from dawn until dusk. But Ming wasn't so poor, and even if he was, she didn't care. She would gladly do the family laundry and feed a family of ten if she could be with Ming. She gazed imploringly at her mother who turned away to stare up at the patch of blue framed by the walls of the air well. As if the sky god might rain down his blessings upon them.

'There's no point in fighting this, Ah Lan, for wilfulness will only bring turmoil. You must be fluid like water, for water defeats the strongest stone in time.'

Yu Lan loosed her grip on the photographs and they fell to the stone floor, landing face up. The old man and his big house, lying in wait for her. Her hand found its way into the pocket of her *samfu*, seeking reassurance. Her mother was wrong. Stone lasted for ever. She twisted the ring onto her finger, determined not to cry. Ming would help her. He was sixteen now, almost a man. He would find the courage to beg his father to arrange a match between them. Then her father would have no reason to sell her to this *towkay*.

She raised her head once more to find her mother still staring up at the empty sky, but Yu Lan knew that she would find no saviour there. Ming had to help her, for there was no one else. Not her mother. Not her brothers. Not the sky god. Not the ancestors. And certainly not her father. She was sixteen and she was alone.

If he couldn't help her, who else was there?

4

NOBODY COULD SAY that Madam Chan was a jealous wife. This room stood testament to that fact. She took a last look around the room that had been prepared for the coming of her husband's concubine. She could have put the girl in the cramped downstairs room where her husband's old amah had spent her last days, except she didn't want to jinx the arrival of their sons in a room that had belonged to a dead woman. What if the old woman's spirit still lingered? She didn't want some old lady spirit inhabiting the bodies of her strong young sons with her bow-legged gait and hairy chin.

The small upstairs room at the western corner of the house might have proved suitable too, except for the late-afternoon sun that turned it into a steam room. Chan Towkay would find the heat unpleasant when he chose to visit, even with the advent of a new fan from General Electric imported all the way from America. Besides, the fan was much better placed in Madam's room at the front of the house where husband and wife often sat playing cards in the evening.

So Madam Chan set up the large room in the northeast corner with windows on two sides to catch the evening breeze. She personally selected a new brass bed in the English style and hung it with a river of pink silk embroidered with dragons and phoenixes, magpies, ducks and any other animal associated with fertility. She had even spotted a couple of eels slithering amongst the menagerie. It couldn't hurt to enlist celestial help. It hadn't worked for her but Madam Chan was a pragmatic woman – perhaps her womb was too shrivelled even for heavenly intervention.

She hadn't stinted when it came to the dressing table and full-length mirror either, for the girl would need to look her best to encourage Chan Towkay's juices. But since she would arrive without a trousseau, there was no need for elaborate cabinets to store jewellery and household wares – a simple wooden trunk would do service for her clothes. Madam Chan released a satisfied sigh. The girl would not be able to say she was ill-treated in the Chan home.

'There's no sign of the girl yet, Madam,' said Ho Jie, surprising her by entering on silent feet. The new amah did have a way of slipping into rooms, her black cloth slippers sliding noiselessly across parquet and stone, her white *sam* and black *fu* blending into the furniture, already almost a part of it. 'Towkay is becoming impatient.'

'Is he shouting?'

'Not shouting, but he threw his chopsticks at Cook because the pickles were too sour.'

'We need not worry then.'

The amah turned up her nose at this comment, as if to say, we need not worry for you but what about Cook? Madam Chan had discovered already that the amah's expressions held a world of meaning. She was far from inscrutable, bordering on insolent in fact. But since one could hardly chastise a servant for the lift of an eyebrow, Madam Chan had to find fault with her needlework or her hairdressing instead. Luckily, she could always find something to complain about.

The woman had been with them for only two months after Chan's previous amah finally fell on the street from old age. The old woman must have been at least eighty and at the end Madam Chan had to tend her rather than the other way about, spooning rice porridge down her throat at every meal because she no longer had teeth and catching the drips as they dribbled down her chin. This task was particularly unpleasant as Ah Po had the nasty habit of chewing betel nut, which meant that her toothless gums were stained red as well as sections of tiled floor where she had missed the spittoon. It was almost a relief to see her go.

Their new amah was a sworn spinster who had combed up her maiden's pigtail into a bun and vowed never to marry. There were more and more of these women about lately and Madam Chan wondered whether the vow was really an excuse for being unable to get a husband. Ho Jie was rather a pork chop with her square flat face and squashed nose. She had been a silk worker in China but once the demand for silk fell, she along with many others had sought work far afield in the promised abundance of the south seas. She had arrived from Shonde County in the Pearl River Delta a few months previously, and come to work at the Chan residence after several weeks spent in a boarding house in Chinatown.

Unlike *mui jai,* the young slave girls sold by poverty-stricken parents, she was paid a salary and could leave whenever she chose. Madam Chan thought that a degree of choice made for a better worker. Not too much choice of course, for that would upset the natural order of things. However, she wasn't quite sure how her new amah perceived that natural order yet and judging by her expression, thought that she might need a little re-education.

'You may go and help in the kitchen. I will watch for the girl's arrival.'

She dismissed the woman with a wave of her bejewelled hand, arm jingling with gold, for in a show of authority she had chosen to wear all her jewellery at once. She had also donned a new *cheongsam*, patterned with white chrysanthemums on a light-blue background and sporting delicate cap sleeves. The girl was young and, if not strictly speaking beautiful, she glowed with health and vitality. Madam Chan meant to glow with the allure of gold.

Her silk slippers sliding upon the parquet, she crossed the upstairs hall, skirting the atrium above the courtyard below, and entered her bedroom at the front of the house overlooking the garden. It was a large and elegant room, as befitted the *taitai*, the lady of the house. Every day Madam Chan offered a prayer to Guan Yin, the Goddess of Mercy, for keeping her husband's widowed mother safely in China. Chan Towkay was a second son and as such wasn't required to live with his parents. He had been sent to Malaya as a young man to seek his fortune and further his family's financial interests. His older brother lived with his parents, so she didn't have to kowtow to another woman in her own home like many of her friends. Her sister-in-law had that pleasure. Nor did she have to listen to her mother-in-law chastise her daily for being barren. However, she did have to put up with regular letters complaining about such a useless daughter-in-law.

Despite these complaints, Madam Chan was the *taitai* and the only person she obeyed was her husband (and only then if she couldn't convince him otherwise). So long as she kept him happy. And she had, for many years. But she could tell that his patience was wearing thin, as thin as his hair. The nagging letters from China and the condescending remarks from friends and associates had begun to chafe. The new *chieh* was her way of continuing to keep her husband happy and getting a son into the bargain. Some of her friends' husbands kept numerous concubines – her friend Madam Tang was required to live with Second and Third Lady Tang – so she supposed she was in good company. Plus she had chosen the *chieh* herself rather than having some idiot girl foisted upon her by a salty wet husband.

The shutters were open, allowing early morning light to bathe the pearl-encrusted furniture and embroidered silks in silver. She crossed to the window and stood gazing down the dirt track that wound up through the jungle. Theirs was the only bungalow within view, the site chosen by her husband for its proximity to the tin mine he owned a few miles away. The house was sited halfway up a hill, looking out to the Klang River valley and beyond. Luckily, jungle hid the ugly gashes in the earth created by nearby tin mines. Nor could she see the Malay *kampung*, with its huts on stilts and chickens scratching beneath, for it was situated further along the ridge. Kong once let slip that workers had encountered several old Malay graves while digging the foundations for the house, but Madam Chan didn't believe it. Her husband wouldn't have countenanced building over a graveyard. Not for all the tea in China. Or all the tin in Malaya. This rumour was merely the gossip of superstitious coolies who had nothing better to do.

Apart from a troop of macaques resting in the shade of an enormous candlenut tree, there wasn't much to see. The garden was dotted with fruit trees: mango, banana, jackfruit, rambutan, papaya and sago palm. Madam Chan had banned the growing of durian for the smell assaulted her nose and she wouldn't have it anywhere near the house. Though she suspected Kong often feasted on it in the shed he shared with the Chevrolet at the rear of the property, for its stink lingered on his clothes and tainted his breath.

Taking a last look down the empty track, she crossed to the enormous bridal bed that dominated the room and lay on its silky coverlet for a rest. The day to come held its challenges. She would need to be at her most forbidding to ensure that the girl knew her place from the outset. A girl who didn't know her place was bound to be trouble.

*

'BANISHED YOU TO the kitchen, has she?' Cook cackled as Ho Jie entered the kitchen. 'Well, don't expect me to be waiting on you. I've got too much to do.'

'She told me to come and help you.'

'Know your way about a kitchen, do you?'

To be truthful, Ho Jie could barely boil rice. She could reel silk cocoons with her eyes closed, yet steamed fish defeated her. She wasn't about to admit that to this cranky old woman, though, not when she needed this job. For two decades she had been a silk worker in the factories of Shonde, labouring eleven hours a day, seven days a week, fined if the thread she wove was uneven or the wrong size, crowded into a dark and airless room with many other women. But at least she was paid for her work. Ho Jie was no man's slave. Until the world demand for silk crashed and she found herself unemployed at the age of thirty-five. But she was smart and she was resourceful and she had got herself across the South China Sea all the way to Malaya and no one, neither a bossy *taitai* nor a cantankerous old widow from Hainan, was going to intimidate her. She was a self-combed woman from Shonde and she was nobody's fool.

'Tell me what you want me to do, Old Woman, and it will be done,' she said, pushing back the sleeves of her tunic.

The cook stared up at her as they took each other's measure, the wrinkled old widow with her gap-toothed cackle and gruff voice, and the wiry silk worker with her neat uniform and independent manner.

'The vegetables need washing. Think you can do that?' Cook said, then ventured companionably, 'Madam is in a mood. Can't wait until her replacement arrives, I expect. Stupid woman, why get a young peach blossom to replace yourself. She should have got him an old hag like me, heh, heh.'

'Why get married at all? Men treat their wives like property.'

Cook paused in her chopping of vegetables to glance sideways with a knowing look and Ho Jie wondered whether she had offended the old widow. After all, she had been married once, but the woman's tone remained friendly as she said, 'True, but you know what they say: "Of the three ways to lack filial piety, not having children is the worst." Madam must be feeling very unfilial to bring a peach blossom into her house.'

Ho Jie felt a pang of sympathy then for this young girl she had never met, brought into the house as little more than a breeding sow for an old man's sons. She wouldn't be *chieh* for all the silk in Shonde. She wouldn't change places with the concubine, not for a big brass bed and a gleaming dresser. For not only had the girl been sold like property, she had been sold into a house where she would be lorded over by master *and* mistress, without even the freedom to leave the house without permission. Severed from her family, removed from her friends. Ho Jie suspected the girl had been given no choice in her future.

She was essentially a slave.

5

JUST SIX DAYS after the visit from the go-between, Ba woke her early, long before the sun crept over the roofs of the shophouses across the road. He entered the room she shared with her brothers and pinched her awake, hissing at her to listen carefully.

'Ah Lan, today is the day you do your duty by this family.'

Even more than the pinch on her arm, the words parted the fog of sleep and woke her with a jolt. She reared up from the bed, swivelling her head in search of danger but finding only her father.

'I've kept you for sixteen years, filling that hungry stomach of yours, putting clothes on your back, and now you must do your part for your brothers. They'll be here for you soon.'

She hadn't realised his plan would be put into motion so quickly. She hadn't known that her life was about to change so abruptly. She needed more time.

'From this day on you will be part of the Chan family. You must do as the *taitai* tells you and be a credit to you parents. There's no going back.'

'But I don't want to leave home, Ba,' she said, her words barely above a whisper.

'It doesn't matter what you want. I am your father. I know what is best for you and this family and it's your duty to do as I tell you. Besides, Chan Towkay is rich. This opportunity is a golden rice bowl for you.'

'But Ba... there's a boy who...'

As the words left her mouth he pinched her to silence.

'What boy? Has this boy's father engaged a matchmaker to speak to me? Has this boy's father spoken to this worthless daughter's father?' he hissed, pressing his face close to hers and spitting out the word 'boy' as if it was poison.

'Not yet. I only told him about... about... Chan Towkay's offer two days ago.'

'Then his father has had two days to make an offer,' he said, with a self-congratulatory smile.

In the face of his smugness Yu Lan didn't know what to say. She was unaccustomed to questioning her father. Even her mother would not challenge him directly. When Ma wanted to sway him to her way of thinking she plied him with his favourite dishes of chicken's feet and steamed pork with cuttlefish. That wasn't an option for Yu Lan.

'He hasn't interfered with you, has he?' her father asked, his eyes boring into hers.

Were kisses interference? Was the press of his body against hers interference?

'No, Ba. No one has interfered with me,' she said, willing herself not to look away.

'And how long have you known this boy?'

'My whole life. He's my friend.'

'So this boy's family have had many years to arrange a betrothal?' he said with a satisfied nod. 'And they're yet to say a word to me.'

'Couldn't we wait? Give them time?'

'They've had more than enough time. I won't give this boy more time to taste the fruit when he hasn't bought the tree. The Chan family has made a generous offer. For your brothers' sakes I can't refuse it. You should be honoured that such a respectable family has chosen you. Would you rather be married off to a coolie, panning tin in stream beds to earn a pittance?' Being reduced to manual labour was her father's greatest fear.

'But he's not so poor.'

'Enough! Stop talking now or you'll wake your brothers. They need to be rested for their studies.'

That was three hours ago, before her mother brushed her hair to a shine and plaited it with flowers. Before Ma packed a rattan case with three sets of clothes and a pair of lovingly embroidered slippers. Now she could hear her mother calling up the stairs, 'Ah Lan, you must be ready! Chan Towkay's driver will be here soon.'

But by this time she was already sneaking out through the kitchen and heading for the narrow lane at the rear of their house, used by the night soil man. Then walking briskly, she headed down Foch Avenue, turning right into Petaling Street, knowing that at this time of the day Ming would be serving customers in his father's *kopi* shop.

When she entered the shop it was brimming with customers drinking glasses of thick sweet local *kopi.* Chopsticks were kept busy with bowls of Hokkien *mee*, the noodles slick with dark, oily sauce. Spoons shovelled hot rice porridge into waiting mouths. Groups of men conversed in loud voices, bowls clattered on marble-topped tables, and stools scraped on the concrete floor, all adding to the noisy hum of hungry people. She spotted him as soon as she stepped inside, stacking empty bowls in a teetering pile to wash later as he squatted by a tin tub at the rear of the shop.

'Ah Ming,' she called softly. He didn't hear her above the clatter but one of the customers did, a man with a huge hairy mole growing prominently on his chin.

'Ah Ming!' the man shouted across the busy restaurant. 'This girl is looking for you,' he said with a chuckle and a wink.

Her friend turned where he stood, the bowls gripped tightly top and bottom, and stared in her direction. He didn't say a word, only blinked a few times as if she might prove to be an apparition who disappeared by the time he reopened his eyes. He didn't look pleased to see her. In fact, he had the look of a street cur expecting to be struck by stones. What had happened to him since she saw him last, sitting under the *banyan* tree outside the Central Market? They had shared a sweet-watered coconut drink and he had stroked the inside of her thigh when no one was looking. He had held her hand as she cried and vowed to speak with his father. To find a way for them to be together.

Yet now he avoided her as if she were a bad smell.

She moved towards him, skirting tables, stools and bustling waiters, and stopped a few feet away.

'Ah Ming, I need to speak with you.'

The entire restaurant was watching them now, aware somehow that the drama playing out before their eyes was just as interesting as the drama of the shadow puppet theatre or a new film at the Odeon cinema.

'I'm working,' he said, nodding at the tower of bowls, oily black sauce smudging his hands.

'It won't take long. Have you spoken with your father?' she whispered urgently.

His eyes slid sideways to a tall man counting money behind the counter. 'We've spoken.'

She nodded once, indicating that he should continue.

'Ba is considering a marriage for me with the only daughter

of his friend, Mister Ng. He hopes to join forces to expand his business. He's been waiting until I was old enough to discuss it with me.' His eyes flitted around the room, resting on anything other than her face.

'But what about the promises we made each other?' she asked, scarcely believing he could go along with his father's plan, this boy who caused her heart to flutter and skip. What about the kisses we shared under the monkeypod tree in the dip of the riverbank? she implored him silently.

'There's nothing I can do. I must do as my father bids.'

She felt the impact of his words as if one of her brothers had punched her. 'We could run away together,' she whispered, surprising herself with her daring. She had never considered this possibility before. She had focused her thoughts on persuading their fathers. The idea of leaving her home above the apothecary shop with nowhere to go was too daunting. But with Ming at her side it suddenly seemed possible. They could scrape together enough money to take a train to Singapore. She could find work helping some other apothecary, while he washed dishes in some other man's *kopi* shop. One day, if they worked hard, they might start a shop of their own.

Without realising it, she had grabbed his arm. Now she watched in distress as he shook it off, setting the tower of bowls to teetering precariously. 'And how would we live?' he hissed. 'Sharing a tin shack over the river with six other people? Scraping by with a bowl of rice and a few slivers of fish each day?'

She was silent for a few moments, not knowing how to counter his argument. 'But you gave me your ring,' she murmured finally, the only thing she could think to say. A ring that had been in his family for generations. She couldn't believe that his gift meant so little.

'You may keep the ring,' he said, suddenly stern. 'It's only a trinket I purchased from Leong's Jewellery Store. A reproduction. It's not even true jade. My family were never archers.' He looked down at his feet, shod in their wooden clogs. 'We're shopkeepers, not warriors.'

She fixed her eyes on his face, willing him to look at her, convinced that he couldn't be telling the truth. She told herself that he would fight for their love, that he would risk a shanty by a river to be with her.

'Ah Ming!' shouted his father. He called to his son but he was looking at her as he spoke. 'You have work to do. Tell the Lim girl to go away.'

His son shrugged, careful not to disturb the bowls again, and said, 'I'm sorry.' Then he turned away, carrying his burden to the back of the shop where the washing water waited. She stood for a moment watching, not daring to run after him, yet afraid her legs would be too weak to bear her from the restaurant.

'You'd better go, little sister. Someone will be looking for you,' said the father, not unkindly, now that he had prevailed. 'There's nothing for you here.'

She realised that he was right. If she didn't have Ming there was nothing for her anywhere.

*

'I'M VERY SORRY we're late, Madam, but the girl wasn't there when we arrived.' The go-between glanced frostily at the girl standing a pace behind her. 'We had to wait.'

To Madam Chan the girl seemed even taller than she had

that day at the clan house, as she stood rigid with shame under her teacher's words. She loomed over the go-between, her pale face and white *samfu* leeching her of all colour so that she resembled a ghost from a fairy tale. For a moment Madam Chan wondered if she had done the right thing in bringing her into the house. Where had that healthy glow gone? The girl looked ill. She might even be contagious.

But surely the ancestors had spoken? And they could hardly be mistaken.

'Where was she?' Madam Chan wondered what on earth a sixteen-year-old girl could find more urgent than preparing herself for a new life with her wealthy consort. 'And why is she wearing that dreadful outfit?' The girl looked like she was attending a funeral.

'She won't say. But she returned to Lim's apothecary shop an hour after we arrived. Her father was inclined to beat her, but I told him that would only put her in a worse state.' Again, she glanced back at the girl who towered straight as bamboo, staring unseeingly ahead. Had she been deceived? Was the girl an imbecile? Yet Madam Foo had examined her and determined she had all her wits and faculties before they made the offer.

'What have you to say for yourself?'

The girl looked at Madam Chan as she spoke but didn't reply. She didn't frown or pout or glower. Rather, her eyes appeared empty of all emotion, as if she had no feelings. Yet to Madam Chan's mind her silence was more defiant than any tantrum.

'Well, you're here now. And no doubt you wish to meet the *towkay*. But first I will make a few things plain.' She paused, giving the girl an opportunity to respond in some way, but she remained standing silently, watching Madam Chan's lips as if they were objects of fascination.

'Firstly, you will address me as *Ah Jie*. Is that understood?'

Madam Chan congratulated herself on her kindness in allowing this know-nothing girl to call her Elder Sister. So at the very least she expected acknowledgement, even gratitude. Instead her gesture was met with silence, which wouldn't do at all. Silence was a virtue it was true, but this girl used it as a weapon. She nodded to the go-between, who, grasping the situation immediately, reached out and delivered the girl a slap on the arm.

'Is that understood?'

'Yes, Madam.'

Madam Chan raised the twin arches of her perfectly drawn brows.

'Yes, Ah Jie.'

'Secondly, you will address my husband as *Sin Saang*.'

'Yes, Madam.'

'Ah Jie,' reminded the go-between with another slap.

'And you will be known as… Sai Mui. Is that understood?' Madam Chan smiled in delight at her cleverness. Referring to her husband's concubine as 'younger sister' was welcoming, but adding the word *sai* emphasised her smallness in the scheme of things. She would be family but she needed to know her place.

'Yes, Ah Jie.'

'Now, Ho Jie, you may bring Sai Mui through to the drawing room.'

*

THROUGH THE DOORS on either side of the family altar, past the intricately carved spirit wall, Yu Lan had a view of the length of the house. She saw past the courtyard with its bright flowerings of chrysanthemum and dahlia, and through to the ancestral hall beyond. She caught glimpses of other rooms opening to the courtyard from the sides, while double doors led from this reception hall to a drawing room on one side and a study on the other where two great iron safes squatted. In the centre of the reception hall stood a marble-topped table and four round stools of shiny blackwood, while four pairs of carved armchairs rested against facing walls.

It was the largest house she had ever entered.

The lady of the house stood before the gilded altar, a porcelain statue of Guan Yin just visible behind her. The lady herself was laden with gold: jangling on her arms, weighing down her ear lobes, collaring her neck. Yu Lan had recognised her immediately as the angry woman from the clan house, the one who had remonstrated loudly with her ancestors. Today she was smiling, her smile more threatening than her anger. It hinted at some deeper emotion lurking behind the upturned corners of her mouth, though as yet Yu Lan didn't know what that emotion might be. No doubt she would find out in due course.

But today she was beyond intimidation, beyond fear. For how can you intimidate someone whose life has been stolen from them? She was no longer an elder sister. Now she was the smallest person in this household, not worthy of her true name.

Her new elder sister turned on shiny slippers and trotted through the double glass doors into the next room, her steps made dainty by the tight-fitting silk of her *cheongsam*. Her servant nudged Yu Lan in the ribs and gestured for her to follow. 'Why do you arrive at your new home dressed in mourning?' the woman hissed, shaking her head in dismay. 'Do you want to anger the *taitai* and her husband?'

Indeed her mother had said the same thing when she descended from her room with her little rattan case, dressed in her crisply pressed white tunic and her brother's *gung fu* trousers. But with Madam Foo, the go-between, tapping her foot in the parlour, and her father fuming in the shop, her mother wasn't about to waste more time. She knew that Ma interpreted her white outfit as defiance; she didn't understand that Yu Lan mourned. For the loss of love. The loss of future. The loss of self. No one else would mourn for the loss of this life she had dreamed for herself. One day, when she was truly dead, there would be no tablet placed on an ancestral altar for her. Not as a concubine. Only a true wife merited veneration by her descendants. It would be as if she had never lived.

Ah Jie seated herself on one of the upholstered western-style armchairs in the middle of the drawing room, her *cheongsam* stretching tight across her stomach. She nodded at the go-between, who nodded at the small table set with a teapot and a single cup, as the servant prodded Yu Lan into action.

She crossed to the table, lifting the teapot and pouring lukewarm tea into the cup. Then approaching the chair, she knelt and offered the tea, symbol of her acceptance into Chan Towkay's home by his wife, the only formal recognition necessary of her new position as his concubine.

'Ah Jie, *yum cha*,' she said dutifully.

The angry woman took the tea. Her rouged lips left a crescent of bright red that obscured the cup's gold rim, as she sipped thoughtfully. 'We'd better find her something else to wear before Sin Saang sees her. She looks like a ghost.'

6

THE COLD WATER was a slap. Yu Lan had drifted through the journey to this grand house on the hill and her meeting with the *taitai* like a sleepwalker, little caring what happened to her. Now the slosh of cold water sluicing her body awoke her senses and her survival instincts. She became aware of the chatter of insects outside the open window, the slippery terracotta tiles beneath her feet, the mosquitoes hovering in the corners of the room, and her flesh dripping with cool water. She also registered that she wasn't alone. The amah was soaping her naked limbs with a wet cloth, all the while keeping up a running one-sided conversation.

'You are very tall. Some men would object to this but the *towkay* won't mind. He's a vigorous man,' the woman said with a giggle. 'I hear them sometimes, in the bedroom. He might be old but he has the juices of a young buck.'

Yu Lan felt the woman's hand stray towards the place between her legs and roused herself enough to push it away.

'If you don't wish me to wash you, do it yourself, little sister. Here,' she said, placing the cloth in Yu Lan's hand. 'The *towkay* won't like bad smells in the bedroom.'

Yu Lan bent over far enough to run the wet cloth between her legs, before dropping it to the floor in a small act of defiance.

The amah clucked her tongue. 'You don't want to anger Ho Jie. Not if you want a friend in this house.' Retrieving the cloth, she finished the job by soaping Yu Lan's legs, before pouring another bucket of water over her head and standing back to look at her.

'It's good that you aren't too thin. Those thin girls are dainty but not built for bearing children. And that's what you're here for,' she said, applying herself to squeezing water from Yu Lan's long hair so that it dripped down her back onto the floor. 'You don't have much to say for yourself, do you? Well, it's not so bad here. The *towkay* is all right. He shouts and sometimes he throws things but he doesn't beat anyone. Watch out for the *taitai* though. She pinches. And she'll always find a way to pay you back if you cross her.'

Taking a towel, she began rubbing vigorously, paying particular attention to Yu Lan's hair. 'Your hair is thick and shiny. Your flesh is firm. This is good. This is healthy. Did your parents come from farming stock? My family have been farmers for many generations but I was a silk worker. My father was too poor to provide me with a dowry. If I hadn't vowed to remain a spinster our landlord would have given me away to one of his cronies,' she said with a shudder. 'And who knows what kind of bad man would have taken me then?'

Throughout this stream of monologue, Yu Lan stood unresisting, letting the words too wash over her. Should she be pleased that she had been sold rather than given away to a bad man? That her body would bring some measure of prosperity to her family? Until her father squandered it at the mahjong table. But this amah still had a family, no matter how far away. And one day she might travel home to China and be welcomed for all her years of toil. Unlike the amah, Yu Lan's family lived only a few miles away but might as well be lost to her now that she had been sold as a concubine.

'If I hadn't become a self-combed woman, my husband's family would have reaped the benefit of my hard-earned income.

Besides, I liked working with the silk and my parents were grateful for my contribution to the family. But… so many silk factories are closing now,' she sighed. Yu Lan's silence was no hindrance to this speech. The amah didn't seem to expect much in the way of answer. Perhaps she was so accustomed to listening that she was pleased to have this opportunity to do the talking. 'There. You are clean and dry. But where is your breast binding cloth? Didn't your mother teach you how to bind your breasts?'

She picked up an item from a pile of clothing set on a stool out of range of the splashing water and returned to her charge holding out a *dudou* of red silk. 'Here, the *taitai* has given you these clothes. Put this on,' she said, nudging Yu Lan in the side with her elbow to hold the diamond-shaped apron in place over her chest while she tied it tightly at the neck and waist. 'That should keep your breasts in one place.'

Next she handed her a pair of red silk drawers, then yellow trousers with bands of embroidery at the cuff, followed by a matching blouse. When she was finished she stood back a pace to inspect the results of her handiwork.

'Not bad. Not a true beauty but not bad. You're lucky. Your father sold you to a rich man. True, you aren't his first wife but you will be the mother of his sons. That's something. Now, your elder sister wants to look at you before you go to the master.'

As the woman continued speaking, Yu Lan realised that from now on her body wouldn't be her own. She would be washed and rinsed, prodded and poked, examined and criticised. Very soon a stranger would impregnate her. One day a child of this stranger would colonise her womb. And then she would never be free.

*

'TURN AROUND, GIRL. Let me see you.'

The amah had deposited her in a spacious room at the rear of the house that smelled like the inside of Merchant Tang's silk store. A gigantic brass bed that might have slept Yu Lan's entire family was set against one wall and hung with rivers of colourful embroidered silk. The shutters were open and a light breeze drifted into the room. If she had been another girl in another house, Yu Lan might have cried tears of joy to sleep in this room, but she would much rather be back in the tiny room on High Street that she shared with her brothers.

The *towkay* sat on a stool at a round table, a glass of honey-coloured liquor in one hand. He sipped thoughtfully at his drink as he gestured for her to turn with his free hand.

'You look presentable. If you please me we'll get on well enough.' His gaze surveyed her from the top of her head to her embroidered silk slippers. 'But you must listen to the *taitai* and do as she bids. She has failed me by not bearing sons but in all other respects she is an excellent wife.' He paused to allow her to absorb his words. 'So don't get any ideas. Now, come here.'

Close to, he was even older than he appeared in the photograph. Older than her father. Perhaps fifty years or more. As old as her grandfather. Dark spots marred his hands and the skin on his neck resembled steamed chicken feet. She knew that when he stood up the thinning hair of his head would barely reach her eyebrows.

'Come here, girl,' he repeated, crooking a finger stained yellow with tobacco.

She stepped closer, powerless to resist, bereft of choices. She had no friends in this house, despite the *taitai's* words, despite the amah's Buddha mouth, snake heart. She knew that if she fought her new master it wouldn't go well for her. If she didn't please him, he might send her away. Not back to her father. She was a commodity now and Chan hadn't earned his wealth by squandering his commodities. If she fought him, she might never see home again. She might never see Ming.

So she chose the path of least resistance, allowing him to inspect her thoroughly, to run his hands up and down her body. He lingered on her buttocks, squeezing and stroking, his finger poking her with a sharp nail. Then he cupped her breasts through the tightly bound *dudou* before turning his attention to the fastenings of her loose blouse. She could tell from the intense expression on his face that his member stirred. She closed her eyes and tried not to see his face behind her eyelids.

'Open your eyes. I want you to look at me.'

He unbuttoned each toggle from its loop, pulling the blouse over her head and throwing it to the floor. She tried to repress the shiver of revulsion that quivered through her body, knowing that it would anger him. She tried to make herself into a statue. But she couldn't help thinking of his bony fingers and dread them touching her. She imagined them as claws raking her skin, gouging deep scratches in her flesh, even though he didn't touch her hard enough to leave a mark.

'That's a good handful here, heh, heh,' he said with a smirk, before turning his attention to her trousers. He untied the drawstring and let them drop to the floor, staring hard at the neat triangle of hair. He ran his hands down over the slight curve of her hips, then motioned for her to step out of the puddle of silk and stand back a distance.

Outside, the jungle steamed in the late afternoon heat, yet Yu Lan shivered, exposed to this old man's inspection. Once she had imagined the wedding night she would share with Ming, the smile lighting his eyes as he unwrapped his new bride. The quiver of his body as he melted into her. She had thought they would explore the secrets of the bedroom together, learning to give each other pleasure. Not like this. Never like this.

The old man stepped back several paces and sat, the better to see all of her. 'Don't cross your arms,' he chided, as he reached one hand beneath the long silk folds of his gown and jerked his hand back and forth. She knew what he was doing. She had seen her brother do the same thing in bed at night when he thought no one was watching.

'Untie those strings,' he ordered, waving his free hand at the ties of her *dudou*. But her hands refused to do his bidding. They seemed to have lost all ability to move, dangling nervelessly by her sides. Even if she wanted to she couldn't comply. Annoyed, he dropped his gown and stood up, crossing the few yards to where she stood and wrenching her around so that her back faced him. She felt his fingers pinching her neck as he struggled with the delicate silk strings, then a tearing sound as he ripped the flimsy apron from her body, before grabbing her breasts and tweaking her nipples between his fingers. She was conscious of twinges of pain all over her torso as his hands rubbed and pulled at her soft flesh. She could feel his member prodding at her buttocks as he pressed against her.

She closed her eyes, willing herself back to the riverbank under the shade of the spreading monkeypod tree, the river lapping near her feet. She tried to summon the feel of Ming's lips upon hers; anything to block the old man and his groping hands from her mind. But he gripped her by both arms and marched her towards the high brass bed in the corner of the room. Then he bent her upper body forward over the silk coverlets and her thoughts, like her body, were trapped.

She felt a hot burning pain as he plunged inside her, ramming himself into the softest tissue of her body. She screamed as he bludgeoned her in a frenzy of thrusting, his body slapping against her buttocks. So hard did he thrust that it seemed to her he must tear something deep inside. And then, just as suddenly as he entered her, he cried out with a shudder and let his upper torso fall upon her back. She felt the stiff silk of his gown pressing against her naked skin and his hot breath snuffling at the back of her neck.

'Heh, heh. Number One Son is in there. I know it.'

*

MADAM CHAN STEPPED away from the door to the concubine's room. Unconsciously, she put her hands to her ears to block out the sound of her husband's groans and the concubine's cries. She knew the sounds of her husband's lovemaking well, and felt a niggle of anger that he couldn't pretend that the business was a chore. Judging by the concubine's squeals, he hadn't had any trouble in that department tonight. She didn't know whether to be pleased or disturbed. For seventeen years they had been on good terms in almost every way. The duties of the bedroom had never been a problem for her. For the most part they had been enjoyable. Her husband liked to indulge in the pleasures of the bedroom and she obliged. Over time she had gently trained him to please her. As far as she knew he had no mistresses, and she knew most of what went on in his life, for it was in the bedroom that he confided his worries, appreciating her sympathetic ear and her insights. Yes, they had rubbed along quite well. And if at times he was difficult and demanding, well, she had servants to deal with that.

The only ripple on the smooth surface of their married life was the absence of children. There had been miscarriages, which she mourned as the loss of not only a child but also posterity. Without children, her husband's line would end. There would be no one to inherit all that he had built, all that he had carved out of the jungle of this uncultured land so far away from the Middle Kingdom. He was fifty-nine years of age and who knew how many years remained to him. And although he never berated her in public, in private she caught him looking at her sometimes with steely resentment in his eyes, as if all their years together meant nothing in the face of her barrenness.

The concubine was her gift to her ageing husband. The concubine would be the saviour of her marriage and the future of the Chan family. Yet she realised now that she didn't want to share her husband's love, not even for the sake of a son. She had loved him faithfully and well all these years. She especially didn't want to share his love with a sixteen-year-old child who had done nothing to earn it.

Madam Chan returned to her bedchamber at the front of the house and pulled up a stool at the table where she had set out tea implements and playing cards. No doubt her husband would be along soon for their nightly game of cards. He would play with his new toy for a while and then he would return to her. He was hers. As his ancestors were hers. As his children would be hers. As his grandchildren would be hers.

She picked up the cards and began to shuffle. The cards would fall as the ancestors willed. There was no need to worry about a know-nothing concubine. This girl was merely a vessel. Chan Towkay's children might one day call the girl Little Mother but she would be Big Mother. No one would usurp that title from her.

7

YU LAN FELT her shoulder being shaken roughly followed by the sound of shutters being flung back and windows thrown open. Outside she could hear someone, presumably the Chan's driver, hawking up that morning's phlegm and a female voice scolding him for being a dirty pig.

'Come, Sai Mui, it's time to get up.'

She resisted the impulse to open her eyes. She had been awake for some time but reluctant to stir beyond the cocoon of this bed. If she stayed where she was she could pretend that the previous day had never happened. If she kept her eyes scrunched tight she could wish herself back to the day before yesterday, when she still had hope that she might find a way to control her destiny. She could still imagine riding in a red sedan chair to a new home above a *kopi* shop, her arms tinkling with wedding gold. She could imagine the gentle touch of a boy's hand upon her hair, the sensation of his fingers stroking the soft skin of her inner arm. She could picture herself serving tea to her in-laws the morning after her wedding, her head bowed in respect, their faces smiling approval.

Burrowing beneath the cotton sheet, she twisted the jade ring that encircled her thumb, comforted by its silky feel. The ring was a symbol of their promise to each other. Yesterday Ming said that it was never passed down through generations of his family, that it was a poor imitation, not real jade. But when she cradled it in her hand, she felt the heft of that stone. And when she slipped it onto her thumb it was slow to warm from her body heat like true jade. Had he lied then, to trick her into loving him? Or he was lying now to trick her out of loving him? She didn't know which answer was more certain to break her heart. She was sixteen and she felt like her life was over when she had only begun her journey. All that lay ahead was an old man's penis and his wife's sharp tongue.

No. It couldn't be true. If Ming lied to her it was because his father was watching. His father must have threatened him. He would never hurt her. He loved her. She could tell from the way he looked at her, the way his body quivered sometimes when he brushed against her. The way her heart hammered in her chest when they were together. These feelings were the truth, not hurtful words placed in his mouth by his father.

She felt a tug and the sheet was torn from her body.

'These sheets will need soaking. So much blood from tearing so small a thing,' the amah said, clucking her tongue. 'I suppose it hurt? They tell me it doesn't hurt so much the second time. And you can always use a bit of spit if it gets too dry down there. Now, time to get up.'

The amah was prodding her now, urging her towards the edge of the bed and the start of a new day. But Yu Lan wanted to hide from that day. She flung out an arm to push the woman away, but her arm was caught and held.

'Heh, heh. You're surprised that Ho Jie is so strong? I may be small but I've been working longer than you've been alive,' she cackled before adding, 'and what's this you wear on your thumb? It wasn't there yesterday. Who gave it to you? A young man, I suppose.'

Yu Lan tried to wrench her arm from the woman's grasp but the amah locked her in a fierce grip, her fingers like iron.

'Let me go!'

'Let you go? If I let you go downstairs wearing your precious jade the *taitai* will have it from you faster than a monkey snatches a banana. It won't look so well on her bony white claws. Ho Jie is doing you a favour.'

Save for her mother, no one had ever done Yu Lan any favours. She paid for her father's rare kindness with her labour. She bargained for peace with her brothers. She fought for her turn with the other children in her neighbourhood. That was how life worked. For a time she had hoped there might be another path for her, but the gods deemed otherwise. You struggled and then you died. This was a fact.

Turning her head, she looked properly at the servant for the first time since she had entered this forbidding house. Small, thin and dressed in neat black *fu* and white *sam*, she looked little different to any other amah, except for the ropy muscles of a labourer that graced her arms. She appeared to be a similar age to Yu Lan's mother, and although she was unmarried her hair was braided and pinned into the bun of a married woman. Yu Lan gazed into her eyes, expecting to see disapproval, but was met with a twinkle.

'Unless you would make Ho Jie a gift?'

'It belongs to me. You can't have it.'

'Then you'd better find a place where snooping noses and prying eyes won't find it. This house is large enough to hold many secrets. How big a secret could a child like you need to hide?'

In the Chans' world, where wealth and the will of their ancestors prevailed, Yu Lan's love was so small a thing she could hide it in her heart for ever. The ring, however, was a different matter. Ho Jie was right. It would kill her to see her ring decorating that woman's hand. So if she wanted to keep it from the *taitai's* clutches it demanded more from her.

'Now dress quickly, for this morning you must serve breakfast to the *towkay*.'

Scrambling from the bed as soon as the amah departed, Yu Lan scoured the room, searching for somewhere to stow the ring. It needed to be a place that wouldn't be shifted, part of the fabric of the house. Under a wobbly piece of parquetry. Behind a loose section of skirting. Inside a hollow in the wall. Somewhere that only she knew. Somewhere safe until the house should fall down around it. For true jade would outlast them all.

*

AS THE *towkay* rumbled contentedly in bed alongside her, Madam Chan drew back the fine cotton sheet and slipped quietly into the adjoining bathroom. She was grateful that her husband wasn't as vigorous as he had been once, for a younger man might have kept the girl busy all night. Instead, he had returned to their room in a self-congratulatory mood, called for a fresh bottle of whiskey and promptly fallen asleep.

In the bathroom, she sluiced cold water over her body then wrapped a batik sarong around her chest. Despite her husband's obvious delight in the concubine's ripe grapefruits, she preferred her own firm plums. She took pleasure in the creamy texture of her skin and the fine architecture of her figure. She was thirty-three years old but looked much younger. Chan might do his duty by the concubine but she was First Lady Chan and if the girl ever forgot this, well, she would soon remind her.

Madam Chan liked to rise early. She didn't care to be caught with bare brows and untamed hair. She preferred to bathe and dress before her husband stirred. It took effort to appear flawless. Effort and a certain degree of discomfort to pluck every recalcitrant hair from her brow each morning and pencil in a perfect arch; to sit perfectly still as Ho Jie applied Mister Marcel's hot irons to her hair, creating the stiff waves that framed her face.

Sitting before the mirror of her rosewood dressing table, Madam Chan applied a fine dusting of rice powder to her already perfect complexion. In her experience, everything had a price and the price for beauty was usually pain. Just as the price for youth was obedience. The price for power was responsibility and the price for respect was ageing. That was the way. Although she gave thanks that she wasn't born in a hick village in China where women crippled their daughters' feet to titillate their men. She was born in the bustling city of Guangzhou, and her mother had more sense. Men might find lotus feet arousing, but tottering about on clothbound hooves wasn't conducive to pleasure for the woman whose feet were maimed.

Her husband was a *towkay*, owner of two prosperous tin mines. But alongside that wealth and prestige came responsibility. If one of his miners slipped and fell into the giant mechanical bucket that dredged up raw earth, Chan Towkay was tasked with writing to that man's family in China informing them of the death. If the pit flooded in a heavy downpour and sliding earth crushed men, Chan had to deal with the aftermath. He was the one who worried about the fluctuating price of tin and pored over the accounts late into the night. The livelihoods of many depended upon him. For how would his miners repay the agents who paid for their passages to Malaya if he didn't provide them with work?

Everything had a price and if you were prepared to pay, surely the gods would reward you. If the price for a son was to share her husband with this girl – then Madam Chan would pay it. For as long as necessary, anyway.

*

'SHE ARRIVED YESTERDAY and already she thinks she is the new Tzu Hsi,' Madam Chan observed as Yu Lan entered the room. 'Ho Jie, in future please ensure that this lazy girl is downstairs in good time to serve breakfast to the *towkay*. We aren't living in the Forbidden Palace and she isn't the new Empress Dowager.'

Yu Lan wondered how the sixteen-year-old concubine Tzu Hsi felt all those centuries ago when court eunuchs left her at the end of the Emperor's bed naked except for a flimsy red robe. How did she feel about being given as a fourth-ranked concubine to the Son of Heaven? One lowly girl amongst many, offered up to the Emperor whenever he felt the urge to spill his seed inside her. She wondered whether Tzu Hsi once had a boy who loved her, a boy who she never saw again.

'The *towkay* may indulge you for the moment but the novelty will wear off soon. Especially if his rice porridge is cold.'

Like her, Tzu Hsi had no choice.

'Now, go to the kitchen and ask Cook to give you the *towkay's* porridge and his favourite accompaniments. He will be down in a moment.'

But Tzu Hsi was the only consort to give the Emperor a son. In the end she was the only one who mattered. She outlasted the Empress. And she outlasted three emperors: a husband, a son and a nephew. For almost fifty years she was the power behind the imperial screen. And they all hated her for it.

'I'm going, Madam,' she said, guarding her words. Whatever she said would be wrong.

'I'm going, *Ah Jie*. Remember, I'm your elder sister now.' The words held an implicit threat. You are nothing beneath my gaze; she could see the thought in her eyes. The woman stared at her with eyes as hard as daggers and eyebrows taut as twin bowstrings, but Yu Lan didn't lower her glance. What could this woman do to her that hadn't been done already? Yesterday her life had been ripped from her. Last night her body had been ravaged. What more could they do?

Turning away without another word, she headed for the rear of the house where she knew she would find the kitchen and the owner of yet another scolding voice. This house was full of them.

'Who's that then?' A wiry old lady with almost as much hair sprouting from her chin as her head stood at a brick stove set against the outside wall of the kitchen. An overhead chimney funnelled smoke from the cooking fire to the outside. Nearby, a red wall plaque and a row of offerings in small ceramic cups announced the Kitchen God's altar. In her mother's kitchen a slip of red paper on the wall represented the god, but here he was given a proper plaque and many gifts. Rows of cooking implements hung on racks suspended from the ceiling and earthenware pots in all shapes and sizes sat on benches and shelves about the room.

'Well, don't just stand there looking like a stupid rice bucket!' The cook spoke Cantonese with a strong Hainanese accent. She looked too small to stir the great wok that hung upon the wall, her arms too skinny to lift the heavy pot of rice porridge that simmered upon the stove. 'Come here.'

Yu Lan walked over to stand at the table in the centre of the room. She became aware that the usual enticing mix of kitchen odours was overlain by something that smelled vaguely dead. Perhaps there was a dead mouse lying under one of the benches or a bird trapped in the chimney. She hoped the smell wasn't emanating from Cook.

'So you're the new girl?' the cook said, lifting an eye from her pot to consider her. 'You just do as Aunty tells you and we'll get along fine. I might even find something pleasing to a young girl's sweet tooth if you do right by me.'

'Thank you, Ah Yi,' she said meekly, for her mother had taught her to respect all grandmothers, even ones with questionable personal hygiene.

'That smelly mess there is the master's breakfast.' The cook nodded at a dish of pickled vegetables and cubes of steamed tofu that had been placed on a table next to a bowl of steaming rice porridge. The tofu was an unappealing grey colour. 'I make the tofu myself. Aunty's secret recipe. The master won't accept anything less. Three months the brine has been fermenting out back.'

'It smells worse than sweaty feet,' Yu Lan said, relieved to discover the source of the odour, but tempted to hold her nose all the same.

'Just how the *towkay* likes it.'

'What does it have in it?'

'Oh, dried shrimp, rotten meat, vegetables, herbs... and the magic ingredient.'

'What's that?' asked Yu Lan, curious despite herself.

'Dead babies' fingernails.'

Yu Lan jumped back from the table before realising that the old woman was laughing at her.

'Heh, heh, heh. I may be an old crone but I'm not a witch, girl. Now hurry up. Don't make him wait. He's grumpier than a two-year-old when he's hungry.'

'I won't, Ah Yi.'

'And then come back for the *taitai's* breakfast. I'm frying up a couple of *youtiou*, to go with her porridge,' she said, indicating the cylinders of dough she was about to deep fry in a spitting wok, 'but she needs to be careful. She'll get fat if she eats too many of these. And the master has new fish to fry too.' The old woman cackled, looking at her properly for the first time and winking. 'The master has new fish to fry indeed. I wonder how the mistress is liking that.'

Holding the bowl of porridge in one hand and the dish of pickled vegetables and stinky tofu in the other, Yu Lan returned to the dining room to discover that the mistress had been joined by her husband who took pride of place in a high-backed wooden chair with curving arms. He was dressed for business in a Western-style suit with a striped tie but on his feet were a pair of cloth slippers.

'I apologise for this lazy girl. She is slower than a three-legged tortoise,' Madam Chan declared, rapping Yu Lan on the arm with her fan as she set the blue and white bowl of steaming porridge in front of the *towkay*.

'Oh, don't be harsh woman, the girl is merely tired,' he said, his mouth curling awkwardly into a smile, as if it was out of practice. 'All this is new to her and she had a very busy night. Take a seat, girl.' He tapped the chair beside him, nodding at her encouragingly.

Yu Lan hesitated, looking to the *taitai* for confirmation. At least the chair was out of reach of her snapping claws.

'But I don't have my porridge yet,' complained Madam Chan.

'Ho Jie can bring your porridge. Let the girl sit. Eat. She'll need all her energy to grow my son inside her.'

Madam Chan bowed her head in acquiescence, for what possible objection could she raise to that? She hadn't managed to produce a son in all these years so now it was left to another. Her face grew even whiter than usual, as pale a slab of fresh tofu, with her red lips a vicious gash in her face. For all her wealth, Yu Lan realised that her new mistress believed she had failed her husband, failed in her duty as a wife. For all her silk dresses and gold jewellery, for all her vicious claws, she couldn't do what any uneducated sixteen-year-old girl could accomplish.

Yu Lan was that sixteen-year-old girl. Her body would be that sacred vessel, the bearer of the Chan future, the repository of Chan hopes. This was her purpose. This was her power, if she were clever. Glancing at the *taitai's* strained face, Yu Lan understood that she wasn't the only one in this room who strove to control her destiny, which meant that there must be some room for her to manoeuvre. She might be 'little sister' but perhaps her destiny wasn't yet set in stone. Perhaps she could still escape this house and find her way to Ming. She could still attain the future she had dreamed. Once Chan had a son, he might release her. Once he had a son, he might be so grateful that he would reward her with her freedom. So long as the *taitai* had no say in it.

The question was... how could Yu Lan ensure that Ah Jie had no say? After all, she had a say about everything else in this house. It would take cleverness and guile, and the ability to close her heart and mind to the old man's greedy pillaging of her body. She would need to be strong. To stay focused on her ultimate goal. She might need to be ruthless. She would certainly need to be cunning.

'I'm sure you put a son in me last night, Sin Saang. Your seed is so vigorous,' she said, summoning the sweetest smile she could muster. 'Don't you agree, Ah Jie?'

8

Hampshire 2015

SARAH PEERED THROUGH foggy glass, trying to follow a dotted white line that snaked into the night like a lifeline. They were on their way to her mother-in-law's house for eggnog and Christmas cheer, but the heavy rain and poor visibility were in danger of leading them astray. The headlights illuminated a canopy of bowed trees that offered little protection from the driving rain, and although there was hardly any traffic on the road, she felt uneasy. She didn't like narrow, country roads on stormy nights. In the city she knew what to look out for, but who knew what dangers lurked beyond the trees.

She risked a swift glance at Nick's profile. He was staring straight ahead, his face relaxed in a neutral expression so that she couldn't tell what he was thinking. Her husband always managed to look pleasant, even while stubbing his toe or arguing with the power company. If Nick were an emoticon he would be the round-eyed, half-smiling one and she would be the eyebrows-raised, kooky-looking one with the grimace.

'Hey, what's up?' he said, catching her glance. 'Still can't get enough of me?'

'Nothing. Just thinking.' She laughed, trying to lighten her mood. It was Christmas but she was still shifting stock in her head.

Reaching across the handbrake, he captured her wrist where

her hand gripped the wheel. 'You think too much. It's the holidays, remember.'

'I know, but Christmas is our busiest time.'

'Your head isn't a warehouse, Sar. Let it go for a bit.'

Returning her attention to the road, she glimpsed a flicker of movement ahead out of the corner of her eye. A flash of white caught in the headlights as something drifted through the trees to her right. She tore her gaze from the road, concerned that the figure – whatever it was – might stray into their path. But it shimmered in the rain for a moment before moving deeper into the forest, finally vanishing from view in a last dance of light and shadow. Perhaps it was a deer. She'd heard that there were white fallow deer roaming the New Forest. A collision with a deer was the last thing they needed. She doubted the deer would appreciate it either.

The danger over, she breathed out in relief, only to be surprised by a staccato bumping sound as the car hit something. Oh, shit.

'What was that?'

'I think you ran over a plank of wood. Don't worry about it.'

A few seconds later the thump-thump of a punctured tyre told Sarah that she did need to worry about it. But that was Nick for you. Never worry about anything and look where it got you.

'Now look what you've made me do,' she said, as she steered the car onto the verge. Of course, she knew she was being unfair. Of course, she knew that it wasn't his fault she had taken her eyes from the road, and she could hardly blame the deer, if that's what it was. But someone had to take the blame for the rain, the traffic out of London and the flat tyre. And he was the only other person present. Nick, being a sensible man, declined to respond. In silence, they both got out of the car, struggling into their jackets. Sarah headed automatically for the boot.

'I'll do it,' he said, popping the boot before she could reach it.

'Maybe we should call the RAC.' She doubted he'd changed a tyre in his life, and a storm wasn't the time to learn.

'No. I can do it.'

Already her hair streamed with water, turning into rat's tails. She could sense the mascara running down her face. This evening she'd swapped her usual straight blow-dry for curling brown tendrils framing her oval face. She'd forsaken her business-like beige shadow and brown liner for a smoky eye, and black flats for high-heeled ankle boots. She'd wanted to look sexy. She'd even shimmied into an early Christmas gift for Nick beneath her little black dress. Dark purple and barely there. She'd wanted to be fun Sarah tonight instead of business Sarah. So far she hadn't made a very good job of it.

Pulling her jacket up over her head, she said, 'God, it's cold.'

'Get back in the car. I can manage.'

'No. You might need me. Besides, I'll only make the car heavier if I sit there while you're jacking it up. I've put on a few pounds recently.' She flicked on the torch, then carried the jack and wrench over and set them on the ground, her new boots slurping through puddles. Nick rolled the spare towards the flat front tyre, flicking up a spray of mud.

'You really did a number on it.'

'I thought something was about to run onto the road.'

With one knee on the ground, and the other foot bracing his body, he placed the jack under the car's frame, manoeuvring it into place behind the wheel well. His hair was plastered to his head like a shiny black cap. The rain coursed down his flaring black eyebrows, neat straight nose and high cheekbones, so that he gleamed in the torchlight.

'I think there should be a little notch there or something.'

'I can do it, Sarah.'

She could take a hint. Sometimes. Moving away a few steps, she stood in front of the car, illuminated by the headlights. She wondered whether it was really a deer that had distracted her. It hadn't looked like one. But what else would be flitting through the forest this late on a rainy night? And she was an attentive driver. Mistakes like this didn't happen to her.

She watched as he picked up the wrench and began loosening the wheel nuts, using his body weight to break the resistance. She smiled to herself at the way he grunted a little with the effort. He was so cute when he had to do anything practical. When each nut was loose he began cranking the jack until the tyre was suspended several inches above the ground. Then one by one he removed the nuts, turning them with his hands, before lifting the wheel from its bolts.

He was placing the wheel on the ground next to the car when she felt it move, shifting a little on the soft verge. Sarah wasn't psychic, but she could see the future playing out before her eyes like a scene from a movie. She could see the jack sliding sideways in the mud, slipping out from under the frame and dropping the car onto its axle. All that weight, sitting on the brake disc. Crushing who knew what mysterious components of the undercarriage.

'The jack is slipping!' she called.

Nick had seen what was happening at the same moment, dropping the wheel and reaching instinctively to prop up the jack with his hands – his beautiful hands – directly under the falling car. Without thinking for once, with a speed and strength she never knew she possessed, Sarah dropped the torch and lunged forward. She grasped the bumper bar with both hands and lifted. Heaved with all her might.

'Get the spare,' she shouted through the sound of driving rain.

Every muscle in her body strained to hold the car. She felt cords of muscle pulled taut from forearm to shoulder. Each second stretched elastically as Nick snatched up the spare and wiggled it onto the wheel bolts. Even then she didn't dare let go. She waited until he fumbled the nuts into place, his hands slipping on the wet metal as he turned and twisted them until they tightened. Only then did she release her grip on the car and step back, holding her stomach, releasing her breath. All those crunches had finally proved useful.

With the wheel in place and the car squatting steady in the mud, Nick stood to face her. Patches of mud darkened his jeans and his wool jacket clung wetly to his body. Behind him the road plunged into darkness and above them the trees closed in like a dark cavern. Ahead, the shining road disappeared into the mist, with rain gleaming like spears of light in the headlamps.

'You look like an angel,' he said.

'I think my halo is soggy.' She shrugged, wincing as she discovered a wrenched shoulder.

'I didn't know how strong you are.'

'Well, who else you gonna call?' she said with a half smile, as surprised as Nick that she had such power in her. She'd never really tested herself physically before.

He walked towards her, throwing his arms around her waist and pulling her close. She nestled against him, searching for a spot of warmth.

'What would I do without you, Sar?'

'I don't know. You'd have to get yourself a substitute, I suppose.' She smiled, not allowing herself to think about losing him, even in jest. But she couldn't help shivering, in her wet clothes, with the freezing rain falling around them.

'Here, let me warm you up,' he said, taking her hands in his and chafing them.

'Your hands are so cold. Your mother's eggnog better have plenty of rum in it.'

'It always does.'

She pressed closer to him. Beneath the jacket, his body was lithe and pliant as bamboo. She could trust him to bend but never break.

'I'm sorry I'm such a bitch.'

'That's all right, sweetheart. At least you're my bitch. I'd hate to be on the other team.'

9

THE LANE WAS awash with shimmering strings of Christmas lights. June's house was second to last, a stone cottage with slate roof and latticed windows set in a rambling garden. Like its neighbours, it dazzled with prancing reindeer and grinning snowmen, but with the addition of a row of Chinese lanterns glowing around the entry porch.

'Ma's excelled herself this year,' said Nick, peering through the car's misted window.

'The snowflakes are new.'

Smoke drifted from the chimney, and through the open drapes Sarah spotted a tree glittering in one corner and the flicker of candlelight. June loved all holidays and celebrated them indiscriminately, probably a result of growing up in a country of so many faiths. She had an entire attic devoted to holiday decorations, dragons nudging reindeer, shouldering pumpkins.

'I hope she hasn't baked mince pies again,' said Nick.

'I wondered why I found half a mince pie in the pocket of your anorak in March.' Rubbing her hands up and down her arms and finding only cold, damp wool, she added, 'I'm glad she has a fire going. I smell like wet dog.'

'Are you all right, Sar?'

'Yeah. I'm fine.' Her right brain was telling her she was fine, and she'd finally relaxed her grip on the wheel, but instinct was saying something different. A crawling feeling beneath her skin told her that something bad was about to happen. She shook it off. It was probably just a delayed reaction. They'd narrowly escaped one disaster tonight; nothing more was likely now. It was merely shock that had set her nerves on edge. 'I'm not the one who was nearly crushed by my car,' she said, returning his concern.

'But I wasn't.' It was true; he didn't seem at all affected by their near miss. He seemed positively jolly, about to begin ho-ho-ho-ing any moment.

Her phone chimed in her jacket pocket. She knew she would probably regret looking at it but it could be a last-minute work emergency.

'Your mum?' Nick asked, reading the truth on her face.

'Uh-huh. Ninth message so far today and we've still got two hours to midnight. "Please bring another Christmas cake. This one tastes funny. They must have put chemicals in it."'

'Maybe we can pick one up on the way tomorrow.'

'You know there's nothing wrong with the cake.'

'More cake for me then.' He grinned, rubbing his hands together. 'Okay. Eggnog here we come.'

Grabbing their overnight bags and June's gift – wrapped in brown paper and tied with a twisted silken cord – they braced for the cold. Now that the rain had eased, the air was crisp with a hint of wood smoke. All they needed was a flurry of snow to conjure a perfect Christmas, except of course for the music issuing faintly through the door. As Nick led the way up the garden path, it became clear that carols weren't on June's Christmas playlist.

'Is that Cantopop? Or K-pop?'

'Nineties Cantopop, actually. My friends grew up listening to their parents' Bowie albums and I was subjected to Sammi.'

'I don't mind it.'

'Yup, except I learned my Cantonese listening to Sammi Cheng and watching Jackie Chan. So the only words I know are "I'll kill you" and "I love you". Not much use if you're trying to order take-away.'

'Well, so long as you know the difference.'

Linking his free arm through hers he smooched her cheek, his nose still chilly. *'Ngoh oi neih.'*

'I hope that's "I love you".'

*

THE FIRST THING Nick noticed, besides the lopsided angel on top of the tree, was that his mother was burning incense. In fact, since his last visit two months previously, she had set up a small altar in one corner of the living room. The antique altar table, porcelain deities and bowls of offerings looked incongruous next to the chintz armchairs. But then, his mother always had embraced diversity.

'Hey, Ma,' he called to her in the kitchen. 'What's with the gods? Are you trying to stink up the house?'

One of the porcelain figures, the benevolent-looking one, he recognised as Guan Yin, Goddess of Mercy. The distinguished, bearded guys must be the Three Pure Ones. There was also a plaque to the Sky God and a couple of old photos leaning against a vase. Studying the arrangement, he wondered what had prompted his mother to return to her Taoist roots. June usually only indulged in the festive trappings. She was all about lion dancers and Santa Claus, nothing as esoteric as spirits. Except for the occasional tot of whiskey.

He was helping himself to a homemade sesame ball from

the altar when she returned from the kitchen with a plate of shortbread.

'Get your mitts off that. Fancy taking food out of the mouths of the gods!' she said, swatting his hand away. 'Have a shortbread.'

'Come on, Ma, you know I love your sesame balls,' he said, winking at Sarah over the top of his mother's head. 'The gods can forage for themselves.'

'Don't be so disrespectful.'

'Why this sudden devotion anyway?'

She avoided his eyes by fussing with the shortbread, sliding a pile of books across the coffee table and setting it down. His mother was a librarian so books lined every available surface of the cottage. Growing up, they had used stacks of books for everything from bedside tables to plant stands.

'Just a little insurance,' she said, returning to stand next to him.

'Wouldn't Prudential be a safer bet?'

She shook her head, making a clicking sound with her tongue. 'Don't think I don't realise you're making fun of me. But I'm not getting any younger. None of us are.' She paused and he caught a flash of regret in her eyes. 'You never know when your time will be up. You always think you have all the time in the world. Anyway… it's good to be prepared.'

'Don't worry. I'll burn hell money for you. I might even throw in a paper Mercedes.'

'Death is nothing to laugh about.'

He leaned an elbow on her shoulder and kissed the top of her head. 'Sorry, Ma, but it's not like you to be so superstitious.'

'I have a lot to be grateful for and you can't be too careful,' she said, flicking him with the tea towel that had been draped over her other shoulder. 'And don't use me as an armrest.' She turned to Sarah and asked with a smile, 'So how is the home-wares business? You look exhausted... and wet.'

His mother knew how hard Sarah worked, and how Nick longed for the worst to be over and the business doing well so they could take a long, lazy break. He admired his wife's passion and stamina but sometimes he wished there was a little less of it.

'Not bad. I'm off on another buying trip next month,' Sarah said, but she was gazing at the altar rather than June. 'I've never seen these,' she said, picking up the two photos and flipping between them.

Nick could see that the first was a photo of Ho Jie, his mother's old amah. She had died when he was a very small boy, but he felt he knew her from his mother's stories. The second one he didn't recognise.

'Is this your family?' Sarah asked, indicating the second photograph.

'Mmm. I was thinking of having it framed.'

'And is this baby you?'

The baby in question was seated on the knee of a woman wearing an embroidered Chinese gown and jacket, her hair styled in stiff waves with gold peeking out beneath her sleeves. The baby was dressed in an old-fashioned smock embellished with lace, and a matching bonnet. Seated next to the woman was an older man in Western dress, dark suit jacket over light trousers and a striped tie, his hair parted severely on one side. To Nick, the clothes looked too dated to belong to his mother's parents. Although since he'd never seen a photo of them before either, they could just be old-fashioned people.

June was frowning at the photograph. 'The baby is my father. With my grandmother and grandfather.'

'You've never shown me a picture of Ah Gung before,' he said, leaning over Sarah's shoulder to examine the photograph more closely, as if he could find some hint in the baby's round cheeks and pointed chin. Some clue to the man his grandfather would become. Some foreshadowing of the grandson he never knew. He was looking for himself in that baby's plump face.

'That's the only one I have and it won't tell you much. He looks like any other baby.'

Nick knew his grandmother had died when his mother was a small child. And that his mother became estranged from his grandfather when she decided to remain in London after she finished university rather than returning home to Malaysia. But apart from stories about Ho Jie, he knew little of his mother's early life and even less about his grandparents. As a kid, whenever he tried to ask about them she changed the subject. After a while he learned not to ask. He wasn't even sure whether his grandfather was still alive, although his mother usually behaved as if he wasn't.

Now he studied the other people in the photograph. Standing behind and to the right, he recognised Ho Jie, dressed in the ubiquitous amah uniform of white blouse over loose black trousers, hair pulled back tightly into a bun. And to the left was a young girl wearing matching blouse and trousers in a small floral print.

'Who are the other people?' Sarah asked.

'The one on the right is our amah, Ho Jie. She brought me up after my mother died. Actually, she was the one who sent me this picture. But I don't know who the girl is. Perhaps she's another servant.'

The girl didn't look happy. Funnily enough, she reminded him of photographs of his wife as a teenager. Sarah always donned her bitch-face for family photographs. Sullen. Bored. Decidedly pissed off. But if the photographer managed to catch her off guard, or if one of her friends had taken the picture, it was a different story – she would be smiling and goofing off. She would be more like the Sarah he'd met all those years ago, sprawled on the lawn, scoffing hot chips. But here the girl was resolutely unsmiling, staring at nothing. Nick wondered what kind of life she'd led for all hope to be absent from her face.

'Did Ah Gung really never try and get in touch with you?' he asked, sensing that the appearance of the altar and the photographs might mean that his mother was softening. Perhaps now was the moment to worm out her secrets, especially if he opened a bottle of her favourite Burgundy. And perhaps thoughts of her father might deflect some of her attention from his news, news that he suspected neither his mother nor Sarah was going to be pleased about. 'I can't believe he just cut off all contact.'

But June's hands curled unconsciously into fists as she said, 'Well, he was old school. Everything with him was about filial piety, obligation, etcetera.'

'I suppose I'm lucky you're so hip then?'

She gave him a scathing look. 'You don't know *how* lucky, my boy. After I refused to return to Kuala Lumpur he never spoke to me again. I wrote so many times but my letters were all returned unopened. Ho Jie was illiterate but even she made the effort of using a letter writer to keep in touch. She was more of a parent to me anyway.'

'Maybe we should have made the trip when I was a kid. You know, if he'd met his only grandson, maybe things would have been different.' Maybe you could have patched things up, is what he meant. Or was that just wishful thinking? Little boy lost thinking, Sarah would say.

'You never knew him, Nicky. You don't know what it was like to grow up in that house... besides, he would never have accepted me as a single mother. He would have been too ashamed.'

As if to shut him up, Sarah elbowed him in the ribs. 'Nick has picked up another session at Queen Mary's, teaching Narrative.'

'That's great, darling.'

'Yup, still only four sessions a week though. It's hardly going to make our fortune,' he said.

'Well, you only finished your doctorate last year. Things are bound to pick up,' Sarah said, sliding her arm around his waist.

'Mmm, about that...' he paused, trying to make up his mind whether to tell them now or wait until they'd had a few glasses of wine. He took a deep breath. He had to tell them sooner or later; might as well get it over with. 'Actually, I've been offered a full-time contract.'

He felt Sarah's arm tense and she looked at him a little strangely. Usually he blurted out good news before he kissed her hullo. Unlike her, he was an amateur at secret keeping. So she would sense there was more.

'That's wonderful news,' said June, giving him a big kiss on the cheek. 'Congratulations.'

'Thanks, Ma,' he said, but he was looking at Sarah as he replied.

'Where is it?' she asked, looking him in the eye and getting straight down to business. She had a sixth sense for the dubious clause in any agreement.

'Monash University.' He wondered if she would recognise the name. Probably not.

'Where's that?'

He'd been pretending for days that she might be enthusiastic, but even before he spoke he knew that he'd been fooling himself. 'It's in Australia, but I've been offered a job at their Kuala Lumpur campus.'

If Sarah looked dumbfounded by this announcement, his mother looked as if someone had trampled over her grave. With her sun-shy complexion, she couldn't be any paler, but she had an expression of such shock on her face that he thought she might be about to have a heart attack. He gripped her arm above the elbow, leading her over to the sofa and helping her to sit.

'Are you all right?'

'Apart from the fact that my son is trying to kill me?'

'Come on, Ma. It's not that bad.'

'I suppose you waited to tell us both at the same time so you only had to face the music once,' said Sarah. 'Good plan, Nick.'

'I haven't accepted. I wanted to talk to you about it.' Maybe he hadn't accepted officially, but in his head he was already making plans – about how they could make their lives work for two years with half a world between them. It wasn't ideal but it was an opportunity he couldn't afford to pass up. So many of their friends were eking out a living on sessional teaching. Tenure had gone the way of tweed jackets and elbow patches. This seemed like a first step in the direction of something more permanent. Something tangible.

'But you're tempted.'

'Yes, I'm tempted.' He shrugged, offering her a tentative smile. 'We could make it work for a couple of years. I know you can't leave London now, but the academic year is short. And there are so many interesting crafts in southeast Asia. You could make an occasional trip out worth your while.' When she still didn't comment, he added, 'It's a fantastic opportunity.'

'I know. It's just that it's so... so far.'

Maybe it wouldn't work if they were newlyweds – or parents – but they were an old married couple now. Together twelve years. Married eight. And Sarah didn't want to consider children yet. He loved her but he knew that he could survive without her. And she could survive without him. At least for a while.

His mother was sitting silently. She clasped her hands in her lap, knees locked, lips buttoned tight. 'It's not for ever,' he promised.

'Isn't it?' She stopped contemplating the backs of her hands to look up at him. 'There's nothing for you in Malaysia, nothing but trouble. Why do you think I never returned?'

He perched on the arm of the sofa, as if his physical presence might reassure her. 'Don't be so melodramatic, Ma. You didn't go back because Ah Gung disowned you. You were too wounded to return, but there's nothing to hurt me there. Kuala Lumpur is a thriving modern city. Nothing bad is going to happen.'

June wasn't reassured. 'It's not safe there.'

'To be honest, it's about more than getting a job. I've felt like I'm drifting for a while now, like I need an anchor. You know the feeling that there's nothing connecting you to the past or the future. Like you're...' he trailed off.

Alone? But that wasn't fair. He wasn't alone. He had a full complement of friends. He had colleagues. He had his beautiful Sarah. And he had June. But there was something missing. He felt disconnected. It was a cliché, but he felt like he needed to find out who he was before he could become who he was meant to be. He needed to find the real Nicholas Chan. And Malaysia, his mother's homeland, might show him the way.

'Maybe I'll find the story I'm searching for there,' he said, looking from his mother to his wife with a shrug of apology. 'Maybe I'll start writing again.' He hadn't attempted any fiction since his undergraduate days. He felt like he'd lost the knack for story. He could only recognise it in others.

June sighed and shook her head. 'The only story you'll find there won't lead anywhere you'll want to go.'

10

Kuala Lumpur 2016

BY THE TIME Nick arrived outside the neat white bungalow hidden behind palm-screened walls, he was beginning to feel like a mouse trapped in a maze. He knew there must be a logical route through Petaling Jaya's labyrinth of roads with its coded numbers instead of street names, but even his GPS seemed in imminent danger of going on strike. All he knew was that the PJ city planners must have been a singularly unpoetic lot. And they certainly could not count. Why the hell was BU 10/1 adjacent to BU 7/2? Did they lose sections 8 and 9?

He let the engine idle, taking a last few air-conditioned moments to slow his breathing before he got out of the car. His friends assumed that he was calm by nurture, if not nature, that it would take a hurricane to ruffle his feathers. Even those who knew him best didn't realise that sometimes it took effort to appear effortlessly relaxed. Especially when you were dropping in unexpectedly on the grandfather you had never met, the grandfather who quite probably was unaware of your existence.

A brass plaque attached to high metal gates read 'Distinguished Home for Venerable Elders' in Malay, Chinese and English, which cheered him up a bit. At least someone here had some imagination, a poetic way with words. Maybe the Distinguished Home for Venerable Elders would have a Refreshing Receptacle of Fragrant Tea on offer. His mouth was dry and his throat parched in anticipation. He had been working up to this moment since he first arrived in Kuala Lumpur, telling himself that he needed to feel settled before he faced the dragon. Hopefully a dragon with less than a full set of teeth.

Opening the car door, he stepped out into a front of warm air, and headed for the intercom that loomed by the gate.

'*Matyeh a?*' What? Clearly, the woman on the other end of the intercom didn't have time for fripperies such as greetings.

'*Neih sik mhsik gong yingman a?*' He asked if she could speak English, predicting that her English was bound to be superior to his Cantonese, which in the last couple of months had progressed to an impressive second-grade standard.

'Can. What you want?'

'I'm here to visit my grandfather.'

'What his name?'

'Chan. Chan Wei Long.'

'Ah... Mister Chan. He here. Can come in.'

'Thank you, I...'

'Quick, quick.'

He slid through the gates before she could change her mind – checking that no ancient Venerables were lurking in the bushes waiting for just such an opportunity to escape – before following a path of stepping-stones that led across a wide lawn of broad-bladed grass towards the front entrance. Next door, a dog set to barking raucously at his presence. The bungalow was bordered on two sides by a wide veranda with chequerboard floor-tiles and overhead ceiling fans that whirred listlessly, stirring the air. Groups of rattan armchairs and small circular tables were scattered about the veranda, many of them occupied by said Venerables who turned at the sound of barking to stare in his direction. He wondered which one was his. Well, he had been waiting thirty-three years to find out, he supposed he could wait a few more minutes.

He pushed through the door to enter a spacious white-walled, white-floored room that doubled as lounge and reception area. A harried-looking woman with short, efficient hair – he guessed she was the sparing conversationalist of the intercom – manned a desk while several Chinese and Indian elders sat about in wheelchairs or armchairs watching a Hong Kong soap opera on maximum volume. In the little time he'd had for television since he arrived, he'd discovered that Cantonese programs were semi-obliterated by at least two sets of subtitles – usually Chinese and Malay – to cater for the maximum audience.

'Ah… good morning, I'm Nicholas Chan. Thanks for letting me in…' he ventured before she interrupted him, saying, 'This way. He on veranda. You his grandson? He not mention grandson. Why you not visit before?'

'I just arrived. I'm from England.'

'Sign visitor book first.'

Dutifully he signed, while she stood tapping her pen against the desk. Then she led him back through the front door, past several groups of residents, to the far corner of the veranda where a lone gentleman sat staring at a mahjong board. He had a thick quiff of white hair and an angular, deeply lined face that looked as if it hadn't cracked a smile in decades. Nick threw a wistful glance towards the gate. This was not going to go down as smoothly as a piece of *pandan* cake, he could see that already.

'Chan *sinsaang, neih yauh loihban*,' the woman said, more politely than Nick had thought possible.

The man looked Nick over from his head to his toes, saying, '*M sik keuih*,' and went back to staring at the little white tiles populating the board in front of him.

'*Keuih haih neihge syun*,' she said, explaining that Nick was his grandson. So far Nick followed the basic gist of the conversation.

'*Ngoh m yauh syun. Ngoh m yauh saimanjai*,' he said, denying all knowledge of any grandchildren or indeed children.

Nick hadn't expected to be welcomed with open arms – well, maybe he had a little bit – but neither had he imagined having his existence denied, and he was surprised by the hurt he felt. Except he wasn't about to give up that easily. From the way his grandfather's shoulders straightened as soon as he was announced, Nick could see that he was a stubborn old coot. Well, he could be stubborn too, when he had to be. And the old man's blood ran in his veins, after all. He looked to his grandfather's carer, about to explain himself further, when she grabbed him by his T-shirt and hauled him over to stand beside his grandfather's chair.

'*Tai keuih*,' she said, directing the old man to examine him. She went on to point out that Nick would be the father of future generations of Chan. Wouldn't Mister Chan like to have such a fine, strong boy as his grandson? Besides, surely any grandson was better than no grandson.

'*M yiu*.' Apparently not.

She lifted Nick's arm and extended it, inviting the old man to feel his muscles.

'*M yiu*.'

She pulled Nick's jaw to open his mouth, inviting Chan to inspect his teeth. 'Not many fillings,' she told him.

'*M yiu.*'

'Would he like me to take off my shirt too?'

The woman frowned, shaking her head. 'No need, lah. He stubborn old man. You want to die with no one to make offerings?' she asked, directing her comment at Chan, in English this time.

Nick expected another growled 'not want' but the old man remained silent for a moment, staring at him, his bottom lip jutting forward.

'He is *gwai lo*,' he said in English, probably to ensure Nick understood that he was being called a 'ghost man', the less than polite, but nevertheless ubiquitous, Cantonese expression for a European. In England, Nick had become accustomed to being called Chinese or Asian. Here, everyone thought he looked more European. His grandfather was telling him, in his not-so-subtle way, that he was an outsider. A ghost man. Well, so be it.

He returned his grandfather's stare. 'I'm Nick Chan. Your daughter's son. Your grandson. Ghost or not.'

The old man picked up one of the tiles, the nine bamboo, and flipped it between his fingers, the veins on his hand popping out amongst a map of lines and liver spots and gnarled joints. Those fingers were long and thin with square tips.

'He play *mahjong*?' the old man asked with a shrug, directing the question at his carer and avoiding Nick's eyes.

'Ask him.' The woman stood unmoving beside Nick, brooking no escape.

His grandfather returned to studying the pieces lined up on the board while Nick waited silently, squeezed between the cranky carer and the stubborn old man, as the seconds ticked on and on. Waiting for an invitation that might never come.

'You play *mahjong*?' the old man asked gruffly, after what seemed like an eternity.

'Yes, Ah Gung, I play.'

'Good. Now we need to find some other *sor gwa*.'

11

London 2016

THE QUESTION CAME out of the blue. A forkful of egg was halfway to her lips, and the waiter had just set a full English breakfast in front of Nick, when he opened his mouth and instead of shovelling in bacon asked, 'When was the last time you felt happy, Sar? Not merely satisfied but really happy?'

They were supposed to be enjoying these last few days before he had to fly back to Kuala Lumpur for the new semester. They were supposed to be revelling in a sunny July morning at their favourite café. Happiness was not supposed to be on the agenda. And she hated it when he put her on the spot like this, while continuing to skip along in his spontaneous, carefree way. Meanwhile she was left feeling ambushed.

'What sort of question is that?' She put down her fork with a frown.

'It's a D and M question. Like the kind married people are supposed to ask each other.'

'You know I don't do Deep and Meaningful, Nick. I get prickly all over if someone even asks me what I'm thinking. A question like that just about breaks me out in hives.'

'Try.'

'All right,' she sighed. 'I'll make an exception for you just this once.' She took a deep breath. 'Well, after five years, my business is finally making a real profit. You've got a teaching contract until the end of next year. I know it's not ideal that we're living half a world away from each other, but it's not permanent. Why shouldn't I be happy?'

'You're not answering my question.'

When in doubt, she'd learned to answer a question with a question. It had been a useful strategy thus far in her life. But Nick knew her too well.

'I don't know what your question means.'

He gave her a pitying look. 'How can someone not know what happiness means?'

She shrugged, tempted to roll her eyes, but that would be too childish even for her. 'Well, I don't. I can quantify aspects of my life that bring me satisfaction. I can list things I enjoy. But I'm not the Dalai Lama. I can't define happiness.'

When he next spoke his voice was filled with quiet intensity, his eyes fixed to the side of her face. 'What brings you joy? What makes your heart skip a beat?' He paused as if searching for a way to explain what he meant. 'Remember how it was when we first got together.'

Of course she remembered. She remembered the feel of her hand in his and the warmth of his breath on the back of her neck. She remembered the way his smile lit up the room when he saw her. But these were facts. These could be measured with thermometers or recorded on cameras, nothing to do with something as esoteric as happiness.

'Remember that feeling of floating on air. When was the last time you felt that?' He reached across the table and captured her wrist, holding her eyes with urgency. Why was he bringing this up now when he was about to leave again? It wasn't fair. Now wasn't the time to have it all out. The first week of his two-week break they'd spent tiptoeing around each other. The second week they'd spent getting used to each other again. She'd seen it in her friends and never thought it would happen to her and Nick. The strained politeness when the sound of his chewing drove her crazy. The false cheeriness when the sight of his dirty shoes in the middle of the living room made her want to toss them in the bin. She'd known it was a mistake to spend so long apart. And now this question.

She looked away, not wanting him to read the truth in her eyes. How could she tell him that she'd never felt like that? Not even when they first met. Her heart had never skipped a beat. Her feet had never left the ground. Before Nick, there had only ever been the racing heartbeat of panic, the feeling that life was being pulled from under her. There was only the memory of her father leaving and her mother reverting to a needy, manipulative child. That was why she'd chosen Nick as her anchor, to hold her steady in a world filled with uncertainty. She loved him, but never with that heady, giddy heedlessness. No one willingly gave in to that, did they?

'What if we have kids? Everything's going well. I really think it would bring us together, Sar,' he said, full of enthusiasm like a puppy.

'Not when we're half a world apart.'

'Metaphorically.'

'I wasn't aware we were apart *metaphorically*.' It was a lie and they both knew it.

'I'll be back in London at the end of next year.'

'Come on, Nick. You know I'm too busy to have a baby now. I can't take time out. Everything is just starting to fall into place.' If she relaxed her grip on the business now it might all fall apart. All that hard work and sacrifice for nothing.

'Maybe not right this minute but soon. We can at least talk about it. Plan for it.'

He was still holding her wrist. Could he feel her pulse race? Could he feel the panic setting in? Talk of children always set her nerves on edge. Couldn't he understand that she didn't want to be responsible for another human being?

She wrenched her wrist from his grasp, knocking over the teapot so that a puddle of hot tea seeped across the table, spilling over the edge and onto her lap. 'Now look what you've made me do! You've got to stop pressuring me. I can't have this same conversation over and over again. I'm just not ready.'

'I'm beginning to think you'll never be ready.'

'Can we not talk about this in public? Please.'

'Why are we even married, Sarah?' he asked, his perpetual half-smile suddenly vanishing.

This was where she should have brought out a speech about loving each other, needing each other and the two of them being enough. But she couldn't find the words. She could only shake her head and pat futilely at her jeans with a paper serviette. It seemed to Sarah then that they had gone from sweet marmalade to bitter anguish in moments. Didn't he understand that safety lay in having him there but not being so in love with him that she would shatter if he left?

On the table between the salt and pepper, her phone buzzed. Her mother's name appeared at the top of the screen. 'Did u get message about the fox...'

*

USUALLY NICK HAD music playing while he worked, but the flat was silent when she returned from work the following evening. It didn't take long to find him, however; their flat had only one bedroom after all. He was sitting on the bed, so engrossed in a photo on his phone that he didn't notice her until she was standing at his side.

'Hey. What's up?'

'Nothing.' He flipped the phone over onto his knee.

She sat beside him, leaning her head on his shoulder and looking up at him. She liked the way his shoulder fit just so in the crook of her neck. She'd missed that while he was gone, that jigsaw feeling of two pieces locking snugly. Like they belonged together.

'You look younger when you smile,' he said.

'That is so mean.'

'I knew that would get to you.'

'Who is it in the picture?'

She had seen already that it showed an elderly Chinese man with a thick brush of white hair and hands knobbed with arthritis. He peered up at the lens as if he distrusted it.

'My grandfather.'

His answer didn't surprise her. For some reason she had been expecting it, or at least something like it. He'd gone to Kuala Lumpur to teach. But he'd also gone to find himself. And finding his grandfather was part of that.

'Who took it?'

'I did.'

'So you found him then.'

'Yup. Ma was holding out on me. Under interrogation I discovered she'd kept tabs on him the whole time. First through her old amah, Ho Jie, and then through his solicitor. She's been sending money home for the last twenty years.'

'I see.' Did she see? Probably not. She would never have sent money to someone who refused to speak with her for thirty years. But June was a different, kinder person. 'I hope you didn't have to resort to water boarding.'

'Tickling and threats of email spam if she didn't come clean.' He looked up at her with a sheepish grin. 'I was going to tell you. But it never seemed the right moment. You've been so...'

'Busy?'

'I was going to say distracted.'

'I'm sorry. I want to be here with you, I really do. I know you'll be gone soon.' It was the truth, but not all of it. Spending time together reminded her that they needed fixing. And she wasn't sure how to accomplish that yet. Maybe it would have to wait until he returned permanently. Maybe she might find a way to talk about children then. Maybe.

'If you're going to plead "work" again I think I might have to erase that word from the dictionary.'

'Sorry.'

'Also that word.' He put his arm around her waist and she didn't try to surreptitiously draw away. She sank into him. He turned the phone face up once more. 'See any resemblance?'

'Handsome devil, isn't he?' she said with a grin. 'What's he like?'

'It's hard to know. He doesn't speak much English and my Cantonese is still like a seven-year-old's. But he seems to like me visiting.'

'Where does he live?'

'In an elderly people's home. His house got too much for him. From what Ma said I expected to find an angry, bitter old man. The first time I went to see him my knees wouldn't stop shaking.'

'But he's not?'

Nick shook his head. 'Not that I can see. He seems more... resigned... more stoic than anything else. Maybe the anger has eroded with age. Shaved his hard edges. That first time, when I got up to leave he reached out to grab me and I realised we have the same shape hands. His might be crippled with arthritis and mapped with wrinkles but we both have small palms and long fingers with square tips. It was weird. Like I could see myself in him. Like I'd found something I never knew I'd lost.'

Suddenly she felt very selfish and it wasn't a pleasant feeling. Mostly Nick seemed so sane, so comfortable in himself that she didn't realise he too was missing a piece. She forgot that he'd never known his father, or his grandfather. She took for granted that June was such a strong presence in his life that he didn't need those foundations. Maybe they'd both been hiding wounds.

'And now, when he's clearly near the end, I realise that I need that connection, Sar. I'm the last Chan in the family. The last one. It might be old-fashioned but that's an uncomfortable feeling.'

12

London 2017

SARAH'S PHONE HUMMED on her desk where her head rested on one crooked arm. Even from this lopsided angle, she could make out Nick's face glowing in the dim light of her office. She should pick up, but he would want to talk. Better to call when she returned to the flat – that is, if it wasn't the middle of the night in Malaysia. She never could get the time difference straight.

She blinked, squeezing her eyes to clear her vision. Last thing she remembered it was late afternoon. Now scraps of light filtered into her office from the green exit sign over the main entrance. It was the second time this week she'd fallen asleep at her desk. Despite hiring a full-time graphic designer, she and James still worked ridiculous hours. The weekly catalogue was due to be uploaded tomorrow and she wasn't happy with the copy. Plus a couple of products would almost certainly need to be reshot. The stainless steel fruit bowl resembled a bedpan and the French linen sheets were looking more like a pile of dishrags.

Blearily she checked her messages. Two from her message service. Two from Nick and three from her mother. 'Please call...' followed by a Malaysian number, Nick's message began. 'The cat vomited on...' read her mother's. What was this thing with her mother and animals? She locked the phone and placed it face down on the desk. She would deal with the vomit problem later.

Across the room another phone shrilled. She let it echo plaintively through the deserted workplace, vaguely aware of muffled conversation when it stopped. So someone was still here then. And all too soon, James poked his head around the partition. Sometimes she thought those make-believe walls were a cosmic joke played on frazzled office workers by interior designers, like the emperor's new clothes, promising everything and delivering nothing but exposure.

'What's up? I thought everyone had gone home.'

Her partner James was textbook handsome but most of their conversation was so wrapped up in spreadsheets and soft furnishings that she rarely noticed. She forgot how symmetrical his features were, how startling his blue eyes. And then she would introduce him to a girlfriend and watch bemusedly as she became transfixed with lust.

'There's a call for you on the land line.'

'Could you take a message? Please?'

'It's from Malaysia.'

'Ah, did Nick say what he wanted? I'm really snowed under.'

'It's not Nick. I think you'd better take it, Sarah. It's someone calling from a hospital.'

She took a moment to digest his words, so that when he placed the telephone in her hand she blinked in surprise. 'Go ahead.' He gave her shoulder a sympathetic squeeze and moved a few steps to wait by the partition. She waved him away, mouthing that she would be fine. How bad could it be?

'Hullo. Sarah Matthieson.'

'Ms Matthieson, this is Doctor Chua calling from Kuala Lumpur General Hospital. I'm sorry to tell you that your husband has been admitted today suffering a head injury.'

She heard the words clearly despite the time lag, but failed to connect with them. Head injuries weren't a part of her world. Soft furnishings, yes. Soft brain tissue, no.

She shook her head to the unseen doctor. 'You must have the wrong person. My husband isn't Matthieson. He's Chan. Nicholas Chan.'

'Yes, Doctor Nicholas Chan. He presented in our emergency department this morning in an unconscious state. He's now in our Intensive Care Unit. You are listed on his Employment Pass as his emergency contact.'

'But my husband's an academic. Why would he have a head injury?'

She must sound like an idiot, but she seemed to have lost control of her thoughts. It was as if her words were a metronome, marking time while she scrambled to find a rhythm of understanding. Nick couldn't have a head injury. He didn't play contact sports. He didn't cycle, certainly not in Malaysia's perennial thirty-five-degree heat. He was an indoor man.

'He wasn't riding a motorbike, was he?' He'd promised her he wouldn't. Everyone knew it was open season on motorbike riders in Asia.

'Apparently he fell off a ladder.'

How could that be? Her Nick was allergic to DIY projects. Literally. The one time he tried to replace a skirting he broke out in hives from the glue. Light bulbs shattered as if by magic in his hands. She was the one who changed the bulbs and fixed the washing machine when it spewed water onto the laundry floor.

'Ms Matthieson, to put it bluntly, I think you should fly to Kuala Lumpur... as soon as possible.' The woman's voice was kind, at odds with her plainspoken words, making their meaning even more brutal.

Surely she must still be asleep? She closed her eyes tight then snapped them open, but she could still hear the doctor on the other end of the line, speaking words that might be English but sounded foreign. She tried to remain calm, keep her pulse steady, her breathing normal. Words like 'brain swelling' and 'intracranial pressure' resonated, but in a disconnected way. Doctor Chua might indeed have been speaking about the wrong person, another Nicholas Chan unknown to her.

After she hung up she fell back on what she did best, tackling the practical. Opening the top drawer of her desk she began rifling through its contents, searching amongst the staplers and bulldog clips for her passport and finding it buried beneath a gilt-edged invitation to her father's sixtieth birthday, a hand-drawn self-portrait of her twin half-sisters (with extravagantly long, lustrous hair) and a batik-covered notebook Nick gave her last time he was home. She hadn't bothered writing a single word in it. Just as she hadn't stuck her half-sisters' drawing to her fridge door or replied to her stepmother's invitation.

'Sar... are you all right?' James appeared at the invisible door to her cubicle.

'Yes. No. I don't know.'

'What happened?'

'Nick fell off a ladder and cracked his head open... he's in a coma.' The words sounded unbelievable, even to her.

James crossed to her side, leaning over in a half crouch to encircle her with one arm. She was conscious of its weight stretching across her shoulders, the soft cashmere of his sweater touching bare skin at her neck.

'Oh my God, I'm so sorry.'

'I have to go.'

'I'll drive you to Heathrow.'

She shook her head. 'It's too late for the evening flight. I'll go home and pack.'

'Let me drive you in the morning.'

She needed to be alone to process. To decide how to think. What to do in the days ahead. To decide how best to help Nick. 'Thanks but I'll get a cab. There's too much to do here. But thank you. You're a rock.'

There was always too much to do here. So much that she hadn't found time to visit her husband since he'd been gone. For fifteen months she'd made excuses and issued tissue-thin promises. For fifteen months she'd pushed the question of her marriage to the back of her mind and shelved it. And Nick hadn't raised it again either, not since their conversation about children last July. The state of their marriage was a conspiracy of silence, one she'd put off addressing until he was home for good. Then, she'd promised herself, they would fix things.

The last time she'd seen him was four months ago. He was standing in the entrance to their flat, keys in hand, about to return to Kuala Lumpur. Fractured light drifted from the Marcel Wanders pendant overhead and their distorted images were reflected in the glass of a large photograph hanging above the console table.

She caught her surprise in the reflection when he grabbed her hand, pulling her close, as she leaned forward to kiss him. 'Promise me you'll come soon,' he had whispered in her ear.

'I said I would, didn't I?'

'When? I need to know, Sarah.'

'I'm not sure yet.'

'You don't understand. I really have to know.'

'I should be able to get away in April.'

Now it was June and she was going. Finally, she would make the journey to the home of his family. Malaysia, a transit point in the long history of his ancestors. From China to Kuala Lumpur to London. And back again. What if she was too late?

13

Kuala Lumpur 1930

IT WAS THE first day of the month by the lunar calendar and Madam Chan's obligations to her husband's ancestors were more exacting than usual. Two days ago she had sent Kong to a nearby farm to obtain a goose, his grandfather's preferred bird. Cook had beheaded, plucked and marinated the goose with orange peel, ginger, soy sauce, five spice and garlic before roasting it outside over hot coals. Grandfather's favourites also included a dish of white-cut chicken with an accompaniment of ginger, garlic and spring onion and several slices of roast pig. She risked a glance at the grainy photographs of the old man and his wife that hung over the altar. Both were pictured sitting in high-backed ornate chairs wearing voluminous gowns, their hair pulled severely back from their foreheads, mouths so sunken that for all intents and purposes they looked like well-dressed corpses. She hoped they wouldn't notice that the pork wasn't home-cooked. Kong had picked it up from a *kopi* shop the previous night.

As well as the sacrificial meats, she had set out a row of oranges, sugar cane, rice and cakes with several cups of tea and rice wine and a pack of cigarettes to keep the old man happy, for apparently he had been a heavy smoker in life. She flicked a last speck of dust from Grandfather's ancestral tablet and called her husband to begin the offering. He lit two joss sticks, bowed perfunctorily before planting them in the urn and disappeared back to his breakfast. Madam Chan would have liked to eat her breakfast too, since she had been up since five that morning preparing the altar, but she had to wait until the ancestors finished theirs.

After allowing a suitable amount of time for them to digest the offerings, she took two red crescent-shaped blocks of wood, rubbed their flat sides together and tossed them to the ground where they both landed flat side down, rounded sides up.

'Aiya!' So much effort and all she got for it was this bad-tempered answer. She threw again. This time the moon blocks landed curved side down.

'Make up your mind,' she said, disappointed with this equivocal answer. She threw once more and this time was rewarded with a satisfactory answer, one block falling flat side down and the other curved side down. In theory she should have waited for three positive answers to confirm the ancestors' satisfaction but she wasn't about to take a chance when her breakfast was waiting. Gathering up a basket of gold paper ingots from the altar, she took them outside where she burned them in an iron brazier before dousing the flaming paper with water so that evil spirits would not gobble up the offerings.

*

THE GIRL WAS being more sluggish than usual. Although the *towkay* forgave her tardiness at breakfast, especially on the many mornings when he had kept her up late the night before with his business, the *taitai* would not be so indulgent. Especially once her husband had departed for work. She would be sure to make the little sister suffer.

'Come along, the *taitai* is not a forgiving woman. Do not make things bad for yourself, Sai Mui.'

'What do I care if she shouts at me or pinches me? It cannot be worse than what that old man does to me,' the girl groaned, pulling the covers back over her head so that the sheets contoured her profile like a shroud.

'A flying moth casts itself into the flame,' Ho Jie reminded her of the old saying with a cluck of her tongue. 'Why not make the best of your situation? Once you give that old man a son you can ask him for the moon and he will give it to you.'

The covers were thrown off in a billow of cotton and the concubine sat up. 'Do you think he would give me my freedom, Ho Jie? Do you think he would let me go?' she asked eagerly. It was the first time Ho Jie had seen a shred of interest from her in weeks. She was probably thinking she could escape to the boy who had given her the jade ring. Stupid girl. Ho Jie thought it most unlikely that the old man or his wife would let the girl go. Not when they had paid good money for her and not while her body was lush and fruitful, capable of bearing sons and fetching and carrying for a demanding mistress. But if she told Sai Mui this, the girl would never get up and then the *taitai* would come rushing up the stairs brandishing her bamboo backscratcher and beat the child across the legs.

'Perhaps,' she said. 'Perhaps he will let you go once you have given him a son.'

'Every night he comes. Every night he sticks his thing in me. And I am so tired, Ho Jie. He is stealing the *qi* from my body to make this son. Soon I am afraid I will have none left.' She collapsed back onto the bed. 'What does it matter anyway?'

Ho Jie realised something she should have seen much earlier.

She had washed Sai Mui's bleeding rags only once since she had arrived at the Chan mansion. And now she was so tired that she struggled to crawl from her bed. Well, well, it would be interesting to see how the *taitai* took this news. And it would be more interesting to be a cricket on the wall when the *taitai* told her husband. After all, two tigers cannot share one mountain, can they?

*

THE SMELL OF roast goose had made Madam Chan hungrier than usual and with her obligations out of the way she turned eagerly for the dining room. But she had only got as far as the inner courtyard when Ho Jie intercepted her.

'What is it now?' she said, trying to ignore the howling of her stomach.

'There is something I think you would like to know, Madam,' the woman said, her face bloated with self-importance – either that or the amah was getting fat. She would have to instruct Cook to reduce her portions of rice. A fat servant led to a lazy servant, she always found.

'Well, out with it! I have a lot to do today. I have a fitting for a new gown and the *towkay* has asked me to purchase him a new hat.' She had an appointment with her tailor for the first fitting of a Western-style evening gown to wear to the British Residents' reception, a fact of which she knew Ho Jie was well aware. The gown fell in soft folds of emerald-green satin and the tailor assured her it was quite fetching.

'The *chieh* has been with us almost three months now.'

Three months too many for Madam Chan; three months of almost nightly visits by her husband to the room at the back of the house. Three months of watching that mule-faced girl stumble about on her big clumsy feet, dropping cups and knocking over vases with her graceless elbows. Why just yesterday she had slipped and fallen while serving tea, shattering one of Madam's precious Chenghua Ming teacups and twisting her ankle so that they had to summon the doctor with his needles.

'You don't need to remind me of that. What is your point?'

The amah paused before answering, lowering her voice to a conspiratorial whisper, 'I have only had to wash her bleeding rags once.'

So… it didn't take an abacus to do the calculations. Three months, one bleeding… which meant that the girl was most likely pregnant and Madam Chan was about to become a mother.

Ho Jie was waiting to see her response, her head cocked to one side, eyes narrowed, watching. She probably had an opinion. But Madam Chan wasn't interested in finding out what that might be. If she asked, the woman would most likely proffer more opinions and then where would they be?

'Does the girl realise?'

'I'm not sure, Madam. She hasn't said anything to me but she doesn't say much to anyone.'

It had become apparent that Sai Mui was a conversational failure. That day after the ancestors spoke and she followed the girl to her home above the apothecary shop, Madam Chan had flirted with the idea that in choosing a *chieh* for her husband she might gain, not only a son, but a younger sister. Someone who would look up to her, seek her advice and chat amiably as she fanned her mistress and mentor on hot afternoons. Yet from the moment she arrived, the girl was a bitter disappointment in that regard, wandering the house like a ghost, her long face and sad eyes haunting them at every meal. If she wasn't made of sterner stuff it might have put Madam Chan off her dinner.

'Hmm, she's not very bright, it is true. Perhaps she hasn't put two and two together yet. Well, do not say anything to her or the *towkay*. Leave that to me. I will take care of everything.'

Despite her detached manner, Madam Chan's heart fluttered. She almost felt like a girl again, a young bride full of expectation. After so many years of embarrassing failure she was going to be a mother. Finally, she could inform her mother-in-law that she was to be a grandmother again. And if it should be a boy... well, her happiness would be complete.

It had to be a boy. It would be a boy. After all her sacrifice, she deserved a boy and she would do everything in her power to get one, even if it meant more grovelling.

'Call Ah Kong and tell him to get the car ready. We have work to do.'

14

YU LAN REALISED that the Chevrolet was heading towards her old neighbourhood. They had followed Lornie Road along the green river bank for several miles, the area sparsely settled on this side of the river, before reaching the steel girders of Sultan Sulaiman Bridge. Across the Klang River, the minarets of the railway station shone white against the sky and the traffic became busier as they headed up High Street into the bustle of Chinatown. As they passed the police station on their right, she thought that perhaps the *taitai* was taking her to visit her mother. Perhaps she had a heart after all. Or perhaps the *towkay* was satisfied enough with her to grant this special outing.

This thought was enough to rouse her from the lethargy that had weighed upon her spirit for many weeks. Most of the Chan household hadn't been unkind to her. The servants welcomed her in their offhand way, the mistress was yet to beat her and apart from his nightly thrusting, the *towkay* treated her more kindly than her father. Some girls would count themselves lucky to have landed in this wealthy household where there was never a shortage of rice and meat was served at every meal.

She knew that she was expected to accept that the big green house on the hill was now her home; that she was no longer a Lim but owed allegiance to the Chan family. She knew that she was expected to accept the *towkay*'s groping and fumbling as the right of a husband, even if he hurt her. She told herself that if she could just find a way to tolerate it, one day Chan might release her. But despite these urgings, she couldn't help feeling that she was possessed. Each night she resisted the urge to scream and fight back by escaping, by detaching her mind so that it floated free from her body to wander old haunts. While the old man thrust deep inside her body, she returned to her childhood home: arguing with her brothers, pounding dried herbs in the shop, or helping her mother chop vegetables. Anything to distract her from reality. She tried to convince herself that it was no more painful than Lou-si's cane. No more arduous than scrubbing floors. She just had to put up with it and one day she might gain her freedom. Except it wasn't true. She couldn't trick herself into accepting his touch. She could only leave her body and let her mind wander elsewhere.

Come daytime, a leaden malaise struck her, sapping all her youthful energy, so that she dragged herself through the days, stomach churning. As if the house itself was making her ill. Yet now, the thought that she might see her mother caused her to sit up straighter on the back seat next to Ah Jie and fix a smile to her face.

'I'm pleased you're looking happier today,' said Ah Jie. She had been in a good mood all morning, accompanying her breakfast with snatches of *song, warbling* Li Minghui's 'Drizzling Rain' in a wobbly soprano.

Yu Lan was torn between asking if they were to visit her mother and fearing that if breathed aloud, her wish would be snatched away. So she did what had proved safest and said, 'I am, Ah Jie. Thank you.'

Kong manoeuvred the car along familiar streets, weaving between rickshaws and bicycles, bullock carts and myriad peddlers, their shoulders bowed under the weight of poles bearing cane baskets laden with fruit and vegetables. Mostly the pedestrians kept to the five-foot way, except where the space became so crowded with hawkers that they decamped to the road, so that here and there a swell of Chinese men clad in *samfu,* darker-skinned Indians and pith-helmeted European men swarmed onto the dusty street. Yu Lan held her breath as the Chevrolet drew closer to her father's shop, thinking how happy her mother would be to see her, hearing in her mind the swift shuffle of Ma's slippered feet across the tiled floor, imagining her tired smile as she saw her daughter for the first time in three long months.

Why then was Kong stopping the car and turning off the engine outside the Guan Di temple, a full block from the apothecary shop? Why did he step from the car and help the *taitai* to slide from the backseat clutching her *cheongsam* awkwardly so that it didn't reveal a glimpse of thigh? Why did the *taitai* beckon her to follow?

Yu Lan trailed in her wake as she bustled past golden dragons coiled around twin red pillars, and two snarling stone lions crouched outside the temple. Nor did she pause to glance up at the fierce generals who guarded the doorway. She stepped heedlessly through the entry and over the red doorsill into the temple with Yu Lan following. Dozens of curling spirals of incense hung from the roof like smoking baskets. A tall brick incinerator burned with paper devotions in one corner of the courtyard, while huge brass braziers sprouted joss sticks like thickets of glowing eyes. The smoke assailed Yu Lan's nose and eyes and curdled her stomach so that she had to clutch one of the red pillars to stay upright.

'Come along,' said Ah Jie, turning away from the God of War, his blessed sword and his minions, and heading towards one of the side pavilions where other gods waited.

She didn't know why the *taitai* had a sudden desire to worship here when she usually prayed at the clan house or the family altar – after all it wasn't New Year or another important festival – but she knew that when Ah Jie beckoned she would do well to follow or risk a sneak attack of pinching and slapping. Perhaps the mistress thought the gods might listen more closely here to whatever new wants she had. And the *taitai* had a lot of wants.

Dropping several coins into Yu Lan's hand, the *taitai* ordered, 'Go and purchase some incense,' before settling herself in front of the altar to Guan Yin, Goddess of Mercy, hearer of all sufferings, protector of women, giver of children. The Goddess smiled beatifically at all who requested her help, a tiny child cradled in her arms as a symbol of her mercy. Yu Lan recalled that Guan Yin was her mother's favourite goddess. The goddess gave her mother hope but mostly that was all she gave. It wasn't enough for Yu Lan. She didn't want to be like her mother.

When Yu Lan returned carrying a thick bundle of incense she found her mistress kneeling before the statue of Guan Yin, two red moon blocks flat side down on the floor before her.

'It cannot be so!' she was saying, her voice tight with fury. Clearly, the goddess wasn't being merciful enough for her liking. The divination blocks hadn't given her the answer she wanted. Gathering the moon blocks to her chest she rubbed them together, then pressed them to her forehead for several moments before tossing them to the floor. They landed quivering, convex side down, causing her to remonstrate with the goddess: 'I could have fed an army with the offerings I have made over the years. Surely you can give me the answer I need now, after all my devotion? Is that too much to ask?'

Whatever she had asked, the moon blocks showed that the goddess was quaking with laughter.

'I am going to give you one last chance,' the *taitai* said.

Yu Lan heard the desperation in her voice and wondered what she wanted so urgently. Closing her eyes, she tossed the blocks to the ground, this time without even offering a short prayer for guidance. Yu Lan watched as the crescent-shaped blocks flipped once in the air to land one atop the other; one flat side down with its partner lying across it rounded side up. Ah Jie opened her eyes, squealing with joy when she saw that the goddess had given her a positive answer.

Turning her face upwards, she regarded the goddess with reverence. 'Thank you, blessed one. Thank you.' Then she turned to Yu Lan, who was standing to the side out of range of any stray benevolence that might come her way. Her gaze travelled from the tip of Yu Lan's head, down past her puzzled face to settle on her belly.

'Let's go again to be certain,' she said with a self-approving smile. 'And you, Sai Mui, you had better pray that the goddess looks upon you favourably now that you are carrying our son.'

The words hit her like one of Kuala Lumpur's sudden downpours. One minute she was angry and disappointed not to be visiting her mother after all and the next her world had changed irrevocably. Her hand found its way to her belly and hovered there uncertainly. She had known that this was expected of her but had tried to shut it from her mind. The weeks had gone by without her noticing a lack of bleeding. Now, as her thoughts clicked into place, she realised that it had been almost two months since she last bled. That was why she had been so tired and listless, why her stomach had turned on her, why her *qi* had deserted her. So many things became clear now that her future was determined. She was to be the mother of Chan Towkay's child.

A son, according to the goddess.

But she did not believe in the largesse of the gods. She hadn't received any of their hard-won benevolence, no matter how fervently she prayed to be reunited with her family, to be granted a chance of love. Ah Jie might think she could engage with the gods and order, beg or nag them into her way of thinking. But Yu Lan believed that they were all afloat, tossed willy nilly upon unpredictable waters. Yu Lan would bear a son. Or she would bear a daughter. Or she would bear no child at all. There was no relying upon the gods. She could only paddle feebly in the hope that she might one day make it safely to shore.

She clutched her belly, wishing herself far away from this beaming woman, her smiling goddess, the beseeching worshippers and the clouds of pungent smoke that assaulted her senses. Swaying, her head lighter than air, she felt her knees buckle beneath her as she dropped to the floor, her whole world fading to black as she landed splayed across the moon blocks that had deigned to determine her future.

15

FOR A MOMENT Yu Lan didn't know where she was. She emerged into light, the sun almost blinding after a dim, smoky interior, so that it took several breaths before she could see clearly. Then she recognised the many-coloured tower of the Hindu temple across the road, and knew she must be in the High Street, standing outside the Guan Di temple. Although she couldn't remember how she had got there. She became aware of a hand on her arm, urging her past two monstrous stone lions that guarded the temple entrance. The hand held her arm in a fierce grip so that she felt like a child unable to escape her irate parent. She almost expected to look up and see her father frowning down at her. Except that it was a woman's scent she smelled, and a woman's red-taloned hand that restrained her. She wondered what she was doing at the temple in the middle of the day when she should be at the shop helping her father, and she felt a niggling alarm, knowing that he would berate her when she returned home.

But on top of the disorientation, her skull felt like an implacable hand was squeezing it, making her head ache and her vision blur at the edges. She needed to get home. Ma would know what to do. Ma would find a wet towel to soothe her temples. She would comb her long hair to distract her from the pain. She would put her to bed, despite Ba's objections, if she believed her daughter was ill.

Yu Lan looked down at the hand gripping her arm and

tried to shake it off, but to no avail. The fingers encircled her arm like talons, steering her towards a large black car where a grinning man stood guarding an open door. He said hullo to her, showing a gap-toothed mouth stained yellow from tobacco, and gestured for her to climb into the car.

'Stupid girl! One minute we are praying and the next she faints. I suppose we will have to take her home,' the woman said.

For the first time since they emerged into the light, she turned to stare at this pale-faced woman holding her arm. Twin curls kissed her cheeks and a *cheongsam* skimmed her body in a sweep of floral silk. Yu Lan felt sure that she knew her from somewhere, and her skin pricked with instinctive dislike.

'Let's get you into the car, Sai Mui.'

The man spoke as if he knew her. His face was familiar too, yet she couldn't place it. A name hovered in her memory just out of reach. His tone wasn't unkind, but she knew that she wouldn't be safe in that car. She knew that it would swallow her up, imprison her in its leather-scented interior. Every hair on her skin lifted in danger. She stared past the big black vehicle with its open door waiting to trap her, searching for an escape route. People lumbered past, burdened with baskets and bags from the market. Others leaned back in rickshaws pulled by thin, wiry men wearing broad-brimmed bamboo hats. And then she saw him, passing by on the other side of the street, carrying a basket brimming with bunches of *gai larn*, *choi sum* and *gai choi*. A boy she knew better than any other, her true friend. He was intent on his journey, not looking in her direction, but surely he would help her if she cried out. He would rescue her from this white-faced woman and the man with the car.

'Ah Ming!' she called.

Louder now to catch his attention above the noise of the street: 'Ah Ming!'

She saw him turn his head to meet her eye, taking in the silk-clad woman at her elbow and the man holding the door of his shiny black car. A fleeting expression of sorrow mixed with something like fear crossed his face. He took a single step towards her then stopped.

'Ah Lan,' he said into the noise of the passing throng. 'What are you doing here?'

But before she could answer, another deeper voice shouted his name and she turned to see an older man with the same protruding ears as Ming. His father. 'Come away!' he shouted, beckoning to his son.

Ming took another step towards her.

'This is not your business. This is only trouble,' said his father, frowning sternly. 'Would you make trouble for us all with the Chans?'

Ming looked to her once more and blinked twice before turning to catch up with his father and resume his journey. She watched as he hurried away, his broad shoulders becoming smaller and smaller as he followed his father down the crowded street. Why did he turn away from her like that? Why didn't he wait for her? Surely he could see that she needed his help.

'Ah Ming,' she breathed, her words smothered by the sound of passing traffic.

'Get into the car,' said the woman. 'Those people are not your concern now.' Momentarily, the woman relaxed her grip as the man with the yellow teeth stepped away from the car and extended his hand to take Yu Lan's other arm. Tearing her elbow from the woman's grasp, Yu Lan headed for the street and her friend. Instinct told her that she had to reach him before he disappeared from view. She had to catch him or he might be lost to her for ever. Forcing her unsteady legs into action, she ran out into the street. She didn't see the dark-green Austin bearing down on her. She only had eyes for a grey *samfu*, worn by a tall, thin boy with too-big ears. Then a whoosh of air and she felt her arm being wrenched from its socket. She was hauled from the path of the Austin to land in the dusty street, her limbs entangled with those of another. She was vaguely aware of burning pain at elbow and knee, the touch of silk against her skin and the angry muttering of a female voice, before the man who had been guarding the car helped her to her feet.

'The things I do for this family,' said the pale-faced woman, levering herself up and brushing dirt from her skirt. 'Look what you've done now. There is blood all over me.'

Her brows drew together like two angry bows as she rounded on Yu Lan, jerking back her hand and slapping her cheek with an open palm. Yu Lan heard the crunch of vertebrae as her head snapped back from the force, shocking her brain and dragging her thoughts to the present. When her head stopped reeling, she opened her eyes to see the furious woman looking down at her bloody *cheongsam* in disgust.

'Madam Chan,' she muttered weakly as everything came flooding back: the smoke-filled temple, the Goddess of Mercy, the waiting car, Ming disappearing up the street away from her and… and… the child that had been planted inside her womb.

'How many times must I tell you to call me Ah Jie! *We* are your family now and the sooner you remember that, the happier you will be. There is no point chasing after phantoms from your old life.'

Yu Lan stood swaying, her eyes closed. If she could only shut them tight enough, perhaps she could wish her world back to the way it had been. But the *taitai* was having none of this. She jabbed her finger at Yu Lan's chest, snapping words in time with the beating digit.

'Do you know what happens to *chieh* who try to run away? They are sent to China or Hong Kong. They are sold to another master, one who might not be so kind. Or they are sold to a Madam who will give them to any man who pays her price. That is what happens to girls who run away.'

Yu Lan tried to block out her words but the *taitai*'s voice was shrill and insistent. 'Is that what you want, stupid girl? To service many men each night until you are old and worn out?' Yu Lan knew her words to be true. She remembered the *rojak* seller's fifth daughter who disappeared from their neighbourhood one day with no word of where she had gone. Like the ten-year-old girls sent overseas to serve as *mui jai* in wealthy Hong Kong households, just as poor families in China sold their daughters to Malaya. Young women who became dead to their families. Little girls who never returned. For it is better to raise geese than girls, so the saying goes.

'And don't think you can bleed all over the upholstery either, or the *towkay* will have something to say about it.'

Yu Lan opened her eyes. She looked down, past the jabbing finger, to her leg where blood seeped through cotton trousers. The leg seemed alien, as if it didn't belong to her, just as this angry woman and the invisible child growing in her belly were no part of her. Yet despite this apparent truth, despite her unwillingness to accept it, she knew that it must indeed be so. She knew that this would be her life now. She wasn't Lim Yu Lan any more.

She wasn't an elder sister. She wasn't secretly promised to a boy with dancing eyes who lived above a *kopi* shop.

She was a little sister. She was Second Lady Chan. She was no one.

She felt a wrench then as if her soul was being torn from her body. There would be no mercy from god or human.

'Let's hope the child inherits its father's brains, for this one is nothing but a stupid rice bucket.'

16

DESPITE ITS COOLNESS, the water stung with the bite of a fire ant. Yu Lan sat on a stool, leg stretched out before her, trouser rolled high, as Ho Jie bathed her grazed knee. The amah had removed her straw slippers, and was murmuring soothing words as she dabbed gently at the dried blood, trying to extricate the grit embedded in the wound.

'Aiya child, so much dirt you could grow vegetables in there. What are you trying to do to yourself? Running out in front of that noisy monster? Those automobiles are a danger to life and limb. You wouldn't catch Ho Jie riding in one. I am not suicidal.'

Yu Lan did not respond to this flow of words. She kept her teeth clamped as the prattle drifted over her head and filtered through the shuttered windows into the steamy afternoon. But if the amah thought she remained silent from pain she would have been wrong. It was despair, not pain, that kept her quiet.

'You mustn't mind the *taitai*. She only wants what's best. If she seems harsh, it's because she worries for your health.'

Worries for the child's health, Yu Lan thought bitterly.

'It's true that the babe is on her mind. She has waited a long time for a Chan son to arrive and she will not risk him now. But you and the babe are one person.' The amah grinned so that her two black teeth showed. 'Don't pay heed to her threats. She won't send you away now. She must take care of you. If you are clever you can use this to your advantage.'

She might not send Yu Lan away while she carried his child, but she might once the child was born. Yu Lan wasn't fooled by the servant's kindly attitude and soft words. Ho Jie pretended to be on her side, but she couldn't be trusted. No one in this house could be trusted. The walls had eyes that watched her, reporting back to the *taitai* her every movement, especially now that she carried Chan Towkay's child.

'You don't want to be here. I understand that. You don't want to be tethered to an old goat like the *towkay*.' The amah finished bathing the broken skin and wound a strip of soft cloth around Yu Lan's knee. Then she lifted Yu Lan's hand from its resting place upon her lap and inspected the scrapes where she had landed in the dirt of High Street. She turned it this way and that as if she could read some message in the palm, tracing a finger along the line cutting deepest into its centre. Then she turned her own hand to the light so that Yu Lan could make out the myriad lines crisscrossing her palm, lines that skirted mounded callouses, gouged chains across her hand. What did she read there? Did she think of her home in Shonde, as Yu Lan pined for the smells of the apothecary shop? Or was she happy to make her way in the world alone?

'You are young. You want to run free. Yet none of us are free. We only fool ourselves that it is so,' Ho Jie said, as if she had read Yu Lan's mind. 'Look at me... I have combed up my hair and vowed not to take a husband but I am not free. I am bound by my vow. I am bound to my family, far away in Shonde. I am bound to my employer. Even the *towkay* isn't free. He must obey the laws of the land and bow to his venerable mother's wishes. But if you are clever you can be *more* free.'

How could you be more free? Either you were free or you weren't. There were no degrees of freedom as there were with wealth. You could be poor or very poor, rich or very rich, or somewhere in the middle. But you could not be a little bit free.

Ho Jie unfurled from her knees to a standing position then walked behind the stool and her injured charge. 'There now, bend your knee or it will grow stiff. I will comb out your hair. That will make you feel better,' she said, as her nimble fingers set to work untangling the knotted strands of Yu Lan's braid. 'That will soothe your poor old cabbage head.'

Despite herself, she relaxed into the amah's touch. Her hair flowed like water down her back as Ho Jie pulled the comb gently through her locks. The comb grazed her scalp in a rhythmic motion so that she felt like she was floating, lulled into a sense of wellbeing by the dual stroke of comb and soft words.

'The old man has to die sooner or later,' cooed the amah, 'and when he does you will be the mother of his son. A son always loves his mother for she has given him life. And if he doesn't, well, the gods will punish him for his unfilial behaviour, won't they?'

Yu Lan closed her eyes and imagined she was back in the cramped air well on High Street, seated on a rickety green stool, with her mother listening to her troubles as she combed out her braid. Even if her mother couldn't make her better, she had made her stronger. She had made her believe in herself. She wished now that they had discussed her future life in the Chan household, so that she could have asked her mother's advice. But at the time she hadn't believed it would become fact. And she hadn't realised that her mother was strong despite her reliance on the gods. Perhaps her mother was just making the best of a situation she couldn't escape.

In those few short days between the matchmaker's visit and her departure for the Chan mansion, she believed Ming would rescue her. That he would find a way to convince his father to let them marry. Now she knew that she had been foolish. If she wanted to be free she would have to rescue herself. Perhaps if she had talked with her mother about her situation she might have been helped to find strength in adversity. Somehow she had to find that strength again, she thought, as she listened to the amah's words. She had to find a new way to give her life meaning. If she couldn't have Ming she must find another reason to live.

'You believe this child is your prison. But if you are clever it could be your salvation. There is no point swimming against the current, little one. Let the water take you downstream, for it will make your journey home that much easier.'

*

THE DRAGON BRACELET glimmered on the old man's palm, catching the stray beams of afternoon sun that stole into the courtyard. Made from twisted strands of gold so fine they resembled lace, the bracelet pulsed with light. Yu Lan had never seen anything so beautiful, although she regarded the beady ruby eyes of the dragons warily.

'It is yours.'

Two dragonheads fighting over a golden pearl formed the clasp of the bracelet. When Chan Towkay broke them apart the bracelet opened upon a central hinge. Then, indicating that she should hold out her arm, he snapped their jaws closed around her wrist. She expected the metal to feel cold against her skin but it was warm, like a living thing.

'Let's hope our son will become a dragon one day,' he said,

stroking her arm, and Yu Lan thought she caught a glimpse of tears in his eyes. Why did all men want their sons to be dragons? Why didn't they want them to be rabbits or monkeys? Or even roosters? If they were all dragons, wouldn't they just gobble each other up?

She turned her hand palm up so that the dragons wrestled each other over her wrist, their ruby eyes flashing in the light. According to folklore, dragons were not only powerful; they were benevolent, wise and just. Somehow that didn't stop them fighting over the flaming pearl of power and prosperity.

'It's very beautiful.'

The dragon bracelet must be worth a great deal of money. Enough money to buy passage to somewhere far away. And where there was one dragon bracelet there might well be another.

'Almost as beautiful as its owner.'

'Thank you, Towkay.'

'You must call me Sin Saang. I am your husband, remember?' he teased, patting her on the buttock with his right hand. 'How could you forget, eh? Especially now that we have made a son.'

It didn't matter to Yu Lan what she called him, for no matter what Ho Jie advised it would not set her free. *Sin Saang* meant 'husband', but it also meant 'mister' and she could find nothing fond in either. But the dragon bracelet might one day set her free, if she found a way to use it.

'You need not be so shy with me now that we've made a child together.' His left hand cupped her other buttock and gave it a squeeze. 'That's something to celebrate, eh?'

Her flesh rebelled against his hand. The muscles in her buttock twitched, longing to escape. Ho Jie advised her to let the river bear her downstream, except the amah couldn't know what that might cost. A confirmed spinster couldn't know what it was like to have this old man consuming her young body night after night, to have his wrinkled hands squeezing her breasts and gripping her thighs.

Slipping from his grasp she moved several steps to stand fully in the light, holding her arm out admiringly, twisting it this way and that so that the ruby eyes winked at her in the sun.

'No one has ever given me such a precious gift,' she said, hoping to distract him from whatever he had in mind, something she felt sure she wasn't going to like. Day or night, he took her whenever he had a fancy or an itch.

'No one has ever given me such a precious gift either,' he said with a sniff.

Now the tears were virtually dripping down his cheeks. He made a show of wiping them away with the sleeve of his long linen gown, for today he was dressed in the Chinese style rather than the stiff Western suit with its high-collared, starched shirt that he usually wore to the mine. He wasn't embarrassed at all by his tears. In fact, they seemed like a matter of pride to him, another sign of his virility. She couldn't understand this man who held his wife and servants hostage with bad temper, who tossed his bowl on the floor because the soup was too salty, or shouted at the *taitai* when he could not find his slippers. Yet he cried like a baby over a mere possibility, a tiny seed planted in a young girl's womb. Yu Lan's mother would have brought out the broomstick if she caught her children crying over nothing like that.

'Husband.'

Both turned at the sound of Madam Chan's voice. She appeared at the bottom of the staircase, her eyes directed at the dragon bracelet glinting on Yu Lan's arm. She did not look happy. Even from this distance Yu Lan discerned the tight line of her jaw and her rigid grasp on the bannister. She looked like a woman ready to do battle. And although her arms jangled and her ears jingled with gold, she looked like she might reach out and snatch the bracelet from Yu Lan's wrist. But what did she know? She was merely a poor shopkeeper's daughter. Perhaps you could never have enough gold.

'Husband, you look tired. Sai Mui will bring you tea.' She used the familiar term *louh gung* rather than the formal *sin saang*. That was her privilege as First Lady Chan.

'I don't need tea. Sai Mui has something far more thirst quenching for me.'

His tongue flicked out to lick his lips as he sidled closer, inching across the terracotta-tiled floor of the courtyard in his slippers. Yu Lan stood rigid, resisting the urge to flee. How she longed to escape. But if she ran they would surely catch her. They would send out Kong with his shiny black steed to round her up. They would alert the constables and notify her father. There would be nowhere for her to run. Now that she carried the Chan seed they would do whatever was necessary if they thought she might escape. And when the child was born and she was no longer needed, who knew where they might send her? For who would stop them? Not her father, for he had sold her. Not her mother, for she had no power. Not Ming, for he had abandoned her. She saw that with all the forces against her she would need more than a dragon bracelet to find her escape.

'Come, Sai Mui, let's go upstairs. I have another gift for you.'

He waggled his eyebrows as he reached for her hand, his dry calloused skin hot against hers. She wanted to snatch her hand away and bury it in the folds of her *samfu*.

'But now that the girl is carrying your child, surely it would be best not to... not to...' Madam Chan released her hold on the bannister and glided across the tiles. She placed a hand upon her husband's outstretched arm, frowning with concern.

'Not to what?' he asked, tearing his gaze from Yu Lan but retaining her hand. Three hands, linked together.

'Not to risk... complications,' Madam Chan clarified.

'Aiya, woman! The girl is not so delicate.'

'I only meant that there was no need now for... no need to risk the baby.'

Chan Towkay made a gurgling sound deep in his throat as he hawked up phlegm. Yu Lan watched as a gobbet of spit was propelled from his throat to land on the shimmering red silk of Madam's slippers.

'Look at the girl!' he spat the words. 'Look at those strong limbs, those womanly breasts. Not like your skinny old bones, your flat chest. She is made for bearing children. Complications... my arse!'

Madam Chan's face lost all its taut possession now. In a matter of seconds her cheeks appeared to slide down her face, her jaw fell and her mouth drooped at the corners. In the face of his disgust, she became an old woman. And as her husband's voice rose in volume, her eyes too welled with tears. Yu Lan saw that they were both at Chan's mercy, but this thought didn't bring her any comfort, or arouse any sympathy.

'Stupid woman! What use are you? I might as well be married to a slab of barbecued pork!' he shouted, flicking her away with a snap of his fingers. 'Why don't you make yourself useful in the kitchen and leave me to decide what is best for this family!'

His wife responded with a dignified nod, dropping the hand beseeching her husband to her side. The only sign of injury was in her watery eyes. But Yu Lan knew from experience that her eyes didn't fill with tears of sadness. She knew that those eyes glittered with rage. Madam Chan may have answered her husband's insults with silence but as she brushed past his *chieh* on her way to the kitchen, one claw darted out and pinched Yu Lan's buttocks so hard she would be marked for days.

Yu Lan knew that she would not be forgiven. She knew that she had made an enemy. And sooner or later she would be required to pay.

17

HO JIE WAS a practical woman. She had to be to survive. And although she too had been sixteen once, there had never been room in her life for tender dreams of love. She could no longer conjure the face of any boy from her village, only the gap-toothed leer of the village landlord as he put his hand upon her arse, or the sour voice of the factory boss as he backed her up against a wall. She knew that there was little love to be had from men. What passed as love in their world was sex dressed up in pretty words. But she couldn't tell the girl this, for she would not be believed. Look at her now, twisting and turning that jade trifle upon her thumb. Ho Jie didn't know who had given it to her, but it did not take a pair of moon blocks to tell her that it had been a man.

Men brought only trouble. And if trouble was coming, better if it came bearing gold.

'Madam says I am to make you presentable for your visit this afternoon.'

What the *taitai* had actually said was, 'Can you make the girl appear more like a woman and less like a sow in front of my friends?'

Madam Chan's idea of beauty was traditional. A melon-seed shaped face, magnolia petal skin, eyes like clear autumn water, winged eyebrows and cherry lips. A body that swayed like a willow branch, with a waist as slender as a sheaf of silk. Like the Han Empress Yan who was so lithe she could dance on the palm of a hand. Ho Jie suspected that any woman light enough to dance on someone's hand was probably in need of a good dinner. She had never met a paragon like this, but she supposed there was always a first time.

The girl, however, looked more like a northern barbarian than a slender Han woman. She should be riding a horse or skating on ice rather than embroidering slippers. Well, short of chopping off her feet, Ho Jie couldn't make her any shorter so she must begin with the face.

'Sit on the stool and stay very still. If you move it will only hurt more.'

Sometimes Ho Jie wished the girl would complain. At least that way they would know she was alive. As it was, she seemed to move through her days more like a ghost bride than a living girl.

Ho Jie reached into the basket at her side and took out a length of white sewing thread. She had learned more than spinning from her sisters at the silk factory. They had taught each other many skills in the confined space they shared. How to plait and pin each other's hair. How to pluck each other's eyebrows. Yes, they had shared many tricks.

Holding one end of the thread between the thumb and second finger of her right hand, she pinched the other end between forefinger and little finger. Then with a twirling motion, she began removing the fine hairs from the girl's face. Sai Mui's face might be round as a moon but at least she would have magnolia petal skin.

'Ow!'

'Finally, it speaks.'

'There are easier ways to kill me than with a piece of thread.'

'I am not trying to kill you, child, only make you beautiful.'

'You might as well catch crabs on a hill.'

'Well, the *taitai* has spoken and when she speaks it must be done. So catching crabs on a hill it is. Now do not move or I might pinch your skin and leave a mark, and then we will both be in trouble.'

Gritting her teeth to hold the pain at bay, the girl resumed her silence. Ho Jie thought that in its way her silence was a wall, shutting out everything and everyone she wished to forget. Perched on a stool, sitting so close that she could see the pores in the girl's skin, Ho Jie wished she could breach that wall. Once she had hoped she might earn enough money to buy the contract of a *mui jai*, an adoptive daughter to care for her in her old age, an old age lived in a house of women back in her native Shonde. There would be no rough voices or violent hands in that vegetarian hall, only soft voices and gentle hands. But exiled here in this uncivilised land, with its swarming mosquitoes and soupy air, that seemed unlikely. Perhaps she and this girl could be, if not friends, then allies.

'Now for the eyebrows.'

Under Ho Jie's skilled hands, the girl's brows took shape until they soared like wings. Her hair was looped in the shape of a butterfly and her ears glittered with gold, but no matter what the amah did, those full lips would never resemble a cherry.

*

MADAM CHAN HAD taken particular care with her toilette that morning. It was the day of her regular domino game at Madam Tang's house and for once she wouldn't have to listen to her friends' chatter of children and grandchildren in silence. She would have her own talk of children to contribute. She could hardly wait to see their faces when she told them her news. In the meantime, as she waited for Ho Jie to bring the girl downstairs, she took tea on the veranda looking out over the garden into the jungle beyond. A troupe of macaques was moving through a yellow cassia tree, the large male standing watch as mothers and babies briefly left the safety of its branches to cross a patch of grass towards the rambutan tree, laden with spiky red fruit.

The morning was mild and overcast, almost tricking her into believing that the day wasn't headed for its usual sticky heat. But Madam Chan wasn't fooled. She wore a loose voile *kebaya* in the Nonya style over a batik sarong, with jasmine adorning her hair. She would not take a chance on sweaty armpits in a form-fitting *cheongsam*, not on this most important of days, when she was certain to be the centre of attention amongst her friends. She only hoped that the *chieh* did not embarrass her, that she could stand quietly fanning her mistress without doing something embarrassing like fainting. Second and Third Lady Tang would wait upon Madam Tang and they could always be counted upon to serve tea gracefully without such attention-seeking antics.

'Good morning, Madam, here is Sai Mui as you ordered.'

Madam Chan didn't turn around at the sound of the amah's voice. Instead she waited for the girl and the maid to appear before her. She leaned back in her rattan armchair, golden teacup poised to her lips, narrowing her eyes as she inspected the maid's handiwork.

'Hmm, not too bad. Her skin is acceptable. And one cannot complain about the hair. A pity we can't do anything about her height, but I suppose height in a son could be an advantage.'

'I have done my best, Madam.'

'Are those her only acceptable garments?' The girl was

wearing a yellow *samfu*, the one purchased for her first night in the house. Madam Chan didn't like to be reminded of that night. 'We will have to order her some new clothes. Perhaps red for good luck.'

As she was speaking to Ho Jie, the girl had turned away to look out over the garden. Stepping off the veranda, she wandered beneath the portico towards the lawn where the monkeys were prising open rambutan and stuffing the sweet white flesh into their mouths. Spotting her, the male barked – three short, sharp sounds of alarm – before leaping from the tree and rushing towards her with his teeth bared in an enraged grimace.

'Aiya! What are you doing?' Madam Chan screeched. 'Come away! Don't you know better than to annoy the macaques? Do you want our son to come out looking like a monkey? Stupid girl! Go back inside!'

She shook her head in dismay at the girl's stupidity. Everyone knew you didn't mess with monkeys when you were expecting. 'Make sure she doesn't get into any more trouble before we leave.'

Clearly her husband's concubine wasn't very bright. But perhaps that wasn't such a disadvantage. Chan Towkay was an intelligent man who enjoyed intelligent conversation. Once their son was born he would tire of his foolish concubine and things could return to normal. And if he didn't… well, she would find some other way to rid herself of the problem. Madam Chan was nothing if not a patient, resourceful woman.

*

THE CLATTER OF tiles being shuffled punctuated the women's conversation. Watching the constantly shifting red and white pips on the black tiles was making Yu Lan dizzy. That and standing in the heat fanning the *taitai* for what seemed like hours, all the time listening to her crow about the coming arrival and how pleased her husband was. You would think she, not Yu Lan, was the one who moved through her days like a leaky boat, bloated with fluid and in danger of sinking.

Sitting around the rosewood table with Madam Chan were her friends Madams Tang, Kwan and Chu. Madam Tang appeared several years old than her friends. The rice powder dusting her face had settled into creases around lips that were rouged to an ageing red bud. Behind the carved and gilded chairs, the Tang concubines stood fanning the ladies. Third Lady Tang was little older than Yu Lan, and smiled shyly at her when Madam Chan broke the news of her pregnancy, whereas Second Lady Tang seemed only slightly younger than the mistress of the house and wore a habitually stern expression.

With the tiles once more shuffled and stacked into piles, the women began placing their bets, chattering excitedly.

'Ah Yin, fetch the photographs to show the ladies,' said Madam Tang, and Second Lady Tang left off fanning to disappear into the family quarters at the rear of the courtyard. The courtyard was paved with shining red tiles and bloomed with potted dahlias and camellias. At this time of the day it was bright with sunshine, but still allowed a whisper of air to enter the surrounding rooms. Opposite the room where the ladies played at dominoes was a family sitting room, furnished with carved teak opium beds scattered with embroidered cushions and several upholstered armchairs in the British style. Yu Lan wished she could lie down on one of the beds and fall asleep, even for a few minutes, to give her tired arms a rest. But each time her fanning faltered, the *taitai* rapped her sharply on the knuckles with a domino tile and a terse, 'Lazy girl, you don't even know how to fan properly. It needs rhythm. Look at Second Lady Tang. She has it down to a fine art.'

Yu Lan wondered how long Second Lady had lived in the Tang household. If she had entered the house when she was Yu Lan's age she had been fanning her mistress for at least twenty years, rubbing that lady's tortured lotus feet with fragrant oil each night and serving her congee each morning. Was that to be Yu Lan's life? Would she be rubbing the *taitai's* feet until she finally died and Yu Lan was set free? She couldn't bear it. Better to die now than be imprisoned in that house with the Chan matriarch ruling over her for the next thirty years.

'Good, here is Ah Yin with the photographs of my son's wedding,' said Madam Tang, her beaming smile cracking the carefully applied mask of face powder.

Second Lady Tang reappeared carrying two gilt-framed photographs that she placed on the table between the stacked dominoes. Yu Lan couldn't help noticing that the concubine's hands shook slightly as she set them down and she wondered why. From where she stood behind Madam Chan's chair, Yu Lan couldn't see the portrait of the happy couple but she had a perfect view of the family portrait taken in the garden of the Tang mansion. Yu Lan expected to see the bridal couple decked out in typical Qing brocade gowns and ornamental headdresses, but to her surprise the bride wore a white lace Western gown with matching white headdress in a Chinese style, while the groom was in top hat and tails. The bride and groom stood in the centre of the portrait, flanked on either side by Madam Tang in a full-length *cheongsam* and a man wearing a mandarin suit, presumably Tang senior. Various guests and family members surrounded the proud parents wearing a mix of Western and Chinese dress. At the very rear of the portrait, her face just visible behind the fronds of a sago palm, stood Second Lady Tang.

'He is so handsome. Just like his father,' Madam Chan cooed.

'We are lucky that his bride is such a talented girl and she came with a generous dowry,' said Madam Tang with a satisfied nod. 'More than ten gold chains and twenty bracelets. Not to mention the lovely porcelain and a brand new Ford.'

It was true that the groom was handsome, but judging from the photograph there was small resemblance to his father and even less to Madam Tang. In fact, if it hadn't been for both men bearing the same high forehead, Yu Lan wouldn't have known they were related. She glanced across at Second Lady Tang who had resumed her position behind the *taitai*'s chair. For a moment their eyes met and in the other woman's gaze Yu Lan detected such sorrow that her breath caught in her throat. Long leaf-shaped eyes just like those of the happy groom. A short straight nose and oval face, which could have been the female reflection of the young man in the portrait.

Second Lady Tang was the groom's mother.

And all the joy of that happy position had been stolen from her. Just as her son had been stolen from her. Just as Yu Lan's son would be stolen from her, unless she could find some way to prevent it. Otherwise she would never grow old with a son to love and honour her.

'You are lucky to have such a gifted son,' Madam Chan said, as she considered the four tiles dealt to her by Madam Tang. She had to decide which front and rear hand combinations would be most likely to beat the dealer.

'It will be your turn soon,' said their host.

As the ladies arranged their dominoes to give them the best chance of beating the dealer, Yu Lan considered Madam Chan's tiles. She might not be adept at reading but she could count, and she saw at a glance that the tiles could be arranged to make a hand of eight and a hand of nine, almost certainly a winning combination.

Dropping her fan to the floor, Yu Lan swayed from side to side, letting her eyes roll back in their sockets. Then lurching forward with a plaintive cry, she buckled at the knees before collapsing upon the table, sending tiles and money skittering across the rosewood surface and onto the floor, so that any winning hand was lost forever in the subsequent confusion.

And as she lay spread-eagled amongst the dominoes, she found within her heart a tiny flame of hope. She would not be like Second Lady Tang, accepting the theft of her child with equanimity. She would not go quietly. Somehow she would find a way of keeping her son. Somehow she would find a way of defeating Madam Chan and taking back her life. If the river did not take her where she wanted to go, then she would find a paddle and take herself, even if she left a storm of chaos in her wake.

18

Kuala Lumpur 1931

THE BEDCHAMBER WAS more crowded than a busy wet market. Women flapped about the bed pecking and clucking, so that Yu Lan found it difficult to understand what they wanted. All she knew was pain and a great lethargy that weighed down her limbs and fogged her thinking. With the shutters and door closed, the room was dim, but she recognised the midwife who had delivered her baby, a Malay woman of middle age, the sleeves of her loose *kabaya* rolled to the elbows, her hair pulled back in a tight bun. She remembered the way the woman had smiled and made encouraging noises as she lay screaming that she was dying, as relaxed as if Yu Lan was a chicken popping out an egg. She did not recognise the other two women who busied themselves with soiled linen and clothes, and a small bundle that might have been her baby but was snatched away too quickly for her to be certain. Ho Jie was there too, issuing instructions in broken Malay that were clearly being ignored.

She wasn't sure how long it had been since the birth. Hours or a full day or more? Time was running and hiding from her. Already she couldn't remember details. Only the cycle of pain and rest, where pain kept getting longer and rest shorter until her body was ripped apart. Why had Ma not warned her? She supposed that if mothers told their daughters the truth they would all run away and no one would ever marry.

Now the pain had settled to a dull ache. She could feel her breasts hot and hard to the touch. She longed for the cooling flow of water over her body, but when she struggled from the bed and staggered towards the bathroom she was firmly returned with a flurry of shouting and arm waving.

'Ho Jie, I'm so hot and my breasts are on fire,' she moaned. 'I need to bathe them in cool water.'

Perching on the edge of Yu Lan's bed, the amah clucked her tongue, saying, 'You cannot bathe until your confinement ends. Surely your mother has told you this. Do you want to let a cold wind enter your body? Do you want to risk aches and pains in your bones?' She put a hand to Yu Lan's forehead, stroking wayward strands of hair from her face saying, 'You don't have a fever.'

'But my breasts hurt so much.' Beneath a simple sarong tied under her arms, Yu Lan felt the hot mounds of her breasts throbbing.

'That is your milk coming in. It will go away in a day or two. The *bidan* and her assistant are here to help you.'

'But where is my baby? Won't the pain disappear if I feed him?'

Yu Lan had been seven when her youngest brother was born, old enough to remember her mother feeding him, his greedy mouth latching on and sucking until he fell asleep at her breast. Old enough to remember helping her grandmother prepare special food and drink for her mother during her confinement.

'Madam has engaged a wet nurse from the village to feed your baby. So you don't need to concern yourself with that. All you need do is get well, recover your strength. Here, let me help you from the bed.'

Ho Jie helped her to stand on wobbly legs, saying, 'This is Kak Kembang. She is the *bidan*'s assistant. She will stay for the full month of your confinement to look after you. The *bidan* will stay only a few days to ensure you and baby are thriving.'

Kembang was a young woman of perhaps twenty-five years who padded barefoot about the room, lighting incense that she placed in a burner upon the floor. She waved a graceful arm in Yu Lan's direction, urging her to come closer. Then she positioned her, standing with one foot either side of the burning incense so that she was enveloped in smoke. She felt like a slab of barbecued pork hanging over a bed of coals.

'What is this for?' she asked, her lethargy compounded by the heady smoke.

'You have lost blood. You have lost heat,' said Ho Jie. 'The *bidan* says we must replace that heat and cleanse you with smoke.'

Except that Yu Lan did not feel very cleansed. She felt like she might faint. Sensing her dizziness, Ho Jie remained at her side holding her steady as Kembang prepared another concoction at a table in the corner. Soon the fragrance of lime and coconut oil infused the air, adding to the cloying scent of incense in the closed and shuttered room. It was all Yu Lan could do to stay upright.

Once the incense had burned out, Kembang beckoned Yu Lan back to the bed where she indicated for her to lie on her back. When the woman removed her sarong, placing warm hands upon her distended belly, Yu Lan made a feeble attempt to push her away.

'She will massage your stomach to help your body return to its proper shape,' explained Ho Jie. 'She will not hurt you.'

Too weak to fight, Yu Lan submitted to these ministrations. The awkward feel of Kembang's hands upon her stomach was followed by the strange sensation of having her torso bound tightly with cloth. Set upon her feet once more, she felt Ho Jie supporting her as a long cloth was wound about her middle. Beginning at her hips, Kembang circled her body with a band of cotton many yards long, knotting the ends each time they crossed in front and tying it off firmly beneath her breasts, until her entire torso was encased by this girdle. It would hold her soft flesh rigid and pull her muscles back together.

Once the girdle was in place, Kembang retied Yu Lan's sarong and returned her to bed propped up by pillows, while Ho Jie served her a warming drink of red date and ginger tea, and encouraged her to eat a bowl of chicken cooked in ginger and sesame oil. During the next thirty days Yu Lan knew she would be expected to eat a great deal of ginger, plus plenty of chicken, pork and other confinement foods to rebuild her strength.

'Where is my baby?' she asked when she could eat and drink no more.

She remembered seeing a red, squirming infant. But she didn't remember feeling his weight upon her stomach. She remembered hearing his first cries, little louder than a kitten, but she did not remember holding him. And then she had heard him no more. She remembered the voices of women, the sound of Malay being spoken and the lilt of Cantonese. She thought she had heard Ah Jie's voice issuing orders, but she could not be sure. What if her son was ailing? What if they had taken him away because he was weak? She needed to see him. She needed to make sure.

'Where is my son? Is he sick?'

'The wet nurse is feeding him. He is a strong and healthy boy. No need to worry.'

'But when can I hold him?'

'Soon. The *bidan* will bring him to you soon. Lie back and sleep now and recover your strength.'

Constricted by the cloth girdle encircling her waist, exhausted from her labour, and shut up in the dim confinement of her room, Yu Lan didn't have the strength to argue further. Closing her eyes, she slumped down in the bed and promptly fell asleep.

*

WHEN SHE WOKE the women were gone. She felt a momentary peace until she remembered her baby, then a stab of panic. Outside she could hear the drum of rain on the roof and in the corridor beyond her room the murmur of conversation. Slipping from the bed, she crept across the parquet to listen at the door, catching the familiar sound of Chan Towkay and his wife speaking in urgent tones. She heard the excitement in the *towkay*'s voice, an excitement tinged with pride. Of course he would be proud, for he had made a son with very little effort on his part. She had made all the effort. Yet she had nothing but this aching emptiness to show for it.

'She will be pleased to receive me no matter how tired.'

'Let her sleep. She has laboured hard and needs her rest.'

'Aiya, how much strength does it take to receive a few words of praise from her husband?'

Yu Lan could imagine his frown of displeasure and the stubborn set of his chin when his wishes weren't immediately gratified. Usually at that point he would throw something. She almost smiled at that thought, and hoped it would be something sharper than a slipper.

'If her body is to return to its youthful suppleness and her mind to calmness, she needs complete rest.'

There was silence for a few moments as the *towkay* considered this. Yu Lan thought that she would be happy to lose her youthful suppleness if it meant no more nightly visits from the old man.

'But I have a gift for her,' he said querulously.

'The gift will be even more precious for the waiting.'

'Tomorrow then. She will be better tomorrow.'

'Tomorrow.'

The sounds of conversation ceased, replaced by the soft tread of slippers as they departed for another part of the house, leaving Yu Lan once more to her thoughts. What had they done with her son? The answer resounded in her head with the voice of certainty: 'They have stolen him. They have stolen him and they will never give him back.'

*

THE MIDWIVES HAD departed for the day, the wet nurse was in the kitchen eating rice, and Madam Chan sat in her favourite chair cradling the concubine's child. Ho Jie had never seen such an expression of pleasure on her face. Usually the mistress's smile was the daggered heart hidden by a honeyed mouth. When she smiled the servants knew that trouble loomed. But today her eyes crinkled with laughter as she cooed happily at the child.

'Would Madam like tea?'

'Later, later. I am getting acquainted with this stinky little piggy,' she said, tickling the child under the chin with her forefinger. 'Such a handsome piggy. He has the Chan nose too.'

The child wasn't stinky, he had just been changed, but Madam was wary of rousing the attention of evil spirits. Calling him a little piggy was designed to mislead any spirits in the vicinity. They would not bother expending their spite on a piglet.

'Perhaps while Madam has tea I could take little piggy to visit his mother?'

'Oh, let the girl sleep. We are paying an army to look after him. There will be time for visits later,' said the *taitai,* waving away the idea.

'She is quite distressed, Madam. I think it would calm her to see the child.'

'It's a good thing I don't pay you to think then. The girl has done her part. I will take over now. She needs to rest and rebuild her strength, and once her confinement is over I am sure the *towkay* will keep her busy producing more sons.'

This one is mine. Madam Chan didn't say the words aloud, but Ho Jie heard them in the tone of her voice. She saw the possessive light in her eyes. The child was hers now and no one was going to take him from her, least of all the seventeen-year-old daughter of a good-for-nothing gambler. Although Ho Jie was a spinster, she had never felt any envy towards mothers, just as she had not envied her married sisters. She didn't need a husband or a son telling her where she should live or how she should behave or what she should do with her money. She could manage those decisions for herself.

'Very good, Madam. I will fetch your tea.'

'And Ho Jie, do not bother me again with that girl's wants. She is lucky that Chan chose her, that she is not married to a poor man, slaving all day after a bad-tempered mother-in-law and a brood of whining children. She is privileged to bear Chan

Towkay's son. We wouldn't want anything interfering with that, would we?'

'We wouldn't.'

'We wouldn't want her to be sent away, would we? For then she would never see the child again.'

'We wouldn't, Madam.'

'So let's not hear any more about the girl's distress. She will get over it soon enough.'

Ho Jie wasn't so sure. Yu Lan was little more than a child herself. There was something fragile about her, like the finest porcelain. She wasn't tough enough to protect herself from a woman like Madam Chan, and she wasn't experienced enough to know how to tempt Chan Towkay to her side. She was a child cast adrift in a dangerous world without the tools necessary to survive.

She needed a friend. She needed Ho Jie.

19

Kuala Lumpur 2017

WHEN SHE'D LAST seen her husband he was brown from the sun. Now, swathed in a hospital gown with tubes and hoses snaking from his body to a bank of machines, he was barely recognisable. The bits of his face that showed were white, almost bloodless.

'Nick?'

She didn't know why she spoke aloud. She'd been told he was unresponsive but it didn't seem right somehow to greet her husband with silence.

'I'm here. At the hospital,' she said, just in case he didn't know where 'here' was. 'It's me. Sarah.' Just in case he didn't know who 'me' was.

The ventilator's plastic hoses were larger in diameter than she'd imagined. More like transparent garden hoses. Other tubes issued from nose, arm, and chest and from somewhere under his hospital gown. Wires connected a finger and sections of his scalp to various other machines, while cloth ties restrained his wrists. Instinctively, she itched to wrench them all loose. He shouldn't be tied down like this. He wouldn't like it. He would want her to get him out of here.

She edged closer to the bed. He didn't smell like Nick. A disinfectant odour overpowered his usual scent of soap, hair gel and espresso. She wondered if she should touch him, whether the invisible microscopic demons inhabiting her body might contaminate him.

'You can touch him,' said a voice behind her.

She flicked a glance over her shoulder to see that a nurse had entered. Clad in blue trousers and long shirt, a dark headscarf tucked inside her collar, the young woman crossed to the end of Nick's bed and took out his chart.

'Don't worry. He won't break.'

'He looks so… fragile.' Almost as if he was laced together by wires, which was true in a way, for the wires and tubes were the only things holding him to the earth.

Sarah reached out a single finger and stroked the back of his hand lightly. When there was no response, she floated her fingers above his hand. So close that static leaped between them. Surely that was a good sign.

Slowly she rested her hand upon his and squeezed.

Nothing. Nothing but warm, smooth skin on a hand that lay limp where once Nick would have grabbed her hand and swung it high as they walked through Camden Market or strolled in Barnard Park on Sunday afternoon, swinging back and forth until she begged him to stop before her arm pulled loose from its socket. Thirty-three and he was still such a child.

Thirteen years ago he'd held her hand for the first time. They'd been sprawled on the lawn in front of the Queen's Building at Queen Mary's College, basking in one of those rare spring days when the sun does more than peek through the gloom. Sarah had been in her first year of marketing while Nick was majoring in English. They shared no classes but Nick, for all his reserve, seemed to know everybody. He was one of those people who listened so well that you immediately felt you'd made a new friend. When she offered him a hot chip, instead of taking it, he took her hand. She was so surprised that she dropped the chips. But she kept his hand.

'Will you promise to keep me in chips?' she'd asked him years later when they talked of marriage. He was the one person who could bring out her inner clown.

The nurse moved closer, chart and pen in hand. She directed her words at Nick but glanced intermittently at Sarah as she spoke.

'Nick? My name is Azra. I'll be looking after you today. Can you open your eyes for me?'

They waited, Sarah fixated on his thick dark lashes as if she could will them open, the nurse moving her gaze between his face and the monitors, watching for a sign. When there was no response, she pressed her pen to the tip of his fingernails and waited again. Nothing. She made a notation on the chart.

'Can you tell me your name... Can you tell me where you are... Nick, could you tell me what month it is?'

To Sarah, the questions seemed futile. Clearly he was floating in another world, biding his time until it was safe to return. But Nurse Azra waited patiently after each question, as if he might suddenly perk up, open his eyes and speak. After several more moments, she made another notation and then, hooking her pen onto her collar, she reached forward to take his hand.

'Nick, can you squeeze my hand and then let go... Can you open your mouth and stick out your tongue?'

Moving closer to the head of the bed, she placed her hand on his shoulder and pinched but he didn't move, not even an involuntary shiver. She pressed on his forehead just above his eyebrow. There was only the sound of the ventilator pumping new air into his lungs and sucking out the old while he lay on the bed like a wax doll. Unmoving. Unreachable.

She made a final notation on her chart before turning to Sarah, her brown eyes smiling.

'How long has he been like this?'

'Since he presented in emergency yesterday. He's lucky the paramedics brought him here, where we have a neurotrauma unit.'

How could she call him lucky when he was trapped like this? But perhaps it was a question of degree. Perhaps she'd seen others who weren't so lucky.

'His housemaid found him. Miss Lau.'

Nick had never mentioned anything about a housemaid. Then again, he hadn't told her about his handyman activities either. She wondered what else he'd neglected to mention. In her head, the fair-minded voice of reason whispered, 'You didn't give him a chance. You barely picked up his messages.'

'Doctor will be here soon. She can tell you more.'

'Thank you. Thank you for everything.'

'Oh and Mrs Chan, we have a few of Doctor Chan's belongings here. They were in his pockets. A key and a few other items.'

Crossing to the bedside cabinet, she unlocked the drawer with a key hanging around her neck alongside her identification tag, and handed Sarah an envelope. Then she held Sarah's upper arm and squeezed.

'I'll be back.' Sarah nodded. 'Make yourself comfortable. And talk to him. Someone may hear,' she said, rolling her eyes upwards. 'Even if he can't.'

After she'd gone Sarah looked down at the yellow envelope. She was holding it so tightly that her fingers were white at their tips. Mechanically, she tore it open, shaking the contents into her hand. Three objects rattled onto her palm: a phone, a key and a ring. The key was of the old-fashioned kind, made of brass with complicated square teeth patterned almost like a Chinese character. It was looped onto a simple steel ring attached to an obsidian amulet, carved in the shape of a Chinese warrior with a fierce, uncompromising visage. The third item, the ring, was made of green jade. Its wide, flat surface was completely unembellished besides a single carved slot.

Apart from the phone, she recognised none of these items. That key would never open the apartment Nick rented. The keyring looked touristy, not the sort of thing he would choose. And the only ring he wore, she'd slid onto his hand almost ten years ago. That ring still glinted on the finger crowned with a plastic clip, connected to a wire, attached to a machine that confirmed her husband still lived.

Other than that she would never have guessed.

*

THE JADE THAT felt cold when she'd first slipped the ring onto her thumb warmed with her body heat. She sat by Nick's hospital bed, unconsciously twisting it back and forth as she watched him breathe. So attuned was she to his breath that her own breathing aligned with the slow rise and fall of his chest.

'Where are you, Nick?' she breathed, her voice barely audible.

'Just ducking out for a pint.' She imagined him answering. She willed him to answer. Just to hear his voice again, even if he gave her one of his rare scoldings. Closing her eyes, she pictured him at the door to the flat, throwing on his jacket and looping his Arsenal scarf about his neck. 'Back in a jif,' he'd say.

But he hadn't just ducked out for a pint. He'd been gone for too long. She should have begged him to return.

'Call me if you need anything.' She saw his teeth flash white in a grin, then the door closing behind his departing back. The image was so powerful that she opened her eyes and was about to take out her phone when she heard another voice close by.

'Ms Matthieson? Sarah?'

She turned at the sound of her name. A middle-aged woman, dressed in a smart suit and white coat with a stethoscope draped around her neck, stood a few feet away.

'Doctor Chua?' she asked, standing to shake hands. It was only then she realised she was still holding the strange key. Transferring it to her left hand, she offered her right.

'I hope you had a good flight and I'm so sorry to have been the bearer of bad news. Nurse Azra tells me that there's been no improvement in the last couple of hours.'

'No. It seems not.'

'We've been monitoring your husband closely. Doctor Haziq, our head of neurotrauma, has been in several times.'

'Thank you,' she hesitated, not sure whether to ask her question, for a question unasked remains unanswered and Sarah wasn't sure she would like the answer. 'Nurse Azra said you'd be able to tell me more about Nick's condition.'

'You must understand that it's very difficult to give you a definite prognosis with an injury such as this. Every patient is different. And at the moment we're not sure of the extent of the injury.'

'I understand that, but when do you think he'll wake up?'

The doctor met Sarah's gaze but she had removed her

stethoscope and was unconsciously twirling it.

'As I said, we're not sure at this stage.'

'He couldn't have fallen very far. It was only a ladder.'

'We understand from the young woman who called the paramedic that he hit his head on the edge of a stone step when he fell. He was trying to repair a crack in the wall near the ceiling. Ceilings can be high in these old buildings.'

What old building? What is she talking about? She glanced from the doctor to her still and silent husband. The apartment he rented was in a high-rise, one of those towering condos that filled Kuala Lumpur's skyline.

'You know me, Sar. Always found those new places a bit soulless,' she heard his voice in her head as she remembered all the places they'd inspected before they bought their one-bedder. She'd been tempted at times by the gleaming and new but Nick was always drawn to the charming and old, despite questionable plumbing.

But the doctor was continuing her explanation and Sarah needed to pay attention. 'Plus in a head injury the impact is only the primary injury. Nick has a fractured skull, but the impact has also caused the brain to crash back and forth against his skull. This can cause bruising, bleeding and injury to the nerve fibres. In Nick's case there has been significant bleeding and a haematoma, or blood clot. Yesterday we performed emergency surgery to repair the ruptured blood vessels and remove the clot.'

'So he should recover now?'

'Sarah, I'd like to promise you that your husband will recover but I can't.'

After the doctor left, Sarah realised she'd been telling her that Nick might die. But Doctor Chua didn't know Sarah. She didn't know how single-minded she could be. Being single-minded was the only thing that had got her through her parents' divorce and its subsequent turbulence. Single-mindedness had brought her Nick and driven the successful development of her company. She hadn't come all this way to lose her husband. It was ridiculous. June would never forgive her. June wouldn't forgive her son either. He'd promised his mother that he'd look after himself and now he'd gone and fallen off some stupid ladder and cracked open his head.

'How could you do something so dumb?' she said aloud.

'Sorry, babe, but the ladder fought back.'

'Why didn't you wait for someone to hold it? Why didn't you…' She shook herself, trying to break this pointless train of thought. Obsessing was dangerous and didn't change anything. 'Oh, Nick,' she whispered.

'Sarah?'

She turned sharply at the sound of her name spoken in an unfamiliar Australian voice. 'Yes?' she said with the lift of an eyebrow, forcing her thoughts away.

A man stood in the corridor, just outside Nick's room. He wore no ID tag or stethoscope so presumably he wasn't a doctor. He was tall and solid and he regarded her gravely from cool green eyes, all the more startling for the number-three crew cut which had reduced his hair to stubble.

'I'm Ben. Mason. Nick's colleague. I just found out. How is he?'

'Not so good. How did you know who I was?'

'Nick has a picture of the two of you on his desk and we share an office so… I see you every day. He talks about you a lot too.'

Of course Nick would have her picture on his desk. Of

course he would talk about her. 'Thanks for coming.' She was unsure what this man expected of her in the way of conversation. She was too sad and tired to make small talk.

'Is it okay if I visit for a minute?' he asked, indicating the bed with a bob of his head.

'Sure, I was just heading off,' she said by way of ending the conversation, her body already turning towards the door.

'Are you staying at the house? It's still a bit primitive.'

She turned back. 'Primitive?' Suddenly the strange key, the ladder and the housemaid began to make a kind of sense.

'You know, half-scraped walls, barely working plumbing and a kitchen without a stove.'

'Which house?' As if Nick had a whole portfolio of houses in Kuala Lumpur.

'The house he inherited. His grandfather's house.' He stepped towards her, one arm extended. Was she making so little sense that he thought she might keel over?

'Oh, that house.' She kept her voice level, trying to hide her surprise. 'I thought you might mean the apartment.' When did Nick inherit his grandfather's house? Without telling her.

'You're probably jet-lagged as hell,' Ben was saying.

'I probably am.'

'Well, my number's in Nick's phone... you know... if you need anything.'

'Thanks, I'll be fine,' she said and turned for the door. She couldn't let herself be otherwise. Because if she allowed herself to sink into those feelings that were waiting to overwhelm her, she might be sucked down so far that she couldn't claw her way back. Yes, she would be fine, except she had lied about not needing anything.

'How did this happen, Nick? And why were you keeping secrets from me?' she asked silently.

'Not keeping secrets, babe. Temporarily withholding information.' He had a slippery way with words, her husband.

Oh yes, she needed so many things. Most of all, she really needed her husband.

20

'MAYBE WE SHOULD ask someone,' Sarah suggested to the taxi driver. They had driven the length of the road several times with no success, looking for the address she'd been given at the hospital. In the mirror the driver nodded agreeably, yet he showed little sign of pulling over. Perhaps he was content to drive up and down for another twenty minutes, so long as the meter was running, passing row after row of red-tiled houses and soaring condominiums with an expanse of unexpected forest in their midst.

'What about that lady there?' she persisted, pointing to an elderly woman sweeping the street in front of her house with a rush broom. She was a very tiny lady. Once she might have been of regular height but now she'd shrunk to the size of a ten-year-old child. And strangely, she appeared to be wearing pale-pink pyjamas with rubber flip-flops on her feet.

The driver pulled over, cutting a bit close for Sarah's comfort, but the woman did not bat an eyelid.

'*Jou sahn, Ah Po,*' he said, winding down his window and hailing her.

'*Jou sahn,*' she answered, briefly halting her sweeping and squinting into the sun so that her face creased into a nest of wrinkles.

There followed a very loud conversation in rapid Cantonese with a great deal of gesticulation. Finally, the woman finished with a few terse words that she repeated three times, accompanied by a shake of her broom. It was a surprisingly frenzied conversation over a simple request for directions.

'What did she mean… gwai oak?' Sarah asked as the driver took off.

'Nothing. Not to worry.'

'She said it three times. What does it mean?'

He sighed, clearly reluctant to translate.'*Gwai nguk*. Ghost house. She says that lane leads to the ghost house.'

By now the taxi was approaching the stretch of forest they'd passed earlier. Sarah had thought it strange to find an expanse of jungle in the middle of the suburbs only fifteen minutes from the city. But from what she'd seen so far, development occurred in a haphazard manner here. Houses skirted jungle, winding up one side of a hill, while the other lay bare. Glamorous apartment towers were planted adjacent to squatters' dwellings.

'She said the lane enters jungle halfway along.'

'That's good. At least we know where to go.'

The driver caught her eye in the mirror. 'She says we shouldn't go there. She says this place is cursed.'

'Well, in the absence of any visible ghosts I'm prepared to take the risk.'

Shaking his head slowly he said, 'Okay, Miss,' and made a right turn into a narrow gap in the forest that she'd failed to notice before.

She wound down her window, hoping to breathe fresh forest air after the heavy smog of the city, but was met by a blast of sticky heat. With the window open she could hear the raucous call of an unfamiliar bird, and the rustle of animals moving through the trees. And then, a mere hundred metres from the turn, a house came into view. Set in an overgrown garden of untended fruit trees and thick grass, the house was encircled on all sides by jungle.

'I guess this must be the ghost house. Can't say I see any welcoming committee,' she said, quirking an eyebrow at the driver in the rear-view mirror.

'Maybe inside.'

'Look, thanks so much for your patience,' she said, handing him the very reasonable amount showing on the meter with the addition of a generous tip. 'Could you come back in say... an hour to pick me up?'

'Sorry, Miss, maybe not in area then.'

'How about giving me your number and I'll call you?'

'Maybe going home soon.'

'I see.' She saw that her driver was more spooked than he'd admit. Clearly, he wasn't prepared to risk a run-in with any ghosts. 'Well, thanks.'

'Better to walk down to the road and call.'

'Good idea.'

Sarah turned towards the house that sat like a sad remnant of bygone glories. Once, the entrance had been adorned by elaborate pillars and wrought-iron gates to keep out unwelcome visitors; now those pillars were shrouded in vines and grey with mildew, while the gates lay in a crumpled heap alongside. Looking up, she saw that a sapling sprouted from one of the upstairs lintels. The faded green paint blended with the surrounding forest so that the entire structure appeared to be absorbed into the jungle. Yet despite this sad state of disrepair, the windows gleamed with shiny, new glass and were barred by the ubiquitous iron grilles that adorned every house in the city.

Clearly, someone had been at work here.

Opening her handbag, she fished out Nick's key, guarded by the ancient Chinese warrior snarling a warning.

'I don't know what other surprises you've got in store for me, Nick, but there better not be a giant Rottweiler behind that door.'

'More a beagle man, myself.'

Hmm. She picked her way through the long grass, more afraid of bugs biting her sandalled feet than ghosts tripping her up, to arrive at a porte-cochère lined with mosaic tiles. The front door stood intact, its heavy wood peeling with remnants of red paint. Clutching the key tightly, she inserted it into the lock, not sure what she hoped to find but desperate to discover some clue, any clue, to help her reach Nick. Wherever he had gone.

*

THERE WERE SMALL signs of her husband everywhere, from his familiar denim jacket thrown over the back of a rickety plastic chair to his gym bag sitting on the floor of one of the upstairs rooms. They seemed alien, dotted throughout this crumbling old house with its mildewed paint and scarred tiles. Like clues to some existential mystery. Or that board game where characters were murdered in various rooms of a mansion with a random assortment of objects. Miss Scarlett in the hall with a rope.

She wandered through the house, losing count of the rooms, most of them empty of furniture apart from a dusty and worm-ridden Chinese altar in one room and a few incongruous pieces from Ikea. There was also a legion of mosquitoes buzzing about, pain telling her that one had settled on her bare arm. She noticed signs of building work too, paint cans and brushes, a toolbox and a stack of building supplies in one of the rear downstairs rooms. And then there was the ladder, leaning against a wall in what she supposed must be the kitchen, furnished with a single gas burner atop a tiled concrete bench, a steel sink and a few simple shelves.

Doctor Chan in the kitchen with a ladder.

The ladder was a regular six-foot aluminium stepladder, the kind you'd find in any hardware store. It didn't look particularly sinister. And yet, surely it must be? Surely as the instrument of her husband's accident it must be evil?

'That's going to the scrap-heap ASAP,' she muttered.

'Tut tut. A good craftsman never blames his tools.'

'I've heard you cursing your computer often enough.'

She stood there on the cracked terracotta floor of this quasi-kitchen in the damp heat thousands of miles from home, staring at a ladder and wondering how she'd arrived at this point. When had they become so alienated from each other that they thought nothing of being separated for two years? Why had she allowed more than a year to pass without visiting him? Why hadn't he told her that the old man had died? That he was mourning the grandfather he had only just found? And how could he embrace his new life without a hint to her that he had inherited a house? One that was reputedly haunted.

Why didn't she know these things? A house wasn't some token vase left by a great-aunt. A house wasn't a bequest for a few quid from a family friend. A house had a life. A history. A future. A house grounded you.

A house claimed you.

And he hadn't said a word about it.

'Why, Nick? Did you think I'd object? Were you worried I might think you were putting down roots? I would never try to stop you pursuing your dreams. You always supported me in mine.'

When friends battled it out over where to live and whose career took precedence, or complained that their partner worked too hard and took them for granted, she and Nick always gave each other space. Maybe they'd given each other too much space.

Hearing the sound of a door closing somewhere in the house, Sarah jumped. 'God, they've got me spooked now.' It was probably Nick's housekeeper. She'd seen signs of occupation in one of the upstairs rooms at the rear of the house. A clothes rack hung with a woman's clothes, a folding table sprinkled with a few cosmetics, and a neatly made bed. Perhaps his handyman activities coupled with his full-time job kept him so busy that he needed some domestic help. And apparently employing a maid was an affordable option in Kuala Lumpur.

Leaving the kitchen, she found her way back through a warren of rooms to the one with the worm-ridden altar. From here she looked across the open courtyard through to the front reception room. A woman stood there, silhouetted by the light of the open door behind her. Black hair hung loose almost to her waist and she wore a long white drift of a dress. She seemed as surprised to see Sarah, as Sarah was to see her.

'Hi,' Sarah said, trying not to alarm her. 'Sorry if I surprised you. I've got a key,' she added, dangling the key before her like a charm. 'Nick's key.'

'Oh, hi.' Rather than volunteering anything further, the woman closed the door and headed in Sarah's direction. She was young and pretty and clearly not dressed for cleaning houses.

'I would have called first if I'd had your number. You must be

Nick's housekeeper. The nurse said that his ah... housemaid... called the paramedic.'

'Oh... I think you must have misunderstood her accent. I'm Nick's *housemate*. Su Lin. Pleased to meet you,' she said, extending her hand.

That hand was tipped with red nails, perfectly manicured. Sarah took it with a smile, racking up another piece of information Nick had neglected to mention. Like Alice, she seemed to have stepped into another world. One where familiar people and objects operate by unfamiliar rules. Where nothing is as it seems, and no one is exactly who they say they are. She had stepped into a world where her husband was refurbishing a crumbling mansion cursed by a ghost. He lived in this haunted house with an ethereal young woman. He had fallen from a ladder and could not be woken. Like Sleeping Beauty or Snow White.

But Sleeping Beauty and Snow White were woken in the end, weren't they? Perhaps she just had to follow the story to its climax and she too could wake Nick.

'Hi, I'm Sarah. Nick's wife,' she said, shaking the girl's hand.

'I thought you might be. It's good that you're finally here.' It was said with a smile but what was up with the word 'finally'? What was this young woman with the wide brown eyes and heart-shaped face inferring? She was Nick's housemate. Was she also his confidante? What had he told her about Sarah, about their marriage? Or was she just being paranoid? There was a family history, after all.

'I'm so glad you were here when Nick fell. I don't want to think about what might have happened if he'd been alone,' she said, determined not to let paranoia seep in. She had to keep her wits about her.

The girl was still smiling, though Sarah detected the slightest twitch at the corner of her mouth and there was nervousness in her eyes that showed in the way she kept glancing away. She wondered what Su Lin was to her husband. She wondered where they'd met and why she had taken up residence in his house.

'So, I suppose I might as well sleep here then.'

Su Lin frowned. 'Most of the hotels in town will be more convenient to the hospital.'

'Yes. But I feel closer to Nick here. You don't mind, do you?'

'No. Not at all. *Mi casa es tu casa*. Besides, it's Nick's house and you're his wife.'

'Thanks.'

'Oh, but there is no hot water. We use the local system. Fill the trough in the bathroom with cold water and bucket it over your head.' Su Lin shrugged, the smile reappearing. 'And the mosquitoes are very bad.'

'Mmm, I already found that out.'

21

WHEN SARAH TURNED on her phone after leaving the hospital that evening, she found six missed calls and six text messages from her mother. They were all in caps.

WHERE ARE YOU?

WHY AREN'T YOU AT THE OFFICE?

I WENT TO YOUR OFFICE BUT JAMES WOULDN'T TELL ME WHERE YOU ARE.

WHY AREN'T YOU AT YOUR FLAT?!!

CALL ME ASAP. AM VERY WORRIED!!! TOTALLY UNACCEPTABLE. YOU KNOW HOW MY NERVES GET.

HOW COULD YOU DO THIS TO ME?

There was also a message from James saying, 'Your mother is on warpath. She ambushed me. Managed to weather interrogation but she's gunning for you. Sorry. How is Nick doing? Hope he's on mend.'

Every time Sarah thought she'd finally worked out how to manage Celia, something unexpected happened and it was just like her adolescence all over again. In those years, Celia had lurched between unnerving optimism that her husband would return, and incandescent rage that he wouldn't. It was Sarah who talked her through the long nights when she threatened to kill herself – or her husband: the threats were interchangeable. It was Sarah who cooked, cleaned and shopped while Celia took to her bed for weeks at a time. People told her that she couldn't blame her father for leaving, but Sarah did blame him. Because he had left her behind.

For two years she hid her mother from Nick. She thought that once he met Celia he would see her differently, like she was incomplete, a person with a piece missing. Eventually, keeping them apart became more arduous than dealing with rejection so she had taken him to visit her.

'Sorry about Mum,' she'd told him on the way home. Hoping that this wasn't the beginning of the end. 'You just have to take her in small doses.'

'You're very patient with her, Sarah. I've never seen you like that before.'

Patient? He thought she was patient. She thought that she was cold and distant.

'I can see now where your reserve comes from. I can see that it was the only way you survived. By keeping something for yourself.'

And he'd kissed her on both cheeks and then on her forehead and then on her lips. Like a benediction. Rather than rejection she'd found love. For some unfathomable reason he seemed to love her more once he met Celia, as if her mother explained her in some way. Rather than running for cover he planted his feet.

But now, accustomed to her mother's hysteria, she was tempted to ignore the messages.

'She's just worried, Sar.' She heard her kind-hearted husband's voice in her head.

'Worried about herself.'

'Yup. But she can't help it.'

'Okay. I'll *call* her later. At a civilised London time.'

By the time she arrived back at the house, she'd managed to put thoughts of Celia from her mind. She had to focus her energies on Nick. A soft glow emanated from the room beyond the courtyard and as she continued through to the kitchen, she caught the delicate scent of chrysanthemum tea and the murmur of conversation.

'There's nothing you can do,' a male voice was saying. The owner of that voice was standing with his back to Sarah, one hand resting lightly on Su Lin's slight shoulder. There was nothing proprietary about the hand. It was the tactile person's way of saying, 'I'm here.'

'But I feel so helpless,' the girl said, the sound of tears in her voice. 'I feel like I need to do something but I don't know what.'

'You got him to the hospital in time. Now we have to wait.' He was so much taller than Su Lin, that he made her seem as small as a child. He bent his head towards her, the nape of his neck thick and tanned. Their heads were so close together that they might have been kissing. The thought gave Sarah a jolt. It was something she hadn't been expecting; that Nick's colleague and his housemate might be a couple.

'Sorry to interrupt,' she said with a slight cough, and they broke apart to face her.

'Sarah,' said Su Lin, wiping away tears with a paper tissue that was balled up in one fist. 'Ben and I have been consoling each other.'

'I see that.'

'I'd suggest a group hug but we've only just met,' said Ben. She wasn't sure whether he was joking or serious. On second thoughts, probably quite serious, judging by the way he opened his arms inviting her in.

'I didn't realise you knew each other.'

'Ben is my PhD supervisor in International Studies. That's

how Nick and I met. Ben told him I was looking for somewhere to live. My family is staying in Ipoh.'

'How is he? Any change?' Ben asked.

Sarah shook her head, unable to find words.

'I wish I could do something to help. He's been so good to me when I needed a friend,' said Su Lin.

'He's a good mate,' said Ben. 'He actually comes running with me sometimes and I know he hates it.'

Nick did hate running. His idea of exercise was literally a walk in the park or a quick session in the gym. And you had to run early in the morning here before it got hot. Another thing he hated. Getting up early.

'You are wearing the ring,' Su Lin said, glancing at Sarah's hands.

Sarah looked down at her hands, clasped tightly in front of her. She had taken to wearing the jade ring, as if it connected her to Nick somehow. Almost as if she could feel his hand imbuing the ring with warmth. Hear his voice. Like a conduit. But why did Su Lin call it 'the' ring?

'The nurse gave me some of Nick's belongings. The key is obvious. But I'm not sure where the other things came from.' She held up her right hand, leaving her left hand with its gold band dangling.

'I saw Nick wearing it just the other day,' said Ben.

'He found it. In this house. It's an archer's ring. You see the slot on the side, that's for holding the string of a bow,' said Su Lin. 'Chinese warriors used to wear them a long time ago.'

'I thought someone might have given it to him. Where did he find it?'

'Hidden behind a broken skirting when he was painting the

room where I sleep. He was going to have it appraised. If it's original and good quality jade, it might be valuable.'

Su Lin looked at her strangely and Sarah realised that she was probably puzzled over why a woman would be concerned about a ring when her husband lay in a coma. She didn't understand that the questions were Sarah's way of learning about a man she thought she'd known intimately and was beginning to suspect she didn't know at all. She had so many questions that she couldn't ask, not without admitting the growing rift between them, that she pounced on those she could. Hoping they might lead her in the right direction. Hoping they might help her track him down and bring him back to her.

'There's a keyring too. I only ask because Nick isn't big on trinkets. Not even ones in Arsenal colours. I wondered if it belonged to someone else.' She fished around in her bag for the brass key with its fearsome guardian.

'Not exactly a handsome bloke,' said Ben.

'That's Chung Kwei, the ghost hunter,' Su Lin said. 'You will find him in every Feng Shui shop in every shopping mall.' Sarah raised her eyebrows and she went on to explain. 'According to legend, Chung Kwei was a scholar who committed suicide by throwing himself at the palace gates after the Emperor denied him high honours in the imperial examinations because he was too ugly.'

'No equal opportunity laws in those days, clearly,' said Ben.

'When it came time for judgement by the Hell King, Chung Kwei was appointed King of Ghosts and charged with hunting out and maintaining order amongst ghosts ever after. Chinese people believe amulets or statues of Chung Kwei can protect them from evil spirits.'

She could feel the key and its amulet like a weight in her pocket. 'But you don't believe in demons, Nick. You don't believe in the supernatural. You tease me if I walk around a ladder or pick up a penny.'

'Nick doesn't believe in ghosts,' she said aloud.

'Maybe he was having a bet each way,' Ben suggested.

'He was really out of luck then, wasn't he?'

The words emerged harsher than she intended and she could feel tears not far away, tears she'd been holding back for days. She'd grown adept at holding back tears over the years and wasn't about to give in to them now. Not in front of strangers.

'Well, it's getting late. I'd better be off,' Ben said suddenly. Perhaps he sensed her mood.

'I'm sorry. I didn't mean to take my anger out on you.'

'No worries, I'm a big boy. My brother says I make a better punching bag than the ones in the gym.' He patted his stomach. 'More padding. Want to give it a try?'

'Maybe next time,' she said with a grimace, 'when I can bring my A game.'

'So can I give you a lift to the hospital tomorrow? I don't have classes until late and I'd like to sit with Nick a while.' He ran a hand through the stubble of his hair; resting the hand on the back of his neck, elbow pointing downwards. She wasn't sure what the gesture meant. Was it boredom? Or frustration?

She had always been frustrating. She knew that. When she was small her father called her his little Mary Mary. It was another kind of shell, she supposed. 'No. It's okay. I'll walk down the road and pick up a cab.'

'Maybe I'll see you there then.'

'Sure.' She liked Ben. His casual charm was infectious, but she didn't want to feel like she had to explain herself or her actions, not to this bearlike Australian. Not to her husband's pretty housemate.

She turned to Su Lin, saying, 'I'm going upstairs to dunk myself with cold water and try to get some sleep. Night.'

'*Jou tau*, Sarah. Sleep well. I put a mosquito coil in your room. Don't forget to light it.'

She crossed the inner courtyard, fumbling in the direction of the staircase by the light of a wan moon. She was just wondering where the switch was when a light above her head flickered a couple of times before flaring into life.

Somewhere in the house someone must have flicked a switch.

22

'IT'S RAINING OUTSIDE,' Sarah told her husband. 'I see what you meant when you said that when it rains here the heavens bombard you. Thirty seconds from the taxi to the entrance and I'm soaked.'

The room in ICU had become so familiar that she could find her way around it blindfold. Pale-blue walls, treetops visible through the window, high-backed green-vinyl chair, nylon curtains shrouding Nick's bed – all were imprinted upon her memory.

'I wondered why they had those deep open drains all over the place. Now I know. Flood control.'

She sat in the green-vinyl chair, holding Nick's hand, barely aware of her damp clothing and wet hair. It was funny how she'd grown more intimate with his appearance in the last five days than she had in all the previous years. Who knew he had a single freckle on the back of his wrist? Or that one eyebrow was slightly higher than the other? She'd always thought of his chest as hair free. Why hadn't she noticed the five individual hairs on his right nipple and four on his left?

'I've been to the house.'

Both Nurse Azra and Doctor Chua had told her to talk to Nick even though he might not understand or respond, to tell him what she was up to and let him know she was there… waiting for him to return. She'd considered not mentioning the house, but not mentioning it seemed tantamount to lying. There were already too many things left unsaid between them. She didn't want to add more.

'I don't know how you came to inherit but I'm sure you'll tell me when you wake up. It must have been beautiful once so I see why you want to restore it.'

She squeezed his hand then, for her reassurance as much as for his, searching his face for some sign that he'd heard her. Despite the house's decrepit state, it felt like one of Nick's ancestors might step through a door from another time at any moment. She didn't tell him about these creepier aspects though. How she would catch a flash of white out of the corner of her eye then discover it was simply a plastic bag that had blown into the house. Or how she would hear a snatch of muffled conversation in Cantonese, then Su Lin would walk into the room watching a video on her phone. The house was making her a bit crazy, actually.

She smoothed the hair back from his forehead. 'Sometimes when I walk into a room, it feels like someone has just left. Except there's no one there. It's not a sound or a scent, just...' She stopped mid-sentence, realising she was talking nonsense, babbling like a superstitious idiot. For a split second she thought she caught a flicker of movement, as if Nick's eyes were searching the darkness beneath his eyelids. Looking for her.

'Nick, can you hear me? It's... Sarah.'

She squeezed his hand again, willing his eyes to open. But there was nothing. Only his pale face, webbed by tubes and wires.

'I've met your friends. Ben and Su Lin.'

Perhaps it was her imagination, but above the rhythmic hiss of the ventilator she thought she caught another tiny sound, like the soft moan of a dreaming man. Almost imperceptible to the human ear.

'Can you open your eyes?' she begged. 'Please. Please open your eyes for me.'

Please wake up. Please come back from wherever you are. If screaming could bring him back she would have shouted until her voice grew raw, but she knew that it was pointless. He would return or he would not. No, that was wrong; that made it sound like he had some control over his situation. Some choice. Like he was paying her back for not coming to Malaysia when she said she would. But this was nonsensical thinking. This was how *she* operated. Paying people back for hurting her. Punishing them for not loving her enough. Nick wasn't like that.

He would return or he *could not.*

'Sarah? I'm glad I caught you.' Doctor Chua materialised next to her, brushing aside the white nylon curtains. Beneath her white coat she wore a pale-blue suit, so that she was almost camouflaged by the hospital room.

'I thought I saw his eyes move,' she said, shaking herself back to reality.

'Did he open them?'

'No, but I think they moved under his eyelids.'

'There's often some twitching and involuntary movement in comatose patients.'

'And I think he might have… moaned.'

The doctor leaned over the bed, her gaze shifting between her patient's face and the monitor as she moved through the familiar questions like a litany. 'Nick. It's Doctor Chua. Can you open your eyes for me… Can you tell me where you are…'

'I'm sorry,' she said when she was done, 'I can detect no response. That doesn't mean there won't be any but for the moment Nick's condition remains very grave. Do you think we could have a word? There's a room nearby where we can speak privately.'

Sarah was still holding on to Nick. She stared at their entwined hands, both pale, his left hand with its gold wedding band, her right wearing the loose jade archer's ring. 'You wouldn't leave me?' she asked him silently.

'I'm here, Sar. I'll always be here.'

*

'I'M GOING TO be very straightforward with you, Sarah, because I believe you need to prepare yourself.' The neurologist sat in a low hospital armchair across the small sitting room from Sarah. On the table between them lay a stack of well-read magazines in a mix of languages, while outside the room, rain pattered on the glass. It might have been cosy, except for the cold vinyl floor, the fluorescent lights overhead and the slightly antiseptic air.

'When Nick first arrived in ICU we believed there was only a slim chance of him surviving the night.'

'But he did survive.'

'He did. And then we believed there was a fifty-fifty chance that he would survive the next few days.'

'And he did.' And Sarah was here. Using all her not inconsiderable will to bring him back. 'And you told me that recovery is a guessing game. That it's difficult to give a definitive prognosis.'

'I did. But it *is* our job to make educated guesses. The fact that a patient is even in the Neuro ICU means that paramedics and hospital staff have successfully interrupted a death. But while the patient remains unconscious we can't know for certain whether he will live, die or recover.'

'I understand.' In theory she understood but in practice she couldn't accept it. She wanted things in black and white. He was either here or he wasn't. Sarah didn't deal in grey. And he'd said he would be here, hadn't he? She always took Nick at his word.

Doctor Chua glanced down at a picture of a light-filled apartment high above the city that graced one of the magazine covers, giving herself time to gather her thoughts. 'Unfortunately, CT scans are showing us that Nick's brain is starting to stroke.'

Sarah barely heard her next words. She'd stopped listening at the word 'stroke'.

'The question is, what's the best course of action now? In Malaysia, the medical team is charged with making the final decision, but we always do this in consultation with the patient. And if the patient is incapable of decision-making, then with the patient's family. We can wait a short while before we make a decision about withdrawing treatment, but if and when we decide to turn off the ventilator, and if he begins to breathe on his own, he will almost certainly be severely brain damaged.'

Sarah managed to dredge a semblance of sense from her brain to ask, 'You mean he will be a vegetable?'

'We refer to it as a "vegetative state" and while we can't say with total certainty that he would remain in this state, we can say that if he did regain consciousness he would be permanently and severely debilitated. I'm afraid that fewer than fifty per cent of coma patients survive and fewer than ten per cent recover completely.'

'But Nick might be one of that ten per cent.'

'The strokes indicate this is highly unlikely. I'm sorry that I can't give you a definitive prognosis. The more we learn about neurotrauma, the more we realise that between survival and death there's an in-between area that's quite grey. And I'm even more sorry that I can't promise you a recovery.'

So these were the possibilities. Death. Limbo. Incapacity.

Doctor Chua frowned in a kind manner, saying, 'And despite the life support, should his brain die, the decision will be made for us and we'll withdraw treatment. The question is, what would Nick want us to do now?'

Sarah sensed that if her hands were resting in her lap, Doctor Chua would have reached out and taken them in hers. She was kind. She was practised in the art of death. But Sarah's hands were locked tightly around her upper arms, resisting both conversation and connection. She didn't know what Nick would want because they had never talked about it. Death wasn't part of their plans. Which meant she would have to decide for him. Yet if she couldn't bring herself to take responsibility for another person's life, a child's life, how could she possibly take responsibility for a death?

'What should I do, Nick? You have to help me,' she implored.

But this time he didn't answer.

*

'SARAH? WHAT'S HAPPENED? You look like you've seen a ghost.'

Ben and Su Lin approached her along the hospital corridor, coming from the direction of Nick's room. Su Lin appeared pale and more solemn than usual, while Ben frowned as he looked at her. As if he could read her mind. Or perhaps he was merely reading her appearance. For she was still shaking and her face felt cold and bloodless.

'No ghosts… not yet.'

She tried to avoid his eyes, but he placed his hand on her bare arm, drawing her attention towards him. It was a large hand, tanned and with slightly ragged fingernails, and it held her in a warm, firm grip. There was nothing tentative about the way he held her. Nothing that indicated he was going through the motions of polite concern. This hand meant business. This hand said, I'm here and I'll be here if you need me.

He was her husband's friend and he wasn't going anywhere.

'What is it with you?' she said, suddenly angry.

'What?'

'You might as well be wearing a sign around your neck saying, "Lean on me."'

He ignored her anger. 'It's not good, is it?'

'No. It's not. I need to talk to Nick's mother as soon as… as soon as…' But she couldn't finish the thought, couldn't find enough breath in her body, as her heart rate quickened and clammy sweat broke out all over her. Somehow she found herself being held upright, despite her wobbly legs, her quaking body, and the sick hollowness in her stomach. She tried to push him away, preferring to lean on a hospital trolley, but he wrapped her in his arms and wasn't letting go.

'Come on, mate, you've had a shock. And when was the last time you ate?'

Su Lin stood, watching them helplessly, an unreadable expression on her face.

'I don't know, maybe last night.'

'I'm taking you for lunch. We'll go to one of Nick's favourite spots not far from the house and you can tell us what happened. Or not. It's up to you.'

'No. I need to stay here. In case he wakes up.'

Who was she fooling? According to Doctor Chua, Nick was unlikely to ever wake up.

'Yeah? Well, I know what Nick would say to that.'

'What?' She'd lost her ability to predict what her husband would say.

'*Sihk faan*,' he said, in what she presumed was bad Cantonese.

'What does that mean?'

'Eat rice,' answered Su Lin, her voice croaky with tears. 'That's the Chinese answer to everything.'

What business did she have with tears? Nick wasn't her husband. He was merely her housemate. She had no more responsibility to him than an acquaintance. She hadn't married him. She hadn't made promises. She hadn't failed him.

23

ONE MINUTE BEN was negotiating a maze of narrow roads through hilly, jungle-fringed suburbia, the next he was pulling up to let them out, before parking in an empty space across the road. In the distance she could hear the faint echo of the call to prayer. The restaurant was covered by a green tin roof with green concrete floor and red plastic tables. It was open to the elements on three sides, but the rain had stopped and the place hummed with diners. The boss indicated for them to wait while a table was reset with orange plastic bowls, chopsticks and condiments. While she waited, Sarah contemplated the menu that spread over most of the rear wall, in the form of handwritten yellow posters and large photographs of various kinds of seafood. Sea cucumber with goose palm and the big bowl feast appeared to be the day's specials.

She sat back in her red plastic chair listening to the musical tones of rapid-fire Cantonese exchanged between the boss and Su Lin. At first there was a back-and-forth about the food and what they were to eat – she assumed so, anyway – but then the man appeared to ask a question about Sarah, for he kept turning from Su Lin to her and back again with a smile and a nod in her direction. Once the ordering was completed, he disappeared into the kitchen.

'He asked if you and Ben were married.'

'I've been in a few times before with Lin and Nick,' Ben said, leaving Sarah wondering why the boss hadn't asked if Su Lin and Ben were a couple.

He returned a few moments later with a pot of steaming tea, which he deposited on the table before turning to her and asking, 'You're married to the English professor?'

'Yes, he lives near here now. Do you know the old house in the lane in the middle of all the trees? He inherited it from his grandfather.'

The man regarded her strangely for a moment and she wondered whether she'd spoken too fast for him to pick up her English, but just as she was thinking of asking Su Lin to translate he said, 'You live there with him?'

'No, I'm just visiting from London.'

'I know the house,' he said with a shake of his head. 'You shouldn't stay there. It isn't a good place. Around here they call it the ghost house.'

She would have snorted if it weren't so rude. 'I know it looks unloved but… a ghost house?' Surely he was too young to believe in ghosts. He looked barely older than her; he wasn't a little old lady out sweeping the road in her pyjamas.

'People think it's an unlucky house. Because of the curse,' he said, matter-of-factly.

There was no doubt the house was unlucky for Nick but not because of any curse. 'Why do they think that?'

'Because of *neuih gwai*.'

'What?' she asked, looking to Su Lin for translation.

'Nothing. It's just a silly superstition.'

'It is… a silly superstition,' the man agreed with a shrug, but he said it with the air of one who thinks the disbelievers are the silly ones. 'Maybe it's just coincidence that people die there. Many people… not just *neuih gwai*…'

'What's a *neuih gwai*?'

'A ghost woman.'

He was about to continue but Su Lin cut him off again and there followed another exchange in Cantonese before he added, 'But no need to worry. People die everywhere.' He turned towards the other side of the room. Another customer had caught his eye and he was about to disappear.

'Sir, just a moment, please. Who died there?' she asked, suddenly needing to know all she could about this unlucky house, no matter how silly or superstitious.

'You don't want to know that, lah! It's old lady stories.'

'Please.'

'The old man's father died there. And his mother. And his wife. And a girl, a long time ago. A lot of death in that house. But the old man, he was more frightening than any ghost.' He shook his head, laughing.

So the old man had been frightening, had he? Perhaps that's why June never returned. She couldn't believe that her pragmatic, bargain-loving mother-in-law would be bothered by a few old ghost stories. There had to have been a more compelling reason for her to stay away for almost forty years, a reason for letting Nick think that his grandfather was dead. Until he decided to come here and find out for himself.

'That's the real reason you took the contract, isn't it?' she said to Nick. 'To search for your grandfather. To connect with your ancestors.'

'Did you know the old man?' she asked aloud, conscious that the boss was anxious to return to his other customers but unwilling to let him go. She felt like she'd been stumbling in the dark, unsure where she was going and who or what she was looking for. She needed something to grasp on to, to guide her.

Maybe he held a clue.

'I went there with my friends as a boy. We threw stones over the fence. Cans, sticks...' he paused, looking a little embarrassed, 'dog shit sometimes... you know how boys are. We wanted to... ah... provoke the ghost.'

'And did you... provoke any ghosts?'

'Only the old man. He was a demon. He came running out with big stick. Says he knows where we live, and he will come and find us in our beds and then we will be veerrry sorry,' the boss said with a laugh. 'We forget about ghosts after that. More scared of the old man.'

'But who do people think the ghost was?'

'Sorry, Madam,' he said, nodding in the direction of another table. 'No more time for stories. Come back another day. Try the sea cucumber.'

After the boss escaped she turned back to find her companions watching her sympathetically. Had she sounded deranged? She didn't know why the house had become so important when her husband was lying in hospital, perhaps never to return home. It wasn't as though she believed in haunted houses, curses or ghosts... and yet... Nick had obviously become obsessed with his grandfather's house. He'd kept it secret from her. He'd begun restoring it when previously he would have endured a single dim, lonely lamp rather than hunt out a ladder to change a light bulb. He hadn't even mentioned his pretty new housemate. Something had changed him. Something had almost killed him. And now Doctor Chua expected her to finish the job.

'How about tea?' Ben suggested, pouring three cups of Chinese tea and swinging the lazy Susan in her direction. 'Or maybe a beer? They have Tiger or Heineken.'

'Just tea, thanks,' she said, conjuring a smile. 'Beer makes me burp.'

'Me too,' he said and burped loudly.

On her lap, Sarah's handbag vibrated gently, the ringtone muffled by leather. She fished it from the pocket, answering at the sight of June's name.

'I have to take this,' she said, pushing back the plastic chair to weave through the crush of diners, searching for somewhere quiet to talk about death.

'You're up early,' she said by way of greeting, settling on a spot at the verge of the road several yards from the restaurant.

'I called as soon as I got your message. Is it good news or bad?'

'It's not good.' For the next ten minutes she tried to keep her voice steady as she described the conversation with Doctor Chua, answering June's questions as clearly as she was able and ending with a simple plea.

'I need you here. Nick needs you here. We can't do it on our own.'

'Which hotel are you staying in?'

'I've moved to the house. Your father's house. Did Nick tell you about it?'

'Yes.' *But you didn't tell me.* 'Nick wanted it to be a surprise. He asked me not to mention it. I warned him that you don't like surprises.' Perhaps her mother-in-law knew her better than she thought.

'Anyway, we can talk about the house another time. After… after…' Don't cry, Sarah. Hold it together. Nick needs you to hold it together.

'I'll be there as soon as I can. But I can't stay at that house.'

There was silence on the line as she paused before finishing with: 'There are too many ghosts there for me.'

*

BY THE TIME she returned to the table, rain was falling again. The waiter set a gleaming platter of crabs, a dish of tofu and a whole steamed fish on the lazy Susan. They were each supplied with a bowl of water and a small hammer.

'Try this,' Ben said, picking up a large crab claw with his chopsticks and depositing it on a plate in front of her. 'And don't be afraid to use your hands.'

She blinked, momentarily shutting out the surreal world around her, the teetering mounds of orange crab, the red paper lanterns, the rain pelting onto a tin roof, the whirring fans and plastic crockery. What was she doing here? Why wasn't she sitting at Nick's bedside, her face lit by the glow and wink of machines, holding his hand and listening as a ventilator breathed for him?

When she opened her eyes, she realised that Ben was offering her a hammer. She regarded it blankly for a second, before grasping it and swinging it high to smash down upon the crab claw. Then the hammer took on a life of its own, bearing down over and over again until the offending claw was nothing but a pulverised mass of cracked shell and oozing white flesh splayed upon shards of broken plastic.

Ben and Su Lin watched in silence.

'I don't think I'm hungry after all,' she said, too consumed with rage to feel embarrassed. There would be time for that later, for normal things like eating, sleeping and acting like an everyday human being.

'No worries. We can grab a bite later. Let's drop Su Lin at the house and then I'll drive you back to the hospital,' Ben offered, taking her outburst in his stride. 'Unless you'd like the crab to go,' he added, with the tiniest crook to the side of his mouth.

In another life she might like him, this laid-back man with the easy humour and obliging smile. Like Nick, he seemed to take life as it found him. Except she suspected that Ben Mason wouldn't mind stirring up a bit of trouble now and then, taking a little risk. He had that larrikin look about him.

But Sarah had no space in her life for like or dislike now. There were no absolutes left at all, only the grey area between life and death.

24

APART FROM THE pale glow of moonlight leaching through sheets taped over windows, her room was dim. For a moment Sarah was disoriented, thinking she was back in the Islington flat and wondering what had happened to her oatmeal silk curtains. Then as her life drifted back into focus she sat up, taking in the room around her with its scuffed parquet floors, faded paint and makeshift furnishings. She heard the *tuk tuk* of tiny green geckoes speaking to each other as they prowled the bedroom wall. She remembered lying awake in this room for hours last night, her mind circling the same question over and over until it wore a groove in her brain. Eventually she must have fallen asleep.

Despite her heavy head, gritty eyes and dry mouth, she knew that if she lay back down sleep would elude her. Better to get up, wander downstairs and try to find something to distract her. Slipping her feet into a pair of Nick's oversized Havaianas, she headed out onto the landing. It was cooler here than the bedroom, the night air permeating the courtyard and flooding it with moonlight. She descended the staircase, one hand sliding down the warm timber bannister, the other clutching her laptop. Reaching the bottom step she turned towards the front living room, but was stopped by a noise. She recognised it immediately as the sound of a woman sobbing, the anguished intake of breath followed by a smothered keening. Surprised, she turned back towards the noise to be across the tiled floor, the shape unfurled itself into a girl, long black hair cloaking her face and shoulders, hands and feet shrouded by her nightgown.

'Sorry to intrude, I didn't know you'd be up,' she said, not sure whether to abandon Su Lin to whatever private grief consumed her, or acknowledge her distress and attempt reassurance. Although Sarah freely admitted that she was about as nurturing as a mother hamster.

Su Lin smeared the back of a hand across her face and glanced up. 'I couldn't sleep.'

She looked incongruous, shrouded in her nightie, folded into an Ikea armchair that she must have dragged from the living room and planted in the middle of all this faded glory. What was she even doing here in this decaying house bequeathed to Sarah's husband by his estranged grandfather? Anyone could see she'd be more at home in an apartment with aircon and wifi and a microwave oven.

'What are you doing here?' The words slipped out and Sarah clapped a hand over her mouth. She couldn't believe what she'd just said, rude and abrasive even for her. 'I'm sorry. I didn't mean it that way. I just...'

Su Lin stared at her, pupils filling her eyes like twin wells of pain.

'I only meant... this place is so sad now... so sad and empty. Wouldn't you be happier staying with a friend? Or family?'

'My family lives in Ipoh. Most of my friends have finished their studies, gone back home or travelling. But I can find somewhere else if you want me to go.'

she meant. His tools, his clothes, his old Nikes by the back door.

'I'd rather be here. Nick loved this house.' Su Lin bowed her head so that her hair covered her face once more, concealing her emotions. 'You know, he used to bring out a blanket and lie on the floor staring up at the sky. In the daytime he liked to watch the clouds drift past and the birds fly over. And at night he stared at the clouds in the moonlight. It was like the house infected… I mean *infused* him.'

Sarah closed her eyes, picturing her husband lying here looking up at the stars. Then she saw Su Lin lying next to him and shut out the thought.

'It's not like you think, Sar,' she felt him say. 'She needed a friend.'

'Nick was very kind to me,' Su Lin continued, and Sarah heard the tears in her voice again. So he'd won her with his kindness too. His dependability. She remembered the feel of her husband's lithe, smooth body pressed against hers and thought, bamboo is stronger than steel or concrete after all. Any sad, lonely girl would be attracted to that.

'Nick is a kind man.'

She told herself she meant to comfort but she also meant to put Su Lin in her place. He was kind to her but… he was kind to everyone. She knew her words could wound, yet what had this girl done that was so terrible other than share a part of her husband's life she had chosen not to? Why did she feel this compulsion to mark her territory?

Any antipathy went over Su Lin's head for she answered simply, 'He is. I felt lost after I finished my degree. My parents wanted me to come home and look for a job near them.'

She was so young. What… twenty-two, twenty-three maybe? Sarah remembered being twenty-two and facing the uncertainty of leaving university and setting out into the world. How frightening it had been, even with Nick by her side.

'I didn't have enough money but I wanted to go on to do post-grad. Nick let me live here in exchange for helping out with some painting and plastering, waiting around for tradesmen. He had trouble getting contractors in. Somehow they all knew about the… the *gwai nguk*.'

'You mean you couldn't get a plumber or an electrician because they were scared of a ghost?'

Su Lin nodded. 'You would not believe how superstitious people are. So he needed someone to hold a ladder for him sometimes… and I couldn't even do that.'

The tears were flowing freely now, the sobs torn from her throat. Sarah didn't know what to do. Her hands dangled uncertainly at her sides. She felt that she should comfort her yet didn't know how. She had no comfort left in her.

'I tried to protect him. I bought charms so that Chung Kwei could chase away evil spirits. I made offerings. You probably think I am crazy, but just in case there really was a curse. It couldn't hurt.'

Sarah took two awkward steps towards her, propelled by a sense of obligation, a simple human obligation to comfort another in distress. Yet she'd been in training her entire adult life to ignore those kinds of feelings. Su Lin was one small step away, one arm's length from a hug.

'It wasn't your fault,' she wanted to say but the words caught in her throat.

'I should have been here to hold the ladder. I said I'd be back to help,' said Su Lin. 'Instead I had coffee with a friend first.'

Yes. You should have been. Someone should have been.

'And Nick didn't wait for me. I don't know why he fell. It wasn't a high ladder. I keep going over it in my head. Did he slip? Did he lean out too far? Didn't he open the ladder fully? Did he place it too close to the steps? I don't understand how it could happen.' Su Lin's explanation was awash with tears so that Sarah found it difficult to separate words from sobs. 'And when I found him, apart from the blood everywhere, he was so pale, so still, that I thought he was already gone...' She looked up again, searching Sarah's face. Was she seeking some kind of absolution?

Sarah felt an invisible force try to lift her arm and pull her towards Su Lin. 'Help her, Sar. Help yourself.' In her heart she knew that Su Lin wasn't to blame for the accident, but she couldn't bring herself to utter the words that would wipe away the girl's self-reproach. Because if she didn't know how to absolve her own guilt, how could she acquit another?

'Nick was a grown man,' she managed finally. 'He made his own choices.'

Su Lin's tears were almost exhausted so her next words rang out clear as a bell. 'But what if he *didn't* have a choice? What if something... or someone... compelled him? What if something pushed him?'

Sarah had no time for superstition and she wasn't about to pander to anyone else's either. This house was old and unloved but it wasn't cursed. All it needed was a coat of paint, better wiring and twenty-first-century plumbing.

'Su Lin, you don't need me to tell you there's no such thing as ghosts.'

Not the kind she meant anyway.

25

AS SHE ENTERED the hotel through a revolving glass door, she spotted June sitting on a plush pink sofa, feet planted firmly on the red carpet. June seemed smaller than when she'd last seen her, or perhaps it was merely the oversized chairs. Amidst the purposeful throng of holidaymakers and business travellers she looked tense and anxious. She had made no concessions to the tropical climate, wearing a tailored skirt, long-sleeved cotton blouse and court shoes. As usual, her hair was styled into a neat bob.

'June,' she called as she approached, 'you look perfectly put together for someone who just stepped off a twelve-hour flight.'

They hugged, perhaps a little closer than usual, and touched cheeks. June's body felt thinner too, which made Sarah feel strangely protective, even maternal towards her mother-in-law.

'They let me check in early and I freshened up,' June explained with a smile. 'How are you coping?'

'I'm all right. I'm glad you're here. I suppose you hardly recognised the city after so long.'

'When I left I never for a moment imagined that I wouldn't return for forty years. And now...'

'It's a different city?'

Neither of them was ready to discuss the reason she was here. That subject was too big and frightening to be tackled head-on. It had to be skirted around, sidled up to, ambushed. But they would get there. They didn't have a choice.

Her phone chimed and she picked it up, thinking it might be the hospital.

'It's my mother.'

'How many messages today?'

'Seven. She's complaining that the man next door is stealing her mail. How does she know this? Because he gets more junk mail than her.' Sarah shrugged, showing her emoticon grimace, and June laughed.

'At least she's predictable in her unpredictability.'

'Mmm.'

'What would she do without you, Sarah?'

'Drive the postman crazy for a start. But enough of my mother, have you had something to eat? Why don't we sit in the hotel café and grab a bite before we go to the hospital?' Sarah suggested. It would give them a chance to talk. And put off the moment when June saw Nick for another hour or two. 'I could murder a pastry.'

*

THE TWO WOMEN sat by a window in the upstairs grill, their lunch forgotten as they pored over photographs on Sarah's phone. The restaurant looked out over Kuala Lumpur's famous Twin Towers and the lush green expanse of KL City Centre Park. The towers filled the view from the restaurant like soaring silver rockets. They dominated the skyline of Kuala Lumpur, visible even from the outer suburbs. And like the Eiffel Tower, London Bridge or the Sydney Opera House, they were immediately recognisable as a symbol of the city.

'The house is in a bad state but Nick has made inroads. I suppose the upkeep was too much for your father. It must be a shock seeing it like this,' she said as June studied the photographs intently. She didn't know whether her mother-in-law was looking for something specific or simply memorising details. Or perhaps, like Sarah, she was still putting off the moment when they would talk about her son.

'I hated that house,' June said suddenly, placing the phone on the table. 'Now it looks on the outside how it always felt, like it was rotting on the inside.'

Sarah didn't know what to say so she merely gave June a questioning look.

'That house killed my mother, and now it's trying to kill my son. I wish he'd never tracked down his grandfather, never inherited the house. Inherited its evil.'

She spoke as if the house was a living entity, yet her mother-in-law was a pragmatic woman, not at all superstitious.

'I'm not sure I understand.'

'You've seen the house. It's surrounded by jungle. It was like that in the 1960s when my mother was still alive. I don't know why he didn't sell it years before that. It certainly wasn't pleasant living there. But he said my grandmother had sacrificed everything for the Chan family and he couldn't betray her sacrifice by giving up the house. He said that it was his birthright, and no one was going to take it from him. But there was never any money to look after it.'

Sarah couldn't remember June ever speaking of her parents. Now she seemed intent on imparting the whole saga, as if once started it must be told. Her Danish pastry lay half eaten on her plate as words tripped over one another in a haphazard manner.

'My father was always bitter that most of the family money was lost sometime before the Second World War. And then when the Japanese arrived things became worse. His father had owned tin mines but by the time my father was grown, there wasn't much left. Just a shophouse in Chinatown, I think. Not enough money to keep the house up, certainly not enough for a gardener. Mostly it was just my mother and Ho Jie doing the work.'

It seemed strange to hear her mother-in-law speaking of amahs and gardeners and tin mines. June had worked as a librarian most of her life.

'So there were always broken pots and old plastic buckets and such lying around and the drainage was terrible. Whenever it rained, water would collect in every small depression in the ground. Perfect for breeding mosquitoes. Even inside, in the courtyard. No one seemed to bother removing dead plants or cracked saucers. My grandmother never threw anything out until it fell to pieces in her hands and my father took after her. So you can imagine.'

She took a deep breath, fuelling herself to continue the story. Sarah didn't know what to say, whether June expected her to comment, and she was puzzled about where the story was leading. What did plastic buckets and mosquitoes have to do with June's mother's death? What did plastic buckets have to do with Nick?

'Anyway, when I was about four years old, my mother came down with a fever. My grandmother was still alive then. I barely remember her and she died not long after of ovarian cancer. So for most of my childhood I was looked after by our amah, Ho Jie. I called her Po Po, since she was like a grandmother to me.'

Sarah wanted to ask a dozen questions, but she held silent. She suspected that June hadn't told this story for a long time, if ever. Now that she'd begun, the words tumbled out. Sarah wasn't about to halt the flow if she needed to get this off her chest. They both needed to be strong and clear-headed in the coming days. They would need each other and Nick would need them.

'I think now my father was so worried about my grandmother that he didn't pay enough attention to what was happening to my mother. He probably thought it was flu. She was young and healthy. She would get over it. Except she didn't. What most likely started as a regular case of dengue fever progressed to a more severe form and...' She took a sip of tea and smiled apologetically at Sarah. 'I'm sorry. I don't know why I'm going on like this. We've got enough to worry about.'

'I don't mind.' She wanted to hear June's story. Now that her mother-in-law was here, she wanted to be closer to her – for how else could they talk about what they needed to talk about?

'I've looked it up, you know. Dengue in its more severe form. The terrible stomach pain, the vomiting, bleeding. That's how my mother died. I blamed my father for not taking her to a doctor until it was too late, even though I know he loved her. But I blame the house more... it's as if it didn't want us there. And afterwards, Ho Jie told me much later, my father found out she'd been pregnant. So I lost my mother and a baby sister or brother.'

In her own way, June was an orphan. 'I can see why you don't want to stay there.'

'Yes, sadness and anger... with the house... with my father. So the first chance I had to get out, I took it. He scraped together the money to send me to university in London and I decided then that I'd find a way to stay.'

Usually so composed, June kept fiddling with her gold bracelet, twirling it around and around her wrist unconsciously.

The bracelet was gold filigree, the flaming yellow of twenty-two carats, with a double-headed dragon clasp sparkling with ruby eyes.

When she saw Sarah watching her she said, 'He gave me this bracelet when I left. It was his mother's. He said it would remind me of home. Maybe he thought in some way that it would bring me back to him. But later, when I told him I wasn't returning, he disowned me. I wrote over and over but he never wrote back. He never forgave me. He was so hard and bitter.' She shook her head at the memory, of a man so stubborn that he would rather lose his daughter forever than forgive her for choosing a different life.

'So when Nick told me he was going to try and track the old man down I was torn. On the one hand I was pleased that Nick might bring about reconciliation. On the other, I was concerned that he might wound my son in some way with that nasty, vindictive streak of his.'

How could someone hang on to anger for so long? But even as she pondered this question she knew that it wouldn't be so very hard. She thought of the unanswered text messages from her father, her mother's many phone calls she let go to voicemail. Resentment became a habit that was difficult to break, because if you give up the habit, if you let go, you might not find anything to replace it. All that anger and resentment might be the only thing keeping you afloat.

'I was worried,' June continued. 'I imagined the old man gloating over the fact that he'd lured Nick into staying by giving him the house. That he might never return to me. I know what people say about that house. They call it the *gwai nguk*. I grew up hearing it called that. Well, that house might as well be cursed as far as I'm concerned. It took my mother, my grandmother and now it's intent on taking my son. That's why I hate it.'

This time, when she looked up from her tea, Sarah saw unshed tears in her mother-in-law's eyes. She reached across the table to take June's hand in hers.

'It was an accident, June. That's all.'

'I don't believe in accidents. Someone has to take the blame. And if it's not my father's fault then it must be the fault of the house. Or the gods. Or the ancestors. Take your pick. The thing I don't understand is… why Nick? What did he do to deserve this?'

She looked down at the golden bracelet circling her arm; one dragon's head consuming its mate. 'That house is full of ghosts. You may not want to believe it. But I've seen them.'

26

IT WAS NIGHT outside. In the hospital room, the lights were dimmed so that shadows lurked in the corners and machines blinked like watchful eyes. Nurses floated in and out, while she and June kept vigil by Nick's side. Standing sentinel by the bed, seeing her husband suspended between life and death, Sarah remembered his words that rainy night on the road to his mother's house.

'You look like an angel,' he'd said.

If she was an angel why couldn't she save him? Why couldn't she find the strength to draw him back to her? She'd tried so hard, reaching out to let him know she was there waiting. Trying to understand his life here. But some force was holding him, trapping him where she couldn't find him, an invisible force that she couldn't fight because she couldn't see it. She couldn't grasp it by the throat and destroy it.

'This is crap, Nick. Stop playing games and come back,' she whispered. He could be so stubborn when he wanted to be. He'd been in her head all week but now there wasn't a peep out of him.

'I knew he shouldn't have come,' June said, gripping Sarah's hand tight, her other hand enfolding her son's.

'No one could have known this would happen.'

'I knew something would happen.'

'It's not your fault, June.'

Doctor Chua finished checking Nick's vital signs and turned

to June. For the first time Sarah wondered whether the doctor had children of her own, whether each time she consoled a mother, she put herself in their place. Even if she felt only a tiny speck of that pain it must accumulate. It must weigh on her soul.

'How can I be the jury that sentences my son to death? How can Sarah?' June whispered.

The doctor returned the chart to the slot at the end of the bed and moved closer to June's side. She placed a hand on her arm, saying, 'You and Sarah aren't his jury. You're simply his messengers.'

'But what if this isn't what he'd want? What if he wants to live, no matter how?' Sarah wasn't sure she'd spoken aloud the words she'd been thinking for days. What if his mind was still working, even though his body wasn't? Except all the doctors had assured them this wasn't so.

'Nick has no chance of a meaningful recovery. We have to remember that he started dying the moment he fell from that ladder and hit his head. We only interrupted that process.'

Sarah searched her husband's waxen face, seeking a sign. If he'd only let her know he was still there. Still Nick. 'Nick, it's Sarah. Remember I love you.'

Despite the doctor's words, she knew that this decision would haunt her all the days of her life. But that was a burden she would have to bear. If she didn't, if she let him linger in this half-life until he grew weak from infection, pneumonia wracked his body and sepsis set in, then she would be punishing him for her need. She had to love him enough to let him go.

Her eyes blurred as she looked up, catching the reflection of a woman in the dark window, a face floating in a nimbus of light, a pale form moving towards them.

'Hi, Sarah.'

She turned to the door to find her husband's housemate standing poised at the entrance, waiting to be welcomed. Framed by the fluorescent light of the hospital corridor she appeared wraith-like, thinner even than a week ago.

'Hullo, Su Lin, I didn't know you were coming.'

'I hoped to say goodbye. If that's okay.'

Sarah wanted to say that it wasn't okay. She wanted to stake her claim. To tell this slight girl with the shining hair and bruised shadows beneath her eyes that there was no place for her here. She wanted to hoard these last minutes with her husband to herself, for although she'd failed him, he was still hers.

But June, her gracious, generous mother-in-law, found her voice before Sarah could tell her to go away. 'You must be Su Lin. Thanks for coming. Nick would be pleased.'

She was right. Nick would be pleased. Knowing him, if he was conscious he would probably make his deathbed a party.

'Pull up a chair,' she said to Su Lin, finding a smile to keep the bitch-face at bay. 'It won't be long now.'

She'd always known that anyone she loved was in danger of being taken away. She should have known that loving Nick was a mistake. But she couldn't have known that mistake would cost him his life.

'It's all right, Sarah,' said June, squeezing her hand tight. 'I'm here.'

Nick had been her guardian and she had been his. And they had failed each other.

*

THAT NIGHT SARAH dreamed she was back at Queen Mary's. She was searching for Nick but couldn't find him anywhere. Sometimes she felt a whisper of air as he turned a corner ahead. Sometimes she caught a flash of his familiar form disappearing through a doorway. But when she followed he was gone. And then, in the way of dreams, she was standing on the floor of the Octagon looking up to the light-filled vault above, when she caught a flicker of movement in the corner of her eye, an image of Nick strolling along one of the narrow book-lined galleries.

Taking the stairs two at a time, her heart pounding in time with her steps, she broke into a run when she reached the first gallery. Frantic to find him, she sprinted a full circuit of the Octagon, but he'd disappeared, only to emerge suddenly on the level above. In the dream, she shouted his name, telling him she was there. But he sauntered on unaware, always disappearing just as she thought she had reached him.

She woke in a tangle of sweat-damp sheets, heart racing, and the dream as etched upon her memory as if the events had actually occurred. 'Where are you, Nick?' she said, punching the empty pillow beside her. She was so angry with him for leaving her, so furious with herself for letting him go. So enraged with whoever, or whatever had let it happen.

Outside it was still dark. The digital clock showed four in the morning, too early to get up. Ever since she'd arrived in Kuala Lumpur, her internal clock, like her life, was topsy-turvy. Only Nick could turn it right side up. And like the phantom Nick of her dream, he was gone.

27

Kuala Lumpur 1932

SHE SLIPPED BETWEEN mango trees, their branches heavy with dangling fruit, skirting spindly limbed frangipani and a row of fan palms that offered little cover from prying eyes. The creeping jungle beckoned, a filtered green world where she could lose herself in the tangle of liana vines and ferny undergrowth. For a girl raised in the crowded streets of Chinatown, the jungle had always seemed a place of danger. It seethed with snakes longer than a grown man is tall, which could squeeze the life from unwary victims. It crawled with giant spiders, voracious enough to eat a small bird. And if you were lucky enough to evade these terrors, there was always the threat of the elusive tigers that prowled the forest's secret ways. Yet for Yu Lan, the jungle's dangers paled in comparison to the terror lurking around every corner of the Chan mansion, for even a tiger was preferable to Madam Chan.

It was early morning and the midwives were yet to arrive from the village. Madam Chan was occupied with her toilette. Ho Jie was helping Cook prepare Chan's breakfast and the wet nurse lay sleeping, the baby not yet awake and crying for his next meal. All this she knew from her silent dawn scrutiny of the household with shoes in hand and heart in mouth. With the sun barely peeping above the wall of green beyond the house it was the perfect time to make her escape. She would have an entire day to find her way along jungle paths towards the city, avoiding Lornie Road, where she would be easily found and returned to captivity, and skirting the nearby *kampung* where she knew Madam Chan had eyes. If she did not escape, her life would become smaller and smaller until eventually she disappeared. She would be less than a know-nothing girl. She would be less than a little sister. She would not be at all.

In the city, Ming would be waiting, waiting for her to find her way to him. He had turned away from her at the *kopi* shop but that was because his father was watching. He owed obedience to his father and needed time to find the courage of defiance. He had run from her on the street outside the temple but that was because Madam Chan and her driver guarded her. He was afraid of their power. And who could blame him? But if she could reach him, she knew he wouldn't turn her away. The jade ring and the dragon bracelet would be her dowry and although she had never left Kuala Lumpur, she knew that Malaya was a big place, covered in forest and surrounded by sea. Somewhere there must be a place where they wouldn't be discovered.

The broad-leaved grass was sodden with last night's rain so that her feet in their wooden clogs slipped, as she hurried across the last few yards of open space and brushed between overhanging fronds to enter the forest. A narrow trail led through the trees, the path barely visible between encroaching shrubs and ferns. Stray tendrils teased her face and her feet crunched in the leaf litter as she was enveloped by the sounds of the forest: the chorus of cicadas, the swish of small animals and a whistling symphony of birds. Hearing a rustle directly overhead she looked up to see a red squirrel nibbling on a cluster of tiny green fruits with a banana-like scent. The squirrel returned her gaze, unworried

on its high perch. And above the squirrel soared the great green canopy of trees, their branches interlaced against the sky.

To Yu Lan, unaccustomed to the forest, it was like entering another world. She drew her eyes back down to earth for she needed to watch where she put her feet. She needed to guard not only against reptiles and insects, but also the massive buttressed roots of the *banyan* and *surian wangi* trees that could trip her up if she did not look out. And she needed to beware of the most dangerous predator of all: humans. A person could lurk behind any of these giant trees, waiting to trap her and return her to Madam Chan.

Wrapping her arms protectively in front of her chest, she continued along the path, picking her way around the twisted ropes of liana, the monstrous roots and fallen branches, starting at every sudden noise. As well as the pressure of breasts swollen with milk, her chest was so tight with anxiety that she was conscious of each breath. The slightest rustle of leaves caused her to freeze and look up, only to see a small yellow bird sipping nectar with its long curved bill, or the flash of pink, white and green feathers of a dove swooping between trees.

Once, after she had been walking for so long that her legs began to tire, she was startled by a swoosh of movement to her left. She swung around, ready to sprint up the path regardless of its dangers, pursued by Kong or a posse of Chan workers (for she didn't expect Madam Chan to totter through the forest in her *cheongsam*). But her fear was for nothing. She had surprised a troop of monkeys feasting on the ripe pink globes of the *jambu* tree. Unlike the macaques, these monkeys were dark grey with creamy chests, and white rings like spectacles circling their eyes. They studied her so intently that for a moment she considered running. The largest monkey swung out along a branch, crouching directly above her, and honked twice. She jumped in fear before realising that the monkeys were probably more afraid of her than she was of them. One of the females carried a brightly coloured baby, all fluffy orange limbs clinging to her back, which made Yu Lan think of her own baby. Her little boy that Ah Jie would steal... if she could.

Although she felt so tired, she couldn't have been walking longer than two hours or so. And now there were soft noises issuing from the bundle tied close to her chest, tiny mewings of displeasure beginning to escalate into cries of hunger. With those cries, her breasts tightened as if someone had squeezed them, and wet patches appeared where milk leaked through her clothes. She knew she must stop before the boy grew fractious and his cries became audible from far away. She knew that babies couldn't be quietened with stern words like younger brothers. Babies were yet to learn the consequences of disobedience.

Choosing an enormous *banyan* tree, she squatted behind its massive roots and loosened the toggles of her tunic. Cradled against her chest by a length of cloth, the boy immediately began snuffling for her breast. She shifted him closer, watching in wonder as his mouth found her breast of its own accord, latching on and beginning to suck, causing a strange pulling sensation in her breast, a stab of pain unlike anything she had ever known. She felt his weight nestled against her body, his tiny lips guzzling from her breast. He was so small. Not much bigger than the orange monkey clinging to its mother's back. Almost but not quite nothing.

She wouldn't have thought that so light a burden could prove so heavy.

*

MADAM CHAN HAD surprised herself. This was a unique occurrence in her life, since she always knew in advance how she would think and feel. Mastering her emotions was a point of honour for Madam Chan. Men might permit themselves to shout and sob and show their anger, but women who couldn't mask their feelings were weak and, more importantly, foolish. For how could you utilise the currency of tears, joy or anger if you could not control your feelings? How could you get what you wanted if you couldn't disguise that you wanted it? Yet here she was, swamped by an emotion so powerful that she was shaken to her core, so overwhelming that she floundered like a child discovering for the first time the essential impotence of her rage.

Madam Chan had discovered love. And even more surprisingly, that love had arrived in the form of a child no larger than a housecat, a small being unable to walk, talk or offer anything in return. The whole turn of events was quite ludicrous and beyond the perspicacity of any divination. As soon as she held the boy in her arms for the first time she knew that her life would never be the same. When his tiny fist curled around her finger, she knew that she could never let him go. Which is how she came to be padding along the upstairs hall in cloth slippers before she had even called Ho Jie to put the irons to her hair. It was how she came to be on her way to the small room at the rear of the house where the wet nurse was installed with her charge. In fact, she was beginning to think she might need to move the baby to the chamber adjoining hers, since the smaller room grew so hot and humid in the afternoons.

Yes, she would definitely move the baby, she thought, as she pushed open the door to the nursery. The sun had barely risen and the room still steamed from yesterday's heat. It couldn't be good for little piggy to swelter like this; he would develop heat rash or worse. The second thing she noticed upon entering was that the stupid woman had slept with the windows open so that the room buzzed with mosquitoes, poised to attack the delicate flesh of her vulnerable little piggy, whose mosquito net had been pulled back from his cot. The third thing she noticed was that although the nurse lay curled on her side snoring lightly, there was no sign of the child. The pretty brass crib with the white lace flounces that she had ordered from the Chow Kit emporium was empty. The wet nurse's arms were empty. Someone had taken her son.

Before the panic set in, before the runaway heart and shortness of breath, she had the presence of mind to check on the concubine, thinking that the girl had probably defied her and taken little piggy to her room. Tripping across the parquetry faster than she had ever moved in her life, she thrust open the door to the concubine's room, her heart beating with hope. But finding no trace of girl or baby, Madam Chan began to scream.

*

YU LAN WATCHED the baby suck, tufts of black hair furring its head as it worried at her breast like a street dog with a bone. She wished it would hurry and finish but it finally released her nipple only to resume crying. Her breast was as deflated as an empty sack, yet the baby was whimpering for more. She rearranged the cloth sling so that it could take its fill of her other breast, wincing as it began to suck, its miniature paw cupping and uncupping her breast. Chan Towkay had put his seed in her and now she had a baby. She saw that its face was squashed-looking and wondered whether Ah Jie had been right when she chastised her for watching the monkeys while pregnant, for the baby did have a certain simian look about it, with wizened cheeks and a large, flat nose. She could see nothing of herself in its features.

Perhaps it wasn't really her baby. Perhaps Ah Jie had hidden her baby and replaced it with this impostor. For after all, if it was Yu Lan's baby she would feel its rightness, wouldn't she? She would feel a bond. Instead she couldn't help thinking that there was something wrong, something missing, but exactly what she couldn't be sure.

'She has stolen your mother love for herself too,' whispered a voice in her head. 'And now you have nothing left to give.'

The baby finished sucking and opened its eyes, twin pools of dark grey. She wondered whether it was watching her face, or the lattice of trees overhead. Or perhaps it was too young yet to see anything but light and shadow. How was she to care for it, this bundle that demanded so much of her? And what if Ming objected to its presence, this baby that was no part of him? What if he turned his back on her again? Staring into the baby's eyes, she searched for some sign of recognition but found nothing.

She stood up, stretching out legs stiff from squatting. Now to add to tender breasts and the discomfort between her legs she found that her shoulders ached from the baby's weight. For the briefest moment she considered untying the cloth sling and settling the baby here on a bed of leaves sheltered by the cradling roots of the *banyan* tree.

'Sooner or later someone will come along,' the voice in her

head assured in soothing tones, 'a boy from the *kampung* out collecting jungle fruits or a man returning from his rubber plantation. Someone is bound to pass by.'

Yu Lan tried not to listen but perhaps the voice was right. Perhaps she had made a mistake in bringing the baby with her. Perhaps he would be better off staying with the Chans after all. He would grow up as the prized son of the esteemed Chan family. If she left him here beneath the *banyan* tree, someone would find him and return him to the house. Then she would be free to find her way unencumbered to Ming. It could be like the last year of her life never happened.

She reached up, her hands poised at the knot behind her back.

Except in the meantime there were so many ways a baby could die alone in the jungle. She remembered the ragged tiger skins hanging outside a shop she often passed in Chinatown. She thought again of crawling spiders and barking monkeys, and she knew that she couldn't do it. Whatever happened now, their lives were linked, hers and this child's. Wherever she went he must follow, for she would not leave him behind. He was part of her. His bones were her bones. His flesh was her flesh. She would grow to love him with time. It wasn't true that Madam Chan had stolen the love that should have been her son's. Yu Lan had only misplaced it for a while. She was bound to find it again.

She resettled the child, adjusting the position of the sling over her shoulders and tightening the knot at her back before stepping out from behind the tree, only to find a man standing on the jungle path watching her. The man was so brown and wizened that she didn't notice him at first. He blended in with bark and branch so that he might almost have sprung from the earth. There was barely any flesh on his body, only bones sheathed in leather and the contours of a skull, prominent beneath paper-thin skin. In one stick-like hand he held a bundle of rattan canes that twitched and vibrated in her direction, as if they contained a life of their own.

Yu Lan's instinct was to run. But she found herself snared and held by those black eyes in their web of wrinkles. He dressed no differently than any other old *kampung* man but she knew immediately who he was. His identity was written in the intensity of his gaze and the energy pulsing through his arm. He was the *pawang*, the village doctor and shaman, and he had been sent to find her.

The twitching sticks slowed to a standstill as the old man took several steps towards her so that he stood directly in her path. He was so close now that she could smell his breath upon her face, warm and hinting of cinnamon and other spices. With his free hand he reached into a cloth pouch that hung at his waist, withdrawing a fistful of rice, which he flung in her direction so that it rained over her head in a hail of tiny yellow grains.

'*Hantu*,' he breathed, blowing the word in her direction with a throaty croak.

Despite the sticky heat, Yu Lan shivered. *Hantu*, he had named her... ghost. She knew enough of the Malay language to understand that word. But why would he call her 'ghost' when she was still very much alive? He was staring at her, looking deep into her eyes, searching for... what?

She didn't have time to ponder this question further. She had to get away before he shouted for the others, for surely there would be others following. If Chan Towkay had called the *pawang*, he would have called out the entire village to find his son. She turned, intending to skirt around him even if she had to venture from the safety of the path, but found her way barred by the familiar form of the Chans' driver, Kong.

'Come along, it's time to go back now, Sai Mui,' he said gently, even as he grasped her arm above the elbow in a grip impossible to escape. 'You have caused a great deal of trouble. The *taitai* hasn't stopped screaming since she found the boy missing. Let's get you home before she has a heart attack and makes everyone suffer more.'

He stood behind her, one hand clutching each of her arms above the elbow so that she felt like a puppet being manhandled forward. Kong was marching her back to where she had started. She stared wildly about her, hoping in her panic to see Ming waiting in the cool green shadows to spring out and rescue her.

'Ming can't save you,' hissed the voice in her head, snaky with derision. 'He is just a boy in a world full of monsters.'

Kong spoke to her again but she couldn't hear his words, she could only see his snapping yellow teeth. How could she escape his jaws? How could she escape the *bidang* and her interminable binding cloth? How could she escape the *pawang* and his twitching sticks that named her *hantu*?

'Become the *hantu*,' whispered the voice, 'be like the phantom and disappear where they cannot follow you.'

'They can follow me anywhere,' she protested. 'I will never escape them.'

'But you know how to disappear. You do it each time the *towkay* puts his seed in you. No one can find you inside your head. And I promise to be there with you.'

28

UPSTAIRS IN THE concubine's chamber, two midwives and a wet nurse cowered from the *taitai*'s rage, a rage that rampaged through the house like a hell demon, quieting to a shuddering moan at times before resuming its eerie screeching. Downstairs, the master paced the inner courtyard, his slippers making flapping noises on the tiles. Every so often he would shout for Ho Jie, ordering her to stop his wife's infernal racket. But what could a mere servant do in the face of her mistress's agony? Nothing except scurry from courtyard to boudoir carrying pots of soothing tea and empty words, reassuring her mistress that her son would be found, while secretly hoping that girl and child would escape. Her mistress wasn't a woman who took life's assaults on the chin. Sooner or later she would seek revenge and if Yu Lan were found and returned to the Chan mansion, Ho Jie feared for the girl's safety.

She was standing in the kitchen pouring hot water into her mistress's favourite white teapot with the pink chrysanthemums, when she heard the hubbub of men's voices emerging from the jungle behind the mansion.

'That will be them then,' said Cook. 'I expect they'll want feeding. They've been out there for hours.' She did not bother looking out of the window to discover whether the search had been fruitful; instead she began scooping rice from the wooden rice bucket into an earthenware pot and washing it in the porcelain sink. She didn't see the group of *kampung* men crossing the grass between the mango trees, the long, wide blades of their *parangs* glinting in the noonday sun, perfect tools for hacking jungle. She didn't see the wizened old man who led them, the man Ho Jie immediately recognised as a figure of importance. He wore the same loose cotton sarong as the other men, the same bare feet and thin beard, but there was something in the way the others kept their distance that showed respect… or fear. She wasn't sure which.

And following the old man, surrounded by *parang*-wielding farmers, came Kong propelling the girl by her elbows. She carried the baby in a sling against her chest, her arms held rigid to her sides as she stared straight ahead, ignoring the men who would return her to her confinement. Even at this distance Ho Jie could see the long, red scratch where a branch had gouged her cheek, and the stray leaves caught in hair that straggled free from its plait. And although the girl was taller than her captors, her limbs long and sturdy, their loud voices, their weapons and their intent dwarfed her. She seemed as much a child as the baby she carried, thought Ho Jie, wishing there was something she could do to help.

For a moment she imagined rushing to her side, sweeping the girl into her arms and spiriting her away to a safe haven. She would take her to the boarding house in Chinatown where her fellow amahs lived between employers. And from there she could find a berth on a ship returning to Guangdong. She would take the girl back to Shonde, where they would find shelter amongst the sisterhood of sworn spinsters in one of the vegetarian halls established for their old age. Yu Lan would be the daughter she never had…

'Have all my servants run off now?' The sound of Chan Towkay's angry voice cut through her thoughts. 'My wife is screaming for her tea and I don't know what I am paying you for!'

Cook looked up from the stove where she was setting pots of rice and chicken to steaming and nodded towards the window. 'Ah Kong is back, Boss, and it looks like he's brought the whole village with him.'

'What? Why didn't someone tell me?' He sprang for the outside door with such speed that he didn't bother to change out of his house shoes, hurling open the door and racing across the grass in his slippers. Ho Jie followed close behind, concerned that in his anger he might strike out at his concubine, and the poor child would have no one to protect her. Although what a simple amah could do against a powerful *towkay* and all those men, she didn't know.

'My son, my son, is he safe?'

'The child is sleeping, Boss,' answered Kong. 'No harm done.'

The *towkay* had reached the group of men now, but he had eyes only for the small bundle cradled against his concubine's chest. Ho Jie had never seen him move so fast as he snatched the baby from the sling so that it immediately began protesting at this disturbance to its cosy world. Clearly Chan Towkay had no idea how to hold a baby, for he dangled the boy at arm's length without supporting his head.

'Let me, Boss,' she offered, reaching for the crying baby.

Satisfied that his son was alive and kicking, he relinquished him into her care, turning his attention to the girl standing before him. But Sai Mui hadn't noticed his presence. In fact, for all intents and purposes she seemed unaware of any of the men surrounding her, even the strange old man standing beside her with the bunch of sticks in his hand. The same couldn't be said of the old man, who appeared to vibrate with suppressed energy. Ho Jie wouldn't have been surprised if his entire arm and its bundle of sticks began twitching at any moment. He was muttering some kind of incantation, his eyes glued to Sai Mui, as the village men sidled further and further away from them both.

'What is the *pawang* saying?' asked Chan Towkay, directing his question at his driver, who was the usual conduit between Chan and the *kampung* men. It was Kong who'd been sent to alert the villagers that morning as soon as the boy's disappearance was noticed. It was he who'd presumably negotiated whatever payment was required and set them to searching the nearby jungle.

'Nothing of importance, Boss. He is an old man. You know how superstitious the villagers are.'

'Clearly he thinks he knows something. What is he saying, man?'

Kong spat a wad of tobacco on the grass, saying with a shrug, 'He says she is possessed by a ghost spirit.'

'It's true that she is possessed of a rebellious spirit, but a ghost spirit?' Chan said with a shake of his head. 'I do not think so.'

'He says someone who wishes her ill has sent the ghost spirit into her. He says it can be cast out.'

'No doubt at a price,' he sighed before adding, 'I do not believe the *pawang's* nonsense, but something is wrong with her.'

Ho Jie knew what was wrong with her. She was taken from her family and given to an old man with a vicious wife who guarded him jealously. She was offered no choice. And now the baby she laboured to bear had been stolen from her.

'The question is, what to do with her?' Chan reached out towards the girl who still stood as though she hadn't heard a word being said around her. He took her chin in his hand, forcing her to look at him. 'What's wrong with you, girl? Haven't you been made welcome in my house? Haven't I been kind to you?' Grasping her wrist he held up her arm so that the dragon bracelet shone for all to admire. 'Haven't I made you gifts? Why would you steal my son and take him into the jungle where danger lurks behind every tree?'

Ho Jie was surprised to see the *towkay*'s eyes well with tears. She didn't know whether he cried for his son or his concubine or both, but something told her now was the time for intervention. That this was the moment when a poor woman like her, sworn to remain a spinster all her days, might save a friend.

'She is possessed only of sadness, Boss, not ghost spirits. I've seen it before, this sadness that overtakes a new mother so that she doesn't know what she is doing. Sometimes she may appear lost to the world, but with time and care she can be returned to her usual self.'

The *towkay* frowned, biting his bottom lip as if he chewed over her words. 'Perhaps you're right. But can I risk it? What if she tries to kidnap the boy again? What if she causes him harm?'

'She meant the boy no harm. See, he is safe, happy and well fed by the look of him.'

He peered again at the child sleeping in Ho Jie's arms. 'It might be better to send her away. The *taitai* would agree.'

Ho Jie scrambled to find some argument that would convince him. The thought of her little sister being sent away made her stomach churn with fear and a lump of sadness wedge in her throat. 'But she is the mother of your son. He will owe her his respect. He must mourn her if she dies, even if no one else does. Would you deprive him of his duty?' she said, appealing to his age-old beliefs in the pre-eminence of family.

'Hmmm. It is true; she is the mother of my son. The *taitai* may be his big mother but she will always be his little mother.'

Momentarily his face softened and Ho Jie sensed him wavering. 'I'll watch over her, Boss. I'll make sure she doesn't cause trouble. I'll help her get better. You'll see, she will become again the sweet young girl you first welcomed into your house,' she promised. Although to be truthful, Sai Mui had never been sweet.

He considered his concubine, her wrist encircled by the gold bracelet and her waist encircled by the empty cloth sling, before turning to the amah clutching the concubine's child to her chest. 'We will see how she fares after the boy's one-month party. If nothing else, I suppose I must see to her welfare for his sake. Perhaps after the party, when her confinement ends, I could take her to the hills for a rest. The cooler air might do her good. But, Ho Jie...'

'Boss?'

'If she repeats this or anything similar, I will have her sent so far away that she will never cause trouble again. And if I cannot find a patron willing to buy used goods, there are plenty of other houses that will take her off my hands. Do you understand?'

'I understand.' She understood all too well that if she couldn't persuade Sai Mui to accept her life, then Chan would sell her to some other master in China or Hong Kong. Or worse, he would sell her to a brothel. She would never see her son or her family again. Ho Jie knew that Sai Mui must understand this too, yet she stood silent and immobile, her face giving nothing away, her eyes fixed on a spot in the distance. She might as well have been a statue. The girl was so stubborn.

'And, Ho Jie,' said Chan, 'keep her out of my wife's way or

there'll be hell to pay.' Turning to his driver he added, 'Ah Kong, get word to those good-for-nothing midwives that their charge has returned and tell my wife that our son is back. Then you can drive me to the mine for a little peace and quiet.'

29

DOWNSTAIRS IN THE courtyard Yu Lan heard Ah Jie's friends cooing over her 'little piggy', Madam Tang's voice squawking louder than them all. 'Ah Ling, you have a good life! Baby is so fat!' she screeched. 'And where is the new mother?'

'Upstairs sulking, no doubt. Since baby arrived she has become glummer than bitter melon.'

'You should have seen Third Lady Tang, when our last was born,' said Madam Tang. 'She could hardly lift her head from the pillow. Give the girl time and she'll come around.'

For weeks Yu Lan had been shut in her room at the rear of the Chan mansion, imprisoned by silk curtains as surely as if they had been bars. Her only contacts had been the midwife and the amah, with occasional visits from the *towkay* who would pet her like a dog and promise her treats before exiting as quickly as possible. She suspected it might have been a different story if tradition didn't prohibit sexual relations during a woman's confinement, for she could see the lust gleaming in his eye despite her lank hair and flabby stomach.

Ho Jie smuggled her son in as often as she could wrest him from his big mother's clutches, and Yu Lan would summon a semblance of joy as the amah handed him to her. As he wriggled and squirmed in her arms, she stretched her mouth into a smile, her cheeks so stiff that she feared they might crack. Try as she might, she couldn't shut out the image of blood oozing down her cheeks and dripping onto his tiny face. She knew this was impossible, that cheeks didn't crack from smiling, but she couldn't get the idea out of her head. Just as she couldn't get those other thoughts from her head, thoughts whispered to her in the long night hours as she lay staring at the ceiling. Thoughts she didn't dare admit even to herself.

Sometimes she would wake after a night of broken sleep thinking she was back in the room she shared with her brothers. She would stretch her arms over her head, looking ahead to a day of grinding remedies in the apothecary shop, washing dishes with her mother in the steaming kitchen, attending class at the clan association in the afternoon, or walking home hand-in-hand with Ming. And for a moment she would be happy. She would be Yu Lan once more.

Now, after thirty days as long as a lifetime, the bindings had been unwound from her stomach and she could wash her hair, take her first bath and leave her room. In the kitchen, Cook and Ho Jie would be working feverishly to prepare food for her son's one-month party. Her baby had lived a full month, a sign that he was strong enough to survive childhood. Now his birth could be celebrated. He could be given his formal name and presented to the ancestors. The astrologer had been consulted and pronounced that Wei Long, Great Dragon, was an auspicious name.

Garbed in a new *samfu* for the occasion, fine cotton in a delicate floral print, with her feet clad in silk slippers, she stood at the top of the stairs looking down upon her son's party. From her vantage point, she watched Madam Tang bending over the baby in his big mother's arms, presenting her hostess with the traditional lucky red envelope for the child. Her *cheongsam* was stretched tight across her backside, the seams in danger of splitting. No doubt the red packet would contain a generous gift, at least as much as the Chans had given for Tang Towkay's last child, his eighth.

'Baby is sooo cute,' said Madam Kwan, handing over her own contribution. The envelopes were emblazoned with gold characters wishing the young recipient happiness, good luck and prosperity. Yu Lan thought her baby would probably rather receive his first walk in the garden than his first red packet but this was tradition.

'You have much luck, Ah Ling. Baby is veerry beautiful,' said Madam Chu. Although to be honest, the baby wasn't looking very beautiful since his first haircut. Yesterday his head had been shaved so that his new hair would grow in thick, leaving only a small brush of hair on top.

While the wives admired the baby, their husbands smoked cigars and drank whiskey with the *towkay* on the veranda. And later everyone would find a seat at the card tables, for a one-month party was the perfect excuse for a little gambling. Yu Lan descended the stairs, unnoticed by any of the women but for Third Lady Tang, who whispered a shy good morning as she made her way through to the kitchen to help serve the snacks.

'Ah, here she is,' Cook said, depositing a tray of red-bean paste cakes in her hands. 'You're looking too thin, girl. If you turn sideways you might disappear. Aunty will have to fatten you up.'

'Thank you, Ah Yi. It's good to get out of my room.'

For the next hour she wandered amongst the Chans' guests offering bowls of longevity noodles, cakes and lucky red eggs until Chan invited everyone out onto the front veranda for a formal portrait. He had hired a photographer for the occasion and there was much confusion at the door as everyone searched for their shoes, before the photographer herded them all into position on the front lawn.

'First we will take the family portrait,' said the photographer to the assembled guests, 'and later we will take a group portrait of the entire party.'

He ushered the Chans to their places on two chairs that had been set up on the lawn next to the house. Ah Jie had chosen to wear a traditional gown and jacket for the occasion, the stiff silk dwarfing her body. The photographer arranged the baby on her lap so that he faced the camera. The folds of an English smock-dress swamped his tiny legs and arms, and Ho Jie had tied a bonnet on his head to protect his scalp from the sun. Seeing him propped on Ah Jie's knee, Yu Lan felt a rush of love for her son. It flooded through her body faster than the rising waters of the Klang River. She felt overwhelmed by it, like nothing she had ever felt before, not even for Ming. Suddenly she couldn't understand why it had taken so many weeks for her to feel like this. It was all she could do not to push her way through the guests, run over and snatch him from the woman's arms. He was her son. He was part of her. And she wanted him back.

'Aren't we forgetting someone?' Chan asked, glancing around the crowd of guests with a frown.

'What do you mean?' asked Madam Chan.

'Aren't we forgetting the boy's mother?'

Although she was hiding behind the other guests gathered in the shade of the veranda, Yu Lan felt Madam's eyes bore into her flesh as she said, 'Sai Mui? But, husband, I thought baby's first portrait would be with his father and his big mother. We can take a portrait of our son with his little mother and his amah later.'

Yu Lan's knees buckled as she felt the woman's words like a blow to the stomach. She would have fallen forward except that someone placed a hand on her arm. She turned her head to see Third Lady Tang standing at her side, sympathy warming her eyes.

'When he grows, he will know who his true mother is,' she whispered.

But Yu Lan recognised the *taitai*'s words as prophetic. Since the day the *pawang* had found her in the jungle she had tried to close her eyes and ears to the truth. With the amah encouraging her, she pretended that when she finally emerged from her confinement, everything would change. She would be welcomed back to the household in her rightful place as Wei Long's mother. She would take Ho Jie's advice and try to make a life in the Chan house. She told herself that she could find a different kind of freedom there, where she was respected as the mother of Chan's children. But now she realised that it didn't matter how many children she gave the *towkay* or how much he came to care for her. It didn't matter how many gold bracelets he bestowed upon her. Madam Chan would always steal her most precious gift.

'You see. It doesn't matter how loyally you serve the Chan family,' the voice in her head goaded. 'While Madam lives, you will always come second.'

30

Fraser's Hill 1932

FOR THE FIRST time in her life, Yu Lan was leaving the city of her birth. In the weeks following the party, the *towkay* decided that the cooler air of the hill stations might cheer her up, clear her head and refresh her spirit. He had business to attend to at a tin mine north of the city so they might as well make it a holiday. Indeed, even the idea of leaving the house and the city lifted her spirits, and now that the car's motor hummed along the open road, she felt her spirit hum in harmony. Although she might not be free, at least she had been released from prison. Is this what Ho Jie meant when she spoke of being *more* free? This inkling of what it could be? This slight lifting of the heart, this loosening of the chest? Even the voice in her head had grown quiet, receding to the farthest corners of her mind where she could barely hear it murmur.

'How long now?' Ah Jie asked the driver from her place in the back seat of the Chevrolet. At first the *taitai* had been reluctant to come when her husband declared that a journey like this was no place for a newborn. She couldn't tear herself away from her 'little dragon'. But when she realised that Yu Lan was invited, she swiftly changed her mind. She couldn't leave her husband alone with his concubine for three days. So not only had she insisted on loading the trunk of the car with half her wardrobe, she had also brought Ho Jie along to see to her clothes and hair.

The amah sat in the front adjacent to the driver, watching the road and handing her mistress cups of tea from a thermos at her feet. Yu Lan sat in the middle of the back seat between master and mistress. The mistress's bony elbows dug into her side at every bump in the road. The master's hands crept up her tunic, while his lips murmured nonsense in her ear whenever he thought his wife had dozed off. Yu Lan knew that he had more than rest in mind when they reached their destination, but right now she didn't care. She had escaped the Chan mansion with its oppressive atmosphere, and the cooler air of the mountains beckoned. Her head felt as if a fog had been lifted from it, allowing her to think clearly for the first time in weeks. She relaxed on the smooth leather seat, letting her attention wander to the scenes beyond the car.

'We'll reach the guesthouse in an hour if the road remains clear, Madam,' Kong answered.

'There are too many bumps. You must avoid them. I nearly bit through my lip at the last one.'

'I'll try harder.'

'See that you do.'

'The man can't be blamed for the road, Old Woman,' her husband said, with a snort, and Yu Lan felt satisfaction stir in her breast. Most men referred to their wives as Old Woman at times, but Ah Jie did not like it one little bit, even when it was said with affection. Clearly, she didn't want to feel old, especially not when she was seated beside her husband's concubine. For the first time since the birth of her baby, Yu Lan felt happy in her skin. She was alive, she was seventeen and with a little luck and a lot of ingenuity, she might change her life for the better.

'But he can be blamed for the driving, Old Man,' she sniped at her husband.

Yu Lan sat silently as the others bickered. They traversed endless miles of plantations, where she watched bare-chested men working amongst the scarred trunks of rubber trees, white liquid oozing from cuts into small cups at the base of the trunks. Sometimes she caught sight of a line of Tamil women carrying metal buckets of latex on their heads, or a European man in his white helmet patrolling his estate. Sometimes she glimpsed the sprawling red-tiled expanse of a planter's bungalow. They passed by *kampungs* where naked children played in the shade under attap-roofed houses and buffaloes cooled their heels in the surrounding rice paddies. Yu Lan marvelled at the sea of slender green shoots sprouting from the waterlogged fields – she had never seen rice growing before – and everywhere were the vast gashes of tin mines ripping open the earth. The source of Chan Towkay's wealth.

They stopped briefly in the town of Kuala Kubu with its rows of brightly coloured shophouses, before beginning the long, slow climb to the Gap. Unlike other towns they passed, the buildings here were new, barely touched by the hot and humid air. Their walls were painted in shades of orange, green and blue, defying the creeping mould of the tropics.

'The British moved the whole town after the floods of 1920,' Chan told them over a cooling glass of *cendol* at a roadside stall just outside the town. Yu Lan relished the taste of sweet coconut on her tongue and the feel of the slippery green noodles sliding down her throat. During her confinement she had been allowed only hot foods and drink. If she tried to sip even a cup of cold water she would have the amah berating her with, 'You will let the cold in and lose all your teeth if you drink cold things!'

Chan's hand stroked her bottom appreciatively as he continued the story. 'The dam broke and destroyed the town, killing more than thirty people, including the District Officer. They say all that was left of him was a single hand.'

'Aiya, so gruesome,' said Ah Jie.

'The stupid *gwai lo* went and shot a white crocodile after he was told not to. Turns out the crocodile was the river guardian so the whole catastrophe was his own fault,' Chan laughed.

'Displeasing the gods, even the native gods, is no laughing matter,' his wife remonstrated. But Chan thought that death was a very funny business – so long as it happened to someone else.

Now they were leaving the rubber estates, rice paddies and mines behind as the road twisted along a mountainside, then traversed a gorge, crisscrossing fast-flowing streams and climbing ever higher into the hills. Bamboo and tree-ferns crowded the lower reaches of the forest while a canopy of trees soared above them and for the first time since she had left her home on Petaling Street, sitting squeezed between the *taitai* and her husband and buffeted by their bickering, Yu Lan's fears receded. The voice in her head grew silent. She began to feel, if not safe, then at least unthreatened.

*

AS SOON AS she stepped out of the car she felt the change in temperature from the city. According to Chan, the Gap Rest House sat more than three thousand feet above the sea, the staging point for the remainder of the climb to Fraser's Hill. Yu Lan could not calculate what three thousand feet might mean. It seemed such a large number. But she could look out over the lush jungle to the foggy slopes of mountains falling away before her, or turn to see more mountains rising even higher behind the white-stuccoed walls of the guesthouse. From where she stood, the forest appeared as an impenetrable barrier of green. The English-style guest house, with its window panes like glass chequerboards framed in black, its steeply gabled red roof and chimney spires, was as alien to this place as the *gwai los* who built it. The mountains belonged only to themselves.

Hearing a series of high-pitched hoots followed by a strange cackling laugh, she looked up. There, skimming the treetops, she sighted an enormous black hornbill, its outstretched wings wider than her arm span, its long white tail like a feathered spear behind. Its wrinkled turquoise neck ended in a great bulbous red bill, so heavy that she wondered it could hold up its head. How wonderful to have the freedom of flight, to be able to glide far above the world, beyond the reach of leopard, crocodile or even the formidable tiger. If she were a hornbill she would fly so far away that no one would find her.

She followed the hornbill's flight with her eyes as it soared above the trees in the direction of the mist-shrouded valley, until a violent crack reverberated through the forest. The sound ruptured the peaceful birdsong and set up a commotion of movement amongst the trees. She glanced away for only a moment to search for the location of the noise, only to look back and discover the great bird plummeting earthwards in a tumble of shrieking feathers.

'Sai Mui, what is it? What's wrong?' Chan asked, releasing his wife's arm and rushing to her side.

She hadn't realised she had cried aloud, the first sound she'd made since they left Kuala Kubu an hour before. 'The hornbill.

Someone shot it from the sky. It's only a bird. Why would they kill it?'

Chan considered her with a frown and she thought that he hadn't heard her.

'Why would they kill a bird that hurts no one? She's only going about the business of being a bird.'

'You are a funny thing,' he said and gave her shoulder a pat. 'They hunt them for their bills, of course, for their red ivory, more precious than elephant ivory. That was a helmeted hornbill. Its bill is so dense that it can be carved into fine ornaments. Buckles and buttons and other knick-knacks. Your elder sister has a lovely red comb carved from it.'

'They killed the bird to make belt buckles?'

He nodded, steering her towards a flight of stairs that lead up to the guesthouse where the *taitai* now stood glaring down at them, her chin thrust forward like a weapon. She tensed her hands into talons at her sides, red nail polish like blood dripping from her fingers. But Chan didn't notice; he had eyes only for her, his concubine, who had given him the most precious gift a man could receive.

'Do not cry, child. It's just a bird. There are many more birds in the sky. You'll see.'

31

'GOOD MORNING, MADAM, Sir. Lovely day,' Chan greeted the British couple already seated at a table by the French windows the next morning. Unlike her husband, Madam Chan didn't speak English but she understood the familiar greeting.

The British couple were of middle years, the man wearing the ubiquitous khaki safari suit and the woman garbed in a floral sprigged dress that barely contained her extremely large bosoms. They looked up from their breakfast, the man nodding in acknowledgement. 'Good morning. Good morning, ladies.'

'What a charming girl your daughter is,' the woman said with a friendly smile in the *chieh*'s direction. 'So delightfully tall.'

Madam Chan thought her husband almost winked as he answered with a knowing look aimed at the British man. 'Not my daughter. But quite delightful, eh?' he said, and was rewarded with a stony glare from the man's wife.

'What did you say to those people?' she asked, once they had taken their seats.

'Nothing you need to know, Old Woman.'

Madam Chan wasn't accustomed to feeling out of place, yet that was exactly how she felt, ensconced in the dining room of the Gap Rest House, sipping the stale and bitter tea of the British and nibbling on charred bread. She turned up her nose at the rubbery eggs and fatty bacon her husband was scoffing like a hungry dog. She wished she were back in her own house sipping a cup of her favourite Dragon Well tea as Ho Jie fanned her with a cooling breeze.

They sat at one of several tables set with ugly white crockery emblazoned with the Government's bullhead crest. French doors opened onto a veranda, while at either end of the room were a sideboard groaning with liquor bottles and a fireplace surrounded by a carved timber mantel. She was accustomed to staying well clear of her own kitchen to avoid the heat of cooking fires, yet here the other guests appeared to revel in the licking flames. The old British woman was even going so far as to bend over and put her hands to the fire so that Madam Chan got an excellent view of her petticoats and the purple veins snaking up the backs of her legs.

Another woman whom she presumed to be about her own age – although very poorly preserved – sat at a second table with two children. She observed with satisfaction the woman's already lined forehead, the beginnings of crow's feet fanning her eyes and the irritating way her children devoted the entire breakfast to whining. Clearly, there was little discipline about the woman's family or person. Madam Chan would countenance neither the lines nor the whining in her house.

But although she felt justifiably superior to these women, she couldn't help noticing the older couple's stony expressions each time they glanced over at the Chans' table. She especially disliked the way the frazzled mother admonished her children in a clearly audible hiss. And why did they keep staring at Sai Mui? The British could be so hypocritical about such things. It was common practice for these British men to keep a mistress, but keeping a concubine in your own home was deemed unacceptable. No matter how much more efficient. And the concubine could double as a servant too.

Yes, the entire situation was most disagreeable. And the kitchen didn't even serve rice porridge.

So Madam Chan was in a sour mood before the day had properly begun. And it wasn't as if she needed further incentives to bad temper with her husband making puppy eyes at the girl and catering to her every whim. Why, he had actually asked the waiter to bring her a cup of Bovril tea, since he'd heard from one of his British friends that it was quite restorative. Now he was proposing an excursion to a waterfall beyond the village of Fraser's Hill where they would be required to walk at least half a mile through the jungle. And all in aid of the concubine's constitution. What about his wife's constitution?

She could see what the girl was about now, running away and causing all that fuss. Ignoring the *towkay* when he deigned to visit her during her confinement. Pretending she didn't notice his caresses. How could she not have seen it earlier? It was so obvious now... if a woman is a little bit bad a man will desire her. And if she is fragile he will want to love her and protect her. Sai Mui was more cunning than she had realised, taking advantage of an old bull eating tender young grass. She planned to make him ache for her and then Madam Chan would be stuck with her forever.

'Will Ho Jie be coming?' the *chieh* had the temerity to ask now as she drank down her beef tea, so disgusting that its odour could be smelled from across the table. That was another thing: the girl was forming an undesirable attachment to the servant and she suspected it was mutual. Something else she must put a stop to before the two formed an alliance and made her life even more difficult. Perhaps she would have to let the amah go.

Except it was so tedious training someone new. Of course, a much more preferable arrangement would be to let the concubine go. How that could be arranged, with her husband mooning over the girl and her newly swollen breasts, she didn't know just at this moment. But sooner or later something would occur to her.

'Would you like her to come?' Chan cooed across the table.

'Ho Jie has too much to do,' she interposed before her husband could make a definitive ruling one way or another. 'I have set her to repairing my green *cheongsam*. I can't possibly wear it in the state it is in. And besides, I thought this was to be a family outing.' She forced her lips into a smile aimed in the *chieh's* direction. 'Just the three of us. One happy family.'

'We are happy, aren't we?' Chan beamed at his wife's sudden good mood. 'And it will give me a chance to spend some time with our little mother here. We have missed each other's company while she was doing her month, haven't we, Sai Mui?'

*

'YOU NEED TO be careful, little one. The *taitai* is eating vinegar,' Ho Jie had warned as Yu Lan took leave of her that morning. She had a worried look in her eye and kept fiddling with her bun. 'Her jealousy is eating away at her.'

Yu Lan thought no more of it at the time, for the *taitai* was habitually sour-faced and she clearly wasn't impressed with the toast and marmalade she'd been served at breakfast. They had breakfasted too late to make the seven o'clock road opening up the mountain and had to wait until nine. The road to Fraser's Hill was so narrow that cars could only drive in one direction at a time. Now the amah's words echoed in her mind as the Chevrolet finally crawled up the mountainside. She sneaked a glance at the woman seated beside her, trying not to catch her eye. She definitely looked as if she had been eating vinegar, with her pursed mouth and that glint of disgust in her eye, but perhaps the winding road had sent her stomach into somersaults. On reflection, Yu Lan wasn't so sure. She had known for a long time that the *taitai* didn't like her, yet she hadn't truly believed that she was jealous. How could you be jealous of someone with so little power?

'You are the mother of Chan Towkay's son. You have given him something she never could. That is your power,' Ho Jie had reminded her as they waited for the road to open, 'that and your youth. No matter how many potions Madam slaps on her face it will not make her seventeen again,' she added with a chuckle. 'So watch out. She isn't a woman to look the other way or turn the other cheek.'

'But she brought me to the Chan house. She chose me.'

'From what I hear, the ancestors chose you. And the madam has a contentious relationship with the ancestors at the best of times. Especially if they dare to disagree with her.'

It was true; Ah Jie could often be heard berating the ancestors as she made her offerings at the family altar. Her elation at the birth of her son didn't extend to gratitude to her husband's dead relatives, certainly not for long anyway. At the one-month party Yu Lan had overheard her boasting to her friends about her own cleverness and foresight in arranging the birth. As if she had carried the child for nine months. As if she had laboured for twenty-three hours to push it from her body.

Yu Lan wished Ho Jie was sitting in the front seat of the Chevrolet nursing the tea thermos, but the amah was tending her mistress's clothes back at the Rest House and couldn't be spared, not for so frivolous a purpose as a drive to a waterfall. Madam had made a point of insisting the outing should be a 'family' occasion, with no need for a servant to accompany them. Although she might call Yu Lan her 'little sister' there was no love lost between them. Why did she suddenly want to get her alone?

'It will be refreshing to take a walk through the forest to the waterfall,' Madam Chan said as the road levelled out and they caught their first sight of the hill station, perched on a steep ridge with views out over jungle-clad mountains stretching to the horizon. Stone bungalows with red-tiled roofs were scattered along the hillside and around the smooth green expanse of a golf course, where Yu Lan saw a few European men at play. The bungalow gardens were bright with unfamiliar flowers and she noticed several ladies out walking with their children, none of them carrying the obligatory parasols of Kuala Lumpur town.

'Stop here, Boss?'

'Keep going to the waterfall. We might stop for a pint at the Maxwell Arms on our way back.'

Madam's mouth was still looking vinegary, whether from jealousy or the thought of drinking beer on their return, Yu Lan didn't know. As they veered off onto an even narrower track she decided she didn't care. After all, what could the woman do on a pleasant walk along a jungle path to a waterfall with Chan Towkay at their side?

After about fifteen minutes of hairpin bends the road came to its end and Kong turned off the engine.

'You want me to come, Boss?'

'Stay with the car. I will escort my wives,' Chan said, looping his arm through Ah Jie's elbow and gesturing for Yu Lan to follow as he headed into the jungle.

A chorus of cicadas greeted them as they stepped onto a path that wound through thick forest. It followed the course of a river that cascaded over boulders in a gradual descent down the mountain. Small lizards poked their heads out from under decaying leaves that carpeted the jungle floor, while the occasional centipede scurried underfoot. Above them the trees echoed with the chatter of monkeys and unfamiliar birdcalls. Here and there clumps of fallen bamboo barred their way and Chan steered his wife around them, urging her to step over the wayward branches, awkward in her shiny high heels. Yu Lan was glad she had worn a pair of rush slippers, in defiance of the *taitai*'s remark that she looked like a coolie. At least she wouldn't trip over her own feet.

The sound of water grew louder as they rounded a bend in the path to see the river disappearing below. They had reached the top of the waterfall. Ahead of them the path descended steeply, while a leafy platform extended alongside them, slippery from the water's spray.

'Oh, do let's look at the view from the top of the waterfall,' the *taitai* exclaimed. 'Here, Sai Mui, take my arm.' Releasing her husband, she extended her arm, palm facing up, accompanying it with a honey-coated smile.

'You two girls go ahead, I'll smoke a cigarette while I wait for you,' Chan said, with a fatherly beam aimed at his two women, before extracting a pack of cigarettes and a gold lighter from his jacket pocket.

The *taitai* stepped off the path and onto the leaf-littered ground. 'My feet are unsteady in these shoes, I may need to lean on you,' she said, suddenly grasping Yu Lan's arm and pulling her near. Yu Lan's flesh burned in warning at her touch.

She was so close as they inched forward along the rocky shelf adjacent to the waterfall, that their thighs touched, silk against cotton. Yu Lan considered resisting, but there was something inevitable about the intimacy of the situation, as if the whole trip had been leading to this moment. She and her husband's wife locked together by his ownership of them both. It didn't matter what she thought about the other woman. She couldn't escape her, just as she couldn't escape Chan or his house. Perhaps her mother and Ho Jie were right... she should let the river take her where it would. There was little point resisting. She couldn't fight what the universe had in store for her.

'Take care!' Chan called from the path. 'The ground may be slippery.'

She let herself be led along the ledge, the world around her shrinking to the red gash of a smile and the roar of crashing water.

'I can see the river falling into a pool below,' the *taitai* said, towing her forward, wobbling a little in her unsuitable shoes. 'Just a little further. Watch where you put your feet, we wouldn't want you to slip.'

They came to a halt where the river churned like boiling water around a large boulder. Yu Lan looked down to see water cascading over the cliff in a spray of white to fill a muddy pool thirty feet below. The sound roared inside her head and she tried to decipher what it was saying to her. If she could listen closely enough, surely the voice would tell her what to do. She was so confused.

'So beautiful. Look, Sai Mui.'

The *taitai*'s fingers dug into her flesh, turning Yu Lan's body slightly so that her tall figure blocked Chan's view of his wife. She could feel fingerprints of pain shooting like heat through her upper arm as the *taitai* urged her to lean further out. To see the beauty below.

'Come closer, dear sister.'

She bent over, craning her neck in obedience to the will of the universe until suddenly her arm was released, catching her off balance. And as she toppled forward, suspended between the then and the now, she felt a hip bump her hip, a knee nudge her knee, a hiss of satisfaction blending with the sound of falling water. She hung in the air, her toes curled into soft earth, defying gravity for a single breath. And in that breath, instinct reached out to grab a sapling clinging to the cliff edge so that she hung precariously over the precipice. The universe wasn't ready to let her go yet. She wasn't ready to go yet.

'Sai Mui!' Chan shouted when he saw what had happened. He hurried towards her, heedless of the slippery ground, as she wrapped herself around the young tree that leaned out over the falls like an afterthought.

'Aiya! The stupid girl stepped off the cliff!' shouted his wife.

Chan grabbed Yu Lan's free arm, pulling her towards him and safety. 'What did you do? Why would you harm yourself?' He hugged her to his chest, saying, 'Why would you want to leave me?'

'Someone pushed me,' Yu Lan heard herself whisper. Or was it the splash of water speaking through her lips?

'Husband, I told you she was crazy.'

'I felt hands upon me.'

'She is a danger to herself and everyone else,' Madam Chan shrieked. 'She tried to jump and take me with her. She is full of nothing but spite and venom. She would take us all with her if she could!'

But Yu Lan knew now where the real danger lay. She did not need a voice in her head to warn her. She did not need the amah's warning either. She could still feel the imprint of that hand upon her arm. Burning her flesh. A knee nudging hers. What she didn't know was how to protect herself from it. Sooner or later Madam Chan would have her way and she was powerless to stop her.

32

Kuala Lumpur 1932

THE *cheongsam* SKIMMED Yu Lan's body in a sheath of red silk. The tailor had embroidered a geometric pattern in gold thread around the sides, hem, collar and front opening, and fashioned button knots out of golden cord. An embroidered collar stood high and stiff about her neck, tight sleeves encased her upper arms to her elbows, and her feet were shod in shiny red heels. Ho Jie had parted her hair to the left, pulling it into a complicated knot on the right side and embellishing it with flowers. Staring at the image reflected in the mirror, she hardly recognised herself. Accustomed to wide sleeves that skimmed her wrists and trousers that covered her legs to the ankle, Yu Lan fought the urge to cover herself. Her arms were bared to the elbow and long slits revealed her legs at the slightest clack of heels across the parquet.

'Aiya, so pretty! The *towkay* will be pleased,' Ho Jie pronounced as she stood back to admire her handiwork. 'You will be the most beautiful girl at the Opera and all eyes will be upon you.'

'You grow funnier with age, Ho Jie.'

A dress couldn't perform miracles. The children at the clan association would still call her 'tall man' and 'stupid cabbage', despite her finery. In fact, they would probably invent some new names if they could see her wearing this long red gown that hugged her body like a second skin. She could hear them taunting her already with cries of 'red banana' or some other name even more humiliating.

'When I walk my legs will be naked. Does the *towkay* expect me to float up stairs?'

'You will have to take small steps, I suppose. At least he didn't insist on the sleeveless version.'

Chan Towkay had sent a tailor to the house to make the *cheongsam* in time for the New Year festivities. Since their unlucky journey to Fraser's Hill and her accident at the waterfall, he had been especially solicitous of her health and comfort. He brushed aside his wife's warnings that she was crazy by saying that it was understandable if she was unwell. A little distraught by her near-death experience. Of course he didn't give credence to her story that someone had pushed her. It was better for everyone if Yu Lan were deemed ill, rather than his wife named an attempted murderer.

He ordered that the wet nurse bring the baby to see her every morning, despite his wife's objections that the boy would grow up confused about who to call Mother. Chan solved that problem by reminding them that Wei Long would call his wife 'Big Mother' and his concubine 'Little Mother'. That way there would be no confusion and both women would be acknowledged. It was a solution that pleased him inordinately so that he celebrated with a glass of Chivas Regal, although it wasn't yet three o'clock. In the *towkay*'s world there was a hierarchy for everything, even love.

Indeed, she saw that Chan believed all problems could be resolved with correct action. Sadness. Anger. Loss. Madness. All could be overcome. If he showered her with gifts, he could buy her love. If he let her hold her child, he could eliminate her sadness. But love and happiness weren't his to give, only hers to struggle for. No matter how many gifts he lavished upon her, he wouldn't give her what she wanted. Nor could he return to her what he had stolen.

'It will be better for everyone if you say no more about being pushed, little one,' he had said, his hand cupping her buttock affectionately. 'You are a good girl and I will keep you safe. I will make you happy.'

'He has stolen your happiness,' whispered the voice in her head, 'just as he stole your maidenhead. That precious gift you wished to save for the boy you loved.'

Her love for Ming seemed so long ago now that she could barely recall his face. He was a sketch of a boy in her memory, tall, with a lean, angular shape, thick black hair and sticking-out ears. She could remember no detail, not the shape of his eyes nor the curve of his lips when he smiled. Sometimes she took the jade ring from its hiding place in her room and slipped it over her thumb in the hope that the cool stone might prompt her memory. But all she could see were fragments. Not enough pieces to make a real boy.

'I can hear Ah Kong bringing the car around. It's time to go,' Ho Jie said, interrupting her thoughts. 'Perhaps a last dab of perfume.' The *towkay* had given it to her as a New Year gift. The amah raised her arm and applied perfume to one wrist and then the other. Then, when Yu Lan showed no sign of moving, she added, 'Well, don't look so eager. I suppose you've seen so many Cantonese operas that you'll be too bored to stay awake.'

Although Yu Lan went often to the temple to make offerings at New Year, she had seen an opera troupe perform there just once, and then only a few performers with minimal costumes. She had certainly never been to the grand Coliseum Theatre to see a performance with professional actors. She should be excited. Yet somehow she couldn't summon enthusiasm for anything any more, not even her son. For months she had felt like a puppet in the shadow theatre, a cutout whose arms and legs were worked by sticks, whose sticks were operated by a puppet master. She moved through the world as a translucent shadow. She had no will or power to act, and her presence made little impression upon the world.

She was a shade. A spectre. A ghost of a woman.

And Chan seemed to like her that way.

*

DESPITE THE EXPECTANT chatter of the audience, Yu Lan took her seat in the Coliseum Theatre for the performance of *Snow in Midsummer* without excitement. At least with the *taitai* on the other side of Chan, she ran no risk of being pinched if she so much as hiccupped during the performance. Not that she could hear much above the clanging and clashing. The orchestra was already in position when they arrived and Yu Lan recognised the two-stringed *gaohu* and *erhu*, a bamboo wind instrument called the *dizi* and of course drums, gong and cymbals. The percussion would set the pace for the singing and dancing.

At the opera she knew to expect not only singing and acting, but dance, martial arts and acrobatics. Except she wasn't prepared for the way the story affected her. She didn't predict that her heart would fill with anger when the young maiden Dou E was forced to marry her neighbour to pay her father's debts. She didn't realise that she would forget to breathe when that husband died and the bandit Zhang tried to force Dou E to marry him. Then when Zhang accidentally poisoned his father, while attempting to murder Dou E's mother-in-law, Dou E was arrested for the crime. She didn't know that her fingers would clutch the seat so tightly that afterwards her hands would ache.

Around her the audience members laughed at the antics of Donkey Zhang and his wicked father as they attempted to bully Dou E and her widowed mother-in-law into marrying them, but she couldn't take her eyes from the tragic countenance of Dou E. She became mesmerised by the actor's stark white face, those wild black eyes haunted by red shadows, those flaring black brows and poignant red lips. When Dou E and her mother-in-law were arrested and taken before the court, Yu Lan almost cried aloud, she was so indignant and filled with terror. Poor Dou E, forced into marriage, bullied by the repugnant Zhang, tortured by the town official and unjustly tried for murder.

What had Dou E done in this life to deserve such harshness? And why did filial piety require that she must take the blame for the crime so that her mother-in-law escaped torture? She had already given her life to save her father from ruin and now she must give it a second time to save her mother-in-law. She couldn't comprehend the injustice of Dou E's fate.

The stage became a blur of leaping soldiers and whirling swords. Drums sounded a martial beat, gongs clanged and cymbals clashed in fury. Bound by chains, Dou E was carried to her execution, her long red sleeves floating like ribbons as she was tossed and turned in the air. When the soldiers forced her to her knees and the official prepared to behead her, Yu Lan almost leaped from her seat. Only Chan's hand on her arm stayed her. Why didn't Dou E save herself, why must she die for someone else's crime? Yu Lan's flesh, encased in expensive red silk, broke out in a sweat. Surely there must be some escape? Why must she accept her fate?

She looked about her, aware that some in the audience would know the story, hoping to see expectant smiles upon their faces, safe in the knowledge that all would be well. But all she saw were tense faces, waiting to see Dou E's fate played out on stage. She covered her eyes then uncovered them, not wanting to look yet lured by an irresistible compulsion to watch.

A sword swung high, waiting for Dou E's last words before striking. Although the condemned girl was prepared to die, she didn't accept her fate. In death she would prove her innocence. In death she vowed to have her revenge. With her last breath she cursed the town, declaring that her innocence would be demonstrated by three miracles. Her head might fall but her blood would not gush to the ground. It would creep skywards to stain the white banner fluttering overhead. And although it was midsummer, snow would fall, covering her body in a cold, white shroud. Lastly, the province that had chosen to treat her with such injustice would be punished with three years of drought.

All these prophecies came to pass.

But Dou E's revenge didn't end there. Following the drought, her errant father returned to the town, having become an important government official. Yu Lan leaned forward in her seat as Dou E's ghost appeared before her father, the actor's long white sleeves billowing behind her as she floated across the stage, alarming her father with her ghostly presence.

The ghost recounted to her father how she had been wronged and demanded retribution. He reopened the case, arresting Donkey Zhang and condemning him to death. Thus her innocence was vindicated and the true criminal was punished. Her ghost was finally able to rest.

The instruments fell silent, the performers left the stage and the lights came up over the audience. But Yu Lan didn't notice. She was still deep in the world of the opera. Tears blurred her vision, dribbling down her cheeks and seeping under her high collar. But she paid them no heed.

'Sai Mui, what's wrong? Why are you crying?' Chan asked, perturbed at the sight of his concubine so upset when he meant for her to be entertained.

'It's so sad. Why did she have to die?'

'She died to honour her venerable mother-in-law. She died to fulfil her duty to her family,' Ah Jie hissed on the other side of her husband, 'like all pious women. You would do well to emulate her.'

Her glare spoke more than her words. It said that Yu Lan had neglected her duty to the Chan family. Yet she regularly castigated her own mother-in-law, who was safely distant in Guangdong. And her unhappy rants to the ancestors were a daily ritual in the Chan mansion. Meanwhile her husband left his piety up to his wife.

'It's just a play. For your enjoyment,' Chan laughed, chucking her under the chin in an indulgent manner, his long fingernails scratching her skin. 'Next time I'll bring you to see a play about war, eh? Or a play about love may be more to your liking. You'd enjoy that, wouldn't you, my little pigeon? We can't have you crying over a play.'

But to Yu Lan, the story was much more than a play. It was a lesson. Not the kind of lesson the *taitai* had in mind either. The voice clamoured in her head. 'You can be more than a puppet,' it urged. 'You can have your revenge on all who wronged you.'

Despite the forces raised against her, she could find a way to overcome them if she was determined enough.

'Husband,' she said, widening her eyes and letting her lips quiver as if she was on the verge of tears, 'Ah Jie is right. I should like to emulate Dou E. I have done my duty to this family by giving you a son, but I have neglected my duty to my birth family. You have spoiled me so much they must think I have forgotten them. My dear mother, who gave me life. My honoured father, who raised me. They haven't seen their ungrateful daughter since I left their house. Perhaps I could pay them a New Year visit.'

The *taitai*'s glare hardened but before she could open her mouth her husband nodded, declaring, 'You are right. We have been selfish to keep you all to ourselves. Tomorrow Ah Kong will drive you to High Street to visit your parents. You shall have red packets for your brothers and a good side of pork for your mother.' He squeezed her knee fondly. 'Your parents shall share in our good fortune. It's the least they deserve.'

'Thank you. You are too generous.'

Later, as she waited for the car beside her husband's yellow-silk clad wife, she felt a hand snake out and pinch her on the thigh. 'Don't think you've heard the last of this. Don't forget what happened to Dou E,' the woman hissed in her ear.

Yu Lan remembered fingers like steel digging into her arm, the feeling of falling. Would it be so bad to wander the underworld like Dou E? At least she would be free.

'You may fool my husband with your big eyes and your pretty tears but you don't fool me. I could replace you with another girl tomorrow and he wouldn't even notice.' With that she snapped her fingers in Yu Lan's face before allowing her husband to usher her into the Chevrolet. Yu Lan was left standing alone under an archway outside the theatre shivering. So many emotions trembled in her body that she couldn't put a name to them all. There was fear and sadness and anger and hatred. And beneath these feelings, running through her body like a current of electric energy, was the desire for revenge.

33

THE CHEVROLET ROLLED to a stop outside Lim's Authentic Herbal Remedy Shop, with its sacks and baskets of dried ingredients spilling out onto the five-foot way. In the distance Yu Lan could hear the clash of cymbals and pounding of drums that heralded a lion dance somewhere in the neighbourhood. Children and adults alike crowded the street whenever a neighbour welcomed the prancing gold and red lions to bring luck to their home for the New Year. She always felt sorriest for the back half of the lion who spent most of the dancing doubled over, and then had to lift his front half high above his head to clamber upward for the promised lucky packet hidden inside the cabbage.

'I will return in two hours,' Kong informed them as he opened the door, no doubt under instructions from his employer. Chan might indulge her with this visit but he would take no chances that she might abscond, not after her failed attempt at running away in those first days after the birth. And her request to bring their son had been met with a swift refusal. On the familiar streets of Chinatown she might have an ally or a haven that he knew nothing about, an ally who would help steal the child away. Here the dangers were familiar ones, for she would hardly be attacked by a tiger on Petaling Street.

Still she was glad that Ho Jie had been delegated to accompany her to her father's shop. She didn't care that the amah was there to guard as much as assist her, for returning to her old haunts would be a trial of knowing glances. By now the entire neighbourhood would know that she was Chan's concubine and the father of his son. To some, the position of concubine to a prosperous man was cause for congratulation but to others it was occasion only for shame.

'Your father will be proud of you, mother to Chan Towkay's eldest son! It is nothing to be ashamed of,' Ho Jie had crowed, as the driver negotiated the Chevrolet through the crowded streets of Chinatown. 'And you bring gifts.'

Indeed, a large piece of roast pork, New Year cakes made of glutinous rice, a box of candy and a bag of mandarins all the way from China rested on the seat between them. She knew her mother would welcome the gifts but still, she was nervous. Would she be received as a married daughter returning on the second day of New Year to pay her respects to her birth family, or would she be shunned as an object of embarrassment, even scorn?

She stepped out onto the five-foot way, ducking under a long red banner wishing all Lim's customers happiness and prosperity. The driver shut the car door, but before resuming his seat behind the wheel he glanced from the shop and back to Yu Lan with a frown. 'If you need to return earlier I will be waiting at Lee's *kopi* shop.'

Already she could feel eyes upon her as old man Chu next door poked his head out from his sundries store. Most of the Chinese businesses remained closed on the second day of New Year but that didn't stop Chu from haunting his shop when he heard an unfamiliar vehicle arrive. And somewhere above she heard shutters creak open so that Chu's wife could get a better view too. Across the street, Madam Ng, mother of Tailor Ng, also chose that moment to venture out onto the five-foot way with a rush broom in her hands, her bowed old legs forming an arch as she swept. She was fortunate that it was the second day, not the first, or she might have swept away all her family's wealth in her zeal to find out what was happening at Apothecary Lim's. Everyone knew he had sold his daughter off to a rich *towkay* to pay his gambling debts, and here she was returning with her gold and her silk and her amah in tow.

Yu Lan fixed her eyes to the ground as she entered the shop, Ho Jie following behind with the gifts. She swept past the fishy-smelling sacks of dried swim bladders, sea cucumber and shark fin. She breathed in the earthiness of ginseng and mushroom, and with these scents came a wave of nausea so potent that she almost vomited into a basket of goji berries balancing precariously on an old crate.

'What's wrong?'

'Nothing. I'd forgotten what home smells like.'

The amah sniffed in the aroma of bark, berry and dead animal parts with a twitch of her nose. 'Mmm. Difficult to forget.' But Yu Lan had forced herself to forget. If she hadn't, she would have cried herself to sleep so often she would be as much a husk as the poor dead seahorses crammed into jars upon her father's shelves.

There was no one in sight behind the counter so they ventured further, Yu Lan calling for her father as she pushed aside the bamboo curtain separating the shop from the room beyond. 'Good morning, Ba.'

Her father looked up from a table where he was unpacking translucent discs of reddish brown *chan su* and storing them in a large glass jar. She noticed that his hair was threaded with more grey than when she had left, and he seemed thinner, smaller than she remembered. Or perhaps it was she who had changed and her father was no different to the day he sent her off with Madam Foo to the house of a man she had never met.

'Ah Lan? Is that you, daughter?' he asked, squinting as if he could not believe his eyes.

'It is me, Ba. *Gong hei fatt choi*,' she said, offering him the traditional New Year greeting.

He dropped one more disc into the jar, then wiping his hands upon his tunic, he said with a frown, 'We weren't expecting you. I don't have a red packet ready.'

'It doesn't matter.'

'I suppose you are married now so there's no need.' Was he being polite in referring to her status as married, or merely rationalising his lack of a red packet? She could never be sure with her father. 'You look… prosperous. Chan's house agrees with you.' He didn't mention the shadows of sleeplessness about her eyes or the hollows in her cheeks. Or perhaps he didn't notice.

'I have a son.'

'We heard that. Chan Towkay must be pleased. And you, daughter, perhaps now you'll see that your father had only your best interests at heart in arranging this match. Chan couldn't get a son from the shrivelled womb of that wife of his, but you've given him one.'

He didn't ask after his grandson. Had no questions about the little boy's health or disposition. In fact, he showed no sign that the child was of any importance to him. The boy might have been no relation at all.

'What do you have there?' His gaze shifted to the basket carried by Ho Jie. He didn't bother to greet the amah or ask who she was – her white tunic and black trousers announced her occupation.

'Chan Towkay sends you these gifts.' It was traditional to take a gift when paying New Year visits and Chan had made certain that the gift for her parents wouldn't embarrass him.

'I expect a rich man like Chan can spare a few morsels. Your mother will be pleased.'

'How is my mother?'

'Same, same. Too much heavy work now,' he said, glaring at his daughter as if she was at fault for leaving her mother to toil alone, so that her poor, mutilated feet ached from all the sweeping and mopping and fetching and carrying.

'Is she here?'

'Where else would she be?'

'We'll take her these gifts then,' she said, turning in the direction of the kitchen where her mother would already be chopping ingredients for her husband's midday meal.

'Did you hear about your friend, the Wang boy. What was his name… Ming? That boy who meant so much to you? I heard about your visit to his father's *kopi* shop,' he said, showing his upper teeth in a shrewd smile.

At the sound of that name, Yu Lan stopped walking towards the kitchen, feeling as if her heart might also stop in its tracks. No one had spoken that name in her hearing since she left her father's house. She felt a small thrill in her heart and held her breath. Had Ming run away to make his fortune? Was he biding his time until he could come for her? All these months she dare not speak his name, but it had echoed in her heart through the long, sleepless nights after Chan left her bed.

Sometimes when she held her son in her arms, gazing perplexedly at his features and wondering how this small scrap of life had emerged from her body, she imagined the boy with a smaller version of Ming's ears jutting from his head, a ghost of Ming's long face and eyes staring back at her. For a moment she would find a kernel of love in her heart for her child. Now her legs grew weak at the memory of lost love. Did he think of her still? Did he retain a shred of hope for a future together?

She felt a hand at her elbow holding her steady and knew that Ho Jie stood at her side, sensing that Apothecary Lim had more to say. Yu Lan returned her gaze to her father's face, observing the twitch of a smile at the corner of his mouth. Her heart quickened its beat. What had happened to Ming? Whatever her father had to say, she suspected she wasn't going to like it, yet she was compelled to listen.

'I've heard nothing,' she murmured.

Her father nodded, unpacking several more discs before clearing his throat and divulging his news. 'That boy… he is married now. To the eldest daughter of Ng who runs the *kopi* shop on Foch Avenue. Wang and Ng arranged it years ago. All that time you were swooning over him, he was already betrothed.'

'He couldn't have known this.'

'He knew this, daughter. His father took him to meet the girl. Everyone knows this.' He watched her face, waiting for a response, but when none was forthcoming added, 'What? You have nothing to say?'

Any words she might have found were lodged in her throat with a lump she couldn't name, her gaze riveted to her father's hand as it stowed brown lumps into the glass jar. The stacked discs caught a ray of morning light from the inner courtyard so that they glowed.

'Wang hosted such a party to celebrate his son's marriage. Thirty tables at least, they say. And the bride's dowry contained so much gold she could barely lift her arms at the wedding. Yes, a very grand affair.'

Ho Jie found words on her behalf. 'I'm sure Sai Mui is happy for her friend. And grateful to her honourable father for thinking to tell her. And now perhaps, she might visit with her mother before our driver returns to take us home.' She didn't wait for an answer, but bustled her charge across the inner courtyard and through to the kitchen at the rear of the shophouse, all the while keeping a steadying hand at her elbow.

As the familiar sights and scents of her mother's kitchen greeted her, all Yu Lan could think about was her father's bony hand placing one disc after another into the giant glass jar. And as her mother hobbled forward to hold her head between her hands and enfold her in thin, strong arms, she barely noticed. She was too overcome by a powerful rage; that Ming had been stolen from her, that he hadn't fought for their love. Rage, that her father had decided her fate; that he had sold her to Chan Towkay. Rage, that the Chan family had robbed her of her son, her future and her hope.

Even her mother's embrace couldn't comfort her. She had nothing left but her rage. And inside her head the voice whispered, 'They have taken everything... now they must pay.'

'Ah Lan, what's wrong? I can feel you shaking,' her mother said, encircling her wrist with one hand while stepping back to examine her face. 'Your heart is racing,' she said after a while, looking to the amah when her daughter remained silent.

'Truly, Madam, she hasn't been herself since the birth. She's so listless, poor child. Sometimes she sleeps through half the day. We've been very concerned for her health.'

'Why didn't you send word?' Madam Lim asked her daughter.

'I would have come.'

She heard her mother's voice as if in a dream, faint and faraway, while that other voice, the voice in her head rang loud and clear. That voice belonged to the real world. 'But they wouldn't have allowed her to come, would they? They have cut you off from everyone you know,' it urged, 'your mother, your brothers, Ming. Remember what happened when you tried to find your way back? They sent that old sorcerer to hunt you down.'

'Ah Lan? Are you listening to me?'

'I am listening, Ma.'

'You should have sent for me.'

'There was nothing you could do.' Once she had believed her mother could solve all her problems, but that was so long ago it might have been another life, one in which her days revolved around the apothecary shop, the kitchen and the clan association. Now Madam Chan circumscribed her life.

'You are very pale and there are shadows beneath your eyes. Childbirth takes a lot from a woman and some need longer to recover than others.'

'We must rebuild her strength,' said Ho Jie, 'and help her adjust to her new life.'

'Are they cruel to her in the Chan house?' asked her mother, fixing the amah with a hard stare.

These women, the only two women who had ever cared for her, were of similar height and age. Small, wiry women accustomed to toil. They had both known hard lives, her mother helping her father in his shop, keeping house and raising three children from the time she was seventeen, while the amah had fended for herself since she was a girl of twelve. Yet of the two, her mother was the more careworn. At least Ho Jie could walk away; she had money of her own. Her choices might be hard, but at least she had them.

'The *towkay* is generous... as long as he gets his way.'

Her mother nodded. She knew all about men and their way. 'And his wife?'

Ho Jie pursed her lips as if she had bitten into something distasteful. 'Madam has her moments. But she dotes on the child.'

Madam Lim waited for her to continue but when there was no more information forthcoming the two women regarded each other in silent understanding. The *taitai* doted on the child but the child's mother was superfluous. Perhaps even an encumbrance she could do without. Now that she had what she wanted, why should she share her husband with another woman?

'Remember what happened at the waterfall?' the voice reminded Yu Lan. 'They tried to make you doubt yourself. They said you were crazy. But we know the truth. We know who pushed you, don't we? And next time you might not be so lucky. Next time there may be nothing to hold onto.'

'I'll ask your father to make up a tonic,' said her mother. 'Once you've regained your strength the world will look different. You'll be able to endure. And you'll find your happiness in your children.'

But she didn't want to endure. What joy was there in a life that must be endured? She had once had a dream, a childish dream that took no account of the outside world. That dream had fooled her into thinking that if she worked hard she could make a life of her own choosing. But she had been wrong.

'You can still choose. You don't have to let them choose for you,' said the voice, the words reverberating through her head like a chant. 'First your father, then the *towkay* and *taitai*, even your mother would choose for you. Your mother would have you endure. Your father would have you obey. But you can make a different choice.'

How? How could she make a different choice?

'And you can make them sorry. You can make them suffer.'

How could she make them sorry? She had little strength any more and no power.

'You can steal their future as they have stolen yours.'

She felt a touch on her shoulder, and realised that her mother was speaking to her once more. 'Come, we'll go through to the shop and ask your father before he comes back for his lunch.'

'Ask Ba?'

'To make up a tonic.'

'Anything to make you well again, little one,' said Ho Jie. 'You want to see your son grow tall and strong, don't you?'

Except she wasn't sure that she did. Besides, as long as he lived in the Chan mansion, how could he grow tall and strong? A house filled with poison, a house ruled not by love but by duty and posterity? Her son would be stunted by its spite. 'Yes,' said the voice, 'a house of poison… a tainted house.'

'Ah Lan?'

'There's no need to trouble my father. I'll make up the tonic. I know exactly what I need.'

*

OUTSIDE RAIN FELL in sheets, churning the road to mud and chasing all but the most urgent business from the streets. They waited under the shelter of the five-foot way for the driver to return with the car, trying to avoid stray splashes in the heavy downpour. Water dripped from awnings to stream along the paving underfoot so that Ho Jie wished she had worn her clogs that morning. The new silk slippers she had chosen for vanity's sake were getting a soaking. She only hoped the basket she carried wouldn't get wet, for it was brimming with the dried ingredients the girl had selected for her tonic.

While the father worked shovelling rice at a small dining table next to the kitchen, the girl spent at least ten minutes opening drawers, dipping into baskets and delving into jars. She set to the task with more enthusiasm than Ho Jie had observed in her for months, her face alight with energy. She considered each choice carefully, before slipping a handful into the basket, moving about the shop with easy familiarity. Then when the basket was laden with fungi, roots, berries and hard brown cakes, she declared, 'I think that will do it.'

Now, as they waited for the Chevrolet to roll into view she surprised Ho Jie by grabbing her free hand and squeezing it hard so that the bones crunched together.

'You're my only friend now. No one else can help me.'

For a moment, Ho Jie wasn't sure she had heard the girl correctly. She was an amah far from home and family. She no longer allowed herself to think in terms of friendship.

'You are my friend, aren't you?'

She felt her eyes water and discovered they welled with tears. She had left her last friend behind in the silk factory at Shonde. Ai Leng, who had lain next to her on the floor each night as they whispered each other to sleep. Ai Leng who had gone to America. Who she would never see again. Now this girl was making a claim upon her affections. Exactly what sort of claim she wasn't sure. For a moment she considered rejecting that claim, for with friendship came loyalty and responsibility, and she didn't know if she was ready to give or receive either. Then as she felt the warm pressure of the girl's hand upon hers, she knew that whatever happened she couldn't help but care about her. And if that meant accepting responsibility and offering loyalty, then so be it. Everyone needed someone to care about, even a self-combed spinster making her way alone in the world.

'You know I'm your friend,' she said.

'The *taitai* doesn't need me now that she has her son. She wants to be rid of me,' Yu Lan paused, her eyes flicking wildly around as if she suspected people were watching her. 'If something bad happens, will you promise to help me?'

'Nothing bad will happen, little one.'

'But if it does...'

Her tone was so urgent, her entire body so rigid with expectation that Ho Jie was suddenly afraid. Perhaps she was right. 'I'll protect you.'

'But if you can't... if something happens to me... I will still need your help.' Yu Lan leaned forward so that she was close enough for Ho Jie to smell the talcum powder on her skin. She felt the girl's warm breath fanning her face, an eyelash feathering her cheek. 'Will you do this one task for me?'

'Yes.'

Lips almost touching the corner of her mouth.

'Do you promise?'

'I promise.'

Ho Jie was good at promises. Twenty years earlier she had combed up her hair and vowed never to marry, never to know a man. She had kept that promise. Now she would do everything necessary to keep another. Even if it demanded the rest of her life.

34

Hampshire 2017

THE HOLE WAS a foot deep. They'd considered scattering the remains in the forest but Sarah worried that the bone fragments might tempt dogs. She didn't know much about dogs, never having owned so much as a goldfish, but she did know they liked to dig up bones. Her mother was always complaining that next-door's beagle buried its bones under her camellias and created chaos digging them up. Then again, Celia was always complaining about something.

'I don't think the hole's deep enough yet,' she said. 'What if a fox digs them up?'

'I doubt foxes would dig up bones this dry.'

Once Nick's remains finally arrived from Kuala Lumpur, June had become quite pragmatic. There was a job to do. So they'd decided to bury them beneath the great oak not far from her house. What better place than the oak where he'd played as a boy? 'Then we can visit him any time,' June had said.

Sarah had purchased a dedicated shrub for Nick at a memorial garden in East London. And they could have scattered his bones in a lake or a river, or tossed them out to sea, so she wondered whether June's desire to bury them near her house wasn't only a way of keeping him close, but also of encouraging Sarah to return. Because without her son, or her son's children to connect them, she and Sarah were no longer related. Nick was the one bothered by the idea that he would be the last of his line. Instead, it turned out to be his mother. Sarah couldn't imagine how she must feel, cast adrift with no one left to tie her to family and no way left to change that. She was an orphan in both directions. Sarah grieved for Nick but she still had family, dysfunctional as it might be. And she was young. One day she might meet someone and finally feel whole enough to produce a child. June would never have another son. She had lost the only one she would ever have.

June had warned him about going to the home of his ancestors, fearful of what might happen there. And then all her fears had been realised in a way none of them could ever have predicted.

'I'll return,' she promised Nick silently. 'I'll keep an eye on June.'

She leaned her shovel against the oak's trunk, brushing specks of dirt from her jeans. 'I think that's deep enough,' she said aloud. Then she tipped up the urn and watched bone and ash pour into the hole. She placed her arm around June's waist and held her mother-in-law as she sobbed quietly for a good ten minutes. She thought back to the day after the cremation in Kuala Lumpur when they'd returned to retrieve his remains. The crematorium had been no plush house of death. There was no disguising death there.

A fleet of funeral vehicles queued outside, while inside the bereaved in their white mourning gear, and Taoist nuns robed in blue, performed last farewells. The night before, the mourners had burned the paper mansions and Mercedes that would accompany their loved ones to the afterworld. Here there was only the plain tiled floor, the utilitarian waiting-room chairs and a hall open to the breeze.

June didn't want to leave this last act of love to a funeral director. Like the other mourners, she wanted to perform the task herself. Something she'd been too distant to do for her father. Too young to do for her mother and grandmother. So the day after the funeral they had arrived at the crematorium to be greeted by two grey metal boxes full of bones. White, cream, brown, faded yellow. Some with veins of ash grey running through them. Some almost translucent. If Sarah hadn't been standing in a crematorium beside her dead husband's mother she might have thought the bones were foraged upon a beach. They resembled splinters of dead crustacean, crushed shells and timeworn pebbles of glass. They didn't look human at all.

So while June took up the waiting pair of chopsticks and began filling the urn, piece by piece, until it was brimming with fragments of bone, Sarah looked on thinking of dead, sea creatures. It was only afterwards, on the flight home, that she felt the full force of his death for the first time, like the onset of pneumonia or a bout of food poisoning. She felt his loss in her aching muscles, her churning stomach and pounding head. She had so little energy that she could barely make her legs carry her down the long aisle between rows of passengers to the restroom.

Even now, four months later, she still felt his loss like a hunger, like waking up with a gnawing emptiness that could never quite be filled. She would roll over, longing to hear him complain that she had stolen all the covers again. She worked sixteen-hour days to fill that emptiness. James had actually threatened to confiscate her laptop if she didn't go home.

'Let's go back to the house for a cup of tea,' June said, after drying her eyes with a tissue. 'I made sesame balls.'

*

'YOU'VE BEEN A good daughter-in-law,' June said as they carried their tea and sesame balls into the living room. Had she been a good daughter-in-law though? She didn't feel like it. She felt that she had failed them both. 'Don't worry about all that old stuff about giving your parents grandchildren. You gave me something more important. You let me hold on to my son. And you gave me your friendship. Some women need to hoard their husband's love. They can't leave room for his mother. But you have a heart big enough to share.'

Even as she smiled at June's words she felt like a fraud. Her heart wasn't big enough to share; it was too small to fit all of Nick's love. Too small to give him the love that he deserved. The heart was a muscle, and everyone knows what happens to muscles that are under-used. They atrophy. They become weak. She had let her heart shrink so that it was too weak to love properly.

'I didn't love him enough. If I'd loved him enough he wouldn't have gone away. And then he would still be here.' The words dripped from her as she stared down into her cup of tea. She didn't know why she was telling June this now, but something made her feel like she owed her the truth.

'Oh, Sarah, love isn't about holding someone back, you know that. I didn't want him to go but I couldn't stop him. My father tried to do that to me and look what happened, we never saw each other again. I wasn't going to repeat that mistake with Nick, no matter how afraid I was.'

'He wanted to have children but I kept brushing him off. If I hadn't, if I'd agreed, maybe he'd still be here.'

'Events have to take their course. All we can do is be our best selves.'

'He made me feel safe.'

June nodded, flicking a wistful glance at her altar. 'You're lucky.'

'I think he made others feel safe because he knew who he was. You gave him that, June. I know he said he felt disconnected but that was an intellectual thing. That was about knowing where he came from. He already knew who he was and where he belonged.'

She was trying to comfort June but now she wasn't so sure that he did know where he belonged. Why had he let that house claim him? Why had he kept secrets from her? Her hand, holding the delicate Royal Albert saucer, began quaking as if her elbow rested on a nerve. She replaced the cup on the saucer and set both on the coffee table. Suddenly she knew the truth.

'The trouble is I don't think I knew who *he* was any more. We'd been together thirteen years. I'd changed but I don't think I registered that he had too. I didn't give him the chance to show me.' She thought back to that brunch in London on his first trip back home. He'd tried to talk to her about how he'd changed but she hadn't wanted to listen. Every time he wanted to talk about the future she'd brushed him aside. Made excuses about work.

'Stop blaming yourself. A ladder killed Nick. That house killed my son.'

Sarah looked across the coffee table to where her pretty mother-in-law sat in her pretty chintz armchair. Her mouth was set in a grim line and her eyes radiated loathing.

'Bad things happen there. I tried to tell Nick that but he didn't believe me. You can't make someone believe in evil.'

June stood and walked over to the altar by the window. Not knowing where the conversation was leading, but suspecting it led into unfamiliar territory, Sarah followed her.

'I told you once before that I saw her when I was a little girl.'

'Saw who?'

'The *neuih gwai*. It was when my grandmother was sick. I didn't know it at the time but she was dying of ovarian cancer.' June picked up a photo frame from the altar. It was the photo of her grandparents with the baby on his mother's knee and the amah standing in the background. She must have had it framed since Sarah visited last. She stared at it for a while, as if communing with her ancestors. Each slight movement of her hand caused the ruby eyes of her dragon bracelet to flash in the flickering light of the altar candles.

'I must have been about five. One night I woke calling out for Ho Jie. The house was so big and silent. So dark and scary. Sometimes I felt like the jungle was encroaching on the house, coming to get me. Now I realise that it was crowding closer because there was no money for a gardener to cut it back,' she laughed. 'Anyway, my father must have been out somewhere that night. So when Ho Jie didn't come, I got out of bed and went downstairs looking for her. And that's when I saw her, the ghost woman. She seemed to be floating through the trees at the front of the house. All in white with very long black hair. And then the next day my grandmother died.' She shrugged and set the photo frame back on the altar.

Sarah didn't know what to say. She had no firm beliefs either way about ghosts but she suspected that if they did exist they would be less physically substantial than the woman her mother-in-law described. More of a presence felt than a floating woman.

'You were young. Maybe you were dreaming.'

'No. I wasn't dreaming. I was so scared that I hid in the upstairs bathroom. Ho Jie found me asleep on the tiles in the morning. When I told her what I'd seen, she said it was probably a neighbour out raiding our fruit trees in their pyjamas. I accepted her explanation at the time but years later, I realised how ridiculous it was. For one thing, there were no neighbours for several hundred yards. And also, the neighbours were terrified of the ghost house, and the *neuih gwai*. No one would risk sneaking into our garden at night, and certainly not in their pyjamas.'

'I don't know what to say.'

June patted her hand, 'You don't have to say anything, love. But you do need to know. That house belongs to you now. And you need to do everything in your power to be rid of it.'

'Su Lin is staying there while I work out what to do with it. She had nowhere else to stay and I didn't like to leave it empty.'

June's hand on hers tightened.

'We had an alarm system installed… but maybe it wasn't such a good idea to leave her there alone.' She'd been thinking about human intruders. She hadn't thought about any other kind of danger. She stared at her mother-in-law's hand clutching hers and then at the photograph of the small family group seated in front of the house, a house June was convinced was haunted. There was something she was missing here. Something that her visual memory was trying to tell her, if she could just decipher it. Over the years she'd developed an acute visual memory, an asset in design. Picking up the photograph, she let her eyes rove over every detail. The severe-looking mother with her baby son resting on her knee; the buttoned-up, ageing husband in his suit;

the black-and-white garbed amah who had loved June like her own child; the sad young maid in her printed *samfu*.

'What did your father say again, when he gave you that bracelet?' Sarah asked, suddenly changing the subject. She indicated the dragon bracelet twinkling on June's arm with a nod of her head.

'He said it belonged to my grandmother.'

'Uh-huh. Now take a close look at the young maid.'

'Wait while I put my glasses on,' June said, walking over to retrieve her glasses from the coffee table. 'Okay. Let me see.'

Sarah watched as she studied the photograph, the sudden tension in her shoulders telling her that June also recognised what she'd seen there.

'I usually only wear my glasses for reading. No wonder I never noticed before,' June said, tearing her eyes from the photo to regard Sarah, 'but the maid is wearing my dragon bracelet.'

They both stared at the photograph. The girl held her hands clasped in front of her tunic, the dragonhead clasp just visible on her wrist.

'So if what my father said was true, this girl was his mother.' She didn't look surprised, rather Sarah saw the knowledge click into place like a jigsaw piece, making sense of other pieces of information.

'And if it's true,' said Sarah, 'maybe your grandparents adopted your father to save this girl from being cast out. I'm guessing that being a single mother was frowned upon back in the day in KL.' She didn't like to suggest that June's grandfather might have got the girl pregnant in the first place, but that's what she was thinking. It was too big an assumption, and they were June's family after all.

'Oh, I don't think you understand how things worked then, love. In China, Malaya and other parts of Asia, even in the 1930s, little girls as young as nine were sold as bondmaids. Young women were sold as secondary wives... or worse. It was quite common for affluent Chinese men in Malaya to have two, three or even four wives. Sometimes they had a wife in China and another in Malaya or Indonesia. So if we're right, then that girl wasn't my grandparents' maid. She was probably my grandfather's concubine. And my father was the concubine's child.'

If the girl in the photo was June's real grandmother, why had June never heard anything about her? Why had no one ever mentioned her... or had they?

'I wonder what happened to her?' June said, tracing the image of the girl with her forefinger. Another family member she'd lost, or never had the chance to know.

Sarah thought back to her conversation with the restaurant owner what seemed like years ago now, but was really only a matter of months. He had mentioned another girl who'd died in the house. Not June's mother or grandmother but someone else. Could that someone else have become the infamous *neuih gwai*, reputed to haunt the house all those years? Could that someone else have been the concubine? The woman in white with long black hair, who five-year-old June saw that night in the garden? Ghost stories usually arise from tragic events. Besides June's mother's death, what other tragedy had occurred in that house?

'When I was in KL a local restaurant owner mentioned someone else who died in your father's house a long time before, a young woman. Maybe it was her.'

June closed her eyes, as if trying to summon memories from forty or fifty years ago. 'You know, I'd forgotten about it, but there was a room in the house that was never used. A lovely room at the back corner with windows on two sides to catch the breeze. When I was fifteen I asked my father if I could move into it since it was bigger and nicer than mine.'

'What did he say?'

'Well, he said no. And then when I produced what I considered were sound arguments to support my case, he exploded. The gist of it was that I was a selfish, ungrateful child.' She wiped away a tear. Her father's words still stung after all those decades. 'Sorry. Later when I went crying to Ho Jie, she said not to be too hard on him. That the room held too many sad memories. I thought that it must have been the room where my mother died and for a while I felt sorry for my father. I thought that perhaps all his hardness came from too much grief.' She frowned and placed her other hand over the golden dragon bracelet so that its ruby eyes were blind. Sarah didn't know if she wanted reassurance or she didn't want to look at it any longer. 'But maybe that's where the concubine died.'

35

A NOISE WOKE her, or perhaps a car's headlights flashing through the curtains. Sarah threw back the quilt and put her feet to the chilly floor, before crossing to the window and flipping back the curtain. Soft light turned her hand milky pale, apart from the translucent green ring encircling her third finger. Outside nothing moved, not even a cat. Across the lane, the neighbour's house was dark, apart from the slate roof gleaming in the moonlight. Feeling uneasy, she ventured out onto the upstairs landing and stood listening. Downstairs she heard the sound of a door opening. Was June raiding the pantry at this time of night? It seemed unlikely. June's bedroom was next door to the guest room so she turned the door handle and peeked in to find her mother-in-law curled up on her side, snoring lightly.

Someone else was in the house.

She took the stairs barefoot, hoping the old boards wouldn't creak under her weight and give her away. Perhaps she was foolish to investigate alone. Perhaps she should have called the police, but she didn't think of these things. Instinct took over and all she knew was that they were alone here and she had to do something. Left unchallenged, the intruder might return when June was alone and she couldn't allow that to happen. Not after what her mother-in-law had suffered already.

In the entrance hall, the front door was closed and the room was still. Sarah could detect nothing amiss. She wandered into to the living room, lit by the soft glow of a burning oil lamp on the altar, then through to the kitchen where she noticed that the back door stood ajar. A light breeze ruffled the curtains over the sink and she felt the hairs on her arms lift. She was sure someone had been in the house, and since she couldn't find any sign of their presence, they must have left. But that didn't mean they wouldn't return.

Rubbing her hands up and down her arms a few times to warm them, she stepped out onto the stone-flagged terrace at the rear of the house. The garden was shadowed in blue by a cloud-hazed moon. Trees, shrubs and the skeletons of garden furniture were silhouetted like props in a shadow play. To Sarah, June's lovely garden had become a place of secrets where danger might lurk behind familiar objects. She couldn't see anything unusual – the only disturbance was a rustle of movement behind some shrubs at the bottom of the garden – yet she couldn't shake off a feeling of wrongness. The cottage sat at the edge of the village, the last house in the lane. Beyond lay the forest.

It must have rained in the night for her pyjama bottoms grew damp as she waded through wet grass. It didn't occur to her that it wasn't wise to traipse through the forest alone on an autumn night in nothing but a pair of cotton pyjamas, especially not if an intruder were at large. Especially not if the intruder turned out to be someone she knew. For although the night was silent, she felt as if she was being called, as if an invisible hand tugged at her subconscious, urging her to follow. While his body lay in a coma in that hospital bed in Kuala Lumpur, Nick had spoken to her silently. Reassuring her. Guiding her. And then he was gone. What if he was calling her again? What if he'd been in the house looking for her? What if he couldn't find his way without her? She had let him down once. She couldn't risk doing it again.

If he needed her, she must find him and help him.

It wasn't far to the oak. A hundred yards across open field, then a faint path through a grove of alder trees to where the ancient oak towered like a spire above the roof of the forest. The oak's girth was so great that two people holding hands would barely contain it. Its lower reaches were scarred by great burrs, while the branches on its eastern side were feathered with lichen that shone pale and ghostly in the moonlight. Beneath its twisted branches, dead wood and autumn leaves littered the forest floor where Nick's bones lay buried.

Yet it wasn't the oak that imprinted itself upon Sarah's vision. Standing beneath the tree, directly above the spot where Sarah had shovelled soil just yesterday, stood a girl. Unlike Sarah, she seemed oblivious to the cold in her filmy white pyjamas. But perhaps her hair kept her warm, flowing over her shoulders and down her back in a cloak of black silk. She was staring down at the place beneath her feet where the soil was disturbed. Her hunched shoulders and frail limbs exuded sadness. But when she turned her face to Sarah she was smiling. It was a thing of triumph, that smile; it said, 'My work here is done. Whatever happens now, you can't undo it.'

Sarah wanted to shout at the girl to go away and leave Nick alone, but when she opened her mouth nothing emerged but a puff of moist air. She wanted to rush forward and push the girl over, pummel her with fists, force her to flee, but her feet were planted in the earth as firmly as the oak's enormous roots. She was as powerless to protect her husband in death as she had been in life. All she could do was stand and watch the girl with the grim smile until finally she turned and disappeared into the forest.

The ghost girl had claimed her husband and now he was

condemned to wander the afterworld with no one to guide him home. Sarah had denied him the children who would have offered him their prayers. She had sat by his hospital bed as the machines breathed for him. She had watched helplessly as his life flat-lined. She had let the ghost girl claim him.

She closed her eyes, and in the dusky shadows behind her eyelids she saw her again. The girl in white. Long hair flowing loose as she floated across the leaf-littered ground and disappeared between the alder trees into the forest.

Neuih gwai. Ghost girl.

Haunting them still.

Just as June had warned.

*

SARAH CAME TO sitting upon a wrought-iron garden chair in June's backyard. She shivered in the cold dawn air, her clothes saturated from the wet grass, the rain-soaked furniture and the tears that dribbled down her face and under the collar of her pyjamas.

She didn't know how she had got there, but judging by the state of her clothes and her frozen flesh, she'd been wandering around outside for some time. She hadn't walked in her sleep since moving out of her mother's house. She hadn't woken up anywhere other than a bed since she'd shaken off the terrors that once stalked her adolescent sleep. Now she felt the disquiet of those years return, like an old scar that ached if you bumped it.

What had she been searching for, wandering the night in her pyjamas? Nick was gone. And nothing and no one would bring him back.

36

London 2017

THE COFFEE MACHINE beckoned with the false promise of renewed energy. Sarah slipped a pod into the slot and stood breathing in the aroma of beans while she waited for them to work their magic. Some days she was so busy that the office became workplace, café and gym all rolled into one. After all, now that she had no one to go home to she may as well be sleeping here. She stretched her arms high, bent backwards and listened as vertebrae crunched. Then she rolled her neck a few times before leaning forward at right angles from the waist and resting her hands on the bench.

When they'd first started the company she hadn't minded the twelve-hour days, but ever since she'd returned from Kuala Lumpur, despite her sixteen-hour days – or perhaps because of them – she couldn't summon the same enthusiasm for hand-carved salad servers and black bamboo picture frames. These objects that furnished her days seemed strangely two-dimensional, priced and catalogued but no longer real.

To her disbelief, when she returned from Hampshire after the weekend at June's she'd begun sleepwalking again. All through her adolescence there had been nights when she woke in the early hours slumped on a chair in the living room. Or her mother would nudge her awake after finding her wandering the upstairs hall at two o'clock in the morning. Now it was happening again.

She supposed she wasn't sleeping well, for obvious reasons, so her nocturnal excursions shouldn't be surprising. One thing was clear though: June was right, and she needed to do something about the house in Kuala Lumpur. It was no wonder she was dreaming about ghost girls bent on revenge. Except that poor girl in the photo wasn't a predator, not even a ghostly one. She had been preyed upon. She had been sold as a concubine to a man older than her father, probably with no choice in the matter.

Well, the best way to combat ghosts was to expose them for what they were. And the best thing she could do for Nick was to sort out the situation with the house. Maybe if she got rid of it everything could go back to normal. If she got rid of the house, she might wake to find these last few months were a dream she was sleepwalking through... Oh, don't be so silly, Sarah, she told herself.

'Are you going to drink that coffee or just stand there admiring it?' James said, sneaking up behind her.

There wasn't much room in the tiny kitchenette and he had never been a respecter of personal space, at least not hers. Now she felt his breath stirring the hairs on the back of her neck. Over the years they'd toiled through so many endless days refining marketing plans, negotiating with suppliers or torturing budgets into shape that he seemed to view her more like a sleek but comfortable sofa than a woman. Then again, she had been married and off limits. Not any more.

'Sorry, lost in thought. I'll get out of your way.'

If she turned around they would be almost touching. If she leaned back ever so slightly she could relax against his chest and lean on him, if only for a moment. She didn't think he'd mind. James was an obliging guy, the sort of man who'd ask a girl out just because she expected it. He never seemed to put much effort or thought into his relationships, he just went with the flow until the flow threatened to take him somewhere he didn't want to go. Still, it might be fun to float along with him for a while. She bet he'd look great in swimming trunks.

It was a tempting thought, to melt against his hard body. It had been so long since she'd arched her body against someone else's. And it didn't have to mean anything. There were inches between them, but she could sense his strength, feel it warming her from the inside out. If she just sank back against him, let someone else carry some of her grief, at least for a little while. Except grief didn't work like that. And she was stupid to confuse grief with sex anyway. James wouldn't.

'You're never in my way,' he said. 'Here, I'll sugar it for you.' He reached one arm around her to pick up her coffee cup. He remained standing behind her for a few more seconds, as if secretly sensing her thoughts, before moving to the bench on her other side. He stirred half a teaspoon of sugar into her coffee, just as she liked it, and handed it to her.

'Thanks, you're a honey.' She wondered if men had a sixth sense for sexual opportunity. Could they smell it like dogs smelled fear? Did James sense the hollow ache that for a moment she'd confused with desire?

'I try.' He smiled and draped an arm around her shoulders. 'How is everything, Sar?'

'You know, not so good. I took Nick's ashes down to June's on the weekend.' They'd worked together for long enough to develop a shorthand that dealt in facts, not feelings. If he said he was leaving the office early, he meant he was too tired to think productively any longer. If she said there were a few glitches in the order management software, he knew she wouldn't sleep until she had it sorted. So now she left him to fill in the blanks about what her visit to June's meant.

'Come over to mine. I'll fix you supper. A bottle of merlot will cheer you up, or at least help you forget.'

'Don't you have a date or something?' He usually had a girl in the wings somewhere. She and Nick had spent many entertaining dinners with James and his girlfriends. The women were always charming and pretty but she'd learned not to get too attached to them. She stopped inviting them for coffee or lunch, because they changed so often. She sometimes wondered whether James's real relationship was with the business, so that he didn't have the emotional energy necessary for a woman. Then again, Nick had accused her of the very same thing.

James shrugged in answer to her question and gave a self-deprecating grin. 'Must be losing my boyish good looks.'

'Never.'

'So you'll come?'

She blew on her coffee to give her time to think, even though it was probably cold by now, since she didn't know how long she'd been standing by the machine dreaming.

'I'm really bad company right now,' she warned.

'I'll take that chance.'

'Soon.' She could hardly stand herself, so she wasn't about to inflict her company upon someone else. No matter how tempting. 'I'm almost there. I'll be guzzling champagne and scoffing oysters before you know it and then you'll be sorry you asked me,' she added with a grin.

'Never.' He stood at her shoulder for a few more moments as if his presence might encourage a change of heart, before saying, 'Well, if you change your mind, you know where to find me.' He gave her shoulder a squeeze. 'There's no weakness in asking for help, Sarah.'

Wasn't there? She wasn't so sure. She could easily let herself fall back into his capable arms, either as friends or... friends with benefits. He was familiar, obliging, very good-looking and he knew her well, at least on the surface. But they were too much alike, too engaged with practical solutions. Too contained in their emotions. He would try to fix her with bottles of wine, distract her with amusing conversation, and surround her with activity. But he couldn't help her deal with her grief. She couldn't talk to him about loss. There was no shorthand for that. She had to fix that all by herself.

37

THE KEY WOULDN'T fit in the lock. She fumbled as she twisted it this way and that. She knew that if she could just align it properly, it must fit. It had to fit. Yet her hand wouldn't stop shaking, her heart wouldn't stop hammering and her breath was coming in gasps. On the other side of the door there was something she had to lock out. Something frightening. Dangerous. She felt its presence like an icy wind on a sunny day or a vicious current beneath still waters. She felt it lurking outside the door trying to get in, and she knew that if she didn't hurry, she would be too late. The thing would break into her house and she would never be free of it. It would haunt her the rest of her days, stealing everything and everyone she loved.

Abandoning finesse, she rammed the key at the lock, trying to force the bit into the keyhole. But all she succeeded in doing was digging the bow of the key into the flesh of her palm. Standing back from the door, she stared down at her hand, still breathing raggedly. An indentation sprouted like a deep chain in her lifeline. Her hand was still shaking and on her third finger, the loose jade ring seemed to quiver. Clutched between thumb and index finger, the key dangled uselessly beside its fierce warrior guardian. A mortise key with an elaborately cut bit. A mortise key for a Yale lock.

Sarah came to awareness with a jolt. There was no one outside her door. No one real. No one flesh and blood. She looked down to see her bare legs with the bottom of one of

Nick's old T-shirts barely skimming the tops of her thighs. She'd been sleepwalking again.

In her sleep, she'd taken the key to his grandfather's house from the bedside drawer. She'd slipped the jade archer's ring onto her finger. And she'd walked into the living room and tried to lock a Yale lock with an old Chinese mortise key. To keep out a ghost.

Despite two decades of precaution, two decades of holding herself together, she was clearly going crazy.

The *neuih gwai* was haunting her. Or at least, whatever the *neuih gwai* symbolised was haunting her. Sarah was a daughter of the post-Freudian age, as literate in psych-speak as she was with the lexicon of the Internet. She wasn't stupid. She knew she'd survived her childhood by turning herself into a crustacean. She'd become a skittish creature with a hard shell, snappy claws, and the ability to scuttle quickly out of danger. That shell had served her well. Until it hadn't.

Somewhere inside that hard shell, there remained a soft centre, and the ghost girl was poking sticks at it.

She wandered over to the sofa, flopped onto the sleek Italian cushions, curled into a ball and closed her eyes. For most of her adult life Nick had been there, a bulwark against danger, against the turbulence of her own emotions. Now, the only thing getting her out of bed each day was the threat of the *neuih gwai* entering her dreams and luring her into the world of crazy. Her mother's world.

She opened her eyes and took a calming breath. From this lopsided angle, her eyes were level with the coffee table. And on it, staring her in the face, was Nick, his cheek pressed against hers, his arms encircling her in a body-lock. It was the photo she'd rescued from his office desk, a selfie taken on a rare weekend away in Scotland. She remembered how she'd protested that her nose was red from the cold and her hair hung in rat's tails from the wind, but he'd ignored her protests, pulling her close, thrusting his cheek against hers and snapping. In the picture they were both laughing so hard that their eyes were slits and their faces were creased into laugh lines. She looked like something the cat had dragged in, and she couldn't believe this was the photo he chose for his desk. For his office mate Ben to look at every day.

Nevertheless, that and his laptop were the only things she'd salvaged from his campus office, leaving Ben to sort through his papers and books. He had offered, and at the time she hadn't had the energy to refuse. Ben kept in touch, emailing her with occasional questions, un-offended if she took days to answer. He was another patient man, it seemed, a man who didn't need to be in control to feel safe. In fact, he'd contacted her just the other day and she still hadn't opened the email.

Maybe she should call him.

She looked at the clock glowing green on the sound system. It was two a.m. That meant it was a respectable ten a.m. in Kuala Lumpur. She would probably catch him at the university. Maybe the sound of a human voice would help chase away her jitters, the voice of someone who'd known Nick as he'd been in those last days. Someone who remembered him. She picked up her phone from the coffee table and scrolled through to his number, then waited for it to connect.

'Sarah? I was just thinking about you.' His accent jolted her for a moment. Drew her back to hot days and nights, pungent aromas and lush tropical vegetation, to places she didn't want to go, yet knew she couldn't avoid for ever.

'Not bad thoughts, I hope. I've been a terrible correspondent. Sorry about that.'

'No worries, mate. We're all busy. And you've got things on your mind.'

She felt an unaccustomed urge then to tell him exactly what was on her mind. To spill out her ridiculous ravings about ghosts and curses. For some reason she was confident that he wouldn't humour her or condescend to her, that he would take these revelations in his stride. Whether she was haunted or obsessed, he would keep an open mind. But then he was speaking again and the moment passed.

'I don't know whether you've had a chance to look at my last email but I found something amongst Nick's papers that you might be interested in… a letter.'

'I have all his writing on the laptop but I haven't had a chance… no, that's wrong… I haven't had the will to look through it yet.'

'Yeah, I miss him so I can't imagine how it's been for you.'

'Difficult. I… um… I feel like I let him down, that I made the wrong decision. That I should have waited longer.'

'Yeah, I suppose that was always going to be the case.'

Why didn't he reassure her that she'd done the right thing; that she shouldn't blame herself? A tiny kernel of anger formed, that he would dare imply she'd made a mistake in letting Nick's life support be turned off, before she realised that he wasn't blaming her, he was accepting her, her qualms and insecurities.

She was letting her inner shrew loose again while Ben simply accepted her, complete with all her inevitable guilt, regret and anger.

'The world throws shit at us sometimes, Sarah, and all we can do is duck. Then go and take a long, hot shower.'

She laughed at his ridiculous metaphor, the first time she had laughed in ages. 'You are such an idiot.'

'I try. But seriously, mate, all you can do is breathe through the shit and wait for things to get better. And they will.'

'You think? Except they're getting worse. I think I'm going crazy... seeing ghosts... feeling paranoid.'

'You need a holiday. Come to Perth. I'm heading home for Christmas if you want somewhere to stay. I can promise you stinking hot days, burning sand and enough sharks to make you really paranoid.'

She laughed again. It was tempting. London and the world of homewares were beginning to feel like a cage. She never thought she'd say that. The brilliant blue skies and fierce sun of Western Australia might cauterise her sadness. The sharks might chase away her ghosts. And she would get a stunning tan as a bonus.

'Thanks for the very tempting invitation, especially the sharks. I'll certainly think about it. Now, what's this mysterious letter?'

In the background, she heard a soft crackle as if he was flicking through a pile of papers.

'I found it inside the pages of Nick's Chinese-English dictionary. It looks like he was trying to translate it.' Ben paused for a moment and she guessed he was scanning the letter. 'My Chinese is pretty basic and I learned the simplified script they use in contemporary China. This is written in the classical script, so I can only make out a few words here and there.'

As he spoke, her skin prickled, like the old cliché where someone walks over your grave.

'Here goes. It's dated 1963, that much I can tell you, and signed with the word for "mother". Apart from that I recognise words for "ghost", "father" and "death". Not very cheerful, I admit, but I thought it might mean something to you.'

It meant something but she wasn't sure what. Yet.

'I can get one of my colleagues to translate it if you like.'

'Yes. Thank you. I'd appreciate that.'

Mother. Father. Ghost. Death. The words gripped her, reeling her in with their portent. She knew in her bones who the ghost was now, the ghost who had haunted Nick's family through four generations. The sad girl whose baby was cradled by another woman's arms, whose presence permeated the house where so many people had died. The house where Nick's life had been stolen from him. The ghost girl might not be flesh and blood, but that didn't prevent her from infecting their lives like an inherited disease. Sarah owed it to Nick to try and heal that disease. She owed it to June.

'I'm coming out there.'

'Where? Perth?'

'No. Kuala Lumpur.'

38

Kuala Lumpur 1932

THE MOMENT YU Lan entered the kitchen to fetch Ah Jie's tea on the fourth day of New Year; the smell of garbage assailed her nostrils. Cook was in the midst of preparing stinky tofu, immersing slabs of firm tofu in the brine made to her own recipe. The tofu would marinate in the brine for at least a week before being deep-fried, giving it a crisp skin and soft, creamy interior. Left for longer it developed a blackish tinge like mould, another of his favourite treats. Chan liked to eat his rice porridge accompanied by cubes of this stinky tofu, pickled vegetables and a spicy sauce. Every few months, Cook prepared a new batch of the smelly brine. To Yu Lan's nose it smelled worse than a combination of rotting vegetables, dead fish and sour milk.

'*Jou sahn*, Ah Yi,' she said, peering over Cook's shoulder while pinching her nose between two fingers.

'You seem very chirpy this morning. What's wrong? Are you sick?' barked Cook, scowling at the intrusion into her domain. If she had her way, no one would enter the kitchen without her express invitation.

'I think I'm feeling better at last.'

'Boss will be pleased.'

'I've decided there's no point being sad.'

'That's good to hear, girlie. You've wandered this house like a ghost for too long. You young people have too much time on your hands. Hard work is the answer.'

'You're very wise.'

The cook gave her a skeptical look. 'This is so, though not everyone recognises it. Now, what do you want? I'm not one of the *taitai*'s cronies. I don't have time to lounge around gossiping and drinking tea. And am I the only one who remembers that it's the fourth day?'

'The fourth day?'

'Yes, the fourth day! The Kitchen God will be back from Heaven today and I haven't had time to make the proper offerings. The *taitai* isn't much help. "Just offer what you think best," she says to me. Offer what I think best? Suddenly now she has a son she doesn't care about the gods,' the old woman grumbled. 'There's too much to do here and too many hungry mouths making too much work.'

The Kitchen God always disappeared from the household on the twenty-fourth day of the twelfth month to make his annual pilgrimage to Heaven, reporting to the Celestial Emperor on the family's behaviour for that year. Cook had sent him off with a bevy of cakes and wine to sweeten his report but now it was the fourth day of the New Year and he was due back.

'Perhaps I can help you. I could learn to make the tofu brine and save you the trouble. Chan Towkay has been so kind and patient with me. I'd like to do something to repay him and I know how much he likes your stinky tofu.'

Cook's eyes narrowed so that only a twinkle of keen brown irises showed beneath her wrinkled lids. Yu Lan wondered if the old woman suspected her motives. It was true; she didn't usually take an interest in Chan's likes or dislikes. Indeed, for months now she had taken little interest in anything.

'I smell more than tofu here. What are you up to, Sai Mui? You think you can steal my recipe and sell it to one of your hawker friends in Chinatown?'

Yu Lan blinked in horror. 'Aiya, Ay Yi! Do you think I would steal from you? Only a heartless person would do that. I want to do something special for the *towkay*, that's all.' She lowered her voice to a whisper. 'And my father has given me some herbs that are said to improve a man's... performance, his manly performance. I know you use herbs in the brine, I thought we might add them.'

'His manly performance, you say?' Cook asked, raising her eyebrows. 'He has got one son from you already.'

Yu Lan nodded. Then added with a sigh, 'Perhaps he tires of me. Or perhaps age is catching up with him for his Yang energy is... failing.'

'Age catches up with us all. This is true.'

'But there's no need to tell him. That would only cause embarrassment.'

She fought to hold the old woman's gaze without blinking as Cook considered her request. 'I promise I'll tell no one your recipe.'

'I learned to make this recipe from my mother, who learned from her mother going back many generations.'

'I understand how precious it is,' Yu Lan said with a smile.

The old woman sighed. 'But since I have no daughter to teach, perhaps it's time I taught someone or when I die my stinky tofu will die with me.'

Yu Lan thought that mightn't be such a bad thing but all she said was, 'That would be a great loss. I hope it will be a very long time before you die.'

'Hmmph, so you say. Well, it's about time for a new batch of brine. Come to me tomorrow and I'll teach you the secret method for making Aunty's special stinky tofu.'

'Thank you. I have much luck.'

*

THAT NIGHT SHE slept soundly for the first time since she'd been taken from her home above the shop on High Street, despite Kong letting off a volley of firecrackers in the middle of the night, something he had done each night since the eve of the lunar New Year. The *taitai* complained to her husband that it woke her, but Chan merely shook his head and said the driver was only letting off steam, and she was lucky they didn't live in Chinatown or she wouldn't get any sleep.

Yu Lan woke refreshed to golden light seeping around the curtains and the chatter of tiny geckoes on the ceiling. Springing from bed, she sluiced cold water over her body and dressed quickly. There was much to do today if she was to put her plan into action. She had let herself be tricked into accepting her lot in the Chan household, cowed into submission by the *towkay*'s power, the *taitai*'s haughtiness and her own paralysing sense of betrayal. Even the amah's friendship had coaxed her into submission. But she was older and wiser than the day she had crossed the threshold of the Chan mansion and offered tea to the *taitai*. She had been taken by a man. She had given birth to a son. She had survived many losses. Now for the first time, she knew that she didn't have to accept this life without question. She was imprisoned in the mansion, unable to leave without permission, but there were other ways to assert her power. If she was brave enough. If she had the will, she could defeat the woman who had stolen her future and in doing so, change all their destinies.

She hummed a snatch of song from *Snow in Midsummer* as she finished pinning up her hair.

'You sound happy, little sister,' said Ho Jie as she entered Yu Lan's room. 'And you have pinned up your braids.'

'I am. I have. I am a married woman now.' She paused before adding, 'Remember you promised you'd help me if something bad happened?'

'I remember,' Ho Jie said, dropping her gaze to the floor.

'Now I shall tell you how you'll do that.'

'Nothing bad is going to happen. You said yourself that you're happy.' The expression on the amah's face became more hopeful as she shifted her gaze upward again, but still she kept her head bowed.

'Because I know that you'll share my burden. That once I am gone you'll fight for me.' She smiled, reaching out a hand to raise the amah's chin so that their eyes met. 'You are my sister, my mother, my friend. You're the only one I trust, the only one who can avenge me.'

Although the amah nodded in silent agreement, Yu Lan saw that she didn't believe her, that she thought these words were another delusion. After the incident at the waterfall, Ah Jie had made it known to the entire household that her husband's concubine tried to leap to her death, and then accused the *taitai* of pushing her. If anything, the servants treated her even more circumspectly after that, for how could they believe the alternative: that their mistress had tried to murder her rival? Better to believe that the rival was unstable, made crazy by childbirth.

So she couldn't blame her friend for her reluctance. It was also true that during the month after the child's birth she had been lost, wandering in a dream world. The birth, the separation from her son and Madam's predatory ways had almost unhinged her so that for a time she couldn't find her way. Well, none of that mattered now. The entire household could believe her deluded and she wouldn't care because she knew the truth. She saw it in the *taitai*'s eyes every time her husband bestowed a gift or a kind word upon her, every time the boy smiled in her arms. Of this one fact she was certain: sooner or later Madam Chan would dispose of her. And she would never know when that day was coming.

She took a step closer so that she could whisper the plan in her friend's ear. 'If I should die, this is what you must do.'

*

YU LAN CLUTCHED a cloth sack as she skipped across the courtyard in the direction of the kitchen. The sack contained a selection of herbs from her father's apothecary shop. Although she had told her mother and Ho Jie that she was going to make a tonic to replenish her *qi* after the drain of pregnancy and childbirth, in fact there was nothing wrong with her *qi*. She could feel the energy buzzing through her body, the blood fizzing in her veins. She felt more alive than she had since… since that last day on bustling Petaling Street when Ming held her hand in his and vowed that they would be together one day. So no, she had no need of a tonic. She intended the herbs for a completely different purpose. She intended the herbs for Chan.

'Here you are,' said Cook as she entered the kitchen, which

at mid-morning was already simmering in the heat. The kitchen windows were barred but unglazed – allowing air to circulate – yet there would be no breeze until late afternoon. Even then, the heat would linger until late at night unless broken by a downpour. 'What have you got there?'

Although she was all too familiar with the bag's contents, Yu Lan opened it and peered inside, saying, 'A little wolfberry, dogwood fruit, wild yam, angelica root, cassia bark, plus some deer antler and dried seahorse to help restore the *towkay*'s Yang energy.' She didn't mention the final ingredient she had selected, the one she had ground to a powder between two large stones from the garden, not wanting to risk using Cook's heavy stone mortar and pestle. And not wanting Cook to question her about the ingredient, she had secreted it in a small drawstring pouch inside her pocket.

'I already include yam for his *qi*, cassia for his kidneys and angelica for his liver,' Cook said with cackle, jabbing Yu Lan in the side with a knowing elbow. 'An old warhorse still yearns to gallop a thousand *li*, eh?'

'You are very knowledgeable, Ah Yi. My father could use you in his shop.'

'You don't get to my age without learning a thing or two. And what I've learned is the body can't do its job without good stomach *qi*.'

'The Chan family has much luck with you in its kitchen.'

'Well, no time to stand here gossiping, let's get started.'

She watched as Cook lifted a stout green earthenware jar onto the table where other jugs, bowls and jars of ingredients waited in readiness.

'First we start with the whey from the tofu,' she said, pouring a clear yellowish liquid into the jar, a by-product of the tofu-making process. 'Next we add a handful of ginger slices, old ginger is best, so that when the brine is ready the ginger will be soft and mushy. Add some bamboo shoots, then some mustard greens and salt. Not too much or the brine will be too salty.'

Yu Lan knew that the preserved mustard greens were already salty, a favourite of her father with his lunchtime rice.

'Now we add the herbs,' Cook said, nodding at the sack. 'Show me what you have there.'

She tipped the contents of the cloth sack onto the kitchen table so that they formed a pile of dried sticks that might have been gathered from the forest floor.

'Hmm, we will have this and this and some of this.'

'And some deer antler?' She picked up a handful of the crisp brown slices.

'Are you sure you want to get the old man's juices flowing?' the old woman asked, raising one sparse grey eyebrow. 'More night-time work for you.'

'The *towkay* needs another son,' she said with a shrug. The old woman wouldn't question the will of the Chan ancestors.

'If you say so,' she said, nodding for Yu Lan to throw the deer antler into the pot before shuffling over to the kitchen trough where a parcel wrapped in newspaper sat. 'And now for the most important ingredient,' she said, unwrapping the smelly parcel to reveal a pile of old shrimp heads which she proceeded to sprinkle into the brine.

'Eee, that is disgusting,' Yu Lan said, trying not to breathe in.

'Wait until it has been fermenting a few months.' Taking a large wooden spoon, she gave the brine a good stir. 'Now we'll place it in the outside storeroom so we don't have to smell it while it does its work getting stinky.'

'Here, let me take it for you. It looks very heavy.'

'You think these skinny old arms are too weak? You young people think you're the only ones with any muscle. I could lift you, girlie, and toss you out the door if I wanted,' the old woman said, shaking a bony finger in Yu Lan's face.

'I have no doubt, but my mother would be ashamed of her daughter if I didn't offer.'

'Hmmph, that's all right then. Take the key from the hook by the back door, but close the storeroom after you or the monkeys will have a feast.'

Wrapping her arms around the jar, Yu Lan lifted it from the table, balancing it against one hip so that it didn't slip from her grasp. Then she stepped out into the back garden. A stone path led to the storeroom that was attached to the rear of the house with a separate outside entrance. When she reached the storeroom, she set the jar on the ground to unlock the door, before picking it up once more and edging carefully inside. Without windows, the room was dark, the only light coming from the open door. She ducked under a meat safe hanging at head level, squeezing between shelves groaning with preserved goods, dried goods and seldom-used utensils. Finally, finding a space on one shelf wide enough to house the jar of brine, she set it down.

She stood looking at the tall green jar for some moments. In the dim light, the jar's bulbous shape might almost have been a funerary urn, glowering there on the shelf. Feeling in her pocket, she closed her fingers around the pouch. There was still time to change her mind if she chose. She could accept the fate the gods had dealt her. She could remain a pawn of the Chan ancestors. But why should she suffer alone when she could be like Dou E and force others to share her pain?

Withdrawing the pouch from her pocket, she opened her hand so that it rested on her palm in an innocuous silken mound. Then, taking a deep breath, she unknotted the drawstring and upended the pouch, shaking it slightly so that brown powder rained into the brine like a death sentence.

Chan su. Toad venom. Enough to stop a heart in its tracks.

39

IT WAS THE sixth day of the Year of the Monkey and the Chans had departed for the temple to pray for good fortune in the coming year. Later in the afternoon they would visit friends, taking gifts of sweets and golden mounds of citrus fruits. Although it was too hot to grow citrus in Malaya, oranges and mandarins were auspicious gifts at New Year and the wealthy imported them by the crate-load from China. Ho Jie accompanied her employers to fetch and carry, while Yu Lan escaped that duty by pleading tiredness from a vigorous session with Chan the previous night. She had learned that this excuse appealed to his vanity.

The *taitai* wanted to take her 'little dragon' along to show him off to her friends, but that would have meant dragging the wet nurse along, and her husband vetoed the idea. Besides, the boy had a powerful set of lungs and while Chan loved him, he loved him better safely tucked in the nursery and out of his hearing. At New Year, when the cry of a child could bring bad luck to the entire family, he wasn't taking chances.

Yu Lan stood at the top of the stairs listening. Downstairs the kitchen was silent, the charcoal stove cold. Cook had worked like a demon these last two weeks, gearing up for the banquet on the first night and all the feasting that followed. Today she had gone visiting, off to see her nephew and his family at the tiny sundries shop they ran on Batu Road, taking a lacquered 'tray of togetherness' brimming with sweet treats like candied lotus root and winter melon, roasted watermelon seeds and dried coconut.

The house was strangely still. Only the occasional birdcall disturbed the silence.

Yu Lan padded along the upstairs corridor to the master bedroom at the front of the house and pushed open the door. Even empty, the room felt as if the *taitai* was still in residence. The smell of her perfume and the gel Ho Jie used on her hair hung in the air. Her possessions dominated every surface and shelf. Tall, glass-fronted cabinets displayed her collections of jewellery and her most precious porcelain; embroidered silk bags and chain-mail purses hung from a coat stand; the dressing table was covered in face creams and hair tonics; and everywhere there were mirrors so that she could always be assured she looked her best.

Yu Lan trailed a hand along the gilded edge of the dressing table until it came to rest upon a tray of hair combs: silver filigree, tortoiseshell, and the intricately carved red ivory of the helmeted hornbill. Ah Jie did not care that the poor creatures died so that she could decorate her head with their casques. She picked up one of the combs and examined the finely detailed carvings of animals and plants. The comb was beautiful, but how much more beautiful were the living animals, soaring high above the forest. Not high enough to escape the hunter's rifle.

Leaving the close and shuttered air of the *taitai*'s room, she drifted next door to the nursery. The wet nurse was deeply asleep when she entered, no doubt resting from the night-time feeds. Yu Lan smelled a trace of Shalimar lingering about the child's crib in an invisible haze of vanilla and citrus. She tiptoed across the room to stand by the crib and look down upon her sleeping son. He was stretched out on his back, bundled loosely in a cotton blanket with only his arms freed. He was so beautiful, this child she had produced with Chan's seed. Sometimes when she stood by the crib and watched him sleeping she thought if she could only take him far away from the mansion, she might find a way to love him. Her little no-name boy, for she couldn't bear to think of him by the name he had been given. Wei Long was too large a name for so small a being. Chan might wish for his son to become a great dragon, lording it over others, but she would prefer that he grew to be a kind man who let others live their lives in freedom. She knew now that freedom was the most precious gift of all, even more precious than love. Love could be its own form of slavery.

Trying not to wake him, she reached out a tentative finger to stroke one cheek, the colour of raw silk. When he was awake he never rested easily in her arms, always kicking and pummelling his fists to escape back to his wet nurse or Big Mother. Yu Lan would hand him back half-relieved, yet also devastated that he preferred someone else. Big Mother. How she hated that title. Yet her son seemed to sense from birth that it was Madam Chan to whom he owed filial love and allegiance, not her. Not his little mother. She was only the vessel who had given him life, whereas the Chans owned him. He would be shackled to them for ever. Even in death he would be forced to listen to that family's selfish prayers. Expected to intercede in their paltry concerns. He would never escape.

'Unless you help him,' whispered the voice in her head.

It wouldn't be difficult, she supposed, not with so small a child.

'The boy will barely make a sound. You can go quietly together, somewhere she can't follow.'

Yes, somewhere safe. Somewhere free.

'He would thank you for it if he could speak.'

It would be a simple thing to lift him from the crib, press him against her chest and hold him there until he grew still. She could turn him on his stomach and push his face into the mattress, oh so gently, until he was silent. Or she could immerse him gently in the deep tub of cool water in the bathroom and wait. None of these methods seemed painful to her, not for so small a being.

'Swiftest would be best,' said the voice.

Yet how might she know which that would be? Her finger traced the line of his cheek, coming to rest on the rosebud mouth, so unlike his father's. In his sleep, his lips parted slightly and he began sucking, pulling her finger into his mouth. And as he suckled she remembered the feel of his mouth locked to her nipple that day in the jungle, how surprised she had been at the strength of those tiny jaws, at his hunger for life. Would he hunger so for life, she wondered, if he knew what it might bring?

'If you leave him, they will make him one of them.'

She couldn't bear that thought. Picking him up, she held him to her chest, making sure she didn't scratch his face with the toggles of her *cheongsam*. He was so light, a scrap of a boy. How could she leave him behind to be ruined by the Chans? To be fashioned into one of them. Better to take him now before it was too late to save him. She held him tighter, cradling the back of his head with one hand. His skull seemed as fragile as an egg beneath her fingers, almost bald but for a few tufts of hair on his crown with his baby hair shorn away.

He wriggled, tiny knees knocking against her stomach,

button nose inhaling silk. She relaxed her arms a little, allowing him more room to move. She would take him for a walk while she decided. Let him survey his domain.

Down the stairs and into the courtyard, where she stopped to let him catch a ray of sun on his face. Madam screamed if she discovered one of them had subjected his pale baby skin to the midday sun. She wouldn't let her son grow brown like a coolie. Yu Lan lifted the boy from her body and raised him high so that his face was lit from above.

'See, the sun can't hurt you.'

He blinked open his eyes, looking up at the sky.

'You won't find any gods up there, only birds.' He smiled at her then. Three months old and already he was a heartbreaker.

Turning, she padded across the tiles and into the reception hall where Ah Jie had greeted her on that first day. Guan Yin stared down at them, with her shiny porcelain gaze, daring them to invade her domain. Holding the boy with one arm, Yu Lan filched a green and white *kuih* from the altar and bit into it, relishing the sweet coconut flavour on her tongue. The boy followed her movements with his eyes.

'Would you like some?' Ah Jie had forbidden them feeding the boy solids, saying at three months he was too young.

She broke off a piece of the soft *kuih* and held it to his mouth, watching curiously as he opened his lips expectantly, then hesitated before closing his mouth around the squishy morsel. For a moment nothing happened. Then he appeared to make up his mind and she watched as his whole mouth and tongue went to work consuming the *kuih*. Squeezing his eyes shut, he shook his head from side to side.

'You don't like it?'

He strained to move his upper body towards the *kuih* in her hand.

'You do like it.'

She fed him another two small pieces until there was none left, then settling him on her hip, carried him through the double doors to the drawing room. Here was the room where Madam had sat her silk-upholstered backside on her silk-upholstered armchair and waited to be served tea by her husband's new *chieh*. And here was the study where the *towkay* kept his money locked in two large iron safes. Then crossing the courtyard once more, fragrant with the scent of potted gardenias, she carried the boy through to the hall where his ancestors presided.

She saw at once that someone had neglected to close the French windows so that only a row of vertical bars kept the outside world at bay. And squatting on the grass beyond the open window was a macaque. It saw them enter but didn't make any move to retreat, even when she took a step towards it. Rather, it bared its teeth in a silent grimace. Suddenly, her son began working his arms, waving them in the air and making gurgling sounds, his eyes dancing. She followed his bright-eyed gaze to the altar where a smaller monkey perched on its haunches, its tail dangling over the edge of the ancestral shrine between two delicate porcelain cups. It was feasting on mandarin, watched impassively by Chan's ancestors, and flicking peel onto the tiles below.

The monkey turned at the sound of the baby's laughter, frozen for a moment in indecision – whether to risk remaining and be captured by the intruders or to abandon the fruit for safety. She could see the animal's thought processes at work as it glanced sideways towards the window, then back to the fruit, its face dominated by large green-brown eyes, close together and framed by a mask-like face. At a long shrill bark from the mother it grabbed one last mandarin from the golden mound of offerings, leaped from the altar and scampered through the bars to safety. Then both monkeys took off across the grass into the jungle.

As she watched her son watching the monkey, she knew that she would not take him with her. Despite the voice's urging, he had a right to live his life. Who was she to take that from him? Her son had made his choice. He had chosen life and she couldn't steal that from him. He would have to stay and take his chances with the Chans and the ancestors. But it would end there. She could at least free him from that eternal duty. Despite the wooden plaque above the shrine exhorting her to 'recall the past', he would have this life and then he would have to make his own way in the afterlife, with no descendants feeding him with offerings and plaguing him for his help. He would never become an ancestor.

There would be no more Chans. One way or another she would make sure of that, if she had to consort with all the demons of hell to bring it to pass. She would curse the tree of their line so that it shrivelled. And when there were no more Chans on this earth there would be no one to make offerings to the *towkay* and his wife, no one to light incense for their souls. Once their bodies had turned to dust and bone, their spirits would wither and die. And then there would be an end to them all.

40

MADAM'S LITTLE DRAGON was perched on her lap, banging a china spoon on the table, when Ho Jie entered the dining room carrying a plate of stir-fried longevity noodles. The boy smiled at her entrance, his tongue protruding slightly from his mouth as he began making gurgling noises. Whether at her or the steaming plate of noodles, Ho Jie wasn't sure. She suspected the latter.

'Where is that lazy girl this morning?' Madam Chan asked, frowning at the plate of noodles. As soon as the dish was set down in front of her she began picking at it with her chopsticks to check that Cook hadn't cut the noodles in the preparation. The long uncut noodles symbolised longevity, and she wouldn't stand for anyone cutting short her life, not even symbolically. 'I knew we shouldn't have left her alone here yesterday. It has made her even lazier.'

'I have yet to see her this morning, Madam.'

'Go and wake her. The *towkay* was asking after her. Now he's left for the mine in a bad mood. So you can blame her if he comes home shouting at everyone.'

'She hasn't been sleeping well. Her dreams disturb her.' Some mornings Ho Jie had to call her three times before she finally emerged from her bed. All her *qi* was being drained from her.

'What nonsense. The girl sleeps too much. And when she isn't sleeping, she drifts about getting in busy people's way. If I put her to work in the garden, digging out weeds, she'd soon sleep better. A few blisters would give her something to moan about.'

Ho Jie thought that Sai Mui would probably enjoy working in the garden with the old Tamil gardener. Better than being shut up inside the mansion with eyes always watching her. But she didn't answer her mistress, keeping her face impassive and her tongue silent. She knew that silence annoyed the *taitai* more than anything.

'And I'm considering what arrangements to make once Wei Long is weaned and the wet nurse returns to the *kampung*,' she continued, flicking a sideways glance at Ho Jie. 'The concubine is useless. She doesn't know one end of a baby from the other, so there's no point expecting her to help with him. Besides, with luck we won't have to put up with her much longer.'

What did she mean, that Sai Mui might not be with them much longer? Where might she be going?

'I think I'll employ a second amah to take responsibility for baby so that you can devote yourself to me. Perhaps you can think of someone. One of your sworn sisters?'

Ho Jie felt a sharp pain in her breast. Take the boy away from her and give him to a stranger? Caring for the boy was the brightest point of her day.

'Is Sai Mui going somewhere, Madam?'

'Somewhere far away, I hope, once the *towkay* comes to his senses. Or if he doesn't, I might have to take matters into my own hands. Then there will be one less useless mouth to feed around here.' She stretched her own mouth into a thin-lipped smile, her eyes glittering with malice. 'Yesterday I saw her putting dried rhubarb root in my tea. If I hadn't caught her I would still be shitting. Who knows what she might do next.'

For all that the *towkay* doted on the mother of his son and her nubile flesh, Ho Jie knew that a sharp tongue could kill without a knife. The mistress had many an opportunity to whisper cutting words in his ear. More and more she grew convinced that the girl was right, the Chan mansion held great danger. If only she could help her escape to safety. But although she might save the money required for a passage to Hong Kong, given a few months, she feared that would not be enough time. Madam Chan's eyes told her that, even more than her words. Even if there was time, she didn't know whether she could persuade the girl to leave without her son. And if she attempted to take him with her, Chan would move heaven and earth to find them and bring them back. She would never be free.

Engrossed in her thoughts, she felt a sudden acute pain shoot through her leg and looked down to see the *taitai*'s nails gouging her thigh through the black cotton of her trousers. The fingers were spread wide in an arched semicircle, resembling a cat's claws hooking into her flesh.

'What are you standing there for? Go and wake the girl!' She twisted away, returning her attention to the boy, who was nestled on her lap, held securely by her other arm. He was batting his spoon in the air and kicking his legs as he gurgled happily. 'U gu gu… u… u… what is my little dragon saying? What does Big Mother's big boy want? What does Big Mother's big boy need?' she cooed, tickling his stomach with her claw.

Ho Jie knew what the boy needed. He needed his mother.

*

ALL WAS SILENT beyond the door to the concubine's chamber. Little wonder that the girl slept late. Bad dreams haunted her sleeping hours so that she emerged each morning with dark circles shadowing her eyes. Sometimes she spoke of voices that whispered to her in the night and Ho Jie would remind her of the old saying that 'Thoughts during the day will become dreams at night'. If only she would let go of her fears and desires, she could restore the harmony between her *qi* and her blood. Too much emotion was bound to cause disease. If only she could quiet her demons and accept her new life, she might stumble upon the path to happiness. And if she accepted this life, surely Madam Chan would leave her be, secure in the knowledge that she would always be Big Mother, that she would always be number one in her husband's affections.

She sighed. She might wish that Sai Mui could accept her life, but she knew it was unlikely. The girl was too fragile to think clearly. Ho Jie longed to comfort her, but didn't know how. Short of escape, she couldn't see a way clear.

She was about to turn the door handle when she felt a faint breeze ruffle the tiny hairs on the back of her neck. She swung around, searching for the source of the breeze, but there were no open windows in the corridor and the doors to the other chambers were closed. Perhaps a stray wind had entered the house below and snuck up the stairs behind her. But she remembered only still morning air as she crossed the courtyard and ascended the staircase to the first floor, air warm with the promise of the hot sting to come.

She hesitated a little longer. Without knowing the cause of her anxiety, she felt her breath catching in her lungs. Her hand froze on the door handle.

'Ho Jie!' shouted Madam Chan below stairs. 'What are you doing up there! Do I need to rid myself of you too?'

This threat galvanised her into action so that she forced the dead weight of her hand to turn the knob and inch the door open a crack. It was the odour that assailed her first, the rank stink of faeces with an underlying sickly sweet scent. She felt the ripple of breeze circling her head, whipping up stray tendrils of hair from her bun, and a tingle of energy coursed through her body. The smell was as potent a warning as a growling dog. It said, 'Stay away. Do not enter.'

The need to know warred with the fear of finding out. She pushed the door open a touch more, revealing a glimpse of shining parquetry and one of Madam's red ivory combs lying forgotten on the floor. Then a little further, so that the shiny brass bedhead came into view, framed by its embroidered silk flounces. For a moment she blinked, not wanting to discover what lay upon the bed. When she opened her eyes, she saw only the empty folds of a quilt. Fighting to draw breath, she edged the door open more so that she could see past the end of the bed and halfway across the room. For a split second her eyes refused to understand what lay before her, seeing only the red, pink and gold hangings draped from the four-poster bed, a rich mélange of silk and auspicious animals. Then her mind registered what her eyes revealed and she knew that her life would never be the same again.

*

THE SCREAM RESOUNDED through the house on one long note of agony, setting Madam Chan's teeth on edge and the baby to whimpering. But by the time she swept up the stairs clutching the babe in her arms, the screams had faded to a pathetic keening even more hideous to her ears. It occurred to her then that from the day the concubine arrived, the Chan mansion had suffered an excess of emotion, strong feelings permeating every corner of the house, from the ancestral hall to the kitchen. Even Madam Chan's bedchamber was suffused with tension where once she and her husband were in perfect accord. He gave orders and she pretended to follow them, just as a marriage should be. But ever since the girl had stepped across the threshold, garbed in her hideous white mourning clothes, an aura of disquiet had descended upon them, disrupting the house's calm and orderly functioning and replacing it with turmoil. She had warned her husband that too much feeling was bound to bring trouble, but the girl had made him soft, even while she made his member hard.

'That stupid girl is scared of her own shadow. It's likely just a spider,' she told herself, even while knowing that no spider could prompt such a dreadful wailing. 'And what is that lazy amah doing about it? Nothing.' Madam Chan was the only person in the house who could be counted on to sniff out problems and order someone to fix them. Left to their own devices, the servants would sleep through fire and flood, and then wonder why they had become ghosts, left to scavenge on the food of the living.

As if they had heard her thoughts, Cook appeared on the stairs brandishing a chopper from the kitchen and the bleary-eyed wet nurse poked her head around the nursery door.

'What is it, Madam? Is there a murderer in the house?' asked Cook.

'Stupid woman. It is only a spider or a snake that has got inside. Wait there. And don't chop anything unless I tell you to.'

Holding the boy to her chest she glided along the corridor towards the moaning sounds, wishing for once that her husband hadn't set off for the mine so early. Usually she was relieved to have him gone, and with him his constant demand for attention, but now she regretted his absence.

She saw that the door to the concubine's chamber stood ajar, and as she drew closer she became aware of an unpleasant odour leaking from the room. Halting a few feet from the open door, she was suddenly conscious of her full bladder and suspected that whatever lay behind the door wouldn't be solved with a barked order and a pinch on the buttocks. Perhaps it would be better to wait for Chan's return, or at the least the return of the driver with the car. Then again, distant water did not put out a nearby fire. She must tackle the problem now or it would surely worsen and neither her ears nor her nose would stand for that.

The keening had become muffled now, as if someone had put a pillow over the wailer's mouth. Madam Chan ventured closer, unintentionally leaning forward onto her toes. She prodded open the door with her free elbow and stood to survey the scene before her.

The amah knelt at the foot of the bed and from her the wailing issued. She had buried her face in a drift of red silk, clutching at the concubine's dangling legs. At first Madam Chan didn't care to look upwards. She concentrated her gaze on the distraught form of her servant, hunched around the legs of the concubine, her hair torn from its neat bun and escaping down her back. Her body shook with the effort of so much wailing and weeping, most unlike the woman's usual haughty dignity. She noticed that the concubine's bare heels brushed the shiny brass rail of the bed-end and the white sleeves of the servant's tunic were stained brown. She saw that the girl had chosen to wear her husband's New Year gift, the red silk *cheongsam* he had ordered made for her. Her husband's generosity had been thrown back in his face. After all they had done for her, this is how the ungrateful girl repaid them. Madam Chan felt the beginnings of rage stir in her abdomen and the bitter taste of bile rise in her throat.

Conscious of the weight of her son on her hip, she placed her free hand upon the back of his warm, furry head and held him against her breast. No matter his age, she didn't want the child to see what was before them. It was enough that she must endure a sight that might scar the boy for life. She braced herself to look up. Not only had the evil girl chosen to hang herself from the conjugal bed, she had purloined one of its corded tassels to carry out the task. A silken cord was looped high beneath her jaw, a knot gouging into her flesh on the left side of her neck. The cord strained so tight from the weight of her body that it would have swiftly cut off the circulation of blood and air, halting the essential flow of *qi*. The concubine was long dead. Her tongue protruded from her mouth in a grotesque manner and dark red lesions spotted her face around the eyes.

She resembled a demon.

She *was* a demon. An evil, vengeful spirit.

Everyone knew that a hanged woman in a red dress desired to avenge herself on those she believed had wronged her. Everyone knew that a hanged woman would return to haunt those who had angered her. Those she couldn't overcome in life she would torment in death, bringing evil luck down upon them and destroying them.

Madam Chan knew exactly who the concubine blamed for her unhappiness. That despicable, ungrateful, ignorant girl. She would be the ruin of them all.

41

SAI MUI WAS looking even paler than usual. If Ho Jie didn't know better she would swear that the concubine had been experimenting with Madam's cosmetics. Yet as the girl drew near, she saw that far from suffocating under heavy dusting from Madam's face powder, her skin glowed with translucent light like the finest porcelain teacup. She glided closer to Ho Jie's bedside, the long white sleeves of her tunic drifting behind her, and parted the fine mesh of the mosquito net to look down upon her friend.

'Ho Jie,' she whispered, so close now that Ho Jie could smell the sweet perfume of her breath, like too-ripe fruit that fizzed on the tongue.

'Where have you been, little one? I've been looking for you everywhere.'

'I had to go away.'

Ho Jie thought of the baby, trapped in her employer's arms. 'The boy cries for you.'

'You may cry for me, but my son has another mother.'

Ho Jie searched for her friend's hand amongst the bedclothes. 'Why did you leave us?' she said, when she couldn't find it amongst the girl's floating white draperies. Why did you leave me? she left unsaid.

'My husband's wife wanted me gone. Now she has what she wanted.'

'Did she send you away?' she asked, but the girl didn't answer.

She had her secrets still. 'The *towkay* pines for you,' she ventured instead.

'He won't mourn long.' Sai Mui laughed and Ho Jie saw that her tongue was black in her mouth. She noticed too the necklace of purple hiding beneath the high white collar of her tunic.

'What has happened to you, little one? You don't look well. You need to take better care of yourself,' she said, longing to hold the girl in her arms and make her better.

'I'm hungry. Will you feed me?'

'I'll go to the kitchen and make you a bowl of noodles.' Ho Jie's culinary skills were basic but noodles she could manage.

'It's not noodles that I need.'

'What do you need, little one?'

'You know what I need. You know what you promised.'

Yes, she remembered her promise, and she remembered the red comb lying forgotten on the floor of the concubine's chamber. Red, like poor Sai Mui's dress. Madam didn't forget lightly either. She didn't forget her possessions and she didn't lose them. She knew the location of everything she owned.

Something must have happened for her to relinquish one of her belongings, something terrible enough for her to leave it behind.

*

SLEEP DIDN'T COME easily in the days following the concubine's death. Some might imagine Madam Chan mourned the girl's death. But does the fox mourn the death of a rabbit? Does the tiger grieve the murder of the deer? She was happy the girl was gone and yet... she feared what might take her place.

Most evenings, she resorted to a nip of Hooper and Sons

Universal Household Medicine to send her off into dreamland, so that she woke each morning with a dry mouth and a heavy head. It was worth it to keep the grotesque images of the hanged concubine from haunting her. Instead of fending off demons in her imagination, she drifted into sleep on a pillow of happy calm. Yet despite the medication, the last few nights she had found herself waking in the early hours, disturbed by something or someone.

It was a feather-light touch to her cheek that dragged her from her dreams that night, the sensation of soft fingers tracing the bones of her face from temple to jaw. Yet she blinked open her eyes to silence. Not a footstep to be heard. An out-flung arm quickly assured her that Chan lay dead to the world beside her. She swung her gaze about the bedchamber, looking for intruders. In the dim light, the room was furnished with nothing but shadows, none of which moved. Only a stray breeze entered from an open window. She could see no intruders. But still there was a sense that someone had been standing by her bed just moments before. The thought was like insects crawling upon her skin.

She rose and stumbled across the room, her hands outstretched to find her way around occasional tables and chairs in the dark. Her mind felt groggy with sleep and the effects of Hooper and Sons remedy, yet she was sure she had closed the windows before bed. Despite the stuffy heat trapped in the room, she had taken to keeping them closed at night. Chan complained that he woke drenched in sweat but he humoured her with a grunt when she pleaded for a just a little longer. Until she could be sure they were safe.

Outside, the frail light of stars lit the grounds, leeching the jungle of colour, and turning the dew-soaked lawn to a grey shimmer. She looked out over the roof of the portico, through the ornamental palms and the candlenut tree to the thick mass of jungle beyond. Nothing moved except the shy flutter of leaves in the warm night air. She relaxed the hand that gripped the window ledge. Perhaps she had been dreaming after all. But wait… what was that? Something floated like a ribbon of white in the periphery of her vision, teasing her. A wisp of ill-wishing clutched at her heart and she turned to confront it. But whatever it was, it had gone.

'Chan,' she hissed. 'Chan, wake up.'

Across the room her husband answered her with a groan. She tripped back to the bed and shook him roughly by the shoulder.

'Chan,' she hissed again, 'there's something moving out there.'

'Go back to sleep. You're dreaming.'

'I wasn't dreaming. I saw it through the window.'

'There are many things moving outside that window. There's a jungle outside that window. A jungle with animals.'

'It was a ghost, I know it. We must call a priest to perform an exorcism.'

'Go back to sleep, woman. You're making yourself sick with this talk of ghosts and you're giving me a headache,' he said, turning his back on her and pulling the covers up over his head. But Chan didn't understand the danger. He hadn't been there. He hadn't felt the malevolence in the room the day of the concubine's death. Her husband was more concerned with earthly foes.

It was up to her to protect their family from the unseen. To protect their son.

Feeling her way around the bed, she let herself out of the

door onto the upstairs corridor that encircled the air well, open to the stars. The amah and her son slept in the small room next to hers. She drifted along the passage and turned the handle to the nursery to see that the narrow bed beneath the window lay empty. The woman was gone.

Crossing the room in three short strides, she peered down into the boy's crib, fearful of what she might find there. What if the concubine had returned for him? What if she had stolen him away to the spirit world? But the boy was there; dark lashes feathering his cheeks, tiny thumb in his mouth. Beneath the surge of love that swelled her heart at this sight, she felt a niggle of irritation that her strong dragon was becoming a thumb-sucker. No matter. He was safe and all was well. That greedy amah was probably pilfering food in the kitchen. She should be as fat as a pig with the amount she ate.

She was about to return to her bed when some instinct stalled her. She stood by the crib searching the room. But there was nothing out of the ordinary to be seen. She heard the soft chirp of a gecko nearby but other than that there was silence. Still, there was a hint of wrongness in the air. Something she couldn't quite put her finger on. Something that made the hairs on her arms rise and her heart beat a little quicker without consciously knowing why. And then she knew that what disturbed her was a smell that permeated the room. The sweet scent of flowers, of jasmine and rose. The foul stench of the concubine's perfume, given to her by Madam's doting husband.

42

KNEELING BEFORE THE ancestral altar, Madam Chan kowtowed three times before creaking upright and placing the joss sticks in a bowl. Her knees had been giving her problems for weeks. It must be all the additional bowing and scraping. She had stepped up her obligations in the three months since the concubine's death, offering prayers day and night to her husband's venerable ancestors. And on the first and fifteenth days of each month, she loaded the offering table with so much fruit that it was in danger of collapsing under the weight. Chan complained that his ancestors couldn't possibly consume so much food and the fruit would spoil before they could eat half of it. But she knew that you could never have too much insurance where ghosts were concerned.

He hadn't been in the room the day the concubine cursed them for ever. Kong had hauled her body down from its gruesome rigging before returning to collect his master from the mine. Her husband hadn't seen the girl's face, her eyes bulging, her tongue poking in their faces, mocking all their kindness. Unlike her, he didn't wake in the middle of the night to the feeling that someone was in the room with them. He didn't spy a flicker of movement in the corner of his eye and turn to find no one there. He didn't catch a whiff of the concubine's perfume on entering an empty room. The hairs on his arms didn't lift in fear at every stray breeze.

Chan didn't believe that the girl would return to haunt them. All he knew was that his poor *chieh* had taken her life in a fit of desperate sadness. Clearly, she had never recovered properly after the birth of their son. Her soul was too fragile for this world. He insisted that she be dressed in white silk for the funeral. He even shed tears over her body as it lay in the reception hall for the required three days and nights.

But Madam Chan knew that the concubine meant them harm, and she was convinced that only the ancestors could protect them. There were spirits everywhere. They roamed the earth causing mischief for humans, but in the nether world they themselves were subject to the whims of greater spirits. If their descendants neglected them, they wouldn't have the wherewithal to feed and protect themselves in the next realm and would wander hungry and adrift. But if their descendants made offerings and prayers to help them, then the ancestors in turn would protect their earthly offspring from evil. It was a reasonable bargain for all concerned.

Madam Chan was a devout wife and daughter-in-law. For years she had kowtowed daily to her husband's ancestors. She had burned paper money to smooth their way in the afterlife. She had offered them the finest food and drink to ease their hunger. And in return she expected them to intervene with the gods on her behalf and bring her family good fortune. Now her skin pricked with disquiet and every hair on her body told her that she needed that protection urgently.

'Haven't I fed you until you could eat no more? Haven't I kept cups brimming with whiskey and wine? Haven't I lit so much incense that I have a permanent cough?' she pleaded with the implacable faces looking down from above the altar. 'Now I need your help. Without it we are all doomed.'

Her devotions complete, she kowtowed once more for good measure before turning towards the dining room to join Chan at his breakfast. Like every other morning, the day was already warm with the promise of the heat to come. Nevertheless, she felt a breeze ruffle the full skirt of the Western-style dress she had donned that morning. Ripples of cool air stroked her skin. She shivered, rubbing her hands up and down her bare arms. Despite her uneasiness, she swung back towards the open windows where heavy drapes belled in the breeze. Something wicked was coming.

The jungle formed a natural border around the Chan property. The garage housing the Chevrolet and its chauffeur squatted over by the boundary, a gravel drive leading from that building to the front gates. And between the drive and the house lay an expanse of broad-leafed lawn and a scattering of fruit trees. There was a clump of banana trees, green fronds waving in the breeze, a single papaya tree standing tall, crowned with orbs of unripe fruit, and under the spreading branches of the mango trees darted a figure in white, its head brushed by low-hanging branches. With wide white sleeves billowing and long black hair whipped by the wind, her husband's concubine flitted barefoot through the trees and disappeared into the jungle.

She clutched her chest. Surely her heart must stop. It was a wonder she hadn't fainted dead at the sight. After all, she was thirty-five years of age and her heart wasn't as sturdy as it used to be. She wished now that she had listened to Ho Jie and let the amah place the concubine's dragon bracelet in the coffin with the mirror and paper travel money for the afterworld. But she had let jealousy have sway and kept it for herself. Now she realised that keeping the bracelet may have been an unwise economy when dealing with a demon.

She took another tortured breath. But her mouth, when she opened it to cry out, was so dry that nothing emerged but a strangled squeak. She tossed a cup of the ancestors' whiskey down her throat – the appearance of the ghost called for extraordinary measures – and tried again.

'Chan! Chan!' she shouted as she ran for the dining room where her husband awaited his breakfast. 'The *neuih gwai*. I told you she was haunting us. And now I have seen her.'

Aiya, whatever would they do? Once a *neuih gwai* latched onto you she would steal all your luck. She would devour your *qi*. She would haunt you until someone hanged in her place. Well, no matter what happened, Madam Chan was determined that the 'someone' wouldn't be her.

'Chan! Chan!'

Her husband looked up from his breakfast with a frown. 'Can't a man eat his breakfast in peace?' he asked, lifting a cube of tofu to his lips with his chopsticks. A half-eaten plate of stinky tofu was set in front of him alongside a steaming bowl of rice porridge. Madam Chan wondered how he could eat at a time like this, when a ghost had entered their lives and their entire future was at stake.

'The *neuih gwai* is here. I told you that girl meant us harm. I told you she was still lurking in the house. I can feel her.'

'What are you talking about?'

'I have seen her. Just now, under the mango trees in the garden.'

Chan did not pause in his eating; slurping down a spoonful of porridge followed by another cube of tofu while Madam Chan's hands trembled with the desire to throw something at him.

'What would she be doing under the mango trees?'

'I don't know what she was doing under the mango trees. She is a ghost. They have their reasons.' She clenched her fists at her sides and took a deep breath. Why was he fixated on mango trees? Didn't he understand the danger they were in?

'You're still in shock. We all are. It was a terrible death. But you will get over it now we are done mourning.'

'Yes, I'm in shock. I'm in shock because I saw the *neuih gwai*.' As she watched him dip the smelly tofu in Cook's spicy sauce, popping it into his mouth and swallowing with a satisfied smile, she found herself wishing he might choke on it. Yes, that was an idea. Perhaps Chan's death would placate the ghost. Perhaps if her husband were to die the girl would leave them alone. She and Wei Long could get on with their lives without vengeful ghosts or tyrannical husbands dogging their lives. She would have the ordering of the household and the mines and no one to consider except her baby son.

But no, she pushed the thought from her mind. She didn't really wish her husband dead, not even to placate a ghost. She was merely angry that he didn't acknowledge the urgency of their situation. Most men were like children where the spirit world was concerned; too seduced by the material world to realise they were at the mercy of unseen forces. She must be patient with him.

'It was probably washing blown from the line,' he muttered, his words gagged by a mouthful of tofu.

'The washing hasn't been hung out yet.'

'A monkey then. A big one.'

'I think I know a monkey from a *neuih gwai*, husband.'

'Aiya, woman! What do you want from me? Haven't you tortured me enough? Didn't you mistreat the girl in your jealousy so that she took her own life? Didn't you steal that one small happiness from me?' he said, bits of white spittle shooting from his mouth.

'I gave that girl every consideration. I gave her the second-best room in the house. I gave her an expensive brass bed shipped all the way from England. But it wasn't enough. She wanted more. She wanted everything.' She could hear her voice growing shrill even as she sought to stay calm.

'But she is dead, woman! Murdered by you. Or if you didn't kill her, you drove her to it. And now you would taint even her memory. Leave her be. You have the boy to yourself now.'

He stood abruptly, almost knocking the porridge to the floor. His face was suffused with red, his jaw wild with rage as he threw his chopsticks in her direction so that they hit her chest before clattering to the tiles. She took a step backwards in surprise. For all his bluster, he had never thrown anything at her before. He reserved that for the servants. And how could he believe that she had murdered the girl?

'What more do you want?' he screamed, his features contorted in an expression as ferocious as any temple guardian.

What did she want? What did she want? She wanted her husband to recognise the evil in the girl. She wanted him to help cast her out. From the moment the concubine entered their house she had intended harm. She had set husband and wife at odds with each other. She had sought to steal Chan's love. Oh, she seemed so soft and stupid but it was all an act. In reality she was cunning as a fox, as fierce as a dragon. If only Madam Chan had seen it in time she would never have brought her into their lives. But she was blinded by such longing for a son that she didn't stop to think things through. She ached for her precious little dragon.

And then, when the girl accepted that she would never defeat her rival in life, she chose to triumph in death. Madam Chan looked over at her husband, searching for the words to make him understand. His face, which had been red with anger, now looked pale and clammy, a sheen of cold sweat filming his forehead.

'You've made me ill, Old Woman, with your carping,' he groaned, clutching his stomach and bending forward. His shoulders heaved and Madam Chan watched in astonishment as a thick gush of yellow liquid spilled from his mouth.

'Cook!' she screamed. 'Ho Jie! Come quickly.' She rushed to her husband's side, throwing one arm around his waist and attempting to lower him to the chair, but he moaned and heaved once again, vomiting the vile stuff into his porridge.

'My stomach. Tell Kong to fetch the doctor,' he rasped, collapsing forward so that his head rested on the table, cradled by one arm.

'Cooook!' She held her husband by both shoulders, fearful that without her support he might slip from the chair to the floor. Her nose inhaled fumes of stinky tofu mingled with vomit.

Cook shuffled into the dining room, sniffing the air and screwing up her nose as she wiped wet hands on a cloth. 'What is it, Madam?'

'The *towkay* is ill. Tell Ah Kong to bring the doctor.'

'I told the boss he has too much heatiness in his stomach, but will he listen to an old woman?' she said, shaking her head in resignation at his stubbornness.

'Hurry, woman!'

'With so much heatiness in his system, no wonder he is angry,' Cook muttered. Then she nodded in agreement with herself before heading back towards the kitchen, and the path to the garage.

Chan groaned again, his voice muffled by his sleeve. Madam Chan watched the slow rise and fall of his shoulders, unsure what she should do, wishing for once that he was shouting at her, berating her in his usual fashion. She could see that his breathing was growing shallow. Perhaps it was dangerous for him to rest his head on the table. Perhaps the fumes from the tofu were stopping him from getting enough air. She heaved at his shoulders, trying to lift him back into an upright position, but he was like a dead weight and his skin, through the light cotton shirtsleeves, was damp to her touch. She should have listened to her instincts and brought in a priest despite Chan's doubts. The priest might have expelled the ghost from the house before she got her claws into them. But because she had been foolish enough to obey her husband now he lay barely conscious in a pool of his own vomit.

She heard a door slam in the kitchen, followed by the sound of running feet thumping behind her.

'Aiya! What is wrong with the boss?' Kong panted, appearing at her side. In his haste, he had forgotten to remove his shoes when he came indoors, and she couldn't help frowning at the sight of his grimy clogs on the clean floor.

Chan began to gasp, one long croak after another. The sound of it set Madam Chan to trembling. 'Sit him up! He can't breathe.'

'I'll lay him on the floor, Madam.'

Approaching from the side, Kong grasped her husband under the arms, clasping him to his chest as he heaved him upwards, before lowering him gently to the floor. Meanwhile, she folded the jacket that had been hanging over his chair and placed it under his head. The gasping had ceased, leaving behind a silence even more frightening.

'He's so pale and still. Is he dead?' She waited, her heart knocking in her chest, as the driver lifted one of her husband's wrists and listened for his pulse.

'His heartbeat is very rapid, Madam. Shall I fetch the doctor?' He looked up at her chewing his lip. He wasn't accustomed to acting upon his own initiative, for that way was fraught with danger.

'The doctor is so far away. Yes… no… where is Ho Jie… where is Cook?' She couldn't stay here alone with her husband. What if he should die? Then she might have to contend with two ghosts.

'Cook is preparing a tonic for the boss's heatiness. I haven't seen the amah.'

'I don't think heatiness is his problem. Look at him! We have more to worry about here than heatiness!' She heard her voice grow shrill again and fought for control. With her husband lying unconscious at her feet, Kong only looked to her for guidance. The *neuih gwai* had brought this trouble upon them, and if she didn't keep her head the girl would destroy them. She must rally the strength of nine bulls and two tigers to save her husband and defeat the ghost of his concubine. She couldn't afford uncertainty.

'The village is closer. Fetch the *pawang*. He will know what to do.' The old sorcerer would know how to defeat a ghost, for he was skilled in the way of demons and curses. And if her husband's ailment were more earthly, then he would deal with that too. 'Hurry! And, Ah Kong…'

'Madam?'

'Next time leave your shoes outside.'

Once the driver had departed, she unwound to the floor, her dress making a puddle of dimity flowers around her. She debated lifting her husband's head and placing it upon her lap but she worried that the move might block his airway. Instead she lifted his hand and placed it upon her knees, surprised at its boniness. She couldn't remember the last time he had held her hand. Her husband was an ageing man. In life, he was vibrant with the power of money and bad temper, so that you didn't notice the thinning of flesh, skin and hair. He was agile with determination, so that you didn't see his slight stoop or the slowing of his gait.

Now as she held his hand in her lap, dappled with the first spots of age, she remembered that he was more than sixty years old. What if his heart failed? What if his brain seized? What if he died and left her and Wei Long to the mercies of a vicious ghost?

'Chan, wake up. Don't leave me now. We have rubbed along well enough together, haven't we?'

His hand was so cold and it seemed to her that his pulse had grown erratic. Bolting like a runaway horse one minute and slowing to the crawl of a tortoise the next.

'Our little dragon needs his father,' she reminded him. And she needed her husband. For all his temper and selfishness, he was hers. Or at least he had been once. And would be again if...

Sliding her fingers around his wrist, scrabbling for the pulse, she thought for a second that she had lost it altogether. Ah... there it was... but slow, too slow.

'Forgive me, husband. Forgive me for being a jealous woman. I will find you a new concubine, a girl with almond eyes and lips like a cherry.' She gripped his wrist tight, trying to squeeze life into him. But though she tugged at his arm trying to hold him back, she knew he was slipping away. His heart was slowing. His breath was running out. And then he was gone.

43

THE *taitai* WAS waiting in her favourite rattan chair on the front veranda. She sat in her usual straight-backed fashion, but Ho Jie had heard her prowling the house at night and guessed the effort it took for her to remain calm. Only the repetitive smoothing of her silk *cheongsam* hinted at her agitated state. Ho Jie watched and smiled.

When the *pawang* appeared at last, having completed his circuit of the house and grounds, the woman leaned forward, clasping her hands in her lap, as if to contain them. The *pawang* clutched a bundle of divining rods, but he dropped the rods to his side as he came to a halt on the lawn a few steps away from Madam Chan. Ho Jie sympathised with the old man, for her body ached from fanning her mistress, so that she would have liked to drop her arm too. The *pawang* ceased the dreadful chanting that had accompanied his tour of the house as he inspected the woman before him. His forehead was so lined that Ho Jie couldn't tell whether he frowned or not, but his weary eyes stared at the *taitai* with concern as he uttered a stream of words in Malay.

'What does he say?' Madam Chan asked Kong, who had followed the old man on his inspection of the house and now stood awaiting further instructions.

The driver spat a wad of tobacco onto the grass, ignoring his mistress's expression of disgust, before answering, 'He says he cannot find any evidence of witchcraft. He has found no sign of blood charms or other magic here.'

'But there must be something. My husband was in excellent health. You saw him every day. He was an ox of a man… and yet to die so suddenly… There must be a reason. His death can't have been natural,' she wailed, sniffing back a tear.

'The boss was in good health, it is true. Only last week he told me, "Kong, the doctor says I am costing him money for I am never sick."'

'And what about the *neuih gwai*? She is here. I've seen her.'

In the days since her husband's death, Madam had become fixated upon the idea that the concubine's ghost had returned to haunt her. She insisted that the girl killed herself purely out of spite, that she had cursed the Chan family with her death and her ghost wouldn't rest until Chan's line was extinguished for ever. Ho Jie listened to her in silence, watching the play of outrage across her features, the widened eyes and furrowed forehead. Anyone would think that she was the injured party, that a poor tortured girl didn't lie dead by her hand. She watched for signs of guilt – a twitch of the eye, or shift of the gaze when she spoke of the concubine's death – and heard again Sai Mui's voice as she confided her fear that Madam Chan meant to kill her. She remembered the red comb lying forlornly on the parquetry, she saw again the sad soul who haunted her dreams, and she knew that even if Madam Chan hadn't placed the concubine's head in the noose, she had driven her to it. Either way she was guilty.

Madam's grief over her husband and her anxiety about the ghost were fitting punishment for her ill-treatment of Sai Mui, and some small repayment for Ho Jie's grief. Let her fear for her life. Let her fear for her husband's legacy. Yet she also knew that despite Madam's fears, Sai Mui would never hurt her son. How could she? She was his mother. She was tied to him by blood. But the more Ho Jie tried to persuade the *taitai* of this fact, the more she believed she was being haunted, until she couldn't rest at night for fear that the *neuih gwai* might harm the baby while she slept. She had even moved his crib into her bedchamber and slept with it next to her bed.

The *pawang* began speaking once more, waving his arms as he launched into a lengthy monologue. Neither of the women understood more than a few words of Malay and relied upon Kong to translate.

'He says that you didn't call him in time. The *towkay* was probably poisoned. He has antidotes for many poisons if he is called in time. He says that he has cured many people of poisoning. Whether it be poison of the catfish or the stingray, the millipede or the toad, he has cured these and many others.'

Kong paused to listen while the *pawang* continued speaking. 'He also asks if you had any dreams in the days before the *towkay*'s death. Any dreams about someone attacking or hurting your family.'

'I dream about Sai Mui. She won't leave me alone,' said Madam Chan. Ho Jie dreamed about her too. It was one way of keeping her near.

The *pawang* became even more animated, shaking the bunch of sticks so that they set to rattling. 'He says that if it wasn't poison that killed the boss then almost certainly a *pelesit* got into him.' The driver shook his head, a pained expression creasing his face as he shivered in distaste.

'What is a *pelesit*?' asked Madam Chan, and Ho Jie wasn't sure that she wanted to hear the answer. She had been in Malaya less than two years, but it was long enough to discover that the local people were subject to more ghosts and spirits than even the Chinese. It seemed to her that there were spirits hiding behind almost every tree and rock, waiting to catch unwary humans.

'A *pelesit* is a terrible parasite. A demon kept in a bottle by an evil *pawang*, fed on the owner's blood so that it does his bidding. Then some wicked person pays that *pawang* to send this demon into their enemies and make them ill.'

'And does he believe that "someone" paid an evil *pawang* to send a *pelesit* into my husband? Someone who wished to hurt him?' Someone like his concubine, she meant.

'The *pawang* asks, did Boss have any symptoms in the days before he died? A rash, spots, cramps, fits, spasms of any kind?'

'Nothing like that. He was his usual self.'

The driver questioned the old man again then relayed his answer. 'Hmm, he does not know the answer then because he didn't have a chance to examine the *towkay* before he died. Might be *pelesit*. Might also be poison.'

Ho Jie cleared her throat, saying, 'But I don't think Sai Mui could engage a *pawang* when she never left this house alone.'

'I don't pay you to think. I pay you to fan! The girl escaped the house once, how do we know she didn't do it again? Didn't escape into the jungle at night to meet someone?' Madam had taken to rhythmically smoothing her dress again.

'She wouldn't harm the boy,' Ho Jie insisted, but the woman ignored her.

'And what if the *pelesit* is still here? What if the concubine continues to haunt us? What will happen to my son? What will happen to my son's son and his son's son? Will we never be free of her?' Madam Chan asked, her voice becoming shriller with each question.

As the driver translated her words, the *pawang*'s face grew grave. They waited while he pondered an answer, his eyes scanning the house and its gardens, before coming to rest upon Madam Chan sitting forward in her chair, hands gripping her knees. He spoke, his eyes fixed on the *taitai*'s face.

'He will do what he can.'

*

THE *pawang* SET up a makeshift altar on the ground beneath the mango trees. Smoke from burning incense and two white candles drifted up into the branches in a thin column. Offerings of food were laid out on a mat made from woven *pandanus* leaves dyed in shades of pink and purple. There were bowls of parched rice and yellow turmeric rice and a live chicken tied at the ankles so that it couldn't escape. The old man sat cross-legged before this altar, hands on his knees swaying as he chanted in a croaky voice. At times his tone was beseeching and at others admonishing. Kong had moved a chair from the veranda to the lawn and Madam sat watching as Ho Jie fanned smoke from her eyes. Kong sat cross-legged on the grass nearby.

After what seemed like a long time, the *pawang* picked up seven small branches of various kinds of leaves and tied them together with a length of bark twine. Then he waved the branches above the smoking incense.

'What is he chanting about?'

'I don't know, Madam. The words are in the language of the spirits.'

'Then what does he plan to do?'

Kong shrugged. 'Magic. He says a *hantu* must be haunting this place. Maybe a *hantu pelak*. Maybe some other ghost. The

Malays, they have many ghosts. Too many to count.'

'Does he believe that the concubine's ghost haunts us?'

The driver suddenly found his clogs very interesting and began picking at a bit of loose rubber that was peeling from the wooden sole.

'Ah Kong?' Madam barked. 'Does the concubine haunt us?'

'The *pawang* says a person's soul is very small, Madam, only the size of my thumb. Who can say where it may go? It may sneak up on another soul and feed from it.'

'Feed from a living soul?'

He shrugged again. Ho Jie watched as he tried valiantly to evade her questions, but Madam was a woman who didn't take 'no' from the gods; she was hardly likely to accept it from her driver.

'Tell me, does he believe that the concubine's soul is haunting us?'

He sighed, his shoulders heaving in resignation before saying, 'He doesn't know for certain but he says that the *hantu pelak* is a ghost who dies by violent means. It haunts the place where it dies… seeking revenge upon those who caused its death.'

Madam Chan's intake of breath was audible and Ho Jie smiled from her position behind her employer's chair. 'Perhaps Sai Mui continues to watch over the boy, Madam,' she said. 'Perhaps she means him no harm.'

'You don't know what you're talking about! You didn't see her. You didn't smell the stink of her lingering about my poor baby son's crib.'

The *pawang*'s chant became louder as he dipped his bouquet of leaves in a thin paste of rice flour mixed with water and shook it out in a spray of droplets that glimmered in the sunlight. Rising to his feet he shuffled over to the nearest corner of the house where he proceeded to paint the masonry with the rice water. Then, transporting the leaf brush in one hand and the bowl of rice water in the other, he marched for the kitchen at the rear corner where he repeated the procedure. Then before they knew it, he disappeared from view around the back of the house, his thin shoulders bowed beneath the weight of his sorcerer's tools.

Ho Jie allowed herself another smile of satisfaction, knowing that her employer couldn't see her. 'Well, a sprinkle of rice water should do the trick. I'm sure we've seen the last of any *neuih gwai* or *hantu pelak* in this house now.'

By the time her employer twisted in her seat to glare at her, she had rearranged her face into its usual implacable expression. Madam Chan could call in as many *pawangs* and mediums as she liked. She could paint every corner of the mansion, sprinkle every tree, douse every rock and still it would make no difference. For she would never be free of the concubine's ghost. Not while Ho Jie had breath left in her body.

44

Kuala Lumpur 2017

IN SOME WAYS Kuala Lumpur International was like any other airport, a crazy carnival of escalators, endless corridors and duty-free shops. But even locked inside its walls, Sarah knew she had landed in the tropics. For one thing there was a mini jungle sprouting in the middle of the terminal. And then there were the women – Malay women in long floral tunics, brightly coloured scarves wrapping their heads; Chinese girls in towering heels and flimsy tops; tanned holidaymakers in shorts and flip-flops; and the occasional black-shrouded mother, sandalled kids in tow.

It was so far from London, both geographically and metaphorically. She could barely believe that only twenty-eight hours ago she had asked James to buy her out and watched his face as he processed the knowledge that she wanted to abandon all they had built together.

'I thought we might really join forces, Sarah. Once you'd... you know...' He didn't have the words to describe her grief. And if it was true that he'd believed they might form a more personal partnership one day – well, she doubted he'd done more than give it a passing thought. He would get over it soon enough. Work or another woman would consume him.

'You'll be all right without me, James,' she'd said, reaching up to pat his shoulder. 'Some other partner will come along. And there's no hurry to pay me out… we'll need to get a valuation, you'll need to re-finance. I'll be all right for money for a while.' He'd looked disconsolate the entire morning but by three o'clock he was back to his usual self, offering to book her flight and ship any extra luggage she might want sent over in case she decided to stay, although his horror-stricken expression suggested that only a mad woman would want to stay anywhere other than London if she had the choice.

So just twelve hours after she'd boarded the Malaysian Airlines flight at Heathrow and thirty-six hours after she last spoke to Ben, she exited customs to be confronted by the usual press of humanity congregating outside Arrivals. She made directly for the exit, the humidity hitting her like a wall as soon as she walked through the glass doors. Outside on the road, triple-parked cars and pedestrians with overloaded luggage trolleys caused a chaotic jumble, and the smell of exhaust mingled with the sticky tropical air.

'Sarah!' She heard her name boomed in a familiar Australian accent. 'Your flight was early. I meant to catch you as you came through Customs.' Ben surprised her by zooming in for a peck on the cheek and a hug, making her conscious that her head only reached his shoulder. He was taller than she remembered. He was more tanned too, and his brown hair had grown out and was bleached by the sun.

'You're looking very sunny,' she said by way of greeting.

'My brother was over so we took off for a few days, surfing in Sumatra.'

'Older or younger?'

'Younger. I have two brothers. One older and one younger. No sisters. Probably just as well for them.'

'Thanks for picking me up, I really wasn't expecting it. You must have got up early.'

'No trouble. I don't have a lecture until tonight. Come on, the car's this way,' he said, grabbing her bag before she could protest.

Once her luggage was stowed and she was ensconced in his Toyota, she leaned back, settling herself for the hour-long ride from the airport to the house. And as he manoeuvred the car out of the airport and onto the freeway, she found that her gaze kept wandering to the man beside her, one strong brown arm on the steering wheel, the other resting on the car's doorframe.

'You're left-handed.'

'You noticed,' he said with a lopsided grin.

She was noticing a lot of things about him this morning: his light-green eyes, his somewhat ratty shorts and in particular the snail's trail of hair on his abdomen that revealed itself when he lifted her luggage into the car. She didn't like the fact that she noticed. Tearing her gaze from this big, cheerful man with his big, cheerful grin, she turned to the scenery flashing by outside the window. And as the car ate up freeway miles, cruising past palm-oil plantations, half-finished rows of shophouses and gleaming white mosques, she tried to refocus her thoughts on what she was doing back here, in this place that had taken her husband. Curled up on the sofa in her London flat, terrorised by her own imaginings, it had seemed like the only way forward, the only way to be rid of her demons. If she rid herself of Nick's grandfather's house and discovered the answers to her questions about his family, perhaps she and June would be free to go on with their lives. Perhaps she would be free to forgive herself for Nick's death.

*

BEN ROLLED THE Toyota onto the overgrown drive of the house and put it into park. While he stepped out, walking around to the boot to collect her luggage, she found that her body was glued to the upholstery. She couldn't shift her legs. It was as if they knew something she didn't. Once she entered there would be no going back; she would have to deal with whatever she found there. Secrets, truths, lies, ghosts, they were all the same, really. All things you didn't want to confront. In returning to the house, she was returning to the truth of her marriage, the secrets Nick had kept from her, the lies she had told herself, and the ghosts of the past – real or imagined.

She clutched her handbag where the key waited like a threat. She wore the jade ring on her thumb like a talisman. Beyond the windscreen, the house glowered at her. In the months since she'd been gone it had merged into the surrounding trees. Long grass grew like a skirt around its walls, saplings sprouted across what had once been lawn. Without Nick to domesticate it, the jungle was taking back its own.

There was still time to ask Ben to turn around, take her back to KLIA to wait for the next flight. She didn't have to be here. Nick was gone; what did it matter if no one ever righted his family's wrongs or discovered its secrets? June would understand. What did it matter if she never came to terms with what had gone wrong in her marriage?

'Need a hand?' Ben opened her door, holding out his hand, large and squarish, and sprinkled with coarse hair. So unlike Nick's long, slim fingers and smooth olive skin.

'No thanks, I'm fine.'

She peeled her body from the seat and headed for the portico. It was only eight-thirty and already the heat was oppressive. Ben joined her in the shade saying, 'You did read my earlier emails, didn't you?'

'Huh? Some of them. Not all… actually, I skimmed.'

'I see,' he said. 'Well, you do know I'm living here at the moment?'

'What? No. I definitely skimmed that bit.'

She must have sounded disturbed because he said, 'I can move out tomorrow if it bothers you.'

'No, not at all, I'm just… surprised.' It did bother her though, the meaning of it, the implications of Ben living in the same house as Su Lin. Despite her airy words, she didn't like it one bit. She didn't like the thought of him putting his arms around skinny Miss Su Lin, no matter how platonic the hug, no matter how casual the peck on the cheek. Su Lin had shared Nick's last months instead of her, his wife. Why should she get Ben too? She knew this was the thinking of a jealous shrew but she didn't care. She would own it.

'I was worried about her being alone here. The house is so isolated.'

'Not you too?' This was all going wrong. Why should she care if he shacked up with Su Lin? He was only an acquaintance. She might never see him again once the house was sold. He wasn't the one who deliberately kept secrets from her. He hadn't lied to her by omission. If he felt protective towards the girl why should she care? None of this was his fault.

'What do you mean?' he asked, staring at her as if he might read her thoughts on her face.

'The ghost, you're not worried about the *neuih gwai*, are you?' she said with a pathetic laugh. 'June thinks the house is haunted.'

'No, I'm worried about more flesh-and-blood intruders. There are too many break-ins in KL for her to stay here by herself. Last month, friends of mine woke up to two men armed with the kitchen choppers looking for jewellery.'

'I'm so sorry. I should have realised from all the bars everywhere. I should never have left her here alone.'

'She's a grown-up, Sarah. She decided to stay. I just thought she might appreciate some company. It made *me* feel better to be here.'

They had reached the front door and Sarah fished in her bag for the key, guarded by its ghost-hunting warrior. She hesitated for a moment, confronted by the door's peeling red paint and all the tragedies it had witnessed. So many deaths, so many lives not lived.

'And also...' Ben continued, his expression unreadable, '... there's Lin's... um...'

She was just about to put the key in the lock when the door was opened from within and Su Lin appeared in the doorway. She was wearing a white cotton sundress with a dropped waist and lace inserts. It bared her shoulders and finished at mid-thigh to reveal slim, shapely legs. Yet despite a cut that draped loosely from a high neckline, the dress did nothing to disguise the bump of her abdomen.

'... condition,' he finished.

'Hi Sarah, it's good to see you again,' she said, but the welcome didn't include a smile. Instead she seemed nervous, backing quickly away from the door to allow Sarah to enter.

'You're pregnant.' There was no point in pretending she hadn't noticed. No point pretending that Su Lin had just got fat, for clearly she was as slim as ever, except for her baby bump. Sarah looked from the girl to Ben, who had followed her in, pulling her suitcase behind him. She supposed a pregnant girlfriend was an excellent reason to move into a crumbling mansion overrun by jungle.

'Are congratulations in order?' she asked, trying for a smile. They were nice people. They deserved to be happy. Only a selfish bitch wouldn't wish them well.

Ben didn't answer, flicking a glance at Su Lin.

'Not to Ben,' the girl said, and her eyes held all the secrets and lies from which Sarah had been hiding. All the truths that she had been avoiding. All the betrayals she had spent her life punishing. In those moments, as Su Lin searched her face for – forgiveness? Understanding? – she felt the pain of her husband's death all over again. She felt his betrayal like a stab wound to her soul and she hated him for it. She hated Su Lin for it. And she hated herself all over again. Her hatred was a bottomless black pool that she could tread water in endlessly. She knew that she could go on hating him and his secret girlfriend for ever, just as she had hated her father, just as she had hated her mother. She could let her grief go, and dive into the black depths of a hatred she hadn't felt since she was a teenager. Not since the day sixteen years ago when she had come home from school to discover her mother had done what she had always promised.

*

CELIA HADN'T GIVEN her daughter time to dump her schoolbag and grab a snack before she was confronted by the sight of her mother sprawled on the sofa, her too-short dress riding up to reveal lacy knickers, the empty foil packets of diazepam lying scattered on the floor around her. Of course, Celia had timed her dramatic gesture so that she would be discovered in time. She may have swallowed an entire box of tablets but she wasn't stupid enough to do so without ensuring that she would be found. She knew she could count on her daughter to phone if she was stopping off at the shops or hanging out with friends after school. Sarah was too well-trained by her mother's tantrums to risk offending. Celia's tantrums could go on for days and usually involved far too much alcohol, floods of tears, screaming matches and, sometimes, embarrassing rants delivered to teachers. Sarah had learned to avoid this at all costs.

Celia had even prepared a note, addressed not to Sarah but to her ex-husband. Later Sarah would read that note, a psychotic outpouring of love muddled with accusation and insult. In her suicide note, Celia reiterated the usual recriminations for her husband's abandonment, the same old vitriol that he had shacked up with someone else, the same colourful descriptions of his new wife, and the very old declarations of undying love. Or in this case... dying love.

But for the moment, Sarah ignored the cream envelope with the floral border, noting only her father's name written on its front and her own name's absence. She pulled down her mother's skirt and checked for a pulse. Then she wiped the vomit from her mother's face with a tissue and turned towards the hall where the telephone sat. Afterwards, she would tell herself that she must have been suffering from shock, that this was why she felt no terror that her mother might die, why she felt no compulsion to rush. For what other sixteen-year-old girl who found her mother unconscious with an empty packet of pills beside her wouldn't panic? Wouldn't feel the strangling grip of terror in her throat? Only an unnatural daughter would feel nothing.

Except it was a lie. She wasn't in shock at all. In fact, from the moment her father had walked out of the house and gone to live with his girlfriend, she'd been expecting something like this. And now that it had happened, she could only feel nauseated that her mother had placed her in this position. Celia was the one who should be wiping vomit from Sarah's face. Celia should be pulling down her skirt and warning her about the perils girls could get themselves into if they weren't careful. Celia was the mother.

But then again, Sarah was accustomed to resenting her mother. She was used to being angry with her father. She suffered all the usual adolescent rage, fanned by the flames of her father's abandonment and her mother's descent into alcohol-fuelled mania. There was no mystery about it. You didn't have to be a psychologist to see it. But now, along with the nausea and the anger, she could taste the bitter vinegar of vitriol on her tongue. Along with a rage that made her teeth ache, she wanted to spit on her mother. She wanted to slap her stupid face and call her vile names. And then she wanted to walk away and never come back.

She would walk out the door and go to her friend Amanda's house, where Amanda's mother would offer her tea and cake and ask what she'd been up to lately. No one would know that she'd been home first. No one would know that she'd found her mother unconscious and abandoned her. No one had seen her enter the house. And even if they had, she could always blame her desertion upon shock. She was only sixteen, after all. And then, when her mother was gone, she would go and live with her father and his sane new wife, Claire, who would remind her to do her homework and impose a curfew of ten on weeknights. Who would cook dinner and drive her to soccer practice.

If she hadn't found her mother in time that is what would have happened. But she had found her in time. And no matter how much she hated Celia for what she had done, for who she was, for the responsibility she had dumped upon her, this fact could not be changed. She had no choice but to save her.

45

ALREADY SHE FELT the sting of mosquitoes nipping her flesh. She slapped them ineffectually, too overcome to care. It had rained in the night and pools of water glistened in the potholes. She smelled the wet leaves and leafy soil crowding in on the lane that led to the house. But she was walking away from it now, down the hill towards the road where she might hail a taxi. Her legs gathered speed, moving faster than her upper body, careering down the hill, running away from all her ghosts.

She stopped when she reached the road where she'd seen the old lady sweeping leaves in her pyjamas on that first day. She wished that she'd listened to her, that she'd asked the taxi driver to turn around, that she'd never found her way to this house of ghosts. Now she turned in the direction she remembered led to the main road, although the profusion of winding dead-end streets made the entire area confusing and mazelike.

The jungle where the house lay hidden bled into the grounds of a curving, multi-faceted apartment tower. She stopped for a moment to wipe the sweat from her face and take a sip of water from the bottle she carried in her bag, looking up and down the road, searching for a taxi. Instead, Ben's Toyota pulled up alongside and the passenger window rolled down.

'Sarah, please get in the car. Come back and talk to Su Lin at least.'

'Why didn't you warn me?' she said. His silence was another lie. Another betrayal.

'It wasn't my secret to tell.'

She began walking again, waving away his explanation and heading towards the intersection ahead. 'So you let me fly thousands of miles to discover that my dead husband cheated on me?'

He rolled the car forward, following her at a snail's pace. Out of the corner of her eye she saw that he steered with one hand, leaning towards the open window, flicking his eyes from the road to her and back again, and she couldn't help imagining that strong hand gripping hers. Those strong arms holding her.

'You needed to know. June needs to know too. And Su Lin wasn't going to tell you. She felt too ashamed.'

She thought of June then, cast adrift in the world with no one to follow her and no one left behind to remember her. She thought of June raising her own child alone. *Did* she need to know? What difference did it make whether she knew about the child or not? It would still exist. Nick would still have the child he wanted left in the world, the child she hadn't given him.

'I don't care,' she said, knowing even as she said it that she did care. Of course she wanted June to be happy and although no child could replace her son, it might make a dent in her sadness. But Sarah didn't have it in her to relent now.

'And I wanted to see you again,' he said.

Her traitorous heart skipped a beat but she ignored it. 'Go away, Ben. Leave me alone. I just make people unhappy.'

She'd almost reached the intersection where the miserable excuse for a footpath petered out. To her left, the road crossed a bridge over the freeway, but she thought she remembered the taxi coming from straight ahead. Ben's car hovered beside her, holding up traffic, so that cars were honking and motorbikes scooting around him. Making a sudden decision, she skirted behind his car and ran across the road to the vestiges of a broken footpath on the other side. The narrow, uneven path fell away here to a deep drainage ditch.

Without looking back to see what Ben was doing, she stumbled over stones and weeds for a few hundred feet before the path picked up again. There were still no taxis in sight, just houses, blocks of flats and somewhere to her left the roar of a freeway. The houses meandered up a hill to her right and at the distant top she could see the sprawling pagoda-like roofs of a temple. A blue sign in Chinese and English pointed to the Thean Hou Temple and she remembered that she'd read about this temple, a popular tourist attraction. Perhaps she would find a taxi there to take her to a hotel or back to the airport.

It was so hot now and the road led her up a steep hill. There was no path, just a drain on one side and a stony verge on the other. It was easier to walk on the road, bypassing plastic rubbish bins, parked cars and barking dogs. Her T-shirt was sticking to her back and she wished she wore sandals instead of her thin-soled ballet flats. The occasional car passed her by but there was no further sign of Ben. It was better that way. Better for him.

By the time she reached a large gravel car park she was breathing hard and the sweat was dripping down her body. A couple of tourist buses were parked here and swarms of people were coming and going. Sooner or later a taxi was bound to arrive. Family groups wandered along the concourse in front of the temple, children clambered over statues of zodiac animals, whilst stalls selling food did a roaring trade. In front of her, the temple rose in tier upon tier of golden tiled roofs. A flight of white stairs led up through red-pillared arches and everywhere there were lanterns and dragons.

The sun and the walk had burned away some of her anger so that she found her legs steering her towards the stairs. Now that she was here, she might as well take a look. Perhaps the calm of a temple might be soothing. Once inside, she discovered that the lower level of the temple was like a busy shopping mall. She ignored the food court and the stalls selling paintings and giftware, to climb further flights of stairs past banqueting halls and a marriage registration office to the prayer hall at the top. On the concourse outside, joss sticks smoked in a large urn with yellow dragons climbing its sides, and the eaves of the pagoda-like roof twisted and turned with colourful carvings. She left her shoes on the steps with everyone else's and climbed the last flight of stairs to the prayer hall.

It was dark after the brilliant sun outside, despite gleaming pillars of light that surrounded each of three deities. There were no gods of war here, just the compassionate faces of three golden goddesses looking down from their altars: *Tian Hou*, the Queen of Heaven, *Guan Yin*, Goddess of Mercy and *Shui Wei Sheng Niang*, Goddess of the Waterfront. Sarah watched as a worshipper approached a cylindrical metal stand and grasped a bundle of flat bamboo sticks sitting in a hole in the middle. The young woman picked up the sticks and dropped them back into the hole. Then she selected the stick that landed highest and after reading the number on it, opened one of the small numbered drawers in the cylinder and took out a slip of paper.

Sarah stood before the Goddess of Mercy, watching as one worshipper after another knelt by the goddess before seeking their fortune amongst the sticks. Sometimes they laughed as they read the result. Sometimes they frowned. And sometimes they selected another stick altogether, clearly unwilling to accept the gods' unfavourable verdict. It was silly, she supposed, but was it any sillier than trusting your future to vision statements and life plans? Was it any more gullible than believing in creative visualisation and positive affirmations? For no matter how successful, how organised or focused you were, couldn't everything be snatched from you in the blink of fortune's eye? You might as well rely on this lottery of sticks.

She waited until she overheard a young couple who looked Chinese, laughing and joking in English before asking for help. They looked to be in their twenties, and both wore shorts and T-shirts.

'Excuse me, can you explain how this works?'

'Sure,' said the guy, in what she thought was a New Zealand accent. 'I'm no expert but I've been here with my mum a few times. First you offer a prayer to Guan Yin before you can ask her a question about your future. Then once you've asked your question, shake the sticks and drop them into the slot. The bottom of the slot has bumps on it so the sticks land unevenly. The stick that lands highest will give you your lot number.'

'In some temples you take the stick to a priest or fortune-teller who'll read your fortune from a book but here it's all self-service,' the girl added.

'Good luck.'

'Thanks.'

She approached the altar and knelt on a cushion provided for that purpose. Guan Yin looked down benignly from her painted face, legs crossed in the lotus position, body enfolded in stiff golden draperies. Sarah already knew the answer to the question she longed to ask. But the gods would only laugh at her. Nick was never coming back. Anyway, even if a miracle occurred and he walked through her door tomorrow she would have to send him away, now that he had betrayed her. No, what she needed to know, the knowledge she needed to help her get through the months and years ahead, was the assurance that one day she would be free of fear and regret. That one day she would no longer be haunted.

'Will I ever feel safe?' she whispered, folding her hands in prayer.

Unfurling her legs, she stepped over to the fortune-telling device, grasping the bundle of sticks tightly in her right hand and lifting them high. Then she dropped them into the slot. One stick landed a fingernail above the others and this one she selected to reveal her fortune. Lot number three. She knew the whole process was pointless, so why did her hand shake as she opened the drawer corresponding with her number? Why did she hold her breath as she withdrew the slip of pink paper that would answer her question and reveal her fate?

> The traveller struggles against the driving rain
> Just like a swallow returning to her nest.
> The swallow builds with clay against the storm
> But her ramparts dissolve to mud – so all is wasted.

She read the poem through twice, puzzling over the meaning. Unlike astrology readings in the daily papers, it wasn't exactly optimistic. It wouldn't go down well back home where everyone was frantically pursuing happiness. This prediction was about struggle, about the futility of trying to protect yourself from calamity. Was she the poor swallow? Had she spent years building pointless walls to keep from being hurt, only to have them come crashing down around her? Had she hidden behind the ramparts of her marriage, only to have her husband taken from her and her trust shattered?

Perhaps the poem was right. She did feel like a traveller in a storm with no refuge in sight. Perhaps there was no hope.

Then she thought about the metaphor of the storm. Was that the poem's real message? The oracle wasn't about the swallow; it was about the storm. It wasn't about the individual; it was about fate. She wasn't the centre of the universe. No one was. You couldn't fight life's storms. You couldn't fight fate. You could only wait. If your home was destroyed and you were drenched to your skin, then so be it. Eventually the storm clouds would clear and the sun would emerge. And then she could rebuild.

*

BEN WAS LEANING against a red pillar at the foot of the stairs when she exited the temple. She would have known his bear-like form anywhere. He was so different to her husband. Nick had been slim, verging on skinny. Ben was built like a brick shithouse, as he called it. Yet he was light on his feet, walking with an easy grace, and his flesh suited him, like a layer of extra comfort. That was it; he looked at home in his skin.

He was sipping from a fresh coconut he'd bought from a food stall and checking his phone while he waited. She told herself that she hadn't expected to see him and walked straight past, heading for a taxi that was just disgorging a group of European tourists.

'Hey, wait a sec,' he said, looking up from his phone.

'Can't wait. I need to grab that cab before it leaves.'

'I'll give you a lift.'

'No thanks.' She threw the words over her shoulder as she hurried to reach the taxi before it pulled away but Ben dumped his coconut in a bin and followed her.

'Sarah, wait a minute.'

She had reached the taxi now. It was an old Proton with sagging seats and the driver had rolled the windows down to save on air-conditioning. 'Can you take me to... um... KLCC?' she asked, referring to the huge city complex that incorporated the soaring Twin Towers. She would think about what to do once she arrived.

'Sorry, Miss. My last fare paid me to wait,' the driver said with a shrug. 'Hard to get taxis here. They all wait to take their fare back. Best if you call. Or use app.'

Ben had caught up with her now, standing close enough to overhear the conversation. 'Need a lift?' he said.

'I'll call.' She'd turned off her data roaming to save money and she didn't have the app anyway.

'It could be a long wait. It's lunch time.'

'Haven't you got something better to do?'

'Something better to do than chase mad Englishwomen around in the midday sun? Not really.'

'I don't understand why you've made yourself part of this. I mean, Nick's gone and he was your friend. Not me. Not Su Lin.'

'I consider Su Lin a friend.'

'So you're following me for her?' She turned to face him, hand on hip, scowl on face. Bitch-face wouldn't be vanquished overnight.

'I'm following you for me, Sarah.'

'That could prove to be exhausting.'

He grinned, one hand on hip, mimicking her. 'Ever since I saw that photo on Nick's desk of you, trapped in your husband's headlock, I thought, she looks like fun. She looks like a woman who's trying so hard to be serious but can't fight her inner clown.'

'You're ridiculous.' She didn't know what to make of his honesty. Why couldn't he just say the polite thing like everyone else and be done with it?

'Probably. But you need to lighten up.'

'Probably. But I have a dead husband,' she said, glaring at him. 'I have a dead husband who I just found out was screwing his twenty-three-year-old lodger.' Or whatever she was.

'Yep. Nick fucked up big time. But he loved you. He missed you. He talked about you all the time, about how smart and hardworking you are. About how bravely you take risks. About how calmly you cope with your crazy mother. About how you try so hard not to be vulnerable.'

'He said that?' Is that how Nick saw her? It almost sounded like he'd admired her, when all along she thought he'd grown tired of her insecurities, bored with her obsessions, frustrated by her reluctance.

'He was lonely without you. And he fucked up.'

She closed her eyes and saw Nick's face, a little blurred. Already she was finding it hard to summon the crisp, clear outlines of him.

'I'm so lonely without him and it's only been six months. How will I get through the rest of my life?' She felt the tears, hot and burning, brimming behind her eyelids. They rolled down her cheeks as she tried valiantly to hold back the dam. And then Ben folded her prickly, sweaty shoulders against his body and pulled her close as the sobs escaped her in breathy gasps.

'It's all right,' he crooned. 'Everything will be all right.'

She doubted it.

'Just get through today and tomorrow and the next day and the day after that... and one day, when you least expect it, you'll find your clown again.'

In that moment, she doubted that she would ever find the girl in the picture again. But she allowed herself to be comforted, to be escorted to his car and helped into her seat, if only to save making a spectacle in public.

'All right, I'll come back to the house with you,' she said as he switched on the ignition and slid the car into drive, 'but I don't want to talk to her.'

Not yet anyway.

46

BY THE TIME they returned to the house, Su Lin had made herself scarce. Her car was still in the driveway but there were no signs of life downstairs, only the creeping sensation that someone had just left the room: a hairbrush sitting next to an empty coffee cup on a small table in the courtyard, an invisible trail of perfume, a bottle of red nail polish on the floor next to a chair.

'Can I make you coffee? We have instant or instant.'

'Do you have a teabag?'

'Sure.' Ben disappeared.

'I got the letter back from my colleague,' he said as he returned with two mugs of jasmine tea. 'I thought you'd be keen to read it.'

'That was kind of her. I'd like to thank her personally while I'm here, if that's possible.'

'I think she was quite intrigued. She asked if she could scan a copy of it.'

He retrieved a buff manila folder from the next room and handed it to her. She opened it to find a single sheet of double-spaced type and the original letter, which she was seeing for the first time. She saw at a glance that it had been written with a brush, in brisk, flowing strokes in traditional characters rather than the simplified version used in mainland China. The ink was faded and the paper creased where it had been folded twice long ago, but the seal was still a brilliant red imprint against the yellowing rice paper. She didn't know exactly what she expected to discover, but her heart was already beating faster as she picked up the translated copy and began to read.

My Dearest Son

I beg that you forgive your mother if I have wronged you. Please do not stint in your prayers for me. You may condemn my secrecy but from my heart I believed it to be best. I considered only the welfare of this family. Once I thought to defeat the ghost who cursed us. I engaged all manner of priests and sorcerers to drive this wickedness from the house of Chan. Yet I failed in my quest. Your wife's death is proof of this, as your father's death was proof. Now you inherit the task of ending the curse. It is my hope that the truth, no matter how painful, will help you.

In the eighteenth year of our marriage, your father took a concubine. To my sorrow, I was barren, so I made room in our lives for this girl. I gave her the second-best room in the house and treated her with kindness. From the moment Lim Yu Lan stepped across the threshold she brought discord. But I welcomed your father's concubine into his house as I welcomed her child. It is true, my son, you are the concubine's child, yet you are the child of my heart and I have raised you as my son. For it was clear from the start that the girl was disturbed. Later she became prone to fits of madness, until one day she hanged herself in the upstairs bedchamber that we keep locked. In doing so, she cursed the Chan family with her suicide. Your father died soon after in terrible agony and you know how the family fortunes declined. Now your wife is dead before her time and I too will leave you soon.

I have seen her, wandering the house and grounds. I have felt her malignant spirit. You must guard your daughter, as you must guard your future sons, for the ghost woman seeks to destroy us all. She would see the house of Chan fall to ruin.

Your loving mother

Seal of Lee Ling Wei

20 May 1963

Sarah looked up from the translated words to see Ben sipping tea and watching her over the rim of his mug. When he saw that she had finished reading, he raised his brows in query.

'You've read it?' she asked.

'Couldn't resist.'

'It's strange to think that a woman writing in the 1960s believed a ghost had cursed her entire family. I mean… the Russians had put a man in space by then. How could she be so superstitious?'

'I think I could rustle up a few people who believe in ghosts. And curses.'

Was it really so strange though? Sarah had seen or dreamed something. She'd begun to believe she was being haunted. June was convinced she'd once seen the concubine's ghost, despite what her amah had told her. And given the series of tragedies that had befallen Nick's family, she could be forgiven for believing it was cursed. Each generation had suffered premature death. Each generation had produced only one child. Or had this belief in curses been a self-fulfilling prophecy? If you fear death, will you do anything to avoid it? Even reduce your risk by not having children so the curse can't follow you?

Even leave your daughter's letters unanswered because you want to keep her safe?

'Do you think I should tell Su Lin?' she asked, not wanting to give the letter credence, and yet... Su Lin's baby was Nick's child. Her baby was part Chan.

'I don't think she needs anything more to worry about right now, poor kid.'

'Me being one of those things?' He saw Su Lin as a child in need of protection. It was so obvious now. How could she have thought they were lovers? It was just bitter, twisted Sarah talking, she supposed. Except Nick had cheated on her... and Su Lin knew he was cheating. But her unborn child – Nick's unborn child – was blameless. The child shouldn't suffer for their mistake. She couldn't inflict that on a baby.

'She hasn't even told her parents yet,' said Ben. 'She's been making excuses for not going home. She's scared how they'll react.'

'She'll have to tell them soon.'

*

SU LIN'S ROOM was in the rear corner of the house. Sarah remembered it vaguely from that first day when she'd discovered Nick's other life, the secret life in which he had inherited his grandfather's crumbling oriental mansion without mentioning a word of it. That day, she had wandered through the mostly empty house, following his randomly scattered possessions like a trail of crumbs.

It was a large room, she remembered, with windows on two sides, and an adjoining bathroom. Only the master bedroom at the front was bigger. Su Lin had unwittingly chosen the room where the concubine hanged herself. Sarah wondered if the girl was beset by dreams as she was. Or was knowledge the precursor to dreams? Perhaps she slept soundly because she didn't know about that other, earlier girl and her child.

She tapped on the door and waited, unconsciously curling her hands into fists at her sides. She didn't know whether the tension she felt was a sign of anger or nerves. Either way, she had to get this discussion over with so that she could decide what to do and move on. She wasn't sure whether she wanted to know the sordid details of her husband's affair with Su Lin, but nothing could be worse than her imagination.

Su Lin didn't call out for her to enter; instead she opened the door, her expression unreadable. If she was surprised to see Sarah standing at the threshold she didn't show it, but Sarah noticed that she cradled her baby bump protectively in an unconscious gesture.

'Mind if I come in?'

'*Mi casa es tu casa*, I remember saying once before.'

'Yes, well, that's debatable, isn't it?'

There was a single plastic chair in the room so Sarah took that, feeling that sitting on the bed would be too weird. The furniture was Spartan – a single bed, the chair, and a chest of drawers – apart from two clothes racks blooming with floaty dresses in myriad pastel colours. The femininity of the clothes was at odds with the monastic furnishing.

'I don't blame you for hating me. Sometimes I hate myself,' Su Lin began, staring down at her naked feet with their professionally manicured toes.

'I don't hate you. He was the married one.' Yet she had hated her. Briefly. Mere hours ago. She'd hated Nick too. But somehow she didn't have the energy or the will for hatred any more. What had it ever brought her except sadness? She rarely spoke to her father. She kept her relationship with her mother on a tight leash. She didn't want to hate a dead man she'd once loved. She didn't want to hang on to all that hatred any more. What was the point?

'But I can't deny I'm sad,' she said.

'Please don't hate Nick either. He didn't mean to betray you. It just happened because he was lonely, and I was there, and he liked me.'

But sex didn't just happen. It wasn't like breathing; it was an act of will. And if Su Lin believed that, then she was being either naive or disingenuous.

'It's stupid, I know, but that's why we didn't take precautions. It took us by surprise. We were both a bit drunk and...'

'I really don't want to know the details.'

'He didn't love me but...' Her words trailed off and Sarah wondered what else she'd been about to say. *But I loved him*. She could almost read the unspoken words on her lips. Anyone would love Nick. He was a loveable guy.

Sarah looked around the bare room, spotted with grey patches here and there where Nick had practised his plastering, dotted with missing pieces of parquetry and broken skirting. For decades it had been closed off in an attempt to shut out a ghost, until Nick decided to let the ghost back in. She switched her gaze to the pregnant girl.

'Is that where Nick found the jade ring?' she asked, indicating the broken skirting with a nod of her head.

'Uh-huh. He was trying, not very successfully, to repair the skirting.'

Sarah wondered whether the ring had belonged to the dead concubine. Had someone she once loved given it to her? Had she placed it there to hide her love from the world? From the woman who had taken her son? She took a deep breath, saying, 'The question is, what to do now.'

'I'll tell my parents soon. They'll be shocked but they'll help me. They love me. But I wanted to finish the semester first because once I return to Ipoh, I doubt I'll be back. I thought if I finished the coursework, maybe I could work on my thesis from home.' She seemed so young in her pretty white dress with her long hair hanging down her back, almost a child.

'What will you tell them about Nick?'

'The truth. At least I can say he didn't abandon me. He couldn't help dying, could he?' She'd been trying so hard to keep her emotions in check but with the mention of Nick's death she couldn't hold back any longer. Unlike Sarah's loud sobs an hour earlier, Su Lin's tears were shed silently, rolling down her cheeks fat and full of remorse for what had happened, regret for a future she would never have, and sorrow for all this loss. Sitting on the flimsy plastic chair, hands hooked under her thighs, Sarah watched her cry. Unlike Ben, she might as well be wearing a sign saying 'Keep off'. But despite her inexperience with solace, despite her recent losses or perhaps because of them, she found herself getting up from her chair and going to sit on the bed next to her husband's pregnant lover. She placed her arm around the girl's quivering shoulders and pulled her close. She could feel Su Lin's heart bouncing rapidly against her own chest, as if it might bound away altogether.

'It will be okay,' she said, realising as she spoke the words that for the first time, she believed them. 'We'll figure it out. Just take one day at a time.'

'I don't know what I'm going to do.'

'It's all right. We'll sell this stupid house. The land must be worth a fortune even without the ghost,' she said, feeling rather than seeing Su Lin's giggle at her words. 'Nick would want to look after you and the baby.'

'I'm so sorry, Sarah. I never meant for this to happen.'

'Don't worry, everything will work out in the end. And I know one person who'll be pleased.'

'Who?' she asked doubtfully.

'June.'

They had all lost Nick but two women would have his child. And that had to be something, didn't it?

*

SOMETIME LATER, AFTER she and Su Lin had made peace and begun to make plans, Sarah retreated to her room and sank onto the bed.

'You really left a pile of shit behind, didn't you? You were supposed to be one of the good guys, Nick.'

'Exception proves the rule, babe.'

She stared at the ceiling, trying to conjure his face in the flaking paint and spots of mould. 'You left me behind too.'

'I'm here. I'll always be here. But you're not alone down there either, you know.'

She thought of all the people in her life, some welcome, some inescapable, and said, 'I know.' Then she picked up her phone and listened as it chimed through the long chain of digits to the other side of the world.

'Hello, Dad? Is that you?'

47

Kuala Lumpur 2018

TO SARAH, THE cemetery resembled a carnival ground more than a graveyard. Family groups were setting out vases of flowers, plates of oranges, polystyrene boxes of brightly coloured cakes, and whole roast ducks, in front of headstones. Paper cups brimming with tea and wine were lined up on tombstones and the air was smoky with incense. And everyone was burning hell money and paper replicas of household appliances for their ancestors to enjoy in the afterlife. Of course, it wasn't a celebration, but it was a festival day. Qing Ming Festival or Tomb Sweeping Day – held on the fifteenth day after the spring equinox – was the time when families honoured their ancestors by sweeping their tombs, weeding their graves and making offerings to sustain them in the afterlife.

Situated on hundreds of acres of gently sloping land not far from the town centre, the Kwong Tong Cemetery offered its residents a lovely view out over the city. It was the oldest cemetery in Kuala Lumpur and many of the early Chinese pioneers were buried there, including June's grandparents, if they could find them. They had been walking for twenty minutes but June still hadn't found the spot where the Chan graves were located. They wandered in the older section of the cemetery, carrying baskets brimming with offerings, a rush broom for sweeping, and umbrellas to protect against the sun.

'I know it's here somewhere. I remember it wasn't far from a gigantic tree.'

'There are a lot of big trees,' Ben said with a wink in June's direction. 'They must all look a bit similar after forty years.'

'I might have to stop for a rest if we don't find it soon, I'm almost melting,' Sarah said, wiping the sweat from her face with the bottom of her T-shirt so that her tanned stomach showed. In the months since she'd returned to Kuala Lumpur she'd spent many mornings trying to wrestle the garden back from the jungle, often wearing little more than a bikini top and shorts, and she'd developed quite a tan. The gardening, and her efforts to spruce up the house, had toned her body more than her years of half-hearted gym sessions. 'We should have come earlier before it got so...' She broke off her complaints at the sound of muffled crying. 'Oh-oh, sounds like someone's hungry.'

The baby was working up a head of steam now, unwilling to be ignored. His cries echoed plaintively across the open ground, catching the attention of a large extended family further up the road. Su Lin tried to comfort him by crooning to him in Cantonese, but he had only one thing on his mind.

'I think I'll sit over there in the shade and feed him,' she said, heading in the direction of a large, shady tree, dozens of aerial roots snaking to the ground. With a whispered 'Sorry' to everyone's ancestors, she made herself comfortable on a nearby tombstone and unbuttoned her shirt to feed her hungry son, discreetly covering herself with a scarf. Sarah, June and Ben wandered over to join her, welcoming the excuse to get out of the hot sun. The Chans had waited decades for this visit; they could wait a little longer.

'If we don't find it soon, maybe we could come back even earlier tomorrow before it gets hot. We've got a few days either side of Qing Ming, haven't we?' Sarah said, looking towards June for confirmation. But June didn't answer; she was staring at the writing on the tomb where Su Lin perched. The gravestone was a simple granite rectangle carved with cloud motifs and several lines of Chinese writing engraved in gold. At the top was an oval picture painted on porcelain of a man in traditional robes. 'June, are you all right?'

'This is it. This is my grandfather's grave.'

Sarah bent closer to study the picture. She could see that the painting was based upon a photograph, and although the man depicted was much younger than the man in the group photograph on June's altar at home, it was the same man.

'Chan Boon Siew. Born 1871. Died 1932. That's him. I remember the cloud carving on the grave too, from when I was a child.' Although the headstone and plinth were quite simple, a low wall curved in a horseshoe shape around it, marking the tomb's boundary. There were other graves of various ages clustered nearby. 'My grandmother and mother should be somewhere around. And Nick said that he had buried my father in the family plot too.'

While Su Lin fed her son, the others explored nearby graves, wading through long grass. 'I think I've found something,' Sarah called out to June when she discovered the rounded shape of a concrete tombstone inset with gold-engraved granite. She recognised the character for Chan, having seen it often enough recently. June and Ben joined her, stepping carefully over camouflaged masonry.

'The grave of Lee Ling Wei. Born in Canton, China 1897. Died Kuala Lumpur 1963. Arrived Malaya 1913 to marry Chan Boon Siew. Devoted mother of Chan Wei Long,' June read aloud. 'She probably was devoted, just not his actual mother.'

According to Ling Wei's letter, her son's actual mother was

mentally unstable. But what sixteen-year-old girl wouldn't suffer mentally if she was sold off to a man old enough to be her grandfather and then had her child stolen by another woman? She must have felt like her family had abandoned her. She must have felt like she had no one in the world on her side. It was small wonder that she wanted to punish those who had wronged her. Sarah would curse the people who did that to her too.

'June, I think I've found your father's grave,' Ben called from further up the slope. He was standing near a block-shaped tomb with a shiny black gravestone.

Leaving Ling Wei behind for the moment, they traipsed through the grass, stepping around the low borders of scattered graves, Sarah leading the way. Pausing to swat at a mosquito that buzzed at her ear, she looked out towards the city, where the tall spire of KL Tower and the twin spears of the Petronas Towers dominated the horizon.

'Great view,' she said to June with a smile. 'Nice piece of real esta... crap!' she yelped, as she tripped over a small gravestone hidden in the long grass. Looking down, she saw the first beads of blood seeping from her grazed shin. 'Damn and bloody damn.'

'What's up?' Ben said, appearing at her side. He squatted beside her to inspect her leg. 'Looks like a surface wound. Want me to kiss it better?'

'Tempting as that sounds, I don't think it would help,' she said, blowing him a kiss that sounded more like a raspberry. 'But I've got tissues.' She'd soon learned to carry a small pack of tissues or risk being caught out toilet-paperless. She bent down to dab at her leg and as she did so, spotted the Chan name amongst the faded characters etched into worn stone.

'June, look at this.'

Peering over Sarah's shoulder, June read slowly: 'The grave of Lim Yu Lan. Born Kuala Lumpur 1914. Second wife of Chan Boon Siew. Mother of Chan Wei Long. Died 1932.'

'So she's here after all,' said Ben, 'buried in the long grass.'

'Well, at least we can do something about that,' Sarah said. 'We can tidy her up a bit.'

'It's a wonder we found her,' said June, 'the headstone is so small.'

Was it a wonder, though? Perhaps it was more than inattention that caused her to find it. Don't be so silly, Sarah told herself mentally, it was only because she'd been distracted by the view that she tripped over the stone. Nothing more than that.

'It's a funny feeling,' June said with a shiver.

'What,' asked Ben, heaving Sarah back to her feet, 'tripping over gravestones? Is there some superstition about it?'

'Probably, but that's not what I meant. It's funny that this poor girl, only eighteen years old, has been the source of so much tragedy. So sad that she was driven to kill herself.'

'She wasn't the first and she won't be the last,' Ben said with a sigh. 'UNICEF estimates that eleven per cent of women worldwide are married before the age of fifteen. And how many of them are coerced? Even in Australia, even in Britain.'

Sometimes Sarah forgot that this was the kind of stuff Ben knew. He lectured in it.

'If only we could go back and fix things for Yu Lan…' June trailed off, shrugging helplessly. Although they'd finally persuaded her to stay at the house, she still believed in the concubine's ghost. She was still convinced that she'd seen her that day when she was a child. Then again, sometimes the events of childhood were engraved so deeply that a lifetime wasn't long enough to erase them.

'We can't fix the past but maybe we can do something about the future,' Sarah said, looking down the slope to where Su Lin sat feeding her baby in the shade of the tree.

*

THEY CLIPPED THE grass short in a ragged patch of lawn around the grave. They cleaned the headstone and June painted over the inscription with a small pot of gold paint and a brush. Then they spread a paper cloth on the grass and arranged the offerings in an inviting spread in front of the headstone. Yu Lan had died long before any of them were born so they didn't know her favourite foods, but they laid out some of their favourites instead: several cups of Ben's favourite chardonnay, a plate of June's favourite steamed rice cakes, several small pyramid-shaped packages of savoury rice that Su Lin loved, a bowl of ripe mandarins, a whole cooked duck, and some of the delicious egg tarts that Sarah had recently discovered. Candles flamed softly in the bright sunlight and they planted a veritable forest of incense so that the smoke wafted skywards.

The sound of firecrackers reverberated through the cemetery as June approached the temporary altar holding several smoking joss sticks. Someone was driving away any lurking evil spirits. She bowed three times, offering a quiet prayer asking for the deceased's blessing. Next it was Sarah's turn to offer a prayer for this young girl, Nick's great-grandmother, whose life had been cut so short. They might never know exactly how she died but they could pray for her.

Kneeling in the grass, she dug a hole with a trowel. Then she removed the jade ring from her finger, placed it in the hole and covered it with soil. 'Don't hate us,' she whispered, 'it's time to let go now.' Yes, it was time to let go.

She backed away as Su Lin passed the baby into June's arms and approached the grave to offer a prayer to her son's long-dead ancestor.

'Forgive our neglect and please bless my son with health and happiness.'

The sun was in Sarah's eyes, but as she watched Su Lin kneel before the concubine's modest headstone, she could have sworn she saw the outline of a translucent figure hovering beyond her shoulder, almost like a double exposure. She blinked and when she opened her eyes the image was gone. Two young women born generations apart, both the mothers of Chan sons. But Su Lin's life was so different. She had chosen to love the father. She had chosen to raise the son.

She would choose her own destiny.

Out of the corner of her eye, Sarah caught a burst of yellow. She turned her head towards the concubine's grave to see that the thicket of incense had flared into life, flames blazing, sending smoke heavenwards. On the other side of the grave, Ben stood grinning. Not at the flaming incense, but at her. She didn't know why he had attached himself to a grieving, difficult woman but he had, and with very little encouragement. Perhaps he was just contrary. Perhaps he liked a challenge. Or perhaps he saw something in her that she thought she'd lost.

Maybe one day, when she least expected to, she would find it again.

Epilogue

THE AIR WAS hot and moist in the small downstairs room at the rear of the house, so that her hair clung to the back of her neck. Gathering the hair that spread over her shoulders and down to her waist, she draped it over one shoulder. Once it had been midnight black, thick and lustrous with youth, but now it was threaded with coarse grey. It was a good thing that Madam's eyesight was foggy or she would have noticed years ago. Once upon a time, she noticed the slightest error, and retribution was swift and decisive.

Sometimes Ho Jie wondered why she continued with this charade, since it had all happened such a long time in the past. Chan was nothing but bones now and soon his wife would join him. And yet... vengeance could be seductive in its own bittersweet way. Vengeance could keep you alive.

The boy would return soon, calling a greeting to her before striding upstairs to visit the woman he called Mother. Although in reality he was a boy no longer, but a man with a dead wife and a child of his own. A daughter largely ignored by everyone but Ho Jie. Madam had no time for daughters. Little sister's curse had rippled through the generations, stealing love and leaving regret in its place. Sometimes she wondered if it would ever end.

She picked up the comb and stood before the small, round mirror hanging on the wall opposite her bed. With her arms upraised, the floating sleeves of her white *sam* fell back to reveal wiry brown forearms. She had always been strong. She had always been alone, apart from that brief time when she found in Sai Mui a friend and daughter. Well, those days were so far away now they might never have been. Sometimes, she thought the girl was nothing but a dream, a fleeting episode of wishful thinking for her and the *towkay*. A nightmare for Madam.

Except for the boy, she might never have existed. The boy and the curse.

A shadow drifted across the face of the mirror, a shadow in red with luminous white skin and a waterfall of black hair. Ho Jie studied the mirror, searching for the girl she had lost so long ago. But the apparition vanished as suddenly as it had materialised.

Neuih gwai. Ghost maiden. Well, the girl had made her choice and they all had to live with it.

Ho Jie dragged the comb through her greying hair, reciting the words her mother had chanted when she first pinned up her maiden's plait into a self-combed woman's bun.

'One stroke for luck
Two for longevity
Three for contentment
Four for safety
Five for freedom...'

Author's Note

CHINESE LANGUAGES ARE tonal. However, no matter which Chinese language is spoken, the written language comprises the same Chinese characters. When Romanised, the tones are indicated with accent-like marks, or numerals, depending upon the Romanisation system used. In this novel I have chosen to render Chinese without the tone marks as they will mean little to anyone who doesn't speak, or isn't learning, Chinese. Most of the Chinese words in the novel are in the Cantonese language and I have largely followed the Yale Romanisation, but without the tone marks. The few words where I use Mandarin are those I believe English-speaking readers may already know, such as *qi* or *feng shui*; or place names, such as Guangdong, that can be found on a contemporary map.

In addition, there are a number of Malay words used in the novel. Bahasa Malaysia, or Malay, is the National Language of Malaysia.

Acknowledgements

IF NOT FOR annual visits to stay with my husband's family in Kuala Lumpur this novel would not exist. So I am enormously grateful to the Kwok family for their hospitality over the last twenty-five years. Thank you especially to my mother-in-law Eng Lan Yin for her reminiscences of growing up in Malaysia in the 1930s, and to my sisters-in-law Kwok Oi Leng and Kwok Sui Lin for their explanations and guidance in matters of culture, religion and most particularly... food. I also owe a big thank you to my brother-in-law Raymond Kwok for all those times he has chauffeured us around Kuala Lumpur and squired us to late-night drinks.

Although I have been writing for decades, the road to publication for my first adult novel has been long, and I would particularly like to thank Jenny Darling for her faith in me over too many years to mention.

A huge thank-you to my agent Judith Murdoch for her knowledge, professionalism and shrewd insights. I value her straight-talking, even when it hurts.

I am very fortunate to be published by the esteemed editor Rosie de Courcy. Thank you so much for knowing just what the manuscript needed. A very big thank-you also to the fabulous team at Head of Zeus for helping to breathe life into *The Concubine's Child*.

Lastly, huge hugs to my husband Vincent Kwok for his loving

support and his patient explanations of all things Cantonese, and to my children Ru and Kit for encouraging me even when the journey seemed endless.

Book Club Questions

1. The prologue is narrated by an unnamed woman. Who did you think she was, and how did your feelings towards her change as the book progressed? What expectations did the prologue raise?

2. How important is the setting to the story? Could it have taken place somewhere else? What did you particularly like about the setting?

3. Yu Lan believes that she and Ming cannot choose their own destinies because 'they were sixteen and their lives did not belong to them'. Can any of the characters in the historical strand of the novel choose their own destinies? What about the contemporary story?

4. When she is sold as Chan's concubine, Yu Lan's mother advises her, 'You must be fluid like water because water defeats the strongest stone in time.' Does Yu Lan agree with her? Would Ho Jie or Madam Chan agree with her? How does this attitude differ to the Western idea of taking charge of your destiny?

5. Gods, spirits, ancestors and ghosts are a recurring presence in the novel. What part do they play in the characters' lives and fates? Compare the contemporary characters' attitudes towards the spirit world with those of the 1930s characters. Do their beliefs change at all?

6. Yu Lan believes that the Chans have enslaved her. Do you ever sympathise with them?

7. In what ways does the opening chapter of the contemporary story foreshadow the events that follow? What hints are there in the first two chapters of the contemporary story that things might not go so well for Nick?

8. Nick says, 'I'm the last Chan in the family.' How are descendants and filial piety important to the various characters in the novel?

9. Revenge plays a central role in the novel. What examples of revenge are there, both large and petty? What does revenge cost the characters?

10. What do you think Sarah is most afraid of?

11. Ho Jie says that, 'Men brought only trouble. And if trouble was coming, better if it came bearing gold.' How pragmatic are the characters in the *The Concubine's Child?*

12. Ho Jie also says of her sisters at the silk factory in Shonde that, '... they had shared many tricks.' What other tricks might they have shared?

13. How would you describe Ho Jie's relationship with Yu Lan? How does it change through the novel?

14. Why does Yu Lan decide that only she can free herself? How does she set about doing so? What is her power? What is her weakness?

15. Polygamy was quite common in Malaysia and China in the first half of the 20th century and Ho Jie speaks of the old Chinese saying that 'two tigers cannot share one mountain'. How does Yu Lan's presence affect the household? Do you think this was inevitable?

16. What did you think was the saddest part of the story? Why?

17. How do the stories and characters, past and present, parallel each other? How do they differ? Why do you think the author chose to use mirror stories?

18. When she returns to Kuala Lumpur Sarah says, 'Secrets, truths, lies, ghosts, they were all the same really. All things you didn't want to confront.' What do you think she means by this?

19. How did you feel about the ending of the story? Was it unexpected? Did it feel complete to you? How is the prologue reflected in the epilogue?

20. Do you think *The Concubine's Child* is a ghost story?